Gothic Blue

'You are a very forthright woman,' he whispered, lifting his mouth away from hers momentarily.

Belinda looked up into his face, then was forced to drop her gaze again. His eyes were too brilliant to bear so close up. She felt mesmerised, and quite weak, and her mouth opened when his touched it once again.

His tongue immediately slid inside the soft cavity, tracing her teeth then plunging deeper to duel with her tongue. He tasted of wine and almonds and something else hard to define yet tantalisingly delicious, and she moaned under her breath as he kissed her. Her body had never felt more alive.

As he continued to kiss, playing and exploring, she felt his hand settle once again on her belly, his long fingers splaying out across her skin. She felt him rubbing, gently circling and fondling the curve of her with his slightly bent fingers.

'Do you wish me to touch you?' he enquired, making the words a part of the kiss. His hand stilled, waiting in readiness for her permission.

By the same author:

Gemini Heat
The Tutor
The Devil Inside
Continuum
The Stranger
Hotbed
Shadowplay
Entertaining Mr Stone

For more information about Portia Da Costa's books
please visit www.portiadacosta.com

Gothic Blue
Portia Da Costa

BLACK LACE

This book is a work of fiction.
In real life, make sure you practise safe, sane
and consensual sex.

This edition published in 2007 by
Black Lace
Thames Wharf Studios
Rainville Road
London W6 9HA

Originally published 1996

Copyright © Portia Da Costa 1996

The right of Portia Da Costa to be identified as the Author of
the Work has been asserted in accordance with the Copyright,
Designs and Patents Act 1988.

www.blacklace-books.co.uk

Typeset by SetSystems Ltd, Saffron Walden, Essex
Printed and bound by Mackays of Chatham PLC

ISBN 978 0 352 33075 8

Contents

This one is dedicated to the memory of Boy, a true friend.

Prologue

*I*t had all begun at the archduke's reception, André recalled. Among the sparkling smiles, the dazzling wit and brilliant music. André had been standing on the sidelines, waiting for his beloved Arabelle to make her entrance, when an unexpected chill had cooled his blood.

Looking up, he had seen a woman passing by, her white hand on her attentive partner's arm. He had thought nothing of it at first; the room was full of such sumptuously-dressed women, and a great many of them were also very beautiful. But then she had turned around and looked straight in his direction and his shivers had changed instantly to a fever. Her luminous green-eyed gaze had cut right through him to his vitals, warming his body in exact proportion to its previous peculiar coolness.

The unknown woman was breathtaking, and her manner more imperious than that of a queen. In a swagged and tiered gown of red velvet with gold embroidery, her shape was delicate yet magnificently voluptuous. Her richly-coiled black hair had a heavy bluish lustre that caught the lamplight as she nodded slightly to him.

Who are you? he thought, then felt bereft as she began

to move away from him, her crimson dress like a vivid banner among the crowds.

A few minutes later, after questioning a passing acquaintance, André had discovered the name of his raven-haired enchantress. She was Isidora, Countess Katori, and her reputation was as dangerous as her beauty. Rumour had it that she practised the magic arts.

This is wrong, he told himself, as his eyes hunted for her across the ballroom, then followed her through the dance's complex figures. This is wrong, he thought, gritting his teeth and trying to ignore his suddenly aching loins.

I should not want her. I must not want her. I'm in love and in a week I'll be betrothed. It was only a matter of moments before his exquisite Arabelle would be here. Witty, radiant Belle, to whom he would gladly pledge his mortal soul.

And yet still the flamboyant countess ruled his flesh. His guilty heart hammered when, from out of nowhere, she appeared like a djinni before him, her full red lips forming a smile that left him speechless.

'Sir, do we not know each other?' she enquired, her voice low and teasing as she doffed a minute curtsey.

'I . . . I do not think so,' he answered, bending over her hand to kiss it, and discovering that her skin was fine as silk. 'Count André von Kastel, madam. At your service,' he said, releasing her, but reluctant to let her go.

'Isidora, Countess Katori,' she replied, her faint accent making her name a long caress. With a small graceful gesture, she nodded towards the nearby dancers, then turned from him and walked away towards them, apparently confident that he would simply up and follow her.

Vaguely ashamed of himself, André fell in step behind her, feeling like a callow boy in his first pursuit of love's wild passion. This daring, handsome countess had effortlessly made a youth of him, but to his chagrin, she had also made him hard. His state of high arousal was surely visible to all around him, but though it bothered him,

2

there was nothing he could do about it. And as they began the measure, he soon forgot to care.

Why me? he thought as they danced. His attire, a plain but well-cut coat and breeches, was subdued compared to most around him, and his title was just one among many others. His looks, though pleasant, he admitted, were not what he would have called outstanding or remarkable. Why on earth had the countess chosen him, a grey-eyed, brown-haired minor aristocrat of somewhat modest height, when the room was awash with dashing dukes and elegant princes?

As the dance progressed, he longed to press himself against her. His swollen member seemed to seek her female heat. From time to time, as the countess found a score of sly ways to insinuate herself against him, he tried to clear his mind of his lust for her and think of Arabelle. He imagined the shock and sadness on his dear one's face as she found him like this with another; he pictured the distress in her lovely eyes as he betrayed her. It appalled him, and yet still he felt helpless. Each time her image came to him, like a vision of grace and salvation, the woman on his arm appeared to sense it, and re-double her sinuous efforts to addle his wits.

Countess Isidora's perfume was like a dense musky cloud that hung around them, and when he thought of Arabelle, the odour subtly thickened. It filtered into his brain like a rich miasmic mist and charged his mind with exciting images that shocked him. Debauchery. Unnatural acts. Frenzied, bestial couplings. He imagined himself naked and stretched out over the countess's smooth white body, her firm breasts jutting upward against his chest. And when, under cover of the fast-moving dance, her lips touched his throat for just one second, he moaned and fought for breath, his senses reeling.

It had been but one brief contact, yet incredibly he felt her serpent tongue all over him. She was tasting him; savouring his skin and its hot, manly flavour. No part

3

of his anatomy escaped her, no secret was left unexamined. Her proximity overpowered him and sapped his will.

Half out of his mind, and unable to resist her, he imagined her lapping his belly and his privates. Her long devious tongue would wind seductively around his member, finding new areas of near-painful sensitivity.

Giddy with desire, André could not believe the messages of his senses. It was difficult to believe that they were still only on the dancefloor. In his dreams they were in a huge bed somewhere, their limbs thrashing, their mouths mating like rabid dogs. When his knees betrayed him, he stumbled towards her and half fell.

'Shall we take the air, my lord? You seem a little uncomfortable,' the countess murmured. Then, without further consultation, she led him towards a long, shadowed balcony.

Within seconds, all André's lustful prayers were answered. Her red mouth plundered his, her tongue darting into it and exploring, while her sure hands led his beneath her skirt. Through swathe after swathe of heavy lace and crumpled silk, he was drawn, ever upward and ever inward, until finally his shaking fingers met her treasure. He felt a nest of crisp, wiry curls, then folded flesh rendered slippery by her juices. She was a furnace, a pool of liquid satin, and her soft membranes flickered salaciously beneath his touch.

Almost numb with delight, André described a small movement with his fingertip, and was rewarded by a savage growl of pleasure. His elegant, high-born countess was twisting her hips like a harlot, and grinding her sex against the fulcrum of his hand. Her churning, scissoring thighs caressed his wrist.

'Pleasure me, my lord,' she demanded, rocking and swaying. 'Put your fingers inside me, before I faint.'

Delirious, André obeyed her, his nose and mouth filled with her spicy, rising vapours. Through what appeared to be a haze, an inexplicable thin blue nimbus, he saw

4

her beautiful face slackened by lust. Somehow – by sleight of hand or by sheer force of will – she had released her breasts from her constricting velvet bodice, and their unfettered fullness gleamed like two pale fruits in the cool night air. Her teats were dark, the brownish-purple of drying blood, and he swore he could see them harden before his eyes.

'My lord!' she cried, her voice slurring as her nectar wet his hand. 'Enter me! I crave it!'

He pushed first one fingertip, then a second, inside her, and her whole body shuddered, then bore down. Her weight and the force of her made his wrist begin to ache, and to brace himself he set his feet apart. But still she was unsatisfied by his efforts.

'Fill me, my lord,' she moaned, her white teeth nipping at his neck. 'Give me more!'

He bore in with three fingers, then with four, and the countess keened like a she-wolf in full heat. Her long, perfumed thighs opened wider to give him access, then closed and locked unyieldingly around his arm.

'I spend, my lord! I spend!' she shrieked, untroubled at being heard by nearby dancers. The silky product of her rapture drenched his palm.

Only seconds later, she was down on her knees before him, her nails ripping at his breeches to free his member. As soon as he was liberated, she laughed wildly and plunged forward, wrapping her crimson lips around his tortured rod.

Never in all his days had André experienced an enclosure so sublime. The throat he was buried in seemed to undulate around him as if each muscle had a distinct and separate life of its own. She was almost swallowing him whole, he realised, and her sharp teeth were pressing perilously against his shaft.

'Madam, I beg of you,' he groaned, half in terror, half in ecstasy, his body thrilled to greater hardness by the danger.

Her only answer was to reach in and grip his ball-sac,

adding another layer of jeopardy to his predicament. He
buried his fingers in the coils of her hair, trying desperately to control her, but he couldn't prevent her from
engulfing him even deeper.

Abruptly, in the heart of his pleasure, André felt an
icy surge of revulsion, of shame and betrayal, and at the
moment of release, he thought of Belle, mouthing her
name and picturing her perfect jewel-like smile. How
could he have done this? How could he deceive her,
damage her, break her faith? As he reached his peak, he
despised himself profoundly.

He had little awareness of what happened in the next
quarter of an hour or so, and of how they made their
escape from the reception. All he remembered was a
racing carriage and a moonless night. The countess's
witch-like presence was like a drug to him, speeding up
time and throwing a veil across his vision.

When they reached her luxurious apartments, she
turned and surprised him. Instead of leading him
straight to her bed and stripping him, she paused, smiled
obliquely, and made the gesture of an accomplished
hostess.

'A glass of wine, my lord?' she queried. 'The pleasures
of the flesh are prone to make me thirsty, and I am sure
they must do the same for you.'

'Yes, thank you, Countess,' replied André, feeling as
profoundly out of his depth as he had done earlier. He
accepted a goblet-like wine glass that was as large and
ornately decorated as a liturgical chalice, even though a
panicked inner voice entreated him not to.

The wine had a heavy, unusual taste – somewhat
bitter and vaguely alkaline on the tongue – but he was,
he realised, just as thirsty as she had suggested, so he
drank it down despite its strange flavour.

When he put aside the glass, composed his thoughts
and turned around, his companion was naked. Catching
his breath, André looked back towards his goblet in

6

confusion. At the reception, their dealings had been so hurried and so fumbled that he could almost believe he had only dreamed what had happened, but now he knew it was all true, and that the pale, curvaceous body before him was a prize he had won; his to enjoy, ripe and ready for the taking.

Yet he still hesitated.

'The wine ... It tastes – ' He swirled the pungent residue around his mouth ' – tainted.'

Isidora looked at him, her green eyes level and unblinking. 'I did add a little tincture to it, my lord, something of my own devising.' She smiled narrowly as he thrust the goblet along the sideboard and away from him. 'But do not worry, it is simply to increase your pleasure.' She paused delicately. 'It will enable you to endure.' Her tongue darted out, more serpent-like than ever, it seemed to André, as the room began to tilt ever so slightly. 'With this in your veins you will last for ever, my dear Count.' She began to laugh in a wild and odd way.

André felt unsteady now, and as they had at the reception, his knees began to buckle precariously. Isidora flew to his side, then helped him towards a couch, one firm breast brushing his arm as he leant on her.

'Who are you?' he asked again, his head spinning as she deftly undressed him.

'I am Isidora Katori,' she said archly, flinging away his shirt then attacking his already torn breeches. 'And very soon I will be your lover for all time.'

'I ... I do not understand,' he stammered, suddenly longing to get away from her but not able to. His brain was sending messages that he should throw her off, grab his clothes and flee these apartments immediately; but bizarrely, his body was helping her disrobe him. And as his breeches came off and were tossed away after the shirt, his penis bounced up in a lewd salute.

'You will,' she said softly, her hands gliding fleetingly over his body before she turned away and poured him

7

more wine. 'Drink,' she ordered, pressing the newly-filled goblet to his lips.

André experienced again that strange phenomenon – his mind issuing instructions while his body ignored them and did the opposite. Silently screaming 'No!', he drank the wine.

When the goblet was empty, Isidora took it from his lips and hurled it to the floor, where it smashed into a thousand glinting shards.

'Now, my lord, you are mine,' she cried, her voice strident as she flung herself across him. 'We need only one final element to complete the process.' With an animal groan, she sank down on to his penis.

The pleasure he felt inside her tight, wanton channel was even greater than that he had experienced in her mouth. Against his will, he writhed beneath her, bucking upward to increase his penetration, while Isidora worked his body without mercy. Her flawless white skin was streaked with shining sweat, and her face was a twisted mask of dark hunger. As he looked up at her, André felt his strength begin to ebb. His manhood was still rigid inside her, but elsewhere he felt a great and surging weakness, like a torrent of tidal water rushing through him. Somewhere in his very innermost centre, he experienced the sensation that every cell in his body was beginning to melt. He was expiring, being snuffed out, his life extinguished; and as he realised it his member leapt and shivered.

A weird, singing light began to rise through every deliquescing part of him, and when it reached his brain, Isidora crowed in triumph, riding his release like a giant foaming wave.

I'm dying, André thought with an odd detachment, and knew that there was nothing he could do to stop it. With his seed still spurting, and his body still jerking, he breathed his last to the sound of Isidora's laughter and the evil pulse of her unholy, gripping flesh.

But as blackness fell and his eyes closed, a stark cold

replaced the fiery heat of sex and he saw an image of poignant horror in his mind.

It was Arabelle, his precious love, and she was calling to him. Her lovely face was glistening with a river of doleful tears and though she was nearby, he could barely hear her voice. There was a barrier of solid crystal set between them.

She's gone too, André realised as it ended.

Arabelle is gone and we never were as one.

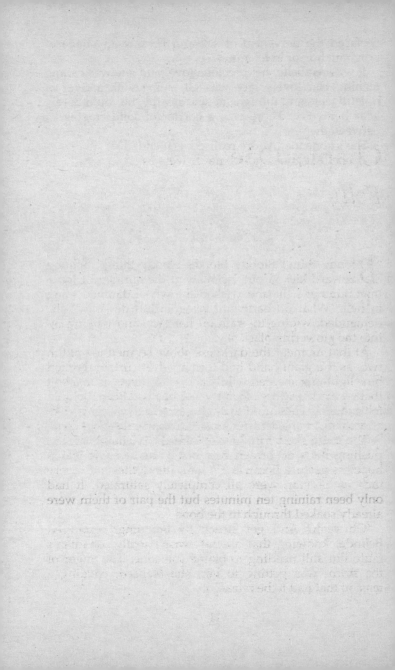

only been raining ten minutes but the pair of them were

Chapter One

Folly

'*B*loody thing! Bloody bloody bloody thing!' Belinda Seward kicked out viciously at the bumper of Jonathan Sumner's car and wished the whole damned thing in hell. 'What on earth are we going to do now?' she demanded, wiping the rain off her face, and looking up into the glowering black sky.

At that moment the darkness above seemed to split in two, as if a giant hand had torn a velvet curtain. Forked blue lightning sheared wildly across the heavens in a bolt that seemed far closer than the last one had been. Belinda felt suddenly convinced that the elements themselves were after them, or at least after Jonathan's ancient yellow Mini.

'We could shelter in the car,' offered Jonathan Sumner, pushing his wet, brown hair out of his eyes. It was a hopeless gesture because his hair, his clothes and every inch of his skin were all completely saturated. It had only been raining ten minutes but the pair of them were already soaked through to the bone.

'Oh yeah? And get struck by lightning?' enquired Belinda, knowing that all this wasn't really Jonathan's fault, but still needing to blame someone. The anger of the storm was getting to her, she realised; creating a tension that had to be released.

They had been lost for an hour or so now, and thunderbolts and torrential rain just seemed to put the cap on things, especially as the Mini – which Jonathan had assured her was reliable – had just broken down and was leaking like a sieve. Their plight wasn't all Jonathan's fault, Belinda had to admit, but somehow she couldn't seem to keep herself from blaming him anyway – something she had told herself she would try not to do.

'Well, I'm not staying here!' she said, reaching into the car for her shoulder bag, then staring first one way down the narrow road they were on, then the other. In both directions the vista was grim, wet and unpromising, so with a shrug, she set off along the route they had been planning to travel.

'What are you doing?' demanded Jonathan, catching her up. 'We can't just leave the car – '

'We bloody well can! I'm not standing around waiting for that pile of scrap to be struck by lightning. I'm going to find us a place to shelter.'

'There's shelter there!' Jonathan grabbed her arm then pointed to the heavy, mournful-looking trees that flanked the road on either side. At that moment, another great thunderflash came, making the trunks glisten momentarily in the teeming water, the knotty bark appearing silver and blue.

'Don't be a prat, Jonathan,' snapped Belinda, shaking him off and spraying water across him in the process. 'Trees are just as likely to be struck as a car is. I'm going to find a building of some kind. Maybe a house or a barn we can shelter in.'

'I suppose you're right,' said Jonathan, falling into step beside her and automatically taking the bag. 'But there doesn't seem to be much life around here, does there? That is, wherever "here" actually is.'

They had lost their bearings quite a while ago, about the same time as the storm had started brewing. It was weird, really; they had been doing quite well up until then, finding all their planned stops and keeping to their pre-arranged itinerary.

As they trudged along the ever narrowing road, chances of finding suitable shelter seemed to narrow too. The trees on either side loomed over them, moving in like tall, battle-blasted soldiers closing ranks around a helpless enemy. Whenever it was possible to see beyond the lines of trunks, there seemed to be very little to see – just desolate fields and scrubby sodden bushes. It seemed so different from the pleasant farming vale they had been travelling through just a couple of short hours ago.

Belinda flinched as another crack of thunder broke right over them, and the lightning seemed to fork both in front of them and behind. She could almost imagine that the little yellow car had just been blasted, and up ahead, the as yet unknown shelter they sought had also taken a bolt of white flame.

'Don't worry, Lindi,' said Jonathan in her ear, as he slid a wet but warm arm around her waist, 'the odds of being struck are astronomical. And if it gets us, at least we go together.'

Funnily enough, the inane remark soothed her, as did the strong male arm. There was something comfortingly solid about it; a safeness and reality that had an unexpected but not unwanted effect. They were both soaked through, but Jonathan's body, close as it was and moving against hers to the rhythm of his stride, seemed filled with an exceptional heat and vibrancy that filtered clean through the wetness of their clothes.

Saying nothing, Belinda let her own body lean in a little closer, and for the first time became aware of strange feelings. The sort of feelings that thunderstorms didn't usually engender.

The beating of the rain on her skin was insidious, and her wet clothes, pressing close against her, created the sensation of a sly but continuing caress. She could feel the water flowing everywhere; teasing her, cascading down across her breasts and dribbling between her legs, soaking a furrow that was already damp with a wetness of its own.

She was acutely aware, too, of the presence of a man beside her. Her brain said it was only Jonathan – her familiar Jonathan, her workmate and sometime lover – but her blood simply sensed him as a male. A strong, lean, muscular form with the pure power of sex between his legs.

Oh God, I'm aroused ... It's insane, but I am! I'm turned on, without trying, just for Jonathan!

There was nothing she could do about it at the moment, but the realisation of her desire almost scared her. She hadn't felt this aroused for many weeks.

As the lightning flashed again, she snuggled a little closer to him, adjusting her stride to fit his as the side of her breast rubbed lightly against his ribcage.

'OK, love?' he enquired, giving her a squeeze.

Belinda nodded, smiling up at him, then laughed as she swallowed a mouthful of warm rain.

'I'm sorry about this,' he went on, glancing up at the blackness of the sky as if it really was his fault. 'I mean ... I serviced the car, and it's in good nick for its age. It must be all the rain on the carburettor or something.'

'Don't worry, Jonathan,' Belinda shouted, competing with another roar of thunder. 'We did say we wanted a change of routine, didn't we?'

Jonathan grinned down at her, then nodded his head towards hers. 'At least it won't spoil your hair.'

'Bastard,' replied Belinda without rancour. They were both still deciding whether they liked her new look or not. After years with long hair, a mad, out-of-the-blue impulse had made her have her red-brown waves shorn to a short crop. It had been a shock to the system, and she still got a surprise sometimes when she looked in a mirror, but on a night like this she blessed her decision. The neat, elfin style shaped sleekly to her skull, and felt

14

far, far better than a dank, unmanageable mass trailing down over her neck and her shoulders.

And her new haircut didn't make her feel any the less feminine. In fact, she felt supremely female at the moment, as if the raving elements had transformed her into a nymph of the storm. She looked up again at Jonathan, just as he turned to look down at her. He seemed puzzled for a second by the heat of her glance, then he smiled, his grey eyes slowly widening in delight. Neither of them said anything, but Jonathan's arm tightened and he gave her a rakish wink.

It was more imperative than ever they find shelter.

After a few minutes more of splashing along the streaming road, it seemed as if some kind spirit in the tempest had been watching out for them. They found themselves by a wall that ran parallel to the road. It was dark and moss-grown, but a wall none the less; a high grey stone boundary that indicated an estate of some kind within, which would be sure to have somewhere they could shelter in, even if it were only a stable or outhouse.

Withdrawing his arm from around her shoulders with obvious reluctance, Jonathan took hold of her hand and by consensus they quickened their pace. Belinda wasn't sure if she was imagining things or not, but the road seemed to wind more now, and the wall with it. A little way on, after a particularly tortuous twist, an imposing set of gates interrupted the seemingly impenetrable stone barrier.

'Looks a bit dodgy,' observed Jonathan. The gateposts were somewhat broken down and the masonry crumbling, although the shape of two heraldic beasts atop each one was still quite clear, especially when the lightning lit them up. Belinda shuddered. The two statues looked like cats of some kind; not the usual lions but some sort of giant domestic cat made grotesquely malformed and ferocious.

'Here, pussy pussy,' said Jonathan with a grin.

'Don't be daft,' Belinda said shortly, a bit shaken by the peculiar stone animals.

The gates themselves were iron, and rusted here and there. They would have been as impenetrable as the wall itself was, but a broken hinge made one of them sag. Where the gate lolled lopsidedly towards the path beyond, there was a gap that could easily be squeezed though.

'What do you think, shall we try it?' asked Jonathan. As he spoke, another huge flash of blue light silhouetted his lean body in his clinging shorts and top, and Belinda felt an answering flash inside her. The strange desire that had kindled while they trudged seemed to flare up again with all the violence of the disorder above them. The sinuous forms of the cats on their pedestals appeared to writhe as if they too were consumed by lust, and though their eyes were only suggested by the stone, Belinda had a notion they were real and watching her. Or something was watching her. Maybe it was the storm itself; like a discarnate intelligence observing its own effects on her body.

'Yes, let's go for it!' she said, her voice rising to match the increasing loudness of the wind and rain. As she moved closer to one of the gateposts, she noticed something she hadn't seen before – the words 'Sedgewick Priory' cut into the stained grey stone.

Five minutes walk up an overgrown gravelled drive brought them out of the trees and face to face with the priory itself.

'It looks a bit grim, doesn't it?' said Jonathan with a resigned shrug. 'I don't think it's lived in.'

Belinda supposed the priory was built in what was termed the Gothic style; all tall brooding turrets and long narrow windows with a multitude of tiny diamond-leaded panes. The walls were dark, dark grey and sternly secretive, and had the same run-down quality as the perimeter wall and its gateposts, a decrepitude that masked a lasting strength. It looked far more like a warrior's fortified residence than it did an ecclesiastical structure, although there did appear to be what looked like a ruined chapel standing a short distance from the house, overgrown with greenery and half in the trees.

'There're no lights,' Belinda began doubtfully, 'but then again it must be the wee small hours of the morning. We were driving for ages, weren't we?'

Indecisive, they stood on the path in front of the house, kept from it by a soggy, forlorn-looking formal garden gone wild, and a series of low but straggling hedges. The house itself seemed to be staring at them, glowering and forbidding their entrance, its windows like lifeless blank eyes.

'I don't think I want to go in there,' said Belinda, pushing the shaggy wisps of her fringe from her brow and flicking away the water running into her eyes. 'I somehow don't think we'd be welcome.'

'But there's nobody in there, I'm sure,' murmured Jonathan, stepping forward and escaping her restraining hand. Belinda was impressed by his sudden boldness but still couldn't ignore the house's bleakness.

'We could break in, I'm sure. At least it'd be dry,' Jonathan said reasonably.

'No! Don't!' cried Belinda, cringing inside at a great wave of strange diffuse emotion. Something in the house had cried out at the thought of violation; it sounded crazy in her mind as she thought it, but nevertheless, it was what she had felt.

'Are you OK, Lindi?' said Jonathan, returning to her and sliding his arm around her waist again. The casual embrace was comforting and very welcome. The dour grey priory had spooked her, and Jonathan's arm was a touch of human warmth.

'Yes, I'm fine,' she murmured in a moment of quiet as the winds seemed to still. 'I just seemed to have a funny feeling about the house . . . the priory. It was almost as if there *was* someone in it . . . and they didn't want *us* in it.' She paused, feeling the quality of her awareness changing. 'Well, not now at least.'

Jonathan looked bemused but seemed to accept her explanation, as he did so often in his easy-going way. 'Maybe you're right. It's probably dangerous anyway. Broken floorboards, rotted beams and such. We might be safer looking for an outbuilding or a shed of some kind.'

'What's that over there?' said Belinda, turning her back on the priory, the hairs on the nape of her neck prickling. Well, as much as they could when they were slicked to her skin with rain. As she squinted through the downpour, the lightning came again in its brightest flash yet, seeming to split the sky with a slice of blue flame. She was at once aware of seeing a small, pale structure that she hadn't seen before, about a hundred yards away across the lawn; and at the same time feeling the thick, almost tangible presence of the greater house behind her, watching her back with its dead, leaded eyes.

'I dunno ... I didn't notice it before,' said Jonathan, turning in the direction of the little building away across the grass. 'It looks like a summer house or something.' His arm tightened and he gave Belinda a reassuring hug. 'Shall we try it? It looks in better condition than the house.'

The grass was waterlogged and squelched beneath their feet, and by the time they reached the summer house their trainers were soaked.

'I wonder if it's locked,' said Jonathan as they surveyed the odd, circular building that stood before them. It looked like a pseudo-Greek temple complete with tall, fluted columns, and its windows were narrow and shuttered. The white painted door was closed and looked as solid as the priory looked shambolic.

'Let's see.' Feeling her own rush of boldness and a determined desire to get out of view of the main house, Belinda tried the door handle, a great globular chunk of cut crystal. After a few abortive twists, it suddenly seemed to click from within, and the white door swung slowly open.

The room inside was circular, naturally, and as Belinda stepped over the threshold the lightning lit it up, bouncing jagged radiance off the pale, painted walls. There was no furniture of any kind, except a low circular divan, upholstered in a faded grey velour, but a second flash of light showed what looked like an ornamental drinking fountain set into a niche at the far side of the room.

'Weird,' whispered Jonathan, following her in.

'But dry,' pointed out Belinda, surprised that the room should be so, given the quality of the torrent outside. 'And there's a bed,' she added softly, feeling a return of the heat that the eerie house had cooled. 'A real bed. Isn't that better than being squashed up in the Mini?'

'Mmm . . .' Jonathan moved closer, as if catching her drift, then looked down at her, nibbling on his lip in a way that she always found appealing, particularly at special times like these. 'Are you tired?'

The logical answer was, 'Yes, of course I'm tired, I've been slogging up and down country lanes in a thunderstorm in the middle of the night', but Belinda found that she wasn't tired at all. She felt exhilarated, fired up by the storm, and strangest of all, aroused by her vague, formless fear of the priory. She felt its presence again, all around her; reaching out from the tall, grey building across the grass and enveloping her in a dark sensuality. Making a low sound of need, a moan in her throat, she pressed her wet body close against Jonathan's.

'Yes . . . oh yes, love,' he whispered as if he'd only been waiting for her signal. His lean, wiry arms snaked tightly around her, and his hands clasped her bottom through her shorts, pressing her loins against a hard, lively erection that she was surprised she hadn't noticed a lot sooner. She felt his breath warm and sweet on her face, then he was kissing her cheeks and her jaw and her lips and licking the trickling drops of rain from her face.

'I don't get this,' he said against her lips as they parted in readiness, 'thunder used to scare me witless as a kid –' He ground his hot crotch emphatically against hers ' – and feel what it's done to me now.'

Belinda felt, and rejoiced in what the thunder had done. Her mouth was open now, sucking in his tongue, feeding on it. Jonathan's body felt harder than it had ever done; more manly, more appetising. Their moisture-soaked clothing was only the flimsiest of barriers between them and she fancied she could see steam rising as the heat of their bodies evaporated the wetness of the rain. Her nipples were like stones against his chest and she felt shameless, wanton. She rubbed herself against him, deliberately pleasuring herself, then parted her thighs, opening them around one of his to massage the demanding centre of her need. She was putting on a show, she knew, but didn't know for whom – it didn't seem to be for her familiar old Jonathan, no matter how much he was enjoying it.

'Oh, Lindi, you're so lovely,' he moaned when she released his mouth, his voice hoarse with surprise. She had sometimes been unenthusiastic lately, but now she felt eager, almost frantic, for sex.

Running her hands around his narrow male waist, she pushed her fingers into the backs of his shorts and slid them down over his rump, caressing the muscles and dipping into his furrow. He was tender there, as most men were, and he cried out loudly when she flexed her wrist, drove in deeper, and rubbed the tiny ring of his anus.

'Please ... Ooh, love, that's too nice,' he chanted, wriggling against her. 'Stop a minute, please ... Oh God, I need to pee before we go any further.'

'Ever the romantic,' crowed Belinda, pressing harder and massaging her pelvis against Jonathan's ready groin.

'Little bitch,' he answered, groaning but obviously

loving what she was doing. He squeezed her buttocks in return, then brought his wet lips down on hers again in a comprehensive, jaw-stretching kiss.

Belinda felt exultation surge through her. Her Jonathan was never like this; never so animal, so uninhibited. It was as if the tumult of the night had seeped into them as the pounding rain had soaked through their clothes.

'Go on then!' she almost shouted to be heard over the rolling of thunder in the air. 'Go and have your pee, then come back to me. I want you!' She abused his body once more – with a squeeze and a press – and felt her belly quiver as he groaned and twisted his wet face.

'Witch!' he hissed, then whirled away and almost ran from the folly, presumably into the undergrowth nearby, to relieve himself.

You're a wimp, Jonathan, she thought, half-fondly, half-despairingly, her head filled with a lewd, enticing picture of Jonathan's stiff, reddened penis and the long, twinkling torrent of his golden water.

What's happened to me? she thought suddenly, banishing the image, yet still feeling its forbidden fascination. She realised that she too needed to urinate, and without thinking she crushed her fingers to her crotch.

The pressure both eased and exacerbated her discomfort, and the sensation was so intense she let out a startled yelp. Pressing herself again and feeling both pleasure and pain and relishing them equally, she almost imagined she heard laughter within the thunder. Someone laughing at her antics and encouraging her; someone feeding off her hunger and erotic wildness. Still holding herself, she whirled around expecting to see Jonathan, but found the folly still empty but for herself.

'Who is it?' she whispered, rolling her hips and feeling hot darts shooting through her belly. 'Who is it?' she said, louder, then bit down abruptly on the question when the closed door of the folly flew open, and the wind seemed to fling Jonathan into the room.

'My turn now,' she said as he reached for her. In her

21

somewhere was the urge to do something outrageous: to drop her knickers and pee in front of him – she knew that he would love it – but the fact that this was somebody else's property cooled her madness. It was enough just to break in and shelter there.

'Hurry then,' urged Jonathan, his penis already rising up.

Out among the trees the blackness was bordering on total. By the light of the flashes, Belinda picked her way to a clearing a short distance from the folly and started unfastening the buttons of her shorts. As she peeled them down her thighs then hitched down her panties and squatted, the incongruity of what she was doing made her laugh.

God, she was wet through in the middle of a rainstorm – why was she so delicately tugging her knickers out of the way and only exposing her bum to the elements? In a few quick movements, she stripped off all her clothes: trainers, socks, T-shirt and shorts, pants and bra. Naked, she stretched her fingertips towards the raging sky, then parted her legs and angled her hips.

The release of her water was a relief so intense she almost climaxed. Whooping with manic joy, she felt the hot golden flood cascade down her smooth, shining thighs and blend with the rain on the grass.

'There! Are you satisfied?' she cried to no one in particular, then almost immediately felt a sense of being watched again. During the next lightning flash, she looked down at her own body and saw it lit weirdly, as if by a strobe, with streaks of blue radiance glancing off her wet skin. Her erect nipples shone like a pair of black jewels, and her pubis was a dark, eldritch smudge. 'Watch this!' she called out to the lightning-filled sky, then pushed her fingertips inward through her sodden female curls to seek out the tiny treasure within.

Gasping, she worried her clitoris roughly until she came, beating her hips to and fro through the downpour and the storm, then rising up on her toes as she peaked.

'Yes!' she called triumphantly. 'Yes, yes, yes!' As her pleasure swooped and spiralled, the black sky seemed to answer, as if roaring out a climax of its own.

'Who were you yelling at?' enquired Jonathan as she re-entered the folly. He was lying on the divan and his hand was near his crotch, so Belinda guessed he had been caressing his penis. He snatched away his fingers as she approached him across the tiles, as if not wanting her to think he needed manual stimulation.

Belinda knew she didn't need it. Her climax in the forest had primed her erotic spirit, and her sex felt empty and in need of male possession. Half throwing herself on to the divan beside Jonathan, she crawled on to her hands and her knees and offered him her body in the most enticing way she knew. Poised on all fours, she undulated her hips, her thighs wide apart and her vulva bare and gaping. Her whole body was wet but her female flesh was wetter still, and she knew that with the next bolt of lightning, he would see that.

Right on cue, the sky opened and pealed, and with a hoarse cry, Jonathan hurled himself upon her.

He slid in with such speed and to such a depth that Belinda was pushed forward and squashed under him. As he pounded her and pushed her, she gnawed the old velour beneath her and gouged it into bunches with her fists.

Gentle Jonathan seemed possessed with the same storm demon that she was, and his thrusts were savage and unfocused. He was hurting her but she was loving it. In seconds, she was soaring back to a climax. Rotating her hips, she shoved her bottom hard against him, then reached in between her legs to rub her centre. As his belly slapped her buttocks, she felt a flash of inner lightning, and as she climaxed, she stifled her screams in the soft grey cover.

'Lindi!' she heard Jonathan sob, then felt him lunge, then lunge again, as he jerked inside her. She was

23

squashed like a star as he shuddered out his pleasure, but in her ecstasy there was no awareness of discomfort.

Floating in stillness and contentment, she felt Jonathan soften and slide out of her channel then roll over to lay his body down beside her. Remotely, she perceived the brutal storm was over.

The sky was quiet and the air was dark, and she and Jonathan were alone in their round, white folly. The night was all peace, and half gone, but to her surprise, she still felt that she was being watched; scrutinised in intense detail, by a pair of eyes that seemed to observe her from within. Brilliant blue eyes that were both hot and icy cold.

Chapter Two
The Eyes of the Night

'*B*elle,' the sleeper murmured. 'Arabelle, my love ... Where are you?' he asked softly, as in his still chest his heart began to beat.

It had been so long, so very long, but suddenly and inexplicably she was alive again, her pleasure like a brightly-burning flame.

How could this happen? he thought as his ribcage rose once, then fell, then rose again, and in his veins the sluggish blood began its flow. It seemed an ocean of time since he had last felt this power, and never, in all the many years of his existence, had he felt it from his sweet Arabelle.

'Oh, Belle, how can this be?' whispered André, sitting up with caution in his ancient, draped bed and gazing across the room through the filter of a dozen silken veils. He couldn't see its outline clearly, but he knew that on the marble top of an antique sideboard stood the intricately-carved rosewood casket that was the repository of all that he had ever loved. He reached his hand out weakly towards it, then gasped and slumped back on the pillows. His energy was dim, and already drained after only the slightest exertion.

Hardly able to keep his eyelids open, André stared

across the room through the veils. There, in the shifting darkness, he saw a thin, blue radiance that surrounded the rectangular box. It seemed to be seeping out through the very veining of the wood and forming a faint aura, an inch-wide cerulean halo.

But if you are still in there, my beloved, thought André in confusion, who is it that I am sensing outside? He turned his head on the soft lawn pillow-case, and looked now towards the window and its heavy velvet drapery. The thick, silk-lined curtains presented no barrier to his acute, inner vision, and he gazed out across the rain-lashed parkland and fixed his attention on the round white folly.

Immediately, he felt life in his lifelessness; the primal force of sex that never failed to revive him. Beyond the pale, columned walls of the little white building, there was someone on the point of making love, and against reason that someone was his Belle.

Fighting disbelief, hope and confusion, he struggled to focus and see her. In his mind there formed the image of how she had looked all those years ago, her lovely face at a very special moment. He saw her fine, harmonious beauty, the soft smile, and the delicate, almost tremulous sensuality of the first time she had permitted him a liberty.

Embarrassed, yet somehow eager, she had unfastened the lacings of her gown and her chemise, then opened them to show him her bosom. Lying in his bed now, a thousand miles and two hundred years away, André could still remember his euphoria, his delight, his instant rousing at the sublime young beauty of her breasts. How perfect her shape had been: how dainty, how pointed, how fresh. He could still hear her sigh as she allowed him to touch her, and his own groan as his passion overcame him.

He had loved her so much, and so much wanted to express that love with his body. He had been angry with himself for the brutishness of his lust, but had been unable to suppress or ignore it. Night after night, he had kissed her gently and decorously, his loins racked with craving. Night after night, he had retired to his bed and jerked his flesh to a long, solitary release with her sweet name and the word 'love' on his lips. They had been close, so close, to the night of their joining, when a dark, seductive evil had claimed him.

'No!' he cried, straining ineffectually and stretching out with his living mind towards the unexplained cause of his revival. Concentrating with difficulty, he retuned his vision on the interior of the folly, then gasped at the sight that assailed him.

Belle, but not Belle. His lost betrothed, his precious flower, on the point of being possessed by another.

Against his will, the image aroused him. Beneath his narrow, resting hand, his flesh stirred as it had not done in a long time. Like the miracle of life itself, his member stiffened and rose, far more vital than the rest of his body.

Arabelle had changed over the centuries, he saw now. Her body was boldly naked and more fully formed, and where once her burnished hair had tumbled in a wave to her hips, it was now shorn to a close, roughly-cut cap that hugged the graceful contours of her scalp. In the very centre of the circular, velvet-covered divan, she was crouched like a bitch before her master, her sex offered to a slim, dark-haired youth.

'Arabelle?' André whispered, his doubts growing stronger. He sent his mind circling the divan, and looked down into the young woman's face.

Yes, the features were the same, but seemed more defiant and a little less fine. The woman who was about to be taken looked much as his beloved might have done a few years after he had last physically seen her, when she had grown and tasted love's invigorating pleasures. This woman had experienced the richness and ecstasy of the flesh that Belle had never savoured, the consummation that Isidora had denied her.

27

'Witch! Foul devil! She-demon!' he hissed, his anger spurring him as sex had done. That black-haired monster had taken away two lives and condemned two souls to two separate kinds of torment. 'Get back to hell. I will not think of you,' he said coldly to his nemesis, and resumed his observation of the lovers. 'Who are you?' he said, as the young woman thrust out her hindquarters and the man behind her took advantage. The slim youth was rough as he thrust into his paramour's lush haven, but even so, André still sensed a mood of great tenderness. This was a joyous consensual act, just as it would have been if it were really Arabelle on the bed, and he himself were the lusty naked lover. The affection between the distant pair seemed to goad him like a new spark of dynamism. Strength returned fully to his hands and his fingers just as stiffness returned to his penis.

Clasping himself, he cried out, 'Yes!' And as if hearing him, the lovers convulsed, their meshed bodies lunging in the so-familiar throes.

'Oh dear God . . . Dear God,' André moaned, joining them in their pleasure, his own spasm so intense it felt like pain. After years spent in the half-life, his sudden release was much too much for him, and with a stifled sigh, he sank back to oblivion. His last awareness was cool fluid on his fingers.

Belinda woke to soft golden light. She smiled at a pleasant warmth on her naked body, and began to stretch and curl her toes and generally wake up slowly and luxuriantly, when suddenly awareness poured into her. With a gasp, she sat up and looked around her, panicked. Where the devil was she, and why was she naked?

Calm down, calm down, she told herself, drawing in deep breaths and trying to work out what had happened. Jonathan's presence beside her and the reassuring familiarity of his body quickly settled her, and as she

28

touched his bare back, he grunted sleepily and stirred a little.

'Trust you,' she whispered, leaning over to kiss the nape of his neck. 'Here we are, stranded in the back of beyond, probably camping out illegally on somebody's property, and are you worried?' She watched him as he mumbled, licked his lips and then buried his face in the grey velour of the couch they had bedded down on. 'No. You just sleep like a baby. As usual . . .'

Yet somehow she couldn't find it in her to be cross with him. For one thing they must have trudged miles through the rain-soaked countryside last night, and that was enough to exhaust anyone. And on top of that, when they had found this, their haven, he had made love to her with all the power of a stallion, and given her a pleasure she hadn't felt for some time. Quite some time . . .

'It's OK, Mr Sleepy,' she whispered, ruffling his dark hair and knowing that nothing short of slapping or kicking him would wake him yet. Then, rising carefully from his side, she stood up and looked around again, hardly recognising the white folly in the morning sun. She couldn't remember whether it was she or Jonathan who had opened the shutters, but whoever had done it had changed the place entirely.

The small circular building was filled with light, and its design, with windows all the way around and going right up to the ceiling, seemed to capture and amplify the sun's radiance. It was like being trapped inside the golden, idyllic essence of summer, and it was easy to imagine the picnics and parties that might have been centred around this charming little structure.

But why have what was so patently a pleasure pavilion in the grounds of a priory? An ecclesiastical establishment? It seemed incongruous.

'Weird,' muttered Belinda, running her fingers through her hair in lieu of a comb and beginning to wonder what had happened to her clothes. Jonathan's shorts, trainers, T-shirt and briefs were strewn across the floor, clearly exactly where each item had been removed, but of her own clothing there was no sign at all.

'Uh oh,' she said to herself, as more memories of last night began to surface. Despite their solitude and Jonathan's complete insensibility, she felt the blood rise into her face in a vivid blush.

Last night, right in the middle of the storm, she had stripped naked in a woodland clearing, then peed herself and masturbated. She could still almost hear her shriek of pleasure.

Good Lord, what got into me? she thought, her fingertips brushing her throat nervously as if trying to twitch up a non-existent collar and hide the pinkness that was rising across her chest and up her neck into her face. She remembered feeling wild and exhibitionistic, and being filled with a strange sensation of being watched. And then, when she had returned to the folly and to Jonathan, she had offered him her body and they had rutted like a pair of animals.

But animals that care about each other, she thought, looking down at him fondly as he turned over in his sleep and began to scratch and fondle at the very member that had so pleasured her last night.

'That's right, get it ready for me,' she whispered to him, feeling naughty, then tip-toed away from him towards the door of the folly.

Outside, the beauty of the day took her breath away. Everything that had been harsh and turbulent last night was pacific and gently sun-kissed now. The grass was vigorously, almost preternaturally, green, and hung with drops of moisture like tiny diamonds. The sky was a delicate eggshell blue tinged with pink, and thin streamers of gauze-like mist were slowly dissipating. Even the grey priory across the park looked quite benign, and not a bit like the derelict hulk of the previous night. Belinda decided to make her way there as soon as she found her clothes.

Retracing her former steps into the woods, looking this way and that and on alert for possible company despite the apparent desertedness of the priory's spacious park, Belinda soon found the little clearing she had encountered last night. Her clothes were there, just where she had abandoned them, the pattern of their falling not dissimilar to that of Jonathan's. She could feel her blood stir again at the thought of how she had shed them and at her own crude and strangely pagan behaviour. And when she had to squat again, she was almost too embarrassed to perform.

Having been taken off in the shade, and sopping wet, her clothes were still in that condition. She shuddered at the touch of the clammy, ice-cold fabric against her skin, but consoled herself that they were at least clean again. She had never liked putting on once-worn clothes for a second time, especially after she had indulged in hectic sex. The vision of a steaming bath full of scented water suddenly presented itself, and Belinda wondered if there was a stream or something nearby so she could have a quick wash before she set off on her exploration.

Better not get lost though, she told herself, turning in a circle on the spot and squelching in her trainers. On all sides the trees were numerous and the woods deep and thick; it was only in the direction of the folly that she caught sight of bright light and open ground.

Back in their circular white refuge, Jonathan was still fast asleep, and much as she would have liked to discuss their situation, Belinda didn't have the heart to wake him. During her absence, he had turned again on the couch, and now lay in a foetal position with his two hands folded so sweetly beneath his sleeping face that he looked a perfect innocent. She decided to walk to the priory and back and give him time to come to wakefulness naturally.

As she set off across the grass, sheer pleasure to be alive made her less aware of her wet clothes and the fact that she and Jonathan were lost. The sun was surprisingly high now, and a light breeze made the bejewelled grass ripple. There were birds singing cheerfully in the woods and she caught sight of a rabbit, or a hare perhaps, sprinting ecstatically along the edge of the treeline. And now, closer up, the priory looked even less like its midnight incarnation.

The building appeared both larger and somehow smaller than it had done last night, spreading out far further than had previously been apparent, with numerous wings, buttresses and even a crenellated turret. But it no longer seemed to claw the sky and loom.

It was still not an 'easy'-looking residence however, and its tall leaded windows with their rounded Gothic arches and tiny lozenge-like panes had a curious and watchful air of latency, as if a presence beyond them lay waiting.

'Don't be an idiot,' Belinda told herself, still studying the priory and frowning. It took her just a few seconds more to realise what it was about the house that had really changed, or seemed different. Last night the priory had seemed deserted, desolate, a blasted ruin; but now, in the brilliant day, although it still wasn't a well-kept building by any means, it certainly looked sound enough to live in.

Pausing to slip off her squelchy trainers, which were taking the edge off her appreciation of the view, Belinda continued to study the priory, her eyes zeroing in on an upper window, where for a moment she thought she saw movement. What if there was actually someone in residence there; someone with a phone, who could help them in their predicament? Barefoot, she began to stride faster.

As she neared the house, Belinda soon found herself in a jungle of flowers and greenery which must have once been a garden. If there were inhabitants at the priory, they evidently weren't keen horticulturists, as both wild and cultivated plants and flowers were growing in a tangled but strangely pleasing jumble. She saw and smelt roses, as well as delphiniums and hollyhocks, but among them were deadly weeds like belladonna.

Reaching a gravel path, she slipped her trainers back on and made her way towards what seemed to be the priory's front door; a massive, weather-beaten oaken affair which stood beneath its own entrance porch. Just as she reached a set of shallow steps, the heavy studded door swung open and a handsome man greeted Belinda with a smile.

'Er ... hello,' she said, suddenly at a loss and able to do nothing but simply stand and stare. The man standing in the doorway was remarkable; a towering, bronzed giant dressed in blue jeans and skimpy white vest. 'My friend and I are lost,' she managed to say at last. 'We spent the night in your folly.' She glanced over her shoulder towards the distant white building. 'I hope you don't mind. We haven't made any mess.' The tall man just smiled. 'I ... I ... um ... I wonder if you have a telephone I could use? Our car's broken down. We need to call a garage and the battery in our mobile phone is flat ... We're supposed to be meeting up with someone soon and we've got to let her know that we've fallen behind schedule.'

The tall man continued to smile, nodding his close-cropped head encouragingly.

Belinda felt uneasy. Why didn't the man answer instead of just standing there like a silent, living statue?

'We can pay for the call,' she offered doubtfully, remembering her shoulder bag was back at the folly.

The handsome giant continued to smile, his large white teeth almost twinkling in the sunlight, his muscled arms gleaming, his eyes –

His eyes. Fighting her growing bemusement, Belinda looked the stranger directly in the eye.

Was this the man she had sensed last night? The watching male presence? There was certainly a mythic quality about him. With his ultra-short blond hair he looked like a Teutonic god just returned from Valhalla in modern dress.

After a few seconds Belinda knew that this wasn't her night watcher. His eyes were a soft brown, and mild, and his expression was gentle and welcoming, despite the fact that he still wouldn't speak to her. The eyes she had seemed to see last night had been blue, a piercing electric blue, and while they had not seemed particularly malevolent, they had possessed a power that could frighten and inspire awe.

Still the man continued to smile, but after a moment, however, he stepped back into the house behind him, waving Belinda through with a gesture of welcome. Feeling she might be making a big mistake, Belinda ventured inside.

The hall in which she found herself was cool, quiet, and rather dark, and looking around she was surprised by its opulence. From outside, the priory looked run-down, even after this morning's improvement, but inside it was well maintained, almost sumptuous. All around her was panelling, in oak or some other rich wood, the carved patterns forming tall arches with curvaceous mouldings. A few pieces of heavyish but gleaming furniture were placed against the walls, and in inset niches hung a number of sombre paintings.

Unfortunately there wasn't a telephone in sight.

'Do you have a telephone I could use?' repeated Belinda as her golden giant closed the door behind them. As she turned round to face him he made his first recognisable response: a slow shake of his head and another smile, this time regretful. He shrugged his huge shoulders, making his taut muscles bunch and surge.

Belinda tried desperately to contain her irritation. How on earth did people survive out here in the back end of nowhere with no telephone? It was almost unheard of.

'We're stuck then,' she said glumly. They would have to see if they could start the car or get directions to the nearest village, then walk there and arrange a tow. And

34

find a phone so they could get in touch with Paula, who wouldn't be too pleased if they didn't phone her soon.

'Could you give me directions then, please?' she asked. She was tempted to ask if the blond giant had a car and could drive them to the next village, but the request seemed a little premature.

The man shook his head again, still smiling the smile that was now getting on Belinda's nerves. Under other circumstances, she would have found the silent blond very attractive – his golden body was as magnificently hewn and solid as the wooden furniture and panels around them – but his lack of co-operation was fast becoming irksome.

'Oh, come on!' she cried, exasperated. 'Surely you can tell me which direction to set off in!'

The blond giant continued to smile but there was a strangely wistful expression in his eyes, and suddenly, as Belinda stared at him, hoping to elicit a response, he made a short chopping gesture, just beneath his chin and in front of his sinewy neck. He did it a second time and slowly shook his head.

Oh dear God, he's dumb! thought Belinda as realisation dawned, and she felt an instant wave of sympathy. Poor man, how awful. What a handicap . . .

'I'm terribly sorry,' she said quickly, 'I didn't realise you couldn't speak.'

The blond man shrugged again, and his immense shoulders rippled.

What the hell do we do? thought Belinda, wishing again that she had brought her holdall, because in it was a biro and a notepad. Presumably her blighted Adonis could write?

As she thought this, her silent companion made a swift gesture that seemed to indicate 'hang on a minute' and strode over to an elaborately-carved table. From a drawer in it, he took a thick sheaf of creamy white paper and a pencil, and grinned at Belinda as if to say he had

35

read her mind. As she moved towards him, he leant over the table and began writing quickly.

My name is Oren, she read, when he handed over the top sheet of paper. His letters were spare and rounded but his writing was beautifully clear. *I am sorry that we have no telephone,* he went on, *but we have little need of one. If you would like something to eat, a bath, and a place to rest a while, my master offers you the hospitality of his home.*

How can he offer hospitality if he doesn't even know we're here? was Belinda's first thought. Unless the movement she had seen earlier at the upper window actually had been somebody watching her?

Her next thoughts were more basic, as she looked up and found Oren watching her expectantly. She had slept well last night, but the prospect of a bath – preferably a long, long soak in flower-scented water – seemed like a mirage in the desert. And she suddenly realised she was ravenous. The last thing she had eaten had been a bag of crisps at about seven o'clock yesterday evening. The vision of a completely wicked and calorie-laden plate of croissants, curls of butter and strawberry preserve became a second mirage, just as vivid and equally as tantalising.

'That's very kind, Oren,' she said, smiling up at him, still feeling a little uneasy, and surprised at such a generous offer made so soon. She wanted to refuse as graciously as she could, but heard herself say instead, 'I'd love a bath, and I'm absolutely starving! I just need to go back to the folly and fetch Jonathan – '

Oren turned to the table and wrote again on a fresh sheet of paper.

Please do not worry. Someone will bring your friend to you. Let me show you to a place where you can bathe.

As soon as Belinda had read the few short sentences, Oren gestured towards the imposing staircase at the far end of the hall, indicating that she should follow him.

Belinda hesitated. This was crazy . . . She didn't know this man from Adam, and she hadn't even met his mysterious master. The pair of them could be serial killers for all she knew. Yet still she found herself walking beside Oren towards the stairs.

'My name's Belinda, by the way. Belinda Seward,' she said as they reached the first step.

Oren nodded and smiled again, and Belinda suddenly felt herself goose-bumping, in spite of the morning's sultry warmth.

It was impossible – but she suddenly had the queerest feeling that Oren had already known her name before she told him. Swallowing nervously, she followed him up the stairs.

Jonathan stretched, then turned over, patting the velour beside him in a blind sleepy search for Belinda.

'Lindi?' he muttered, opening his eyes when his fingers didn't find her. 'Lindi, love, where are you?' Sitting up, he glanced worriedly around the folly.

There was no sign of her, except her bag, a few feet away from the couch, and that reassured him. She was around somewhere; probably slipped away for the same reason she had left the folly last night. Shoving his hand through his tousled hair, he grinned to himself, remembering her return.

Even now, in retrospect, her passion astounded him. And not only hers. Not for a long time had he felt so full of desire, so strong. His own forcefulness had increased his physical pleasure, and it had seemed to have had the same effect on Belinda. Never before had she responded with such wantonness, so wildly and with so few inhibitions.

'We ought to get caught in thunderstorms more often,' he said aloud to himself, reaching down to touch what memory had stirred. But as he handled himself lazily and felt his flesh swell and harden, he was suddenly surprised by the sound of a female laugh.

Snatching his fingers away from his penis, Jonathan looked around again. The soft laughter had definitely been female and for a moment had seemed to sound quite close, but it hadn't been Belinda's throaty chuckle. As he was pulling on his shorts and underpants, it rang out again, and this time he was able to discern that it came from outside, among the trees, and that it had a curious tone to it – an odd muffled quality, as if the amused person were trying to suppress her own giggling.

Jonathan wriggled into his T-shirt, stepped into his trainers, then made his way quickly to the door of the folly, bent on finding the unknown laughter's source.

Outside, he could see no one, but he heard the laugh again, and it seemed to be coming from the woodlands to the rear of the folly. Following what looked like a faint and overgrown path, he set off along it as stealthily as he could. The air among the trees was moist and fresh, and the atmosphere pleasantly cool for what seemed already to be a scorchingly hot day. Jonathan breathed deeply as he walked, enjoying the green, mossy scent of the woods.

After about a minute, he caught sight of something pale flashing among the sturdy trunks of the mature trees around him, and guessing it was the origin of the laughter he speeded up, while still taking care to proceed quietly.

All of a sudden, he found himself almost on top of the woman he sought. As he crouched behind a tree, hidden by the tall grass and weeds that grew around it, he saw that what he had thought was one woman was really two.

They were hardly more than girls, actually: two slender blondes – a little alike, cousins possibly – who appeared to be a few years younger than he was, possibly about eighteen, or perhaps nineteen or twenty.

Both were clad in thin white dresses and they were sitting on a patch of soft turf at the side of a slowly-flowing stream, kicking their bare feet playfully in the water. They were each as beautiful as wood nymphs, both in their faces and in their lightly-covered bodies, and Jonathan's penis rose again to salute them. And though their actions and their naturalness made it seem as if they weren't aware of his presence, Jonathan's sixth sense seemed to tell him a different story. Why else would they suddenly abandon their innocent splashing and lean towards each other for a kiss? A prolonged and very sensuous one on the lips . . .

Jonathan clapped his left hand across his mouth to keep in his exclamation, and with the other he reached down and touched his groin. He had often dreamed about watching two women making love, but never before had he really seen it happen. His cock stiffened and strained until it ached beneath his fingers, while on the riverbank a magical tableau was enacted.

Although in many ways the two blondes looked alike, as they kissed, distinctions became apparent. One was clearly a little older and more confident, and she controlled both the kiss and her companion. The younger girl – who wore her hair loose as opposed to her friend who wore hers in a soft ponytail – was more acquiescent, and the way she used her hands and her lips was more tentative. Her touch was cautious, almost subservient, and she allowed her mouth to be forced open by her friend's bold tongue.

To his surprise, Jonathan found himself wishing that it was he who was being kissed so forcefully. He suddenly felt a profound need to surrender somehow. He wanted to be taken, made to accept caresses rather than give them, and to perform solely for another person's pleasure. He wanted to be rolled on to his back, on the turf, as the younger blonde was being made to, and he wanted to lie there and be kissed and touched and stripped. Then be ridden until he cried out in wild release.

At the thought of that, his penis leapt and almost unmanned him, but by an effort of will he staved off ejaculation. He bit his lip, clenched his fists at his sides and tensed every muscle in his suddenly burning body. He closed his eyes as if to banish temptation, but behind his eyelids he still saw the two blonde beauties.

I'm sorry, Lindi, he thought to his absent lover. She had only left him for a little while. She might only be a matter of yards away, exploring. Yet already he was as good as being unfaithful.

But wasn't it almost Belinda's fault? he reflected suddenly. He hadn't felt this hungry for sex in ages, and thinking back to last night, and the storm, he hadn't really felt amorous then until Belinda had suddenly sidled up close and pressed her body against his. It was she who had changed the parameters, she who had set his mind to thoughts of lust.

An indistinct cry brought him back from the storm-tossed night.

The two blondes were gazing at each other intently now, as if passing messages with their eyes, the older one looming over the younger. As Jonathan watched them, hardly breathing, the older girl unbuttoned the front of her lover's cotton dress and drew apart the bodice like a pair of white wings.

The younger, more submissive girl's breasts were exquisite. Not large, but firm and unsagging, even when lying down. They seemed to challenge the very air with their fresh and perfect curves and the twin cherry-coloured peaks that delicately crowned them. And the older girl did exactly what Jonathan wanted to do. She leant over her partner and began to suck hard on one nipple while plaguing the other with her swiftly moving fingers.

Jonathan had sensitive nipples himself, and his own tiny teats seemed to stiffen and tingle in sympathy. Still clutching one hand to his groin, he used the other to tweak his small, brown crest.

As the blonde woman rolled her friend's nipple between her finger and thumb, Jonathan aped her action. Delicious darts of feeling shot down to his belly as he pinched himself, and seemed to increase the building pressure in his groin. He found himself shifting his bottom slightly where he crouched, and he prayed that his two love-nymphs wouldn't hear him. He felt his penis jerking dangerously in the cage of his underpants, and he knew that at any moment he would have to set it free.

And still he could do nothing but watch the show.

The girl beneath was writhing now, her slender legs scissoring, her hands travelling rabidly over the hair, the back and the shoulders of her busy companion. The two were completely intimate but – Jonathan realised with surprise – quite unspeaking. They both made odd little muffled groans and gasps, but there were no endearments, no questions, no words of praise. Not even when the older woman sat up, lifted the other's skirt, and without pause or warning jammed her hand between her squirming lover's legs.

The assaulted one gasped as if someone had knocked all the wind out of her, and it was no wonder, Jonathan realised. Not one, not two, but three fingers had been pushed inside her vagina; very quickly, in one untempered thrust. He could see the penetration perfectly from his hidden point of vantage; the young woman's smooth legs were as widely spread as she could get them, and her body arranged as if especially for him to see.

Unable to help himself, Jonathan pushed his hand inside his shorts and underpants and began rubbing at his stiff and aching penis. The sight before him on the riverside was so raw, so real and so erotic that he knew now he would experience agony without release.

What the two blonde girls were doing before him was not a bit like his preconceptions of lesbian pleasure. What he had imagined was a slow, ritualistic build up. Love-making that was stately and gracious; prolonged; almost dream-like. But instead the older one was ... well, she was fucking her friend – there was no other

41

word that could adequately describe it. She was using her whole arm and hand in a powerful sawing motion, working her wedged fingers inside her partner and crudely stretching her.

And her partner was loving it. She didn't say so, but her movements spoke for her. Jonathan watched, rapt, and with his fingers tightly clamped around his member, as the younger girl lifted herself on her hands and feet, and began to swing her body to and fro, almost forcing herself on to her lover's stiffened hand. She was strong and limber, and she reciprocated the action of the other woman's shoves as if trying to take the entire marauding limb inside her. She seemed intent on immolation; on being entirely and comprehensively possessed.

Although neither woman spoke or even cried out, other than the most formless of grunts, it was obvious when the younger of them climaxed. Her body went rigid and her beautiful face contorted as she lurched forward in one final frantic jerk. As Jonathan watched her, almost hypnotised, her smooth belly rippled and her bare toes gouged the earth.

It was too much. He had already seen far more than he should have. Slumping to the ground, he began working his own hips back and forth in a motion that echoed the blonde girl's thrustings. His cock was a rod of iron now and he had to give it easement; swivelling awkwardly, he revealed it to the air, then groaned as a vagrant breeze caressed his glans.

His need to climax was urgent, more pressing than he could remember in a long time, and as he pumped himself, he almost forgot his wanton wood-nymphs. Jerking his hips in ungainly circles, he pushed his penis through his fingers, focusing solely on the sensations he created.

It wasn't until the perfect moment, when his rushing semen jetted out in long white strings, that he thought again of his two companions in the forest. And opening his eyes, he looked up and suddenly saw them.

Like two mysterious blonde phantasms, they were standing over him and watching, their slender bodies naked, their pretty faces wreathed in smiles.

Chapter Three
The Magic Interior

When they reached the landing, Belinda stopped in her tracks. At the head of the stairs was a large and quite arresting oil painting; a picture of a man in period dress who had eyes that were the bluest she had ever seen. As she stared up at the image, half-entranced by both the eyes and the commanding image that the subject presented, she became aware that Oren was beside her, also – seemingly – transfixed.

'Is he one of your master's ancestors?' she enquired, turning her attention to the equally eye-catching man at her side, the tall sculpture in living golden flesh.

To her surprise, the mute shook his head, his own warm brown eyes twinkling as if he were privy to some private joke.

'Well, it's a fabulous picture anyway,' she said, taking a step forward for a closer look. Although she was no costume expert, Belinda guessed the man to be wearing eighteenth-century clothing. His expression was both solemn and challenging, and his hair was long, caught into a tail at the back, and had a strange whitish look to it, as if it were dusted with narrow streaks of fine powder. He had on a coat of navy blue velvet, with a high stand-up collar and sloping away tails, and he cut a dashing figure in pale breeches and high boots.

He was a handsome man, in both face and body, yet it was his eyes that drew Belinda's attention. They seemed to bore right into her, directly from the canvas, their colour brilliant and their intensity astounding. There was sadness in those eyes but they also made her feel profoundly vulnerable, so much so that she was forced to turn away. Almost as if he had read her mind and her fears, Oren smiled back at her reassuringly, then gestured that they move on along a corridor to their left.

Still disturbed by the portrait, Belinda followed her guide.

Who is he? she wondered, still captivated by the blue-eyed man. She was aware that the house around her was unexpectedly well-maintained and exquisite, but she felt too fazed to note its decor's more subtle features.

The man in the painting, she realised, had exactly the same blue eyes that she had seen last night in her dream or whatever it was. They were the eyes that had watched her making love with Jonathan.

Don't be crazy, Seward, she told herself, almost running to keep up with Oren's long stride. As they turned a corner and started down a spacious oak-panelled corridor, she saw that a whole row of portraits hung there, and all, it seemed, of either descendants or antecedents of the man at the head of the stairs.

The family likeness was uncanny. The nobleman in eighteenth-century breeches and boots was the very image of the one who now wore the garb of an Edwardian dandy. Strong genes, thought Belinda, pausing before a painting of yet another family member, dressed in a morning suit from the turn of the century. This man had much shorter hair but it still had the same almost dusted look to it, and he carried a top hat, suede gloves and a cane. There was the same arrogant melancholy in his blue eyes.

I'd love to have been able to meet you, thought Belinda

as she tore herself away from the picture to follow Oren. Any one of you. Your eyes, they're out of this world somehow. So beautiful, so brilliant, so alive, even if only in a painting.

At last, she and Oren seemed to have reached their destination, and he pushed open a door then ushered her through into a bedroom.

Belinda gasped. The room was breathtakingly sumptuous and about as far away from last night's impressions of the house as it was possible to get. Everything around her was luxuriously ornate and made no excuses for being so. She was in a pleasure chamber, a temple of sensuality, a retreat created to please and be pleased in.

Wherever Belinda looked she saw velvet, brocade, rich carpeting and the choicest of rare antique furniture, every piece softly gleaming with polish. The colour scheme was womb-like reds, ruddy pinks and vibrant corals, with ornamentation – wherever possible – in gold leaf.

'Wow!' she said, at a loss at the sight of such magnificence.

Oren just smiled and made an expansive gesture which seemed to indicate 'enjoy'. Then, while Belinda stood and stared, still unable take it all in, he retreated, leaving the red room with only a pause for a shallow bow.

What now? thought Belinda, staring around at the chamber that contained her, then walking over to the bed and sitting down.

This wasn't the sort of guest accommodation she would have expected for someone who had literally wandered in unannounced. No, this was the sort of setting a wealthy man would commission for a loved one, either a wife or a treasured mistress. It was a place for trysts and the long, lazy rituals of passion; it seemed to echo with the cries of past desire.

Rolling on to her back, Belinda kicked off her trainers,

46

stretched out on the crushed velvet bedcover and studied the elaborate mouldings of the ceiling. What would Jonathan think of all this when he arrived? she wondered. If he arrived . . . Oren had implied that someone would fetch him. But who? The whole priory had an odd sense of desertedness about it, even here in its magic interior which was so different from the way it looked outside.

Something unusual caught her eye as she tilted her head back, and sitting up and twisting round she looked more closely at what appeared to be a set of velvet curtains, a couple of yards deep, that hung against the wall over the carved head of the bed. It seemed strange for them to be there as the windows were all on the other side of the room, and immediately her curiosity was piqued.

Shuffling up to the pillows, she reached for the gold tasselled pull-cord that hung by the curtains and gave it a slow, steady yank. Immediately, as if on a well-oiled modern track, the curtains parted to reveal what was behind them.

It was another portrait. Another handsome man of the same blue-eyed lineage.

The pose this time was far more casual and naturalistic, fusing a modern look with an antique background and clothing. The man in the picture appeared to be half-sitting, half-lying on the same bed that Belinda was on, or one very like it. He was leaning back languorously against a mound of crimson pillows, his expression vaguely sleepy. And though his eyes had the same hint of sorrow that pervaded the portraits of his relations, he was also smiling a smile of satisfaction. His hair was long, loose and slightly tousled, and he wore just breeches, stockings and a voluminous cloud-white shirt that lay open to show his slightly hairy chest.

It was the most erotic image of a man that Belinda had ever seen.

A woman painted this, she thought suddenly. A

woman he was involved with. He looks almost as if he's just been making love.

Turning around again, Belinda slid down to the bed's wooden footboard, and leant back against it to stare up at the unknown man.

He really was exceptionally good-looking, and would have been so as much today as in any age. His features were strong and candid, with a slightly snub nose and a generous, sensual mouth. As ever his eyes were an electric, lightning blue, only this time they were hazed, as if with passion.

'God, you're beautiful!' whispered Belinda, noting the way the pale *déshabillé* clothing only accentuated the fine structure of the man's body. He was well built – athletically 'chunky', she would have called him – although the contemporary term seemed inappropriate somehow. And there was no denying the promise of his virility; a substantial bulge deformed the smooth line of his breeches . . .

On this bed, she thought, feeling a faint stirring of lust in her belly. At some time in the past, her unknown blue-eyed paramour had made love to a woman on this bed. Closing her eyes, Belinda imagined him first smiling, then stretching, and then rising up from his resting place among the pillows and beginning to strip off his few items of clothing.

It was the ultimate romantic fantasy. To be taken in these magnificent surroundings by a powerful, courteous lover from a bygone age. She pictured him naked, his hair loose, looming over her, his strong body primed and ready for sex.

'Mademoiselle, I must possess you,' he might whisper as his elegant hands peeled the clothes from her body. When she was as bare as nature intended, he would probably kiss her all over, touching his lips and his tongue to her every sensitive zone. Modern men thought they knew it all where sex was concerned, but something told Belinda that this nobleman from the past possessed

48

more knowledge and erotic skill than all her small band of contemporary lovers put together.

It was the eyes that made her think that way, she supposed, sliding down to lie flat on the bed, her own eyes still locked with the blue ones in the portrait. The man in the picture had a gaze that was full of experience. She knew beyond a shadow of a doubt that he had a whole gamut of poignant memories to draw on: passion, love, excess; conquest, loss, sorrow. There were lifetimes of wisdom in that look.

'Who are you?' she whispered again, as in her fantasy he began to caress her. Pushing up her T-shirt, she cupped her bare breasts, imagining that her hands were those of the man on the wall above her.

As she squeezed gently, she caught her breath. Her palms and her fingers felt suddenly and inexplicably cool. Not cool within, but simply cool against the skin of her breasts. Her nipples puckered at the sensation, tingling deliciously. The coldness seemed to spread, even as she acknowledged it, moving down over her midriff towards her belly. Opening her eyes, she looked to see if one of the long casement windows was open and letting in a draught.

One window was open, but the day was calm and the curtains hung still and heavy. Belinda shuddered, not from the cold, but from a strange excited fear. With shaking fingers she unfastened her shorts and eased them down, with her panties, to her knees.

Was it wishful thinking or was there a presence in the room with her? Belinda thought of all the tales of the supernatural that she had read in her lifetime and wondered if her own close encounter had finally arrived. It was something she had always wanted to happen, something she had often hoped for, in spite of the continued opposition of her rational mind. She had never truly believed in the supernatural but what was happening to her now felt incredibly real. The coolness flowed down over the skin she had just bared and seemed to soak in through her pores and tickle her innards like chilly fire.

'It's you, isn't it?' she said accusingly to the portrait, half-expecting the man to be laughing. But still he simply smiled his teasing smile. 'Oh my God,' she croaked, twisting on the bed as she felt something almost liquid seem to flow into her vulva. The texture was honeyed, yet cool; insubstantial yet paradoxically tangible against her burning sexual membranes.

What's happening? What are you doing? she thought frantically, pushing her fingers into her furrow to try and authenticate the sensation she was feeling. Her flesh was running wet but it was warm to the touch; she could not detect the chilly unction from the outside but could only feel its strange effects from within. With a groan she began rubbing her clitoris, massaging it slowly with the silky thrilling coldness.

Helplessly aroused, Belinda circled her hips, enjoying the constriction of her tangled clothing around her knees and the thrill of a peculiar dual reality. She could see that she was alone in the room but within her mind she was convinced that she had company. The blue-eyed man from the portrait was with her. As she slicked her aching clitoris she felt his hand upon her breast, long fingers cradling it, his thumb pressing against her nipple.

'You devil ... You devil ...' she whispered as the mysterious coldness aroused her teat and her vulva. The fluid, viscous chill was overflowing between her legs now, its ghostly trickles running down across her anus. 'What are you doing to me?' she begged as her sex-flesh rippled. It felt as if someone was pouring cooled syrup directly on to her, relentlessly filling her sensitive channel until she was awash. 'Oh God, stop it!' she cried, knowing in her heart that she really wanted more.

The ectoplasmic essence was oozing inside her now, creating chills of cool sensation within her body. She could feel it in her vagina, pushing and welling, and more subversively, sneaking its way inside her anus.

The invisible substance was rising into her and filling her, creating pressure on hidden pleasure nodes in her sex.

Looking down between her legs, Belinda tried to see the flow of fluid, imagining it blue as its cool nature suggested. But all she could see was herself.

With her thighs as far apart as her makeshift shackles would allow, she had a perfect, uninterrupted view of her womanhood. She was wet and her love-juices were glinting on her sex and on her fingers, yet there was no sign of the ghostly inundation. She could feel it and feel the tension it created, but all that was visible were her genitals, pink and normal in their arousal.

'Oh please . . .' she groaned as the pressure still increased, and her beleaguered clitoris seemed to swell beneath her finger. It was pushed out now, like an insolently proud berry, as if there really was a volume of fluid massed behind it. Increasing her efforts, she pounded hard on the tiny organ.

'You! You bastard!' she cried, focusing again on her blue-eyed nemesis as she climaxed and the urgent forces instantly dissipated. Kicking her legs and cupping her vulva, she thrashed and moaned and rode the waves of sweet release until they mellowed.

'You . . .' she muttered vaguely when the tumult was over, and she sat up, still bare-bottomed, on the bed. The man in the portrait looked exactly as he had before she had begun her self-pleasuring, but somehow she sensed that a change had taken place. He still looked ever-so-vaguely unhappy, but there seemed to be a faint glow of hope about him too.

'You!' she said again, studying the painting in search of a more tangible change. 'You did something to me . . . You've done something. What is it?'

The handsome blue-eyed man seemed to mock her, to challenge her.

'I'm not crazy, I'm just tired,' she told herself, trying to take hold of her innate lucidity. 'It's just the novelty

of this room, or hormones or something . . . Imagination.'
Shaking her head to clear it, she began pulling off her
clothes, then stood up, looked around the room, and
wondered where the promised bathroom was.

After a moment, she realised that there was a door set
into the panelling on the far side of the room, and beside
it was a fine Chippendale chair with what looked like a
silk robe laid across it, something she could have sworn
wasn't there when she had first entered. Frowning, she
crossed the room and picked the garment up.

It was a kimono, a very beautiful one with the traditional square sleeves. And on the back of it was
embroidered, in fine silver thread, the design of a rearing
mythic beast. Discovering a tall mirror – something else
she had not noticed before – Belinda donned the robe
and looked over her shoulder to admire the skilful
embroidery. It was an eagle-headed gryphon most probably, she guessed, although her knowledge of mythology
was somewhat sketchy.

Jonathan will know what it is, she thought, turning
from the mirror and cinching the robe's belt.

Remembering her boyfriend, she wondered where he
was now. Had he been brought to the priory, as Oren
had so calmly informed her in his note? Or was he still
fast asleep in the folly? Belinda glanced at her wrist, then
remembered her watch was in her bag which she had
left behind when she had set off exploring.

What on earth was the time? It seemed as if hours and
hours had passed since she had first entered this house
and then this elegant, red-hued room. And yet it was
probably still early. She could not 'sense' the proper time
as she usually could, even when she looked out of the
window. The sun was shining but its radiance was
diffuse, as if it were veiled. The whole sky seemed to
give off a luminosity, a brilliant blue that lit the landscape and the gardens. She had the weirdest feeling that
she was trapped in a bubble, and that the priory and its

grounds were a place out of time. She ought to worry, but she realised that she couldn't be bothered . . .

Opening the inset door, she found, as she had expected, a private bathroom; beautifully appointed and with well-kept antique fixtures.

'What? No blue-eyed men on the wall?' she said to herself as she began to run a bath.

Bathing took quite a while, not only because Belinda had felt sweaty and grubby after twenty-four hours without a proper wash, but also because the old-world fittings in the bathroom intrigued her.

The bath, the handbasin and the lavatory pedestal were all enormous, gleaming creations made out of white porcelain; archaic in appearance but supremely efficient in function. What's more, the water had been piping hot and abundant, and Belinda had discovered a cache of luxurious but unbranded toiletries which catered for her every feminine need. The soap and body lotion had been scented with camellias, the face lotion had been rich and silky, and the toothpaste had had a faint but delicious taste of herbs. The towels had been the thickest she had ever handled in her life, and as soft as a baby's breath against her skin.

Clean, refreshed and revivified, Belinda returned to the red and gold bedroom – to find yet more surprises awaiting her.

On the bed lay a beautiful if rather old-fashioned set of clothes: a dainty calf-length shift-like garment in white cotton – which Belinda suspected was Victorian under-wear rather than a present-day dress – a pair of rather loose-legged knickers in oyster-coloured silk, and a pair of flat slippers embroidered with a mandala design on each toe. Not much, but when she had put them all on at least she was decent, or partially so. The loose shift was extraordinarily thin and her nipples were clearly visible through the cloth's fine weave. When she smoothed the shift down against her body, she felt both unsettled and delighted by its daring.

Of her own things there was no sign at all now, and she could only assume that Oren, or someone, had slipped into the room while she was bathing and taken her grimy, over-worn clothing to be washed.

She had also been left a meal: a tall glass of milk and several slices of home-baked bread, thickly spread with butter. Plain fayre, and taboo in an age of diets and cholesterol, but somehow exactly, and uncannily, what she fancied. The milk was rich and frothy and the bread still warm. The butter was creamy yellow and tasted of sun.

The only thing she wanted for now was company.

Still unsure of the time, Belinda didn't know whether the food was breakfast or lunch, or even afternoon tea, but that didn't stop it satisfying her hunger. When she had consumed every last delicious scrap, she began to feel restless and fidgety, and she went to the open window, hoping to see Jonathan as he crossed the park to join her.

There was no sign of him, or of anyone else. But what did catch her eye was the formal garden.

It was lush with flowers, a brilliant tapestry of colour, but as she sniffed the rising scents, she frowned in puzzlement.

How could she have missed all this last night? In the thundery downpour, all she had noticed was sparse shrubbery and rain-lashed bushes. The brilliant floral hues wouldn't have shown up well in the dark of course, but all she could remember was a sterile, tangled wasteland.

Must have had something else on my mind, she reflected wryly, watching a flock of chattering birds sweep across the park.

'So? What next?' she demanded of her blue-eyed companion, as if the vivid portrait had life and could advise her.

The man's image regarded her silently, his ambiguous expression a silent provocation. Belinda shook her head, realising that she had genuinely half-expected him to answer.

She certainly couldn't lurk around in this room all day though, simply waiting for Jonathan to turn up.

Feeling an amorphous sense of longing, mixed with something akin to fear, she opened the heavy door and stepped out into the oak-lined corridor. To her left was the way to the great staircase and the lower floor, which was the logical direction to take if she hoped to find Jonathan or Oren or perhaps even the owner of the priory; and to the right was uncharted territory. Her conscious mind said 'go left, get things sorted out', but to her surprise she ignored it and turned right, her footfalls silent on the thick carpet runner.

After a moment, she found herself in a long, airy gallery filled with more portraits and a vast treasury of *objets d'art* and antiques. Once again, heavy velvet drapes hung from ceiling to floor and kissed the edge of a richly-patterned carpet. Brilliant sunshine from the windows cut into the design in bright slices, but in the shadows the darkness seemed over-dense. Belinda felt the hairs on the back of her neck prickle for no apparent reason, and squaring her shoulders she headed resolutely for the first patch of light.

'Blue Eyes' – as she realised she now thought of him – was once again the principal subject of the portraiture, but there were also several likenesses of women. Or 'woman', to be correct, in the form of a slender, gentle-eyed beauty whose long, intricately-coiled titian hair and creamy skin looked peculiarly familiar.

'I don't know your boyfriend, but I do know you,' said Belinda, standing in front of one of the pictures which showed the lovely woman in a green velvet gown. 'Although I'm damned if I know where from.' The sense of recognition was at the very edge of her consciousness, and when she tried to reel it in, it became less and less accessible. The more she tried to place the woman, the less she seemed able to; and after a moment or two, the conundrum made her head ache. Rubbing her eyes, she moved further along the gallery.

The owner of the priory had some beautiful but very strange things. Statues of gods and goddesses from the Ancient Egyptian pantheon; a long series of painted wooden representations of animal-headed deities. Gilded boxes, their lids open to display the mummified creatures that lay within: cats, snakes, even a wolf. Huge crystal vessels displayed in pairs, their attenuated spouts entwined. Stuffed birds in glass cases, caught in attitudes of flight and conflict. Two half life-size human figures, male and female, cast in gold and portrayed having sex on what appeared to be an altar.

This last item made Belinda shudder and blush, even though there was no one around to make her feel embarrassed. The copulating figures had been created by a master craftsman. Every detail was perfect, ecstatic, almost alive; even down to the grimaces of pleasure on the two gilded faces, and the intricately moulded genitals, which were fully visible as the pose had caught the outstroke. The man's thick penis pierced the woman's stretched vagina.

Looking more closely at the mating pair made Belinda's belly quiver, and she spun around when she seemed to hear laughter.

But the gallery was empty.

This is crazy, she thought. It's all the eyes in the portraits that are making me feel as if I'm being watched. There's nobody here. I'm quite alone. It's imagination –

A door creaked, and she whirled again, her heart pounding, her throat tight, her mouth dry.

'Who's there?' she called out, noticing for the first time that a previously-concealed door at the very end of the gallery was now gaping open a little. 'Who is it?' she asked, then a thought occurred to her. 'I'm sorry if I shouldn't be here . . . I couldn't find anybody . . .'

There was no answer and the open door moved no further. Belinda crept apprehensively towards it, then stopped dead when she heard a second sound.

It was a faint cry; the sort of indecipherable moan one might make while having a nightmare. Belinda's hand froze on the edge of the door as she wondered what lay beyond it in the dark.

Screwing up her courage, she pushed the door a little further open and discovered that the area behind it wasn't in total blackness. From somewhere up above, a faint shaft of sunlight illuminated a vestibule and the steps of a steeply-rising staircase that doubled back on itself again and again and again. Belinda made her way to the foot of it, then paused, listening carefully for more sound. None came, so she put her foot on the first worn step.

'Here goes,' she whispered, beginning to ascend, and knowing that both the cry and the situation had made her nervous. More than nervous. She felt genuinely fearful, but also, inexplicably, quite aroused. Beneath the flimsy shift, her bare nipples were hard and puckered.

Still straining to hear any faint sound, Belinda climbed the stairs as slowly and carefully as she could. The switchback construction of the staircase made her feel giddy, and she clung on for dear life to its rather insubstantial handrail. Beneath her, the stone steps struck a chill through the thin soles of her slippers.

Halfway to the top, judging by the quantity of steps that remained when she looked upward, there was a small landing and an anonymous panelled door. She considered turning the handle and looking into the room beyond, but instinct told her it wasn't her goal.

It took her a further minute of vertigo to get to the top, and when she did she had to stand for a few minutes breathing deeply and still clutching the thin iron rail. She was in the turret she had observed from outside the priory, she presumed, and which seemed to consist of two storeys and two large rooms. When she could at last catch her breath and her heart rate had settled, she realised she was standing on a second small landing and that the door before her must lead to the upper room.

It's just like a fairy-tale, thought Belinda, placing her hand on the massive iron ring that opened the door. Still not sure she was doing the right thing, she turned it and the door swung open silently and smoothly.

The chamber beyond was also stone lined, but its walls were hung with huge tapestries. Between these, more of the omnipresent deep-pile velvet curtains were drawn across the windows, and several thick candles in elaborate stanchions lit the room. Belinda absorbed all these facts in the space of a couple of seconds, before she focused her attention on the centre of the chamber, where there stood a great bed, all swathed around in what seemed like dozens of thin gauze draperies.

A naked man lay on the bed. A perfectly naked man with long, tousled hair and a face that she already knew too well.

Blue Eyes! thought Belinda, biting her lips so she didn't exclaim aloud. With slow, silent steps, she crossed the room then pushed her way carefully through the many layers of gauze.

In the flesh, the slumbering man – who was obviously the latest of his line – was much more striking than any of his painted forebears, even though the family likeness was still incredibly strong. His skin was very pale and his hair rather oddly coloured in that it appeared to be quite dark but thinly streaked with blond. His powerful limbs and torso were classically formed. Unable to help herself, Belinda centred her attention on his genitals, and was shocked when she saw his penis was half erect. Even as she watched, it twitched disturbingly and rose up further.

Although she couldn't see the sun now and didn't know the time, it suddenly seemed strange to Belinda that the man before her should be asleep during the day. Was he ill? she wondered. Was that why he had not been around to greet her? She peered more closely at his queer, unnatural pallor.

The sleeper looked almost as if he had spent many years indoors. There was no hint of tan about him anywhere, although paradoxically, he did not look unhealthy. His body was muscular and appeared to be in a hard and well-toned condition; it was only his unweathered skin that made him look like an invalid.

And there was certainly nothing fragile about his penis, which seemed to grow ever more rampant by the second. Belinda caught her breath when the man stirred slowly, then touched himself.

Standing at the foot of the bed, she almost swayed with excitement and arousal. The sleeper was a supremely attractive man, and the way he handled his genitals made her own sex twitch and weep. Longing to reach into her borrowed panties and caress herself, she felt weak with desire as she watched the drowsy man masturbate; fondling his hard length in extended, grace-ful strokes. Belinda felt a real need to hang on to the bedpost to stop herself falling, but she dare not do it for fear of disturbing her companion. As he began to writhe among the sheets, she heard him mutter; a string of foreign words and then what sounded like a name – 'Belle' – which he cried out with increasing force and anguish.

Belinda expected the man to wake at any moment; to open his eyes – which she had no doubt at all were brilliantly blue – and find her standing there watching him. The sensible thing was to sneak away; now, while he was still too far from consciousness to perceive her. But she was so bewitched by the sight of him that she stayed.

He was squirming now, twisting his powerful-looking body against the mattress as his clasping fingers con-tinued their steady work. Unable to stop herself, Belinda reached down and pressed the heel of her hand against her pubis, trying to stanch the sweet ache of mounting lust.

'Belle! Oh, Belle!' cried the tormented figure on the bed, before launching into yet another frantic, impenetrable chant. He was lifting his bottom now, pushing his penis through his gripping fist, as his heels gouged and scrabbled against the bedlinen. When his cries and exhortations became one long strangled groan, Belinda looked away; not embarrassed, but too moved by his beauty to watch his climax.

Eyes tightly closed, and with her hand at her crotch, she waited in frozen immobility to be discovered. But when discovery didn't come, she opened her eyes again, but still felt unable to face the figure on the bed. Ignoring the heavy frustration in the pit of her belly, she darted glances around the peculiar gloomy chamber, then stopped dead, her breath caught yet again.

On top of a massive mahogany sideboard, a little way from the bed, there was a small carved box made from a lighter, more rosy-toned wood. It was an unremarkable thing, and Belinda probably wouldn't have noticed it save for the fact that it was glowing in the dark. It was pulsing with an unearthly blue radiance that – when she turned again to the sleeper – she realised was synchronised exactly with his breathing.

Her desire almost forgotten, she could do nothing but observe the weird phenomenon. What the hell was happening? Was it a trick of some kind or her imagination going crazy again? The box was definitely radiating in some way, the rhythm of its pulses uncannily regular. Half of her wanted to move closer and investigate but the other half knew better and held back. There was a special, personal bond between the sleeping man and the delicate blue light, and Belinda suddenly had the feeling she was intruding. Turning silently on her heel, she moved away towards the door, feeling an odd mix of enchantment and true terror. Once through the door, she closed it as quietly as she could, and – her earlier

60

vertiginous feelings forgotten – raced down the round staircase at breakneck speed. She was gasping for breath as she almost burst into the gallery.

Collapsing on to an oak settle, she took in deep lungfuls of air and tried to think clearly and calmly.

What had she got herself into here? Who was the handsome, sleeping man, the one she had just seen masturbate to orgasm? And what the devil was in that luminescent box?

Suddenly Belinda felt very frightened and out of her depth. She really needed to see Jonathan's dear and rather ordinary face and to hear his pleasant, sensible voice outlining a reasoned explanation for what she had just seen.

Beginning to think more clearly, she realised that if someone really had been sent to fetch Jonathan at the time she had encountered Oren – what felt like many hours ago now – then surely her boyfriend must be here in the priory? Somewhere in the labyrinth of rooms and corridors?

Squaring her shoulders, Belinda set off determinedly along the gallery, not looking up at the blue-eyed portraits that seemed to watch her.

What she needed now, she told herself, was normality and reassurance. A bit of comfort from a man whose eyes weren't blue.

Chapter Four
Reassurance

'Where have you been?' demanded Jonathan, as Belinda strode into the opulent crimson sanctum that she supposed she could now call 'her' room.

'I might ask the same of you,' she snapped back, thrown off balance by terseness when she had hoped for understanding.

Jonathan was lying on the lush red counterpane. His feet were bare, and he was wearing a rather baggy white T-shirt and khaki shorts. His dark hair was slicked back and wet, as if he had just that minute stepped out of a shower. As she approached him he swung himself up so he was sitting on the edge of the bed. He appeared fazed by her belligerent response.

'I'm sorry,' Belinda said, relenting. Jonathan looked as confused as she felt, and they were both at sea in a strange situation. It seemed stupid to fall out over nothing. 'I was having a look around while I waited for you to turn up. Oren told me he'd sent someone to fetch you.'

'Who's Oren?' enquired Jonathan as she sat down beside him.

Alerted by something odd in her boyfriend's voice, Belinda studied him more closely, and noted that his expression was guarded.

'Well, it's hard to say,' she began, watching Jonathan start to blush, and wondering what had caused it. Last night, perhaps? What they had done in the folly had been fairly wild. 'I don't really know who he is,' she continued, keeping her own expression neutral while she considered reasons for Jonathan's embarrassment. 'He seems to be a servant of some kind, although he's not what you'd expect as a butler. He met me at the front door when I first arrived. It was weird, really, he almost seemed to be expecting me,' she said, realising as she spoke that it had been true. Her appearance had caused the big mute no surprise. 'Anyway, he welcomed me on behalf of his master, and showed me to this room. Which was pretty clever of him, considering that he doesn't seem able to speak.'

'You mean he's dumb too?'

'What do you mean, "too"?'

'The two girls who came to fetch me can't speak either.' He was pinker than ever now. 'But ... Well, it just seemed the simplest thing to come with them.' His eyes slid away from Belinda's, and he began picking at an invisible thread in the bedcover.

Something had obviously happened between Jonathan and these unknown, unspeaking 'girls'. Belinda could tell that, but own feelings rather surprised her. Her natural response should have been suspicion and anger, but somehow the idea of Jonathan with other women was exciting. She experienced a peculiar inner surge at his undisguised guilt; a superiority that, to her surprise, was quite arousing.

'Did they bring you to this room too?' she enquired in neutral tones. 'I assume you managed to tell them we're together?'

'I told them ...' he began, then paused, making a track on the velvet bedspread with his finger. 'But I'm not sure they understood me. I seem to have been given a room further along the corridor. They insisted and it was easier not to argue.' He looked up, frowning. 'So when

I'd taken a shower, I did a little exploring of my own and found *this* room ... And it just "felt" as if you'd been here, I don't know why.' He shrugged his shoulders and looked around. 'This is some weird set-up here, isn't it?' Belinda nodded, still watching him. 'I mean,' he continued, 'last night it looked like a total run-down heap ... and it still looks a bit dumpish on the outside. But inside – ' He gestured roundly, as if to take in the whole of the priory ' – well, it's like a palace. The furniture alone must be worth millions.'

'You're right there,' observed Belinda. 'I've done a little exploring myself and the whole place is just crammed with paintings and antiques and all sorts of weird and wonderful treasures.'

'You know ...' Jonathan hesitated, taking her hand. 'It might be rather nice to stay here a while. We certainly seem welcome.'

Belinda examined the idea, realising she had unconsciously been feeling the same way herself. It was tempting, but there were some practicalities to be considered. 'What about the car? We've got to get it fixed. And we can't just forget about Paula, you know,' she said, referring to the friend they had agreed to meet. 'She'll be wondering what's happened to us.'

'She could come here,' suggested Jonathan.

Belinda shook her head. 'We can't just invite someone *else* to stay. It isn't our house. And whoever owns it might want *us* out today.'

Even as she said it, Belinda knew she was wrong. She didn't know why or how she felt it, but she had a weird instinct that the priory's 'master' – the sleeping man in the tower – desperately wanted them, or maybe just her, to stay in his house. A wave of desperation swept through her; not her own but emanating from elsewhere. She felt cold, very suddenly, and shivered.

'Are you OK, love?' said Jonathan, shuffling closer and sliding his arm around her. 'You haven't caught a chill, have you?' He touched a hand solicitously to her brow.

'No, it's all right. I'm fine,' she answered, despite the fact that she was experiencing a weird mix of emotions. Puzzlement; foreboding; excitement; arousal. They were all swirling around inside her, and she couldn't understand where such a medley was coming from. Especially the huge rush of desire, which had just arrived, like a cyclone, out of nowhere. She had gone from a state of being mildly turned on by Jonathan to wanting him passionately, all in the space of a few seconds. Twisting in his hold, she slid a hand around the back of his neck and drew his face towards hers for a kiss.

Jonathan balked, his eyes filled with questions, then succumbed as Belinda tightened her grip. She could almost taste his confusion as his willing mouth opened, but he accepted the strong probe of her darting tongue. She felt him sigh as she pushed him back on to the bed.

In the tower, André von Kastel opened his eyes and smiled, feeling vital energy begin to flood through his body. 'I am in your debt,' he said, thanking his distant guests.

Stretching, he tested his capabilities. He was limber, and physically more powerful now, but not back to his full, normal strength. Though the curtains were tightly closed, he sensed that it was afternoon, so there was still some way to go in his restoration. When night fell, he would be all that he had ever been, thanks to a pair of stranded lovers beneath his roof.

Slowly, cautiously, he sat up, feeling a little fragile at first but after a moment gaining control of his equilibrium. Pushing his fingers though his hair, he untousled it a little, suddenly longing to bathe and refresh himself, and to dress again in newly-laundered clothing and to feel it crisp and clean against his skin. For all his peculiar affliction, he was still, in baser matters, completely human, and during his long sleeps he perspired like any man. What's more, there were splashes of dried semen on his belly and his thighs, and its lacquer-like consistency tugged at him minutely.

Can I stand? he wondered, swinging his bare legs over the side of the bed. Leaning heavily on the carved oak bedpost, he put his weight on his feet and pushed his shaking body up to a standing posture.

His head spun and his knees felt like jelly, but reaching out from within, he drew more strength from his unknowing guests. They were inducing great pleasure in each other now, with their caresses and their strokings, and their growing rapture was a well-spring he could draw on. Bracing his legs, he stood straight, just swaying slightly.

André was just about to take his first step when there was a soft knock at the door. After a moment it swung open to reveal Feltris, the youngest and shyest of his three silent servants. She was carrying a silver tray with some small objects on it, and she bobbed a curtsey before stepping across the threshold. The blonde girl's footsteps were feather-light and perfectly noiseless on the carpet, and as she advanced she smiled sweetly and seemed to glide. André smiled too. On the tray were a number of china trinket boxes, and he already knew what they contained.

Placing the tray reverently on the sideboard beside the rosewood box with its enchanted blue glow, Feltris went straight to André and knelt down to kiss his feet.

'You are as clever as you are lovely, Feltris my sweet,' he said quietly, urging her to rise again. 'Thank you very much for anticipating what I need.' Then, feeling weak again, he sank back down on to the bed, bringing a look of sharp concern to the mute girl's face. 'Do not worry,' he said, drawing her down beside him, then accepting her supporting arm around his shoulders. 'Our new friends will soon make me feel better.' He looked at her steadily, then winked to reassure her. 'They are very passionate. They will suit me very well.'

Glancing across at the blue-glowing box, André wondered whether to tell Feltris of his suspicions about the newly-arrived young woman, then thought better of it. He could be mistaken or it could all be wishful thinking – a figment of his desperate hope. And it was likely that Oren had already described to Feltris the special significance of their new visitor, and that the servant too was aware of what might very well soon be possible.

Against his will, André's hopes surged wildly inside him, and with them came his reborn libido. His cool blood raced and his penis began to harden.

'Caress me,' he whispered urgently to Feltris.

Making a wordless murmur of assent, Feltris reached down and took his member in her fingers, delicately strumming him with all her considerable skill. As she fondled and stroked him, André slumped back among the bedclothes, his body arched and his bare feet kicking against the carpet. Hazed by pleasure, his thoughts flew irresistibly back across the years . . .

He remembered a night in summer, on a bench in a rose arbour, when he and Arabelle had eluded her hawkish chaperone. Her beauty and her freshness, and her innocent, open-mouthed kisses had inflamed him to a point where he had lost his reason. Unable to stop himself, he had released his manhood from its constrictions. He could still hear her startled squeak of horrified wonder.

'What is it, André? What's the matter with you?' she had demanded, her lovely eyes agape as she stared down towards his penis. 'Are you ill?'

'No . . . There's nothing wrong,' he had gasped. 'This is what happens when a man loves a woman in the way I love you.'

'But I don't understand,' Arabelle whispered, still absorbed by his towering, aching member. 'Are you in pain?'

'No . . . Yes . . .' he stammered, as confused by his intense feelings as she was. 'It's difficult to explain, my darling,' he continued, feeling the blood pound in his

67

heart and in his penis. 'It does hurt, in a way, but it's a pleasant kind of pain.'

Arabelle frowned and bit her lip, regarding his uncovered staff as if it were a serpent. Not an ugly beast, but a snake that was as beautiful and hypnotic as it was deadly. Despite his extreme discomfort, André watched her, fascinated, as she lifted up her slender hand towards him.

'Is there anything I can do to help you, my love?' she said, her eyes never leaving his erection.

A thousand things, thought André, imagining a scene where he swept up her perfect young form in his arms, then lowered her gently to the greensward before them. A scene where he lifted her skirts and petticoats, parted her smooth thighs, then plunged his tortured flesh deep into her softness. A scene where he rode her body until they soared in mutual ecstasy.

'Just this,' he whispered, taking her narrow white hand and folding it around his stiffness.

'It's so warm,' he had heard her whisper. 'So warm . . .'

And suddenly her words came to him across the echoing void of history, as his body rushed to pleasure in the here and now. Even as he ejaculated, he was aware of the poignant irony of certain contrasts. His coldness that had once been so warm; Feltris's dexterity compared to the hesitant innocence of Belle. Waves of sensation poured up through him as his essence pumped and spattered, but in his heart, he was weeping for what was lost.

'Oh, Lindi, yes . . .' moaned Jonathan as she ground her crotch against him. 'God, that's wonderful! Please do it to me! Oh God!'

Belinda looked down dreamily and smiled. They were both still dressed but she was squatting astride Jonathan's hips in a far from elegant crouch, massaging her clitoris on his erection through layers of cloth.

You're just using him, she thought, closing her eyes,

throwing back her head and swirling her pelvis. He's just an object, something hard to get off on. You're a slut, girl. A nymphomaniac. Try to be kind.

As if privy to her inner debate, Jonathan cried out plaintively. 'Please, Lindi, please!' he begged, bucking up against her, his hands on her thighs. 'Take your knickers off. Let me get inside you.'

About to comply, Belinda froze. She didn't so much hear a second voice in the room with them as much as just feel a presence. Her eyes snapped open and she looked up towards the wall.

They were closed! she thought wildly. When I came in, those curtains were closed!

The red velvet curtains were wide open now, and maybe always had been, but the portrait that they flanked drew her attention. The blue-eyed man seemed to be challenging her again, the subtle curve of his sculpted mouth a mocking quirk.

'Who's in charge here?' she almost heard him say, his eyes glittering like shards of aquamarine beneath his lashes. 'Are you going to obey him, indulge him like the perfect obedient little servant? Or seize the moment, be a goddess . . . impose your will?'

You devil! she cried inside. Who are you? The cool, languid figure in the painting was most definitely the sensuously sleeping man in the tower. She knew that now, and realised that she had known it since the moment she had seen him on that great curtained bed.

Yet how could they be the same? This was the twentieth century, the 1990s, and above her, in the portrait, her nemesis wore the garb of yesteryear – an authentic costume from well over a hundred years past.

Was he in fancy dress?

It was an explanation, but not an adequate one. The condition of the paint itself suggested that both the picture and the clothing it portrayed were contemporaneous.

So how could 'Blue Eyes' still be alive and look so young?

'Please, Lindi!' came Jonathan's pleading voice again, breaking into her muddled thoughts and eccentric fancies. She felt his searching hand find the edge of her knickers and suddenly felt a great upsurge of anger – a rage that seemed to double her sexual need.

'Shut up!' she shouted, fetching Jonathan a hard slap across his cheek. 'Just shut up!' she hissed, feeling his hands drop uncertainly from her body. Looking down, she saw his eyes were bright and staring.

Is that better? she thought, circling her pelvis as she looked up again at the enigmatic, blue-eyed figure in the portrait.

There was no answer. The paint was simply paint again, formed into an image that was handsome but inanimate. 'To hell with you,' she whispered, then leant forward to concentrate on subduing Jonathan. 'So, tell me about these girls you met,' she whispered into his ear. 'Were they pretty?'

'No ... Yes ... Sort of,' he answered, moving guiltily beneath her, his hands disempowered and fluttering helplessly against the counterpane.

'Pretty enough to fuck?' she purred, putting her face close to his cheek, then catching the lobe of his ear between her teeth. Their bodies were contiguous now; her bare arms were resting on either side of his head and her breasts were pressed against his torso. Shimmying, she massaged her nipples against him, rubbing their tips over the muscularity of his chest.

'Well?' she persisted, not sure why she was asking, but asking anyway. Perhaps it was to vindicate certain feelings she had experienced in the tower – her instant desire for that naked, sleeping man.

'I didn't mean to, really I didn't,' faltered Jonathan. Belinda felt his penis twitch and lurch as he stuttered out the words, the tiny movements a subtle stimulation. Spreading her thighs wider, she bore down harder, loving the fact that her actions reversed their roles. She was the protagonist, the instigator; she was taking advantage of the man who lay beneath her, employing his desire and his hardness like a toy.

'But you did, didn't you?' she taunted him. 'I leave you for a moment and all you can do is stick your worthless dick into the nearest female body that's available.' She jammed her own female body down on to him. 'You didn't even have the decency to wait for me.'

'It ... it wasn't like that,' Jonathan gasped, half-whimpering and half-groaning as she tilted her vulva against him.

'Then what was it like?' She wriggled, making a minute adjustment to her awkward position that sent a wave of sweet sensation racing through her. Her teeth closed carefully on Jonathan's vulnerable earlobe, and his body shook with concentrated tension. He was just a second away from losing all control. 'Jonathan!' she prompted, pulling delicately with her teeth as she pushed down firmly with her crotch.

Jonathan's 'Oh God!' transformed itself into a long, falling moan, and through their clothing, Belinda felt his trapped sex pulsating. As he throbbed, she felt a sudden rush of warmth.

Afterwards, it took several minutes for Jonathan to compose himself, and knowing his sensitivity at such times, Belinda remained motionless on top of him. When he stirred again, she resumed her line of questioning.

'Tell me what happened, Jonathan,' she persisted, kissing his neck.

'I heard a noise. Someone laughing ... It woke me up.' His voice was slower now, more mellow, but still sounded just a little shell-shocked. 'I thought it was you at first, but after a minute or two, I realised it wasn't.' He paused a moment, then moved his hips, pressing his soft and sated member up against her. He shuddered as if enjoying his own stickiness. 'Anyway, I got up and followed the sound until I found myself at the side of a stream . . . or a river . . . Anyway, whatever it was, there were two girls there sitting on the bank. They were laughing and kissing each other.'

'Was that all?' asked Belinda, feeling an unexpected frisson of emotion. She would have liked to have been there to see those girls.

'No. No, it wasn't. They did other things too.'

'Such as?' Belinda asked, even though she was now several steps ahead of him. She had an inner picture of the two women caressing each other's bodies wantonly, their fingers probing and exploring. Her sex fluttered uncontrollably as she imagined them.

'Well, one of them – the older one, I think – she put her hand up the other one's dress and started touching her.'

'Just touching?'

'No, it was more than that . . . a lot more.' As Belinda straightened up, she saw Jonathan was smiling, his face slack and dreamy. Between her legs, she felt his flesh return to life. 'She was really . . . really working her,' he continued, his breathing quickening. 'Shoving her fingers right into the other one's vagina. Fast. Hard. It was just as if she was fucking her with her hand.'

Belinda made a sudden decision. 'Show me!' she commanded, rolling off Jonathan and lying down beside him. 'Show me what they were doing.'

'I could see her fingers going in and out,' murmured Jonathan, still shifting slowly and sleepily on the bed.

'Show me!' Belinda reiterated, dragging her skirt up to her waist and pulling at Jonathan's hand until it was lying against the crotch of her panties. 'Did she have knickers on?'

'No, she was bare beneath her skirt.'

'Do it for me, Jonathan,' said Belinda, jiggling her lower body so his hand moved on her sex. 'Take my pants off and do the same to me. I want it. I'm aching . . . Just do it!'

Galvanised, Jonathan sat up, his expression intent.

With unsteady fingers he grasped the waistband of Belinda's borrowed French knickers, then – while she lifted her bottom to make things easier – he pulled them down over her warm, perspiring thighs.

'That's enough,' she said when they were bundled at her knees. 'I can't wait any longer. Push your fingers inside me.' The panties hampered her, but she opened her legs as wide as she could for him, then leant on her elbows, craning forward, to see her own sex and the fingers that approached it.

Jonathan looked nervous. He glanced from her face down to his hand and then at her vulva. Belinda saw his fingers flex as he lifted them towards her body, then he seemed to stare at his own hand as if didn't belong to him, as if it was someone else's hand entirely. Frowning slightly, he blinked once or twice, giving the impression that he was wondering if he was seeing things.

'How many fingers did the woman by the river use?' Belinda asked crisply, to bring Jonathan out of his fugue. She couldn't wait any longer. If he didn't act now, she would have to do the deed herself.

'Th-three,' whispered Jonathan.

'Then you use three,' she decreed, lifting her hips with an imperious little jerk.

Still appearing confused, Jonathan touched his fingers to her entrance, his actions diffident, unassertive, unsure.

'For crying out loud!'

Belinda almost snarled with frustration, feeling a contact so faint it was almost ghostly; a tantalising tingle when what she required was brute male force. Jonathan's fingertips were pale against the orchid pink of her sex-flesh. She looked fiery and his pallor looked like ice.

Suddenly, another wave of empathy washed over her. She was burning between her legs, and she longed for the cool, cool touch she had imagined earlier in this room, the liquid chilliness she had so associated with Blue Eyes. She couldn't see him any more, but she could well believe that the portrait was 'alive' again, and watching closely as she gave her body to her boyfriend. She felt her innards jump impatiently with need and defiance, and with a hungry moan she thrust her sex towards its goal.

Jonathan's fingers slid into her. First one, then two, and finally, with a wiggle, three. Ignoring the discomfort, she dug her heels in and pushed down harder.

'So, what else did they do?' she asked hoarsely, gripping Jonathan's wrist for dear life, denying him the ability to move. She wanted him to be still for a few moments, perfectly still, so she could savour the sensation of being stretched.

'I-I don't know,' said Jonathan, his voice edgy with the sound of new arousal. 'I sort of lost track of them for a minute – '

'How so?'

'I was turned on ... really hard. I-I had to do something about it...' Embarrassment made him stutter again, and his fine trembling passed right into Belinda, through the medium of the fingers inside her sex.

'And was that all?' she probed, already beginning to feel she wanted more.

'No ... Not exactly.'

Tugging his hand away from her and letting it drop, Belinda moved up on to her knees again, so that she was beside him. Feeling sure of herself, she pushed Jonathan backwards until he was once more lying down.

'And what does that mean?' she enquired, slithering her knickers down her calves and off over her ankles, while trying to avoid looking up towards the wall – towards those blue eyes that followed her every move.

'Well, I was recovering. Getting my breath back and all,' continued Jonathan, watching her closely now. 'I was just lying there and suddenly they pounced on me.'

'They what?' Belinda laughed, genuinely amused by the idea. If Jonathan had looked as helpless yet at the same time as virile as he did now, she couldn't imagine a woman who wouldn't attack him. He was sprawled on the red counterpane, looking every inch her abject victim, while his penis tried to bore out through his shorts. Suppressing her smile, Belinda reached for the elastic at his waistband.

As she pulled down first his loose, cotton shorts, and then the briefs beneath them, she wondered who the clothing belonged to. All Jonathan's own clothes were presumably still in the boot of the Mini, and she didn't recognise anything that he was wearing.

Had Oren lent him some clothes? It was possible, but unlikely. The silent servant was well over six feet tall, and in proportion to that his build was broad shouldered and massive. Jonathan was no wimp – in fact he had a rather good if somewhat wiry body – but beside the golden Oren he appeared boyishly puny.

This lot must belong to Blue Eyes, she thought, pulling the borrowed shorts and underpants down to Jonathan's trainer-clad feet and leaving them there, bunched untidily around his ankles. The two men were very similar in size, she realised, even down to the dimensions of their genitals. Both were sturdy and carried the promise of satisfaction.

'They pounced on me,' Jonathan repeated, wriggling his bottom and making his penis sway. He had his eyes closed as if trying to improve his memory. 'I was lying on the grass . . . A bit like this . . . I had my cock out.' He reached down, his fingers brushing his risen flesh, but Belinda caught his hand and replaced it with her own.

'And then what did they do?' she said, exploring the oiled silk texture of his fine, penile skin, and working it very slowly up and down.

Jonathan made an odd little hiccuping sound and grabbed a couple of loose handfuls of the bedcover in his fists.

'They did what you're doing . . . and other things,' he whispered, his voice thin and breaking. 'They kept stroking me. Touching me. Everywhere.' As Belinda slid her gripping fingers down him towards the pit of his

75

belly, he went rigid and rose upward, his body arched. 'Oh God . . . Oh God . . .'

'And what else?' She kept him stretched, taut. His swollen glans crowned his straining shaft like a hard red fruit.

Jonathan made several unintelligible noises, then passed his tongue around his lips as if hunting for words to express his feelings. 'One of them kissed me – it was the older one, I think. She kissed my lips and forced me to open my mouth – ' Belinda blew on the tip of his penis, and his heels kicked and dragged against the coverlet. 'And the other one got on top of me and fucked me.' His body bowed again, raising his member towards her.

'You mean like this?'

With speed and a nimbleness she had never realised was part of her, Belinda released his erection then neatly leapt astride it. Her thin, borrowed dress billowed around her like a boat-sail, and at the last second she reached beneath herself to place him. She was so wet he plunged in easily and sweetly.

Oh yes!

She didn't speak the words, she didn't even think them, and Jonathan seemed beyond speaking them entirely. Yet still the exultation rang around her, and she couldn't avoid looking upwards.

The portrait looked exactly the same as it had done when she had first revealed it. The same, yet unspecifiably different. She didn't know how to describe it, but Blue Eyes was watchful again, and she got the impression he was well pleased by her pleasure. A rush of energy flushed through her like a rolling bolt of lightning, and she could almost believe the portrait was its source. She was Blue Eyes' instrument, the living wielder of his power.

Laughing, she shook her hips and felt incredible sensations at her centre. Jonathan whimpered and reached for her, but she swept his hands away and drove down harder on his penis. When she was settled, she whipped her dress off over her head.

There! she thought in triumph, arching her back, cupping her breasts and circling her pelvis. How do you like me now? she demanded silently of her watcher, meeting his painted gaze just as the euphoric spasms sparked.

I like you very well, he seemed to answer inside her mind.

'Yes, I like you very well indeed,' repeated André. He smiled into the smoke as it rose towards the ceiling, stirring the thurible's contents with his narrow black-handled dagger.

Creating an enchantment had been easy, the words and actions as natural as breathing, despite the length of time that had passed without chance to practise. Selecting a perfectly-dried rose petal from a heaped pile on a silver salver, he crumbled it slowly and added the fragments to the flames.

A single strand of hair from each of the lovers – culled by the observant Oren when he laundered their dirty clothing; several desiccated rose petals; one drop of mercury; one of blood, his own; and a little water from a stream that crossed hallowed ground. These were the constituents, the simple, easily-obtainable substances, which he burnt together to create the desired objective – unprecedented lust and sexual pleasure for his new young house guests.

As he stirred, André considered Belinda's ruminations on power. He heard her thoughts perhaps more clearly than she did, but her misconceptions brought a new smile to his lips.

'It is not *my* power you feel inside you, Belinda,' he whispered to the orgasming girl, as – in another part of the house – she cried out plaintively at her peak. 'The power is yours, my dear. It is simply *I* who feed on *you*.'

Fresh smoke ascended from the tiny pyre in the

thurible, and breathing it in André felt a dizzying rush of vigour. His body, naked but for the embroidered silk mantle around his shoulders, was suddenly imbued with a rising, reborn strength. His skin prickled; his penis stiffened. Every sinew, every muscle, every nerve-end – even the individual hairs on his head – seemed to snap with a vivid life and health. In the darkness, his limbs and torso appeared to glow.

It was purely temporary, this state of revivification, he knew that. The effects would persist in him for the duration of the lovers' current sex act, then linger on for the couple of hours that followed it. The experience was transient at this stage, but while it lasted it was as heady as vintage wine. And in character, it was infinitely more delicious.

Laughing softly, André prepared to slake his thirst. There were more enchantments to be cast if he were to grasp this opportunity, and certain circumstances must be biased in his favour. Using his dagger, he swept the contents of the thurible into an alabaster bowl, and after murmuring an oath of purification, he set up a second enchantment in the shallow bronze dish. The first constituent was another strand of young Jonathan's dark hair.

'Forgive me, my friend,' he said, as he first coiled the hair then dropped it on to the vessel. 'You must sleep. I need your companion all to myself for a while.'

Humming softly to himself, he began his second arcane task. It was good to wield his gifts again at last.

78

Chapter Five
An Audience with the Count

A knock on the door roused Belinda from a light doze. She was not so much asleep as resting her eyes – letting herself drift and just not thinking – and in consequence she was fully awake in half an instant. Sitting up, she grabbed Jonathan's shoulder and gave him a shake.

The knock came again, but despite her best efforts, Jonathan would not wake up. Belinda was used to his ability to sleep on a rail almost and snatch impromptu naps whenever time permitted, but this deep, near coma-like slumber was frightening. She grabbed both his shoulders and shook him as hard as she was able.

No effect.

'Miss Seward?'

At the sound of her name, Belinda grabbed the sheet and pulled it up across her breasts. What could she do? She and Jonathan were naked, their clothes were all over the floor, and the black kimono she had worn earlier was across a chair at the far side of the room. She opened her mouth to call out, 'Just a minute' but instead, to her horror, she cried, 'Come in!'

Before she had time to call out a second time, the heavy oaken door swung open, and a familiar figure stepped across the threshold into the room.

Belinda's heart raced. She supposed, in a way, that her visitor was the one she had been expecting; but it was still a shock to see him standing there, smiling.

Her visitor had his streaked blond hair caught back in a ponytail, and he was wearing clothes now – a white shirt, blue jeans and black boots – but he was definitely her naked dreamer from the tower, the latest representative of a line of blue-eyed men. And he seemed filled with male amusement at her plight.

'I am sorry. I appear to have disturbed you,' the newcomer said softly, his distinctive eyes glinting. 'But I could have sworn I heard you call out for me to enter.' He grinned, his expression keen and knowing, as if he was perfectly aware of what had happened and had probably even caused it.

'I-I did. Call out, that is,' Belinda stammered, feeling both alarm and excitement in equal measures. Blue Eyes was just as impressive awake as he had been sleeping, but his mischievous smile was completely unexpected. All the ancestral portraits had looked pensive and melancholy, and even if they had been smiling, it was a smile tinged with palpable sadness.

And not one of the portraits had done justice to his family's remarkable eyes, which in the living, present day individual were a blue so intense it was borderline unnatural. They were ultramarine, cerulean, lapis-lazuli; every vivid shade of blueness in one colour. They seemed to flash as if fired by an inner electicity, and they were certainly the ones that had haunted her dreams.

Feeling panicked, Belinda looked down at her body, and realised another disturbing fact. The sheet that covered her had slipped somehow, in spite of the fact that she had been gripping it as if her life depended on it. Her rounded left breast was now completely on show again, its nipple noticeably hardened and dark. When she looked up again, her blue-eyed host did too.

Belinda tugged up the sheet. 'I-I – ' she began, then bit

her lip. What could she say? What could she do? She was trapped.

'Perhaps this is what you require,' he said, lifting the black robe from the chair and bringing it across to her. His booted tread was inaudible on the thick Persian carpet as he wended his way among the tangle of discarded clothing.

Belinda began to reach out for the robe, but her host stopped a couple of yards away, a guileless expression on his manly but strangely pallid face.

The bastard! He wants me to get out of bed for it! thought Belinda furiously. Well, all right then, she proclaimed with inward defiance, thinking of the moment a while earlier when she had boldly abandoned her dress. Whoever you are, you've asked for it!

With as much grace as she could muster, she slid from between the sheets then turned around and held out her arms behind her, inviting her host to slip the silk robe on her. Without touching her once he complied, but he was smirking when she turned back to face him, having knotted the sash in a doubly secure bow.

'The robe becomes you,' he commented, taking a step back as if to appraise her appearance. Belinda got the impression he was a shrewd judge of beauty. Or at least that he considered himself as such. Arrogant beast! she thought, cursing him again.

'Thank you,' she said tightly. It was difficult to know where to start in a situation like this, and ludicrously, she found herself holding out her hand. 'We haven't been properly introduced, have we?' she said, feeling an insane urge to laugh. 'I'm Belinda Seward. And this – ' She nodded over her shoulder at the still comatose Jonathan ' – is my ... my boyfriend Jonathan Sumner. We're both indebted to you for taking us in,' she added as an afterthought, wondering if the master of the house had even realised he had guests.

A second or two later, another thought occurred to her, one that shook her even more than her host himself did. He had called out to her from the landing by name, but how on earth could he know it? The only way Oren could have told him was by means of a written report.

Full of doubts now, she hesitated with her hand, then experienced a peculiar phenomenon. She had been going to withdraw it, but suddenly, and as if her whole arm had a life of its own, she lifted her hand again and held it out towards her host.

As he took it he made a movement that was entirely European; a tiny, barely perceptible heel click as he lifted her fingertips and conveyed them to his lips. When mouth met flesh, he looked up at her through his thick, dark lashes, his wicked eyes as bright as blue stars.

'André von Kastel. At your service,' he murmured, his mouth still hovering over her hand. His breath felt strangely cool against her skin. 'Welcome to my home,' he added as he straightened, releasing her fingers with an unfeigned reluctance. 'Or perhaps I should say my latest home. I have travelled considerably throughout my life, and this house is just the latest of many.'

This was his longest speech so far, and for the first time she became aware of his accent. It was delicate, very slight; a mere twisting around the edges of the words that made her insides clench and quiver. Like many women, she had always had a penchant for continental men – whether actors, singers or politicians. There was something worldly about them – a quality that was both polished and vaguely savage – which this André von Kastel clearly possessed in abundance. He was one of the most impressive men she had ever encountered, even though he was casually dressed, and appeared – on closer inspection – to still be a little fatigued.

Sleeping Beauty, she thought, grinning at him and knowing she was probably making a complete fool of herself. Did I wake him? Am I the first woman he's seen for a hundred years?

'Have I missed a joke?' he asked, returning the grin

and looking even more devastating as a set of laughter lines bracketed his blue eyes.

'No, it's just me being silly,' she replied, twisting the sash of her robe.

'In what way?' He was still smiling, still challenging her.

'Well, what with your accent, and the name, and the boots and all – ' The way his jeans were tucked into his soft, calf-high, black leather boots lent his appearance a vaguely cavalier quality ' – you're a bit like a prince in a fairy story. Especially with the long hair too,' she finished lamely.

And that was another thing, she thought, in the split second during which his smile broadened and he seemed to be preparing to respond. When she had seen him in the tower, his hair had been darker, she was sure of it. More brown, less blond. It was drawn back sleekly from his face now, but it was clearly a good deal streakier, almost platinum in places, as if he had spent day after day in hot sun. Maybe he's bleached it? she mused, recognising the thought, when it came, as bizarre.

'I am flattered,' he replied, making that tiny, almost Prussian bow again, 'but I am merely a rather poorly-connected count. Perhaps not even as much as that any more. My home country no longer exists.'

'What do you mean?' asked Belinda, silently upbraiding herself for a curiosity which could well alienate him. She and Jonathan had blundered their way into this house uninvited. They were here on this man's sufferance alone. Puerile remarks and personal questions weren't appropriate.

Count André appeared unperturbed. 'Merely that it is gone now,' he said with a shrug. 'A casualty of the redrawing of Eastern Europe, I am afraid. Which probably leaves me as simply "*Mr* von Kastel".'

'"Count" sounds much better,' Belinda said impulsively. 'Much more glamorous – '

'Why thank you,' he said. 'I shall endeavour to live up

to my title.' He reached out for her hand again, then kissed it, the application of his lips far more determined this time, pressing the print of them like a brand into her skin.

Belinda was nonplussed. The touch and the kiss were intensely erotic, even though the contact not much more than minimal. While he was bent over her hand, she seemed to see him back in his tower again, sprawled naked on his bed and caressing himself, and when he straightened up, she found herself glancing at his crotch.

As if he had noticed her ogling him, Count André gave her another of his impish white smiles. 'May I offer you a glass of wine?' he asked. 'We could retire to the library and get to know each other a little, and leave your young friend – ' He nodded to Jonathan, who, as if he had heard, turned over in his sleep and nuzzled his pillow ' – to his rest.'

'Yes. I'd like that,' replied Belinda, very aware that he was still holding her hand and that his thumb was gently stroking her knuckle. It almost felt as if he were rubbing her sex.

'Come then,' he said, giving her hand a last squeeze before releasing it. Spinning on his heel, he led the way to the door.

As she accompanied her host along the corridor to the big double staircase, Belinda was torn between studying him and taking another look at his forebears. Seeing the living man, awake now, made her realise how strong the family resemblance really was. The von Kastels of yester-year were almost identical to her handsome companion; so much so that the portraits could well all have been of him. The likeness was so exact it was uncanny.

Count André's good looks were also puzzling in another way. What made him beautiful to the female eye was difficult to quantify. Taken individually, his features were pleasantly formed, almost ordinary apart from his eyes, but the whole sum of him was nothing short of devastating. He wasn't tall, but his body looked strong and sturdy, and his way of moving was as aristocratic as his title.

'Are these all your ancestors then?' she enquired, gesturing to one of the portraits.

André turned as he walked, and gave her an oblique glance; a strange, assessing look that she didn't quite understand. 'Yes, they are all von Kastels,' he affirmed, but there was something as undecipherable in his voice as there had been in his eyes. It was almost as if he were telling a minor lie.

It was the first time Belinda had entered Sedgewick Priory's vast library, her previous explorations having been upward through the house, not downward. The room was quintessentially Gothic, decorated in a heavy ornate style which should have seemed sepulchral, but which in fact felt unexpectedly welcoming. Also a surprise, given that it was summer, was the large fire that was burning in the hearth. The bright, orange flames gave off a cheerful dancing light that flickered across the wealth of gleaming wood panelling and the glass panes in the front of the tall bookcases. A full suit of armour stood in one corner of the room, and dotted around on various tables and sideboards were mementoes and knick-knacks that must have been gathered by all the family over the centuries. Some of them were stranger than others. On a mahogany brass-bound secretaire stood a glass jar containing a stuffed and mounted animal, but not one that Belinda could recognise. It seemed to be half-lizard and half-wolf, and completely and utterly fearsome, and she couldn't understand why anyone would want it around them. She supposed that one of those blue-eyed von Kastels must have hunted it and shot it at one time.

Above the fireplace were two beautiful swords, suspended in a cross shape. They weren't the rapiers or fencing foils that one might have expected from a continental heritage, but what appeared to be Japanese fighting swords, a pair of immensely long and sharp *katana*.

Some previous von Kastel had obviously been a daring world traveller and brought back these death-dealing souvenirs of Japan.

'Do you prefer red wine or white wine?' enquired the present von Kastel, moving across to a beautifully-inlaid, bow-fronted sideboard and indicating an extensive selection of bottles.

'White, please,' answered Belinda, wishing that somewhere in the opulent beauty of the library was a concealed wine cooler. She wasn't a connoisseur, but she hated warm wine.

'A good choice,' Count André responded, giving her another of his curious looks, almost as if he were listening to something that she herself couldn't hear.

As he turned away and applied his attention and a corkscrew to the wine bottle, Belinda took advantage of the opportunity to observe him, out of range of those piercing blue eyes.

His bearing was elegant and his small movements as he eased out the cork were spare and effortlessly economical. He reminded her very much of the best type of character she had seen in costume dramas – a confident courtly man, but not a fop or a libertine. There was something very classical about him, despite the modernity of his boots and blue jeans. Jeans that fit him superbly, she noticed, admiring the firm, tight contours of his buttocks beneath them, and the way they formed faithfully to the musculature of his thighs.

It was a bit strange to be analysing his body now, in clothes, when she had already seen it stark naked, but in some ways she was seeing a different person. The André on the bed had appeared feverish, almost weak, as if suffering from some debilitating long-term disease, while this one was radiant with disgustingly good health. The tiredness she had noticed a few minutes ago had dissipated now, and she could almost feel waves of strength pouring off him. It was as if he had an aura of some kind, and it was provoking her. She squeezed her eyes almost closed and tried to see it, but there was nothing there but a fit, handsome man.

From where she had chosen to sit, on a vast brocade covered sofa, Belinda could see her host in profile, and as she watched him, he suddenly touched his fingertip to the bottle and frowned.

Yes, it's warm, she thought, isn't it? I would have thought someone like you would have had a cooler around somewhere.

As she thought those words, André turned towards her, regarded her thoughtfully for a second, then returned his attention to the bottle, first clasping it in both hands, then running his tapered fingers up and down it. After a moment, he smiled and poured out wine into two glasses.

'Here, try this,' he said, as he joined her on the sofa, holding one of the glasses out towards her. 'The grapes are grown in a region quite near to where I originally come from, I believe. It is quite sweet but I think you will enjoy it.'

Belinda nearly dropped the glass when she took it from him. It was cold, as if the wine inside had indeed been sitting in an ice bucket.

Count André grinned again and spoke a brief, unintelligible toast, presumably something from his own language. The word sounded a little like *prosit*, but with a curious part-gutteral part-musical inflection that Belinda didn't think she could have mimicked if she had tried.

'Cheers!' she said, then put her glass to her lips.

The wine was chilled to exactly the right temperature. Belinda was so surprised that she drank half of it at one swallow, hardly noticing that it was also sublimely delicious.

'It's cool,' she said, staring at the pellucid golden fluid.

'So it is,' replied Count André, lifting his own glass and staring at her intently over the top of it as he took the minutest of sips.

Suddenly Belinda desperately wanted to ask him how that was. She was prepared to swear that the various bottles had all been in the room for quite some time, and yet this wine was at the perfect low temperature for its character. The word 'how' formed on her lips, but she found herself unable to utter it. Her tongue felt unwieldy and locked in place somehow, and all she could do was see again that strange double-handed pass that André had made up and down the wine bottle.

The man's a magician, she thought, then told herself not to be ridiculous. He was just a good host who thought ahead. He had probably had the wine brought up from the cellar a few minutes before he had come to her bedroom.

'So, Belinda, are you and Jonathan betrothed?'

'What a quaint expression. You mean engaged, don't you?' she countered. 'No, we're not. But we have known each other a long time.'

'A long time,' he murmured ruminatively. 'Hmm. And what would you call a long time?' His dark brows lifted, and Belinda noticed that unlike his hair, they were not beginning to grow blonder, but remained dramatically dark.

'Three years.'

'That's not a long time,' he said lightly, swirling his wine in his glass. 'How long have you been lovers?'

It was a radical enquiry from someone she had only met a few minutes ago, and the Belinda of last week might have resented it and perceived her bumpy relationship with Jonathan threatened. But now, to her surprise, she faced the intimate question with equanimity.

'Three years,' she said evenly, then took a long sip of her wine as the man beside her digested her admission.

'And does he please you?'

'Most of the time.'

'Only most? A woman like you should be pleased all the time . . .'

'I don't know what you mean by "a woman like me", but I live in the real world, Count, and I don't expect miracles.'

'Perhaps you should,' he said, still rocking his glass, still watching the way the wine clung to its rounded inner contours.

Belinda was watching his hands. She seemed to see that pass again. Up and down the bottle. Lingering over the glass and subtly changing its contents. Involuntarily she imagined a similar gesture performed over her body, and this time it was the induction of heat, not cold.

She looked up into his eyes and actually saw the heat burning in their depths like a volcanic blue flame.

He's a mind reader, she thought, then admonished herself again for abject foolishness. This was the twentieth century, the age of hard science and rationality. Zoroastrian magic powers didn't exist, even if you desperately wanted them to.

Count André was still looking at her, his eyes alight with a peculiar, dark-toned excitement.

'What?' she demanded, feeling shaken.

'I was just wondering what you would look like naked.'

'But you've already seen me naked,' she pointed out, feeling mildy insulted. He had seen her body a few minutes ago in the bedroom. Was it so unmemorable that he had already forgotten it?

He shook his head, as if he was confused and trying to clear his thoughts, then gave her a curious and endearingly crooked smile.

'Ah yes, of course I have,' he conceded, 'and you are indeed very beautiful.' He frowned for a moment, and something sombre seemed to enter his expression, a cloud of fleeting sorrow that dulled every part of him. 'Your Jonathan is a very lucky man. Blessed, I would say . . .'

His eyes went unfocused for a moment, as if he were looking straight through her body to another reality; to another Belinda. He put aside his glass, then slowly, oh so slowly, he reached out his hand towards the knot of her sash, touched it, and seemed to make it unfasten. The overlapping panels of black silk slid apart, and there was a ponderous, eternal-seeming silence.

'So beautiful,' whispered the count at length, his fingertips hovering an inch or so above her navel. Belinda felt the skin there begin to flutter, and the nerves in it grow excited and sensitive. Her vulva, so near, became moist. She saw his nostrils flare and knew he could scent her.

The moment was volatile and precarious, as if they were both in violent, agitated motion even while their two bodies remained still. Then Count André's hand moved, infinitesimally, and he was touching the tender curve of her belly and sending an instantaneous jolt of pleasure to her sex.

Belinda gasped, and the count snatched back his fingers.

'Forgive me,' he muttered, reaching for her robe, as if to close it. 'I have gone too far. I am sorry.'

Belinda was too shocked to speak, but her alarm was because the caress had ended, not begun. The sensation she had experienced from just a single fleeting touch had taken her breath away. It had moved her and beguiled her in a way that would have normally taken long minutes of industrious love-making. And its cessation was instantly unbearable.

She realised she was still holding her glass, so she put it down on the carpet at her feet. Then, without thinking, or even trying to, she simply lunged forward towards him, putting her half naked body directly into his arms so there was no way he could withdraw or reject her.

For a moment, Count André remained passive, accepting first her kiss, then her embrace, as she slid her arms around his waist. His mouth tasted very sweet to Belinda's hungry lips, and the scent of his body was like roses. She felt his arms move up and grip her, then effortlessly and with grace, he swivelled her body, disengaging her hold on him, and turned her until she was sitting on his lap. Belinda could not work out quite how he had achieved this, all without breaking the kiss, but the position made her feel tiny and vulnerable. The whole of her naked torso, as well as her thighs and belly, were now displayed and accessible to his touch.

'You are a very forthright woman,' he whispered, lifting his mouth away from hers momentarily.

Belinda looked up into his face, then was forced to drop her gaze again. His eyes were too brilliant to bear so close up. She felt mesmerised, and quite weak, and her mouth opened when his touched it once again.

His tongue immediately slid inside the soft cavity, tracing her teeth then plunging deeper to duel with her tongue. He tasted of wine and almonds and something else hard to define yet tantalisingly delicious, and she moaned under her breath as he kissed her. Her body had never felt more alive.

As he continued to kiss, playing and exploring, she felt his hand settle once again on her belly, his long fingers splaying out across her skin. She felt him rubbing, gently circling and fondling the curve of her with his slightly bent fingers. He was nowhere near her sex yet it was affected, the delicate folds becoming swollen and very wet.

'Do you wish me to touch you?' he enquired, making the words a part of the kiss. His hand stilled, waiting in readiness for her permission.

Belinda could hardly believe what she had done. She had leapt straight from being in bed with one man to surrendering her body to another. There was no way she could resist this fascinating aristocrat, this stranger who was so honest yet so mysterious. She whispered 'yes' under his lips, then eased her thighs apart to give him access. As his hand slid lower, she heard him sigh so poignantly it was almost a sob.

'It has been so long,' he murmured, his mouth straying

91

across her cheek and settling just below her ear. 'So many, many years . . .' His fingertip began gently inveigling its way through her pubic curls, moving cautiously as if her flesh were made of crystal and might shatter with rough treatment.

The approach was far too cautious for Belinda's liking. She suddenly felt ravenous for his caress. She wanted this strange, strange man to lay his hands on her so she could come to know him through the contact. She wanted to absorb him, drink him in, understand how he could seem to know her so well; even though they had only met a few minutes ago. She surged on his knee, lifting her pelvis and circling it to encourage him, and pushing herself upward against his hand.

'Hush!' he said into her ear, his breath a cool wind against her brow. 'Not so hasty. I will pleasure you, my sweet Belle, but we must go slowly. Bide our time. We have waited far too long to rush our joy and waste it.'

Belinda didn't really understand what he was whispering about. Who had been waiting? And why had he suddenly called her 'Belle'? Her mother had called her that many years ago in her childhood, but she was dead now and no one had used the name since. Not even her boyfriends. To Jonathan, she was always 'Lindi' at times like these.

The thought of Jonathan shocked her back into the reality of her situation. She was sprawled half-naked across the knee of a man she had met less than thirty minutes ago. She was about to let him touch her sex.

Oh no, oh dear God, he had closed the final gap and he was touching her! She wanted to struggle away, apologise and grab her belongings, then get out of this house as fast as she was able.

How could she do this? How could she betray her dear, patient, long-suffering Jonathan just when everything was starting to look up for them?

But the count's clever fingertips were too artful to resist, flickering over her, both hot and cool at once, and

92

invoking shallow ripples of ethereal stimulation. Belinda moaned hoarsely when he stroked the pulsing heart of her, then buried her face against his white shirt as she came.

It had all happened with so little warning that she was barely prepared for the intensity of her pleasure. She felt tears on her face as her body throbbed and glowed, and she clung to the count, to André, as if the safety of her very soul depended on him. The release, and the feelings it roused in her, seemed out of proportion to the relationship they shared.

What relationship? she thought as she regained her equilibrium. Snuggling against his chest, she felt almost giddy from the scent of his cologne, an intense and voluptuous essence of rose that suited him despite its feminine sweetness. I have no relationship with this man, she told herself, and I don't know him. At all. I must be insane to have allowed him to touch me.

'I'm sorry – '

'Forgive me – '

The apologies, hers and his, came out simultaneously, and suddenly Belinda could see if not broad humour in the situation, then at least a lighter side to it. She sat up, drew back a little way along André's knee, and looked him rather shamefacedly in the eye.

'What on earth must you think of me?' she said, plucking at the satin robe and managing to close it. 'It must seem very "loose" of me, allowing you to touch me like that when we've only just met. I really can't believe myself. I-I threw myself at you.'

He touched her face, smiling wryly, then took the ends of the robe's sash and fastened it for her.

'No, Belinda, the fault is mine,' he said, his face shadowed with some indefinable, yet clearly painful emotion. 'You reminded me of someone. Someone I miss desperately . . . And for a moment, I thought you were she, and I lost control of myself.' He was looking down, staring at the loose black bow he had formed, but Belinda could almost swear she had seen tears. Then he looked up again, and his blue eyes were pacific and untroubled. 'I must ask you again to forgive me.' Without warning, he slid his hands around her waist, and rising himself, lifted her effortlessly on to her feet. 'Will you do that? Shall we forget what just happened? And begin again ... as good friends?' He held out his hand again, the same hand that had touched her so beautifully. 'I promise I will try to behave myself from now on.'

Once again, the transition from one dynamic to another was staggeringly fast. Belinda had a strong urge to shake her head in an attempt to clear it. Had she imagined what had just happened? Perhaps it was a fantasy? A dream of some kind. She was tired and confused, what with the breakdown and the storm and all. Maybe what she thought had just happened had really occurred only in her mind?

At a loss to frame a reply, Belinda allowed her hand to be taken and this time squeezed in affirmation instead of kissed.

'And now, I believe it is time to dress for dinner,' the count said briskly, offering his arm. 'May I escort you to your room?'

'Yes. Of course,' she answered, still feeling befuddled by the change from intimacy to courtesy. She took his arm, as indicated, and allowed herself to be led back the way they had come earlier.

'You are free, and welcome, to stay here as long as you wish, Belinda,' he said as they began to ascend the stairs. 'The storm last night was unusual, I believe. Apart from it, we have been enjoying a spell of quite clement weather. I am sure that you will find the priory very restful.' He turned to her, his smile slight, but latent with unexpected significance. 'As I do.'

'That's very kind of you, but – ' The words died on her lips. For a moment, she seemed to see the places she and Jonathan had planned to visit, their itinerary mapped out before them, and Paula, waiting in puzzlement for their call. Then, inexplicably, none of it interested her any more. She looked around her: at the polished panels of the landing, the rare furnishings, the lavish pictures, then finally back to her smiling enigma of a host. 'I'd love to stay,' she heard herself say, 'and I'm sure Jonathan will too. He said only yesterday that he was getting fed up of driving. It's very kind of you to ask us.'

'It is my pleasure,' replied André quietly, stepping back and making another of his minute bows. 'It is a long time since I had such – ' He paused as he straightened, and his blue eyes seemed to flare even brighter ' – such compatible company.' He stepped back, still looking at her intently. 'Until dinner then. The dining room is to be found directly across the hall from the library. *A bientôt!*'

French as well now, thought Belinda as her host turned on his heel like a cavalry officer and strode away down the landing in the direction of the stairs that led up to the long gallery and his tower. And just what other talents and accomplishments does he possess? she pondered, turning the huge cut-glass door knob and opening the door to her room.

Fool! You damned fool!

André cursed himself as he ascended the stairs to his eyrie, taking them two at a time in his impatience, and making the most of his current strength and vigour.

The temptation of Belinda Seward had been too great for him to resist in his newly-wakened and not yet fully-adjusted state. The girl was so much like Arabelle, her body so sweet and so gently rounded at breast and hip, that it had been almost like caressing his beloved again. As he entered his chamber he gasped aloud with yearning, praying with all his heart that he had not gone too far and too fast and ruined everything. As ever, for reassurance, he glanced towards Belle's rosewood casket, but its blue glow was subdued and quiescent.

Could Belinda Seward really be the one? he thought, drawing aside the veils around his bed and tying them back. Had he finally found a woman who was fully compatible? He flung himself on the bed and considered the prospect.

They had been close from time to time, he and Arabelle, and enjoyed a few all-too-brief interludes of stolen communion. But these episodes were almost as painful as they were comforting. To hold Belle in his arms again and touch her and give her pleasure meant everything to him; but on each occasion they had known their happiness was transient. There was always the knowledge that in a few moments it would all be over again, and she would lose her hold on her host and have to leave. It seemed cruel to even attempt being together under such circumstances, but the state of missing her hurt him so hideously that he couldn't forgo even the slightest chance of happiness.

Should he wake Belle? Tell her what he had found? He turned again towards the box and the crystal vial that lay within it, but his mind was still full of doubt. It would be too cruel to inspire her hopes just yet. Perhaps it would be better to wait until he was sure. Sure that Belinda Seward was the woman who could help them, and also certain that he wasn't going to spoil everything by snatching too greedily for the sustaining pleasure he so needed. Covering his face with his hands, he tried to relax his taut body and find the stillness and composure to think clearly.

But such quietude was difficult to achieve and his mind remained active, pondering and ruminating incessantly in the blackness behind his fingers. Once again, he felt the urge to reach for Belle.

Suddenly, he sensed a change in the room's solemn ambience. He dropped his hands from his face, sat up, and stared towards the casket, his hopes rising as the fey blue light intensified and into the silence came the answer to his invocation.

My love, you are awake. Are you troubled?

Her voice was as gentle and animated as it had been in life, and it soothed his anxious spirit with a sense of peacefulness and stoicism he could barely credit given the parameters of her existence.

'Yes, I am troubled,' he answered, speaking aloud as seemed natural when her voice sounded so real to him. 'I think I may have found her, my love. The one who can help us. She seems a perfect match but I cannot help but be afraid.'

Afraid to die? Arabelle asked, her voice soft and steady in his mind.

'No, never that,' he answered. 'I shall be glad of it when the time comes . . . No, what I am afraid of is that I may harm her. This Belinda. She is so much like you, my darling. I could be fond of her, perhaps, had you never existed, and I have to question my right to risk her life.'

Arabelle remained silent but he sensed that she was listening patiently, letting him take his time.

'And yet if I do not try, you can never be released, my love!' he cried out, feeling torn a thousand ways by his emotions.

Hush, my André, do not fret, Arabelle soothed. *If this thing is meant to happen, it will. Perhaps, if you are open with her . . . if you tell her of our plight, and let her choose, she will help us of her own free will.*

'Perhaps you are right,' murmured André, lifting his hands away from his face and staring at them. Those fingers had touched Belinda Seward a little while ago, but many decades in the past they had once caressed Arabelle. He could still remember the superlative softness of her skin, the way she would sigh when he stroked her and blush when he pushed and took liberties. Her erotic soul had just been stirring and growing when they were parted, and each time they had been together he had sensed her wanting him and becoming more daring. The fact that they had so nearly been one

97

flesh, yet never been allowed to achieve that precious goal, was like someone plunging his black-handled dagger into his chest again and again, in blows that hurt and bled and went on hurting, yet which could never give the release he so craved.

Do not torture yourself, my love. Remember what we shared with pleasure, not sadness. Arabelle's voice echoed in his mind like a clear, high bell, a sound so lovely that he started feeling better. *Look forward with hope, my André, and take comfort where you can ... I truly believe that all may yet be well.*

André still had his doubts, and he knew that his wise, all-perceiving beloved was fully aware of them, but as he sent his mind across the years and imagined her sweet body in his arms, his heart grew calmer and he closed his eyes and smiled.

Chapter Six

Nemesis

*L*eaning back against the fragrant, kid-skin upholstery of her chauffeur-driven limousine, Isidora Katori closed her painted eyes and smiled in satisfaction. Her narrow, gloved hand stole momentarily to her cleavage, where beneath her clothes rested her talisman of Astarte.

To an observer, she appeared completely tranquil, as she always did, but on the inside she was a mass of swirling passions.

She had found him again! Her fallen angel. Her object of desire and hate. Tapping the precious medallion with her finger, she considered him: the only man who had ever defied her, and who had obsessed her for decade after decade. André von Kastel, who she had changed and damned for ever.

Drowsing in the opulent comfort of the long black car after a tiresome flight and an exhausting stay in Paris, she had sent her mind roaming through the aether, and suddenly hit the mental signature she sought. André was awake somewhere, in this country of England, and quite close; his consciousness a beacon she could follow.

Sending her imagination back over the years, she could still see his face as she had last seen it, in every beautiful, graven detail. She could taste the rage in his newly-blue eyes; savour his sorrow and his desperate confusion. He had still desired her while he hated her utterly. And that, to Isidora, had been her purest, most gratifying triumph.

'Are you OK?' enquired a voice beside her, snapping her reverie and banishing André's tortured countenance.

Isidora opened her eyes and viewed her companion with momentary annoyance.

Who was this worm? What was his name? She couldn't even recall it. He was just a handsome face on the plane, a clean-cut yuppie – fresh from successful business no doubt – who had made a pass at her after too much champagne. Isidora had felt wasted after the debauch of Paris, but even so his gauche advances had amused her. And his expression, on seeing her limousine, had been a picture.

'Yes, thank you – ' She paused, trying to remember ' – Miles. I'm just a little tired, that's all. Paris was . . . fatiguing. Delicious but fatiguing. But don't worry – ' She hesitated again, then laid her gloved hand delicately on his thigh, quite high up ' – I'm very resilient. I have a strong constitution.'

'Oh . . . er . . . great,' Miles replied, his eyes bright and eager but bemused. He really had no idea what she was doing to him, she realised; no inkling of how controllable he was.

Withdrawing her hand, Isidora lounged back again and studied her prey through her long black lashes.

He was presentable enough, she supposed, although with André in her mind he appeared bland and characterless. Miles was slim, smooth and well groomed, and under normal circumstances she would imagine him to be the acme of masculine self-confidence. But these weren't normal circumstances, she thought creamily, picturing him naked, vulnerable and afraid. At her mercy, as André should have remained instead of cursing her, tricking her, and taking flight.

Enough of negativism, though. André was near, far

nearer than she could have hoped for, and as she knew she was a psychic blank to him, there was no way he could be aware she had located him. She could bide her time, then strike out and reclaim him as and when she chose. Having waited so long, she could approach with stealth, then reveal herself when it was too late for him to flee.

And in the meantime, she had her handsome yuppie. A connoisseur of ever-changing fashion, Isidora admired Miles's loosely-tailored designer suit and the way it hung on his well-toned body. She imagined him working out in some exclusive gym or health club; sweating designer sweat, no doubt. He would be sweating for her too, soon enough, she thought, relishing the scenario she was beginning to have in mind. He would sweat, he would cry out, he would lose the mastery of his own body. She would enjoy him, and when it was over he would adore her.

'So, is there anyone waiting at home for you, Miles?' she enquired, sitting up again and turning to him, giving him the full force of her brilliant green eyes.

'Yes, there is actually,' he replied, a little cockily.

Isidora felt like laughing out loud at the rather smug way he said it, as if he were boasting that he was a man of the world and fully accustomed to cheating on his partner. In a little while, he wouldn't be feeling quite so full of himself.

'Then why not ring her?' she suggested. 'Let her know that you won't be rushing to her side.'

Miles frowned, clearly affected by some of the guilt Isidora had intended him to feel. He took a minute mobile phone out of his briefcase and quickly punched a number. Isidora kept her eyes on him as he spoke into the mouthpiece, enjoying the charge of his discomfort and sexual confusion. She continued to watch him closely while he concocted a garbled and implausible reason for not hurrying home. Faint but sharp words

101

indicated that the other party was not happy with the delay, and Isidora sensed Miles's ambivalence.

'It's OK. All sorted now,' he said, snapping the phone shut jauntily in a vain effort to show her he was his own master.

'I never said you could stay the night with me,' she pointed out, watching the words bring a blush to Miles's cheeks.

'But – '

'We'll have to see, won't we?' she said, cutting him off. 'If you please me, I may want to keep you a lot longer.'

He opened his mouth to protest, but Isidora was on him before he could speak, taking control of his lips and pushing her tongue between them. In shock, he allowed her to plunder him, his own tongue retreating as she kissed him aggressively. He tasted of the champagne they had both consumed.

When they broke apart, Isidora pulled away, still smiling, and took out a lace-trimmed handkerchief from her bag. With it, she blotted all trace of him from her red-painted but completely unsmeared mouth.

'We're here,' she said expressionlessly, placing the handkerchief in his hand as the limousine pulled up outside her building. He was still holding it when the chauffeur opened her door and helped her to alight.

The fact that she possessed a prestigious penthouse in a prestigious building in a prestigious part of London clearly impressed Miles. As they ascended in the bubble-like lift, he glanced around him, grinning with excitement and drinking in the sight of one of the city's most exclusive views, as well as the understated symbols of wealth all around him.

Once they were inside her living room, he attempted to kiss her, but much as she relished his untutored mouth, Isidora swung away and left him standing alone, briefcase in hand, like a pupil on his first morning at the 'big school'.

'A drink, perhaps?' she enquired, moving across to her varied selection of alcohol and drugs.

'Oh . . . Yes! Great!' he answered, shifting the briefcase from hand to hand, as if not sure what to do with it. Isidora refrained from offering to take it, and after a few moments he put it down beside a chair.

'Wine?' she enquired, reaching for a bottle of red from the wine rack and picking up a corkscrew before he had a chance to express a preference.

'Can I do that for you?' he asked, as she set the device against the bottle's neck. He was attempting to appear suave now and gain an advantage. Isidora was amused. Couldn't he tell that he had never had a chance?

'No,' she said, watching him, her eyes level as she deftly relieved the bottle of its cork.

Turning away to pour the wine, she could sense him fidgeting behind her. What would he do if I put a drop of one of these in his glass? she thought, eyeing the row of tiny vials that stood on a low shelf out of sight of the rest of the room. They contained her own devised potions: aphrodisiacs, mood-altering compounds, preparations to aid sexual performance or to make a victim sleep. As she considered a mixture to increase Miles's suggestibility, Isidora couldn't prevent herself from thinking about another of her alchemical creations; one she had employed long, long ago, before he was born.

No! She needed no esoteric assistance to master this young cavalier of the 1990s, and she would not think of that blue fluid she had once made use of.

'Here,' she said, turning to Miles and holding out a large crystal goblet full of wine.

Miles accepted it, sipped gratefully, then seemed to realise he should have waited and made a toast. Isidora said nothing, took one sip from her own wine, and put it aside. Then, with neither modesty nor flourish, she began, very calmly, to remove her clothes.

First went her gloves, then her chic veiled hat, then her jacket, revealing the draped black moiré blouse she wore beneath. She held Miles's gaze as her fingers sought its row of black pearl buttons.

'Oh yeah ... Great!' he burbled, gulping down his wine and abandoning the empty glass before plucking at the lapels of his jacket.

'Wait,' commanded Isidora, her voice soft yet threatening.

Miles licked his lips, still grinning broadly. The fact that she appeared to be doing a strip was clearly a treat for him, and he made as if to sit down in one of her low, leather-covered chairs to enjoy it.

'I said "wait",' she reiterated. 'Exactly where you are,' she continued, savouring his gasp as her blouse slid down her arms.

Isidora was wearing an ice-grey basque beneath her outer clothing, a sleek but sumptuous creation that most women would have found uncomfortable to wear for any length of time. She, however, enjoyed the fierce embrace of its tightly-laced panels and the way her breasts were displayed by its flimsy quarter cups. More pleasurable even than that, though, was the secondary effect of its rigid, relentless boning. Her internal organs were constricted, and bore down heavily on her pleasure zones from within. Her vulva felt like a ripe fruit, constantly pouting open, and her clitoris was an aching pushed-out stud. Her swollen bladder, from the in-flight champagne, only enhanced the dark, erotic tension.

'Wow!' said Miles, as she retrieved her gloves and pulled them back on again, smoothing the thin hide very carefully over her fingers.

'I'd prefer it if you didn't speak,' Isidora said conversationally, sliding a gloved hand beneath each bulging breast to cup herself, then rolling each nipple between a leather-clad thumb and finger. 'I require concentration and quiet, Miles. Your undivided attention.' As the sensations built inside her, she closed her eyes and swirled her hips, gyrating elegantly on her narrow-tipped high heels.

Although she could no longer see him, Isidora studied her young admirer with her inner eye. He was gaping at her; ogling like that schoolboy she had likened him to earlier. At his groin, his fashionable trousers had begun to tent. She could almost feel the nerves twitching along the medians in his fingers. He was longing to touch her, or failing that, touch himself.

'I wouldn't do that if I were you,' she said as he lifted his hand, about to press it to his crotch. Her eyes snapped open, and she fixed her gaze on him.

'Isidora?' he began querulously. 'What's going on? I don't – '

'Silence!' She cut him off, his thunderstruck expression exciting her.

'But – '

This time she silenced him with a look using the full force of her sparkling eyes and her fierce beauty. His hands dropped to his sides and he looked shame-faced.

'That's better,' she said, giving her nipples one last pinch, then beginning work on her narrow pencil skirt. She unhitched the placket, slid down the zip, then let the whole thing slither down to her ankles.

Once again, she silenced Miles with a chilling look, and saw him bite his lips to keep in his exclamations.

Standing in a crumpled pool of linen and satin lining, she knew she looked the very rising goddess. The steely-coloured basque ended just above her navel and her long legs were encased in hold-up stockings, but between these two she wore no other garment. She could feel Miles staring hard at her luxuriant pubic bush and the shimmering ooze of juice that was already trickling through it. She saw him lick his lips as if imagining her flavour.

Ah yes, my dear naïve little Miles, you will get to taste me, mark my words, she thought, stepping neatly out of her skirt and shoes, then slipping her feet back into the slender high heels. You'll use that soft mouth in my service until your jaw aches.

'Stay there,' she ordered softly, realising he was once again about to move. Retrieving her wine from the drinks table, she took a long refreshing swallow, then removed a glove and dipped her fingers into the glass. When they were sufficiently moistened, she opened her legs a little and rubbed her throbbing clitoris.

The weakish alcohol tingled only a little but the pressure alone was enough to make her climax. She groaned gutturally as waves of pleasure passed right through her. Her distended bladder edged each one with a delicious pain.

'Thank you, goddess,' she murmured to the deity whose image rested between her breasts, as self-possession returned from out of chaos. Withdrawing her scented fingers from the niche between her legs, she lifted the talisman and pressed it to her lips. 'For everything,' she added, thinking of a blue-eyed nemesis whose soul would soon be hers.

Opening her eyes, she surveyed her pleasant if rather nondescript diversion. Ah well, he would pass a little time.

'Come,' she murmured, holding out her left hand to Miles and smiling narrowly.

And like a willing lamb for the sacrifice, he walked towards her.

Where on earth has he gone? thought Belinda as she stepped into her bedroom. Jonathan was nowhere to be seen, the bed had been made, and her clothes had been picked up and spirited away out of sight. The casement window stood open to the sepia-toned twilight and there was a strong scent of pot-pourri in the air. The room no longer smelled of sweaty sex.

'I suppose I'd better get ready for dinner then,' she muttered, wondering just who had been in and tidied up. One of Jonathan's blonde friends, she presumed, or perhaps the silent but strangely friendly Oren.

She was just about to shuck off the black robe and see

106

if she could find anything suitable to wear for taking formal dinner with a continental blue-blood, when there was a soft rap on the door.

Not again! thought Belinda, tempted not to answer. Who was it this time?

'Come in!' she called out resignedly.

The door opened and two young women entered. Two beautiful blonde women who smiled at her warmly but didn't speak a word. One was carrying a notebook and a pencil, and the other had her arms full of clothing.

These were Jonathan's silent paramours, Belinda realised, the wood-nymphs with whom he had frolicked by the river.

'Er . . . hello,' said Belinda doubtfully, unsure of what to say to them. Could they even hear, given that they were mute? Oren had perfect hearing but that didn't mean to say that these two could also hear. 'My name's Belinda,' she offered tentatively, patting her chest, then felt awfully self-conscious. What if they both understood her perfectly and were insulted?

To her relief, the smiles of both the young women broadened, and the taller one, whose flaxen hair was tied back in a ponytail, gestured gracefully with the pencil and notebook, then quickly wrote a few words on the first blank page. Holding out the notebook, she showed them to Belinda.

My name is Elisa, the girl had written. *And my cousin's name is Feltris. Our master has sent us to assist you in any way you require. We have brought fresh clothing, so you may bathe and change for dinner.*

As Elisa took back the notebook and placed it to one side, the younger girl, her cousin Feltris, stepped shyly forward with her burden. As she must have done with the shift and the French knickers Belinda had worn earlier, the graceful blonde began to lay out the clothing on the bed. This time there was more though, and Feltris arranged each item with tender care. Belinda was astounded at the sight of such beauty.

107

The first garment was a dress; an ethereal shimmering thing that Belinda was instantly compelled to touch. Constructed from layer upon layer of embroidered silk gauze, it was a glorious blend of peach and orange in colour, and cut in a low-waisted Roaring Twenties style with a straight bodice and an intricately-scalloped hemline. The dress was lined in satin and when Belinda bent to examine it more closely, she discovered it was hand sewn, every facet of it individually crafted. There was no label and no indication of either a designer or a brand name, and something told Belinda that the dress was an original, deriving from the Jazz Age itself. What she was being given to wear was a genuine haute couture antique, and was probably worth hundreds if not thousands of pounds.

'I can't wear this,' she protested, itching to stroke her fingers over the exquisite fabric but afraid to. 'It's too precious. It should be in a museum.'

But the girls just nodded their heads and smiled, encouraging her to examine the dress more closely. Elisa took Belinda's hand and put it gently against the shining silk.

'OK. If you say so,' Belinda conceded, her senses thrilling to the delicate smoothness of the rare and feather-light fabric.

The lingerie was a match for the dress: elaborate, fabulously fragile and so lovely it made Belinda gasp with pleasure. An ivory chemise and long knickers in crêpe-de-chine were both encrusted with soft flounces of lace and tiny embroidered roses. There was a suspender belt too, which was just as pretty, and stockings in off-white woven silk. For her feet there was a pair of satin ballet pumps the same colour as the dress, and beside them lay a tiny matching bag, a lace hankie and a scented corsage.

'And you shall go to the ball, Cinders,' murmured Belinda, transfixed by the beautiful clothes and accessories. So much opulence for one simple dinner.

But what if the count had guests? What if his melancholy solitude was just something she herself had conjured up? Despite the initial image it projected, he had a lovely home; it was a perfect venue for entertaining and parties.

And yet somehow she still knew he was lonely and that all this finery was purely to please him. Maybe not Cinders after all? she thought, lifting the chemise's shoulder strap and discovering it was as light as the very air around it. I'm being decked out and adorned to suit his taste and his fancy, like a concubine being prepared for her master.

Strangely enough, the idea didn't repulse her. Instead she felt an electric anticipation; an excitement that flowed and flowered between her legs. Clutching the black robe closer around her, as if her arousal might be visible, she turned around to face the two waiting cousins.

'OK. I'm ready. What's next?'

Elisa's answer was to take her by the hand and lead her to the bathroom, with Feltris following silently behind them.

Once inside, the two worked as a team, setting out fresh towels and apparently unopened toiletries that seemed to have replaced the ones used earlier. Belinda frowned at the evidence of such efficiency. So far she had encountered only Oren and these two, but the count's establishment seemed to function as if there were scores of household staff in attendance. It was yet another mystery to add to a lengthening list, and as she pondered it, she realised Elisa was reaching for her robe.

Belinda hadn't really thought about what the other woman had written in the notebook, but now she panicked and clutched the thin black silk around her. She had shared communal showers often enough, but she had never actually been bathed by a woman, at least not since the days of her earliest childhood. And judging by what Jonathan had said, the cousins were lesbians: they would not look at her nakedness with cool detachment.

'It's OK, I can manage from here,' she said nervously, trying to snatch back her sash from Elisa's grasp. 'Thanks very much, but I'm used to looking after myself ... Really.'

But the blonde girl would not be gainsaid. With great deftness and determination, she teased the sash back out of Belinda's hold, then handed it to Feltris, who was standing close beside them. Smiling, she reached forward and touched Belinda's face, then leaned towards her and kissed her on the cheek. It was a very soft kiss, but full of reassurance.

Confused, Belinda released her grip on the robe and allowed Feltris and Elisa to peel it from her, revealing her body bare and flushed from their little tussle. She felt an overpowering urge to try and cover herself – with an arm across her breasts and a hand shielding her pubis – but she realised that would only make things worse. Acting like a shrinking violet would only emphasise the fact that their sexual nature scared her. If she behaved nonchalantly, they wouldn't realise she felt threatened.

Yet as she stepped forward, trying to smile, she felt dizzy. Something seemed to rush through her like a wind, and she had a sense of being transformed, transmuted, utterly changed. For a moment she could have sworn she saw Count André's blue eyes – not outwardly but within her mind – and a smile that was kind but gently mocking.

'Oh dear,' she gasped, swaying in the trailing edge of the experience, and almost immediately two pairs of arms were confidently supporting her. In a moment, they had her sitting on a chair.

Pressing her hands over her face, Belinda tried to analyse what had just happened. Something *had* happened, but the more she tried to think, the less she seemed to know. She only knew that now it was over, she felt much better, and lowering her fingers, she looked out and down into a pale and lovely face.

Feltris was kneeling in front of her, an expression of concern across her fine-boned elfin features.

Oh God, she's gorgeous! thought Belinda, astounded at the revelation. The younger girl was so pretty, so sensuous. So desirable.

Desirable?

But why not?

Trembling, Belinda reached out and touched Feltris's silky hair, then slid her fingers through it to cradle the back of the girl's head. Their gazes locked, and in Feltris's grey eyes Belinda saw tenderness and a kindly, encouraging lust. Without a second thought, she leant forward and began to kiss her.

I'm kissing a woman, thought Belinda, savouring the delicately fresh flavour of her companion's minty breath. The girl's lips were soft, almost the texture of rose petals, and they seemed to melt and flex beneath the contact of her own. Belinda felt Feltris's tongue dart into her mouth, flick around playfully, then seek out her own tongue. Automatically, she engaged it in a duel, and felt the young woman's slender arms come up around her.

Without the slightest awkwardness or need to consider her actions, Belinda slid forward, her mouth still pressed to Feltris's, and allowed herself to be guided to the bathroom floor. The embrace seemed so much easier in a horizontal position, and as she went on to her back, she felt Feltris rise up over her and continue the kiss in a dominant, man-like style.

Belinda was acutely aware of her nakedness – and that it gave her joy. She wrapped her arms around Feltris and pressed her bare breasts tight against her, then wriggled her bottom on the bathroom floor as she opened her legs. Feltris made a crooning, happy sound.

What's happened to me? thought Belinda dreamily, feeling her vulva open up like a sun-kissed flower. I'm lying on the floor without any clothes on, and I'm kissing

111

and being kissed by another girl. It's wonderful . . . but what do we do next?

As if she had heard the question, Feltris answered it by shifting her body sideways and making Belinda groan a protest into her mouth. She felt doubly exposed without the mute girl's warm presence lying over her, and the fact that they were still kissing seemed to exacerbate her nudity. Feeling profoundly lewd, she stretched her thighs wider and swung her hips.

After a moment, she felt Elisa move in between her legs, a warm presence with experience and gentle hands. Belinda quivered as the older woman kissed her thigh, then kissed it again, but this time closer to her quim.

Oh no . . . Oh dear God, oh dear God, she's going to lick me, thought Belinda, as Feltris began sucking on her tongue. The two clever cousins were working as a team now, each conspiring with the other to give her pleasure.

Belinda tried to cry out as Elisa prised her open, delicately folding back the fleshy petals of her womanhood; but her protest was absorbed by Feltris's lips.

I can't . . . I can't bear it . . . The words rang in Belinda's brain because there was no way she could utter them. She tried to kick out with her legs but Elisa held them easily, then sank her soft mouth into Belinda's tender sex.

Cunnilingus felt just the same as it did when Jonathan used his mouth there; just the same, yet as different as night from day. Elisa's tongue was smaller, slyer, and supremely nimble. It seemed to find areas of responsiveness that neither Jonathan nor Belinda – with her own fingers – had ever encountered. Roving the entire length and breadth of her sexual landscape, it lingered here and there, and in other places made quick and darting forays. Within just moments it was far too much and Belinda climaxed.

The women held her tightly through the waves of

sweet sensation; gentling her body with their wordless sounds of comfort.

I can't believe what just happened to me, thought Belinda, as the spasms faded and she was able to relax. Utterly content, she was aware of her two companions sitting by her, one on either side, and she almost purred when Feltris stroked her brow. It felt so right, and so appropriate, and the more she thought about it, the more she wondered why she had never had a female lover before.

Perhaps it was just that she had never met the right woman? Or never met that woman when she was feeling so receptive? As she was now, in this weird but lovely place.

All of a sudden, she sat up and laughed out loud. Elisa and Feltris looked puzzled for a moment, then joined in, their laughter a little muffled but still sexy. They smiled and touched her, as if they too had been struck by a revelation.

'André von Kastel . . . you devil!' cried Belinda, throwing her head back and gazing up at the moulded ceiling. 'It's you, isn't it?' she demanded of the absent nobleman, having not the slightest doubt that in some way he could hear her. 'You've changed me. Made me like –' She looked from one beautiful face to the other '– making love with women. I've never had the slightest inclination before, but suddenly I-I'm different.'

At that moment, Elisa rose fluidly to her feet and reached down to draw Belinda to hers too. Beside them, graceful Feltris stood up also.

'What is it?' asked Belinda of the silent Elisa, looking her straight in the eye. 'Has your master called? Told you to hurry?'

The blonde woman smiled placidly, her eyes lambent and slightly teasing. With a lovely dance-like gesture, she pointed towards the bath, and as she did so, Feltris sprang forward and turned on the taps.

'OK, I get the message,' said Belinda, moving forward,

aware that there was no way she was going to be allowed to bathe herself now. Even if she had wanted to. She smiled with pleasure as she realised her friends would be joining her, and as she tested the water, they were pulling off their dresses.

Forty-five minutes later, Belinda stood before the looking glass in the bedroom next door, studying the image of a woman she had never seen before. A new woman, transformed by antique magic.

In theory, the orangey-peach dress should have been hideous with her titian colouring, but in practice it was just the reverse. The strong, fruity shade seemed to light up her hair, her eyes and her lips and give her pale complexion an almost ghostly glow. In her flapper's gown, she looked every inch the Jazz Baby, just as if she too – like her mysterious host – had stepped straight out of a portrait. It was a portrait she hadn't seen, but she was sure it existed somewhere.

'Boo doo pee doo,' she murmured to her reflection, and touched the strands of hair that were curled forward across her cheeks, emphasising her bone structure. Behind her, Elisa frowned, then reached around and made a minute adjustment to the same curl.

If she looked special, Belinda realised, it was because she owed much to the efforts of Elisa and Feltris. They had bathed her, perfumed her and preened her; assisted her with every last ritual of a woman's intimate toilette, including some that had been more intimate than others. She had balked and blushed to the roots of her hair several times during the process, but always, within a moment or two, she had unwound. Until today she would have found it difficult to understand how she could communicate with someone who didn't speak, but she found it easy to get on with the two young women. Not only were they friendly, they were also amusing, and their silence had a sly and jaunty humour. They were incredibly sensual too, and attuned to the erotic

114

possibilities of even the simplest task. There had been slight delays, more than once, while they were getting her ready.

Turning from the mirror, Belinda glanced at each of her friends and asked, 'There! Will I do?'

Elisa smiled and nodded, her eyes dark and expressive, while Feltris, who Belinda had discovered was the more demonstrative of the two, stepped forward and pressed an airy kiss to her powdered cheek. Elisa wagged a warning finger at her cousin, but Feltris had been careful. Neither Belinda's gleaming hair nor her delicate make-up had been disturbed.

'So?' she queried again, and both girls kissed the tips of their fingers as a sign of approval.

Belinda turned again to the mirror.

But will *he* be impressed? she wondered, studying the sleek straight lines of the exquisite embroidered dress and the way it suggested rather than clung to her body. She smiled. Of course he will. How can he resist? she thought, remembering that intriguing mix of impishness and courtesy. The way he had kissed her hand, then later touched her body –

He?

'Good God,' whispered Belinda, amazed at her own thoughts. It was Count André she was daydreaming about, not Jonathan, her own boyfriend. It seemed disloyal, but there it was. Her thinking mind wanted to abhor the idea, but her instincts – and her subconscious – had suddenly overpowered her intellect. She was far more concerned about the opinion of a rather evasive stranger than the approval of a man she had been close to for years.

This place is changing us, she thought, glancing at the two beautiful women who stood to either side of her. Me and Jonathan, the pair of us; we're no better than each other. We've both been led astray.

Whatever next? she thought, turning around as a loud knock at the door surprised her. Another seduction?

André? Oren, perhaps? Someone I haven't even met yet?

But what puzzled her most was how little guilt she felt.

Chapter Seven
Curiouser and Curiouser

When the door opened she discovered her visitor was Oren and not Count André as her subconscious had hoped for and expected.

The tall, blond servant clearly didn't sense her disappointment though, because his smile was broad and cheerful. Nodding respectfully, he then glanced behind her to Feltris and Elisa and an unmistakable glint lit his eyes.

They're lovers! Curiouser and curiouser, thought Belinda, imagining the three of them together. They would make quite a sight, she was sure it; all blond, good to look at, and uninhibitedly full of life's joys. She could just picture their three golden bodies, meshed and contorted in pleasure. Who did what to whom? she wondered, speculating helplessly. Oren was so immense, so tall and broad – what would it be like with a lover so strong and huge?

Although the good-natured subject of her musings seemed prepared to wait indefinitely while she daydreamed, Belinda gave herself a mental shake.

'Have you come to escort me to dinner?' she enquired of Oren, who made an expressive sweeping gesture, indicating that she should follow him.

Enjoying the swish of the shimmering antique dress against her silk-stockinged calves, Belinda stepped out into the corridor, then turned to bid farewell to her beautiful new friends. Elisa and Feltris smiled back at her, then each blew kisses, their dark eyes full of what had happened in the bathroom. It isn't over, they seemed to be saying. And the next time will be even more delicious.

'Oh boy,' Belinda whispered almost silently, as she and Oren made their way along the corridor. The tall, Nordic servant was a pace or two ahead of her, and she got a shock when he turned and eyed her knowingly.

'Are you their – ' What could she say that didn't sound intrusive? 'Are you their friend?' she finished lamely.

Oren glanced at her, his eyes mocking her naiveté.

'Their cousin, then?' She couldn't bring herself to be any more explicit.

He nodded, then made an odd little circling gesture with his fingers, which seemed to say 'a bit more than that'.

'Oh ... Yes, I see,' Belinda murmured, wondering again what it would be like to make love with him. He was a colossus but he was obviously considerate and gentle. And he looked good enough to eat in the clothes he wore this evening: white denims and a white piqué polo shirt, both of which enhanced the bronze-like sheen of his skin.

Goddamnit, Seward, get a hold of yourself, she castigated silently. What on earth had got into her since she had arrived here? She could think of nothing but sex and bodies. Bodies and sex. Shouldn't she be worrying about Jonathan? Finding out where he had so suddenly disappeared to?

'Excuse me,' she said, touching Oren's massive golden arm. 'I was wondering what happened to my friend? We were together earlier, but then he sort of vanished.'

Oren paused in his stride and nodded, and when they reached the top of the stairs, he steered her towards another long landing instead. Halfway along it, they stopped before another heavy oak door – much like the one to her room – where he knocked softly, then opened it for her to enter.

Jonathan's bedroom was luxurious – perhaps not quite as much so as her own red and gold room, but still strikingly opulent and comfortable. The predominant colours were rich, masculine greens, and significantly there were no portraits of the distinctive von Kastels. The only pictures were one still life and one landscape.

The bed Jonathan lay in was like a woodland bower hung with greenery. He was fast asleep and his face looked angelic against the snow-white lawn pillow-case.

'Johnny?' Belinda called out softly as she approached the bed. 'Johnny, are you all right?'

Jonathan stirred slightly and muttered something indecipherable, but he didn't wake up. Belinda turned to Oren, who had followed her into the room.

'What's the matter with him?' she asked, feeling concerned. Jonathan was a great one for taking a nap whenever he got the chance, but she had never seen him sleep quite this deeply. What was more, it was well into the evening now, she realised, judging by the twilight she could see descending beyond the window. And Jonathan was a night person; he usually perked up about this time.

Oren smiled calmly. Launching into another of his eloquent mimes, he described meeting Jonathan on the landing a short while ago and then discovering that the young man felt dizzy.

'And you asked Count André to see him?' said Belinda, understanding the account but feeling puzzled. 'What could *he* do?'

Oren made a stirring motion and a few slow, flowing passes with his fingers, then pointed to a white beaker that stood on the bedside table. Frowning, Belinda remembered André's strange performance with the wine bottle, and she picked up the white mug with real alarm.

119

There was a strong smell of herbs clinging to the interior of the beaker, a scent that was quite pleasant and minty. Belinda guessed it had contained a tisane.

'Was it a medicine of some kind?' she asked.

Oren nodded.

'Something Count André made?'

He nodded again.

Whatever next? she thought, reaching down to touch Jonathan's brow. The man's a doctor now, as well as a magician.

And obviously a good one, she decided. Jonathan's temperature felt perfectly normal, and he seemed to be sleeping contentedly. It was a shame to wake him up just for the sake of it.

'He must need the rest,' she observed, then leant over and kissed her boyfriend's smooth cheek.

As Oren led the way back to the head of the stairs, Belinda felt guilty that she hadn't noticed Jonathan's weariness herself. He had done most of the driving so far on their trip, and obviously the strain had tired him out.

When they reached the ground floor, she was ushered once again into the great library – where the sight of the leather sofa made her blush. It seemed only a moment since she had sat there half-naked on André von Kastel's lap.

The count was waiting for her. Standing before one of the tall bookcases, he had an open leather-covered volume in his hand, and appeared deep in thought. He frowned suddenly, then flicked over several pages. Belinda cleared her throat to attract his attention.

When André looked up, the first thing she noticed was that his blue eyes were serious. The teasing quality she had seen earlier was conspicuous by its absence, and there was again an obscure aura of sorrow about him – something intense that came from deep in his psyche. He smiled to welcome her but still the sadness lingered.

'Good evening, Belinda,' he murmured, closing his

book, setting it aside and coming towards her. 'How lovely you look. You truly are a sight to fire the spirits.'

When he reached her, he bowed over her hand again, clicking his heels. Belinda's heart pounded as his lips caressed her fingers.

André too had changed for dinner, and was now clothed from head to toe in black. Black silk shirt, black trousers and black shoes. Surprisingly, he was tie-less, but he was wearing the most elegant of antiquated dinner jackets, which suited him so beautifully that Belinda caught her breath. His weird, striated hair was hanging loose around his shoulders, but despite its bleached look it appeared glossy and well kept. Belinda could have sworn it was even blonder than before.

'Thank you,' she said in answer to his compliment, feeling disturbed that he clung on to her hand.

'You are worried about your friend, are you not?' he said, giving her fingers a small squeeze before finally letting them go.

He's reading my mind again, thought Belinda, still feeling his firm, cool grip. 'Yes, I am rather. Johnny's usually so fit. It's not like him to come down with something.'

'Do not worry,' said André, his eyes hypnotic and soothing. 'I have examined him and basically he seems quite healthy. He is simply a little over-tired.' His mouth quirked very slightly, as if he was suggesting that *she* was the cause of Jonathan's tiredness. 'I gave him a herbal tonic. Something that will make him sleep deeply and renew his strength and vigour.'

'Thank you,' murmured Belinda again, her eyes sliding away from André's, unable to cope with the intensity of his look. She glanced around at the massed ranks of books. 'I didn't realise you were a doctor.'

He shrugged and somehow managed to capture her eyes again. 'I am not one.' He smiled, a little crookedly. 'I have a little medical knowledge but I am by no means a physician. Simply a dabbler in certain – ' he paused,

121

his brilliant eyes dancing ' – therapies that have stood the test of time.'

'I'm very interested in alternative medicine – herbalism and aromatherapy and suchlike,' said Belinda quickly. It wasn't a lie. Standing here with André, she suddenly *was* interested. 'Do you have any good recipes and potions you can pass on?'

As she spoke, that strange shadow seemed to pass across his face again, but it disappeared just as swiftly when he replied.

'I would not exactly call them recipes,' he said, smiling, 'but there may be one or two things I can teach you. After dinner, that is.' He looked across to Oren, who seemed to be waiting for his orders. 'And now, I think, we shall have some champagne.'

This time, funnily enough, the wine was in an ice bucket. Belinda hadn't seen it when she had entered the library, but she noticed it now on the sideboard, coolly embracing a familiar, shapely bottle. With characteristic efficiency, Oren uncorked the frothing wine and filled two glasses without spilling the tiniest drop.

André took the two crystal flutes and handed one to Belinda, dismissing his servant with a slight nod as he did so. 'Not from my own country this time, alas,' he said, as he clinked his glass to hers, 'but delicious nevertheless. To your health, Belinda,' he murmured, 'and happiness.'

'What about long life?' she asked, as they sat down together. She felt intoxicated on just one sip of wine. 'Isn't that usually a part of the toast?'

André looked away then put his glass down by his feet. When he looked back at her, he seemed a mass of mixed emotions. His cultured face bore traces of irony, thoughtfulness and humour, as well as his slight but ever-present melancholy.

'Would you really want it?' he asked, his voice low and intent.

'What? You mean long life?' she countered, surprised

by the sudden fire in the question. 'Well, yes, I suppose I do. Doesn't everybody?'

For a moment, André didn't answer, and Belinda got the impression that she had lost him somehow. Or somewhere. He was sitting right next to her – handsome, charismatic and desirable – but it felt as if she were seeing him across a huge gulf, a division of time and space it was impossible to quantify.

Belinda felt frightened. In spite of what had happened here on this very couch, she did not know this man at all. She also had a feeling that if and when she came to know him fully, her present fears would seem as nothing by comparison.

'There are some to whom long life is a curse,' he said quietly. Then he reached down to retrieve his wine and downed it in one long swallow, his throat undulating sensuously as he drank. 'More champagne?' he enquired, on his feet again so fast it made her jump.

Belinda looked at her glass. She had hardly tasted the wine at all. She took a quick sip, then held it out. 'Yes, please,' she said, smiling as brightly as she could in an attempt to lift the suddenly sombre atmosphere.

'I'm sorry,' she said, when André returned with the wine, 'I think I've said something to upset you ... but I'm not quite sure what.'

'It is I who should be asking forgiveness,' he replied, his smile returned and his blue eyes unclouded and brilliant. 'I am being a poor host. I allow my worries to intrude at the most inopportune moments.'

'If you want to talk, it's OK, you know,' Belinda suddenly heard herself say. 'I know I'm a stranger ...' Colour flushed in her cheeks. She hadn't acted like a stranger earlier, when she had allowed him – and encouraged him – to touch her. 'But sometimes it's easier to tell your troubles to someone you don't know than it is to tell them to a friend or a loved one.'

For several seconds André stared at her unblinkingly. Belinda felt he was studying everything about her; her every thought, her every memory, her every hope and desire. 'You are a very kind and sensitive woman, Belinda,' he said softly. 'Perhaps I will confide in you. In a little while.' He smiled again, his eyes cheerful and full of promises. 'But first, we should enjoy our dinner, I think.' Draining his champagne, he put aside the glass, then rose to his feet, extending his hand to her like the courtier he most probably once had been.

He's like a prince in hiding, thought Belinda as she accompanied André to the dining room. A dissolute prince, banished for some unspeakable crime of passion and doomed to solitude for the rest of his days. It was a desperately glamorous image, she knew, and made him utterly fatal to women, especially imaginative ones like her, who loved tales of high romance and gothic mystery.

She was laughing by the time they reached their destination, and André gave her an amused look, as if once again he knew her thoughts exactly.

'OK, I admit it,' she said, as André drew her chair out and waited until she was comfortable before taking his own seat. 'You . . . and this place . . . I hate to admit it, but it really gets to me. I've got an ordinary life, an ordinary job, and I meet ordinary people. All this is like something from a book,' she said, gesturing around her. 'A foreign nobleman. A crumbling but fabulous house. Antiques. Gorgeous pictures.' She paused, realising she was gushing, and appalled by it. 'You've got me at a bit of a disadvantage. Really.'

André laughed, a merry, husky sound that seemed to dispel the last echoes of his sadness. 'It is I who is at a disadvantage,' he said, laying his hand across his chest. 'I am at the mercy of your beauty, your compassion . . . and your open-mindedness.' He hesitated, as if debating some thorny inner point. He seemed on the very edge of revealing something, something which Belinda sensed was crucial. 'You have much that I want, Belinda, and much that I need,' he said at last. 'I am your servant, believe me.' He bowed his head momentarily. 'And I would do anything to keep you here in my company. Anything.'

He spoke with such emphasis that Belinda felt chilled. The words 'do anything' seemed to chime around the room and envelop her, despite the fact that he had spoken only quietly. It was a relief when Oren entered the room, bearing their first course on a large chased silver tray.

The meal was light and delicious but Belinda scarcely noticed the fine cuisine. It was as if André had put a spell on her; she could do nothing, really, but watch him and listen to his voice, and answer every question he asked about her. Revealing virtually nothing about himself, he seemed to effortlessly coax everything from her. Her past history; her present thoughts; her future hopes and dreams. Almost the whole of her life – even down to some of the most intimate details she had never told anyone about, ever – was described over the perfect food and heady wine. And when they were finished, she could hardly believe what she had disclosed.

Has he hypnotised me? she wondered as she studied the tiny coffee cup before her and smelt the divine aroma it exuded. It certainly seemed that way. She had just talked and talked and talked, while André had remained enigmatic, and listened.

He had also, she noticed, eaten very little of his excellent dinner. Just a few morsels here and there, and then only taken for her benefit, it seemed. As the strong but sublime coffee began to clear her fuddled head a little, Belinda had the most extraordinary idea ever.

He's not human, she thought, watching André push away his plate and fold his table napkin.

Suddenly, all the books she had read and the films and television shows she had seen seemed to conspire and produce an extraordinary conclusion – Count André von Kastel was a vampire, a ghost, or some other nether being who possessed strange powers and did not take ordinary nourishment.

Everything seemed to point to it. He slept during the day, he barely ate, and she was almost convinced that he had done some kind of magic trick with the wine that afternoon in the library. Plus the fact that he lived alone, in seclusion, with only three dumb servants to attend him, in a house that was crammed with peculiar artefacts. He even came from the appropriate part of Europe.

Belinda began to shake when André rose to his feet and walked around the table towards her. She felt foolish, letting her fancies control her, but when he stood over her, smiling slightly, she couldn't move a muscle and she couldn't seem to speak.

'What is it?' he asked softly, putting out his hand to her. 'Are you afraid of me?'

Belinda licked her lips. She was caught in the thrall of a being who had the combined sexual magnetism of a dozen cinematic Draculas, and even if he were just a man after all, she was sure that wouldn't lessen her growing fear of him.

'Belinda?' he prompted, making a tiny gesture of encouragement with his fingertips.

'I-I'm sorry, I think I've had too much wine,' she said, finally finding the strength to take his hand. 'I started imagining the silliest of things just then.' She stood up, half-expecting to swoon or something, but found herself quite steady on her feet.

'Tell me about them,' said André, tucking her hand beneath his arm and leading her to the door. 'Entertain me while we stroll on the terrace. I always enjoy a walk after dinner.' He patted her hand, his fingers cool but corporeal.

'It's too stupid. I couldn't tell you, really,' she insisted, as he led her along yet another corridor she hadn't been along before, that seemed to lead right through the centre of the priory.

'Try me,' he urged, as they reached an iron-studded door that surely only a man the size of Oren could master. 'I have heard many a tall tale in my time ...

And told my fair share too.' He grinned and released her arm. Then he opened the huge door without effort.

The terrace that lay beyond was broad, stone flagged, and lit by a string of what appeared to be oil-burning lanterns. The sky was dark now, a rich shade of indigo, and the brightest of the stars were breaking through. A three-quarter moon rode above them like a sail. Belinda breathed in and smelt the perfume of many flowers, a rich fragrance that seemed to blend with André's cologne.

'This is so lovely,' she murmured, then hurried forward towards the elaborately-carved stone parapet so she could look out over the gardens beyond.

Why didn't I see this earlier today? she wondered, discovering that in the distance and to her left was the folly. She had approached the priory in broad daylight this morning and seen no evidence whatsoever of this long terrace. The whole house seemed to be remaking itself by the hour.

As she leaned over the parapet, she sensed rather than heard André join her. 'You were going to tell me what you had been thinking about,' he said, sliding his arm around her waist as if it were a perfectly natural thing to do with a near stranger, and as if they were about to take up where they had left off in the library. She felt his mouth brush the hot skin of her neck.

'I . . .' Feeling almost faint, she swayed against him. His lips were still against her throat, and filled with her insane notions of earlier, she expected him to attack at any second.

'Why do you fear me, Belinda?' he whispered, feathering a soft kiss against the line of her jaw. 'I am not what you think I am, believe me. I am just a man who is entranced by your beauty.'

He knows! thought Belinda as André turned her expertly and put his arms around her body to embrace her. He knows I thought he was a vampire. That I still think he might be one.

Cradling her head, André pressed his mouth to hers, probing for entrance with his tongue as she yielded. Belinda tried to keep her mouth closed and her brain sent the message to her lips, but with half a sigh and half a groan, she felt them open, admitting him to explore and taste her moistness.

The kiss went on for a long, long time, and as she enjoyed it, Belinda seemed to see a stream of inner pictures. Erotic images of herself and the man who held her.

First, she saw the way she must have appeared this afternoon: half-naked and sprawled across André's lap, moaning and crooning while he stroked her. Then, a second later, she seemed to be kneeling before him, on this very terrace, taking his strong, erect penis into her mouth. She could almost feel his fingers clasping her head as he thrust savagely, seeking the back of her throat, and she could almost taste the salt-sharp tang of come. The vision of fellatio melted then and changed to a picture of her leaning over a bed somewhere, possibly the red and gold one in her room, while André caressed her naked buttocks. He was teasing her, playing with her; dipping his fingers into her slit from behind, then drawing them up and back to fondle her pouting anus. To her horror the tiny portal seemed to welcome him, relaxing lewdly as a single digit entered.

The fantasy images were so real and so vivid that her body couldn't help but react to them. She groaned around André's intruding tongue and rubbed herself involuntarily against him. In response, his long, graceful hands sank immediately to her bottom, moulding her cheeks through the glistening dress, and pressing her to him.

Whatever his nature or strangeness, he was possessed of a living man's erection, and Belinda felt it bore into her belly. There were several layers of fabric between them, yet it was one of the most exciting sensations she had ever felt. He was like rock against her – like steel, like diamond – and despite the masking barriers, she seemed to feel his shape.

Massaging him with her body and feeling his fingers caress her buttocks in return, she began to see another set of pictures. But this time they were all of André only, in his tower room, fondling his penis until he came. She saw again, in every detail, the way he had arched with pleasure and squirmed like a wild man against the sheets. She almost seemed to hear his incoherent out-cries, his mutterings and exclamations in his own language. She saw him rising towards his climax, his body growing more and more tense as he strained to reach it, but at the instant he seemed to get there, the image faded. As she gasped in disappointment, he broke the kiss.

Panting for air, Belinda slumped against André's straight body, feeling grateful for his strength in her own weakness. She almost felt as if she had just had an orgasm herself, the rush had been so huge. She had certainly never been kissed like that before, and to her dismay, she felt a sudden urge to weep.

Confused, Belinda snuggled closer than ever, and as she buried her face in the hollow of André's shoulder, his hand came up and stroked her hair to soothe her. She heard him whisper something, his voice sounding vaguely Germanic but nevertheless flowing, and she realised he was speaking in his mother tongue to calm her.

'What are you doing to me?' she pleaded, drawing a little way away so she could look at him.

André looked at her steadily, his face appearing chis-elled in the uneven radiance from the oil lamps and his eyes glowing with a fire both light and dark.

'I do not want to hurt you,' he said at length, using his thumb to brush away her tears. 'Only to arouse you, and enlighten you – ' he paused, a hint of a plea forming in the brilliance of his gaze ' – so you can help me.'

Belinda sniffed and he produced an immaculate white

cotton handkerchief from his pocket and put it into her hand. Dabbing her eyes, she tried to think straight and ponder the significance of the words 'help me'.

It was the second time he had intimated that he needed her in some way, but Belinda couldn't begin to see why. She crumpled his snowy handkerchief, then frowned and tried to straighten it, knowing that there was no way she could put off asking the question.

'What are you, André? And why on earth would you need *me* for anything?'

He looked away towards the distant woods, as if seeking the right way to approach a difficult answer in their depths.

'I am just a man, Belinda,' he said eventually, still staring out across the gardens and the park, 'but I need you because – ' He paused, then turned fully away from her to face in the direction he was looking. His hands settled on the parapet, his fingers first splayed then gripping the stone tightly. 'You are beautiful. Desirable. Exquisite. I need your pleasure in order to be strong.'

It was Belinda's turn to seek an answer in the beautiful darkness. What did he mean by 'your pleasure in order to be strong'?

'I don't understand,' she said in a small voice, studying the shadows. 'You say you need my pleasure. Does that mean you are a – ' She couldn't say the word. It sounded ridiculous. Such things only existed in books and on celluloid.

'A vampire?' he asked, moving close behind her, his mouth brushing her neck just like the blackest Nosferatu's.

'Yes.' She was trembling again and gripping the parapet just as André had. She could feel his breath ruffling the fronds of hair at the nape of her neck, and the beating of his heart where his chest lay against her back. Both of these seemed to deny her mad suspicions.

'No, I am not a vampire,' he said, pressing a brief kiss

130

to the lobe of her ear, 'although I can well imagine what it must be like to be one.'

Belinda could not speak. Her shudders doubled and re-doubled. He was skirting the issue. There *was* something wrong with him. Something different. She felt herself about to fall, to crumple face down over the parapet, but André's arms were around her again, holding her tightly against his body. His strangely cool body and his so very human erection.

He was still as hard as ever as he pressed himself against her, massaging his stiffness into the crease between her buttocks. 'Oh, Belle,' he whispered, 'I need you so much.' His hands moved away from her waist where he had held her, one sliding up to cup her breast, the other going downwards.

The fear Belinda felt seemed to have aphrodisiac qualities. She was still terrified but her body began to rouse. Her nipples stiffened, peaking beneath the fragile fabric of her dress and her chemise, and between her legs the silken moisture welled. When André pressed his palm against her pubis, she jerked and whimpered.

'I c-can't,' she sobbed, not knowing why she was trying to resist. What was the point in defending a barrier he had already breached? Hadn't he 'fed' this afternoon, when he had touched and stroked her; hadn't he been nourished by the orgasm she had then experienced?

'But you can,' he told her, his hands moving guilefully to squeeze and massage. 'It is so easy. I would never hurt you.'

Belinda went limp in his grasp, her body seeming to melt as the sensations quickly mounted. Her breasts were aching now, swelling inside the silk of her bodice, and her vulva was a pool of simmering heat.

'Oh André! André!' Moulded against him, she no longer cared who or what he was. He was simply caressing hands and a male body, superbly strong and fragrant.

131

Suddenly there were too many layers of clothing between them. Still held, she struggled in his grip, trying to reach the fastenings of the priceless period dress.

'Hush,' he murmured. 'Let me. It will be easier.' He took his hands from her body in an instant and set to work, deftly undoing the tiny buttons at the back of her dress.

Without André's hands on her, Belinda felt feverish, and she moaned for the return of his fabulous touch.

'Patience,' he said into her ear as the dress fluttered down on to the stone flags beneath them, forming a pale, fluid pool around her ankles. Too impatient even to step out of it, Belinda pressed her thinly-clad body back against him and circled her hips to work her buttocks against his penis.

'Touch me,' she begged, tugging at the cobweb-like chemise and knickers. 'I want you to touch me. Please. Like you did before ... I want to feel your fingers between my legs.'

Somewhere far back in her mind, Belinda was appalled. She was pleading and grovelling like some helpless nymphomaniac, calling out for a virtual stranger to lay his hands upon her sex. It wasn't like her, but it didn't seem to matter. She was another person here, transformed by André, her magician, into a thing of pleasure, pledged only to serve his whim. As his fingers slithered beneath the chemise, she grunted, 'Yes!'

Hunting among the layers of delicate silk, André soon had his hand inside her knickers, and with unerring efficiency, he worked it down to find her quim. One finger wiggled its way through the sodden curls of her pubic forest, and when it found her, Belinda crowed with lust and triumph.

'Oh God! Oh God!' Her cries rang out loudly in the mystical blue-black night, her bottom jerking as André flicked her clitoris. She was a breath away from orgasm, a heartbeat from coming gloriously and freely, but he

132

kept her hovering, his touch wicked and as light as swan's down.

'Oh please,' she begged again, kicking her legs, heedless that she might tear the priceless gown around her feet. 'Oh please, André, please, I need to come. I can't wait. I'll go mad if I don't!'

One arm held her tight around her waist while the other slid loosely to her side. 'Don't worry, my beautiful Belinda,' he purred into her ear. 'You will have your release. But it will be all the sweeter for a little wait. A little craving.'

Belinda kicked again, sending the peach-orange dress flying across the flags. 'You beast! You bastard! You really are a monster!' she howled, squirming and squirreling against him. Her sex was on fire and so engorged it seemed to hurt. She hissed 'I hate you' as he draped her forward against the parapet.

'Be still,' he ordered her, his voice soft yet seeming to resonate with command. She felt his hand lie flat against the small of her back, and though he held her lightly, she seemed to lose the will to move.

Belinda quivered finely as she lay prone across the parapet, toweringly furious yet more aroused than she could measure. She bit her lip as André stood behind her, and she sensed him studying her bottom. After a short pause, she felt him plucking gently at her knickers, then easing the fine, slippery fabric slowly downward.

When her drawers were around her ankles, he lifted the pretty embroidered chemise up to just beneath her shoulders and with a few deft tucks and twists, he secured it there. When that was done, she heard him step back to admire the view.

'Oh God,' Belinda moaned again, as she imagined the shocking vista before his eyes.

Her bottom and her thighs were completely on show, while her suspenders and her stockings enhanced their bareness. She could feel the fragrant night air flowing

133

playfully across her vulva, its cool caress a blessed balm to her burning heat.

'What are you going to do to me?' she asked defiantly, fighting hard to keep the quaver from her voice. 'Beat me or something? Smack my bottom ... I'm sure that's just what you decadent aristocrats live for – a chance to humiliate the lower orders.'

'How wrong you are,' said André, his voice soft and far closer than she had realised. 'I only want to give you pleasure.' She could swear she felt his breath upon her back. 'Although if to be beaten *is* your pleasure, I would be far more than delighted to oblige you.'

'Don't be ridiculous!' she cried, yet at the same time she imagined his hand crashing down upon her buttocks. The idea should have been horrendous; revolting. But suddenly, against her will, she seemed to want it. She felt her sex-flesh pulse and flutter at the thought of André smacking her bottom, and her hips began to weave of their own accord. She pursed her lips to prevent her voicing her wayward urges.

'I know ... I know ...' His voice was soothing and she felt the brush of his dinner jacket against her thighs. 'Perhaps I should beat you?' He seemed to reflect for a moment. 'But not just yet. Tonight we will enjoy a simpler pleasure.'

He *does* know, she thought, feeling herself sink to a delicious nadir of shame. He understands what I want before I do. He anticipates the way I think and what I feel. How will I ever keep a secret while he's near?

Chapter Eight
Indigo Secrets

'*R*elax ... relax ...' murmured André, his long hair tickling her back as he sank to his knees at her side. 'There is no need to keep secrets from me. I have no wish to harm you.'

Belinda stiffened involuntarily. The more André confirmed his strangeness, the more her fear of him increased. And as the fear grew, so did her arousal.

He must be able to see how much I want him, she thought, unable to prevent her thighs from shaking. She could feel his breath on her now, his cool breath, like a breeze that teased her naked bottom. His face was just inches from her vulva. She imagined him flaring his nostrils and drawing her scent; her strong female odour. She could smell it herself, so André must be drowning in it. She pictured him studying the engorged folds of her sex then putting out his tongue, pointed and mobile, to taste and lick her. The idea made her cringe with shame, and yet, with all her might, she craved it. And in acknowledging that need, she knew that he too knew what she wanted.

But still he kept his distance. Inches seemed like feet or yards. His breath and his masculine aura seemed to tantalise and caress her, but his fingers and his tongue remained aloof.

'Well, do something if you're going to!' she cried, unable to bear the waiting any longer. She felt like an exhibit in a gallery or some infernal experiment in responsiveness. Was he waiting to see how wet she would get without the benefit of contact? Was he waiting for her to crack and reach to touch herself? Or perhaps to have an orgasm, just from need?

'Patience,' he whispered, laying his fingers on her flank. 'You are so beautiful. Let me admire you a moment, before I pleasure you.'

Belinda let out a low, frustrated cry. Her swollen sex was calling to him, begging for him. She kicked her legs and felt her knickers at first constrain her then slide off over her shiny satin ballet pumps, one foot after the other. Kicking them away, she edged closer to the parapet, trying to press her pubis against the stone and get relief.

The hand on her thigh moved inward, fingers splaying, thumb beginning a rhythmic stroke. It moved back and forth, less than an inch from her anus, sliding over the sensitive skin with ineffable lightness. As she groaned, his left hand mirrored his right, and then both his thumbs were working in concert, stroking the area around her rosy entrance with the greatest care.

Belinda pushed back towards him, feeling both her sex and her rear portal pout rudely. Her body seemed to speak of its own accord. Choose! it demanded of him. Take me! Take whatever you want . . . it's yours . . . take everything!

The thumbs edged closer together, right into the channel, their soft pads brushing the forbidden opening. Liquid gathered in her vulva, pooling as it never had before, then became too much to be contained and overflowed. She could feel her sexual juice trickling down her inner thigh and landing in a sticky puddle on the stone. Shame made her whole body flush, but it

136

made no difference. The fluid only ran faster than ever, oozing out of her like honey from a jar.

'Oh please! Oh please!' she begged again, unable to bear being touched yet not touched, being viewed but not allowed to come, being so wet and needy she was running like a river. 'Oh please,' she grunted, shoving her whole body towards him and tilting up her hips.

His answer was to dig into the flesh of her bottom with his thumbs, exert a measured, devilish pressure, then slide them outwards again, parting her lobes like a ripe peach. Her sense of being exposed increased exponentially as the entrances to her body were stretched wide, but she urged him on by pressing backwards and stretching them wider –

When his tongue touched her sex, she almost fainted.

It was just the very lightest contact at first. His tongue-tip was furled, extended, probing like a dart into her sacred inner sanctum. Moving like a hovering, nectar drinking bird, it circled the snug mouth of her vagina, then seemed to flatten and lap at her welling fluids. The feeling was so sublime and so longed for, she began to come.

As the pulsations lashed her vulva, she felt André grip her tightly and his tongue point again and dive inside her. Squirming, she reached beneath herself and rubbed her clitoris.

'Yes!' encouraged André, his cultured voice muffled against her bottom.

Belinda rubbed harder, her whole body in manic, jerking motion as the sensations spiralled up to a new intensity. She could hear herself sobbing, shouting, grunting; her sex seemed to be a mile wide, a vast landscape of pure, lewd pleasure; every inch of it beating like a misplaced heart.

The next moment, she felt André withdraw his tongue from her vagina then slither it backwards until it rested against her anus.

Oh no! screamed a scared little voice inside her; then

suddenly the same voice was howling out anew in perfect ecstasy. Furled again, and as stiff and determined as before, his tongue breached the puckered aperture between her buttocks.

'Oh no! Oh no! Oh no!' she crooned, appalled by the power of what she was experiencing. This was an unthinkable taboo. It couldn't be happening. She couldn't be feeling such pleasure because he was doing *that* to her. She couldn't be coming even harder than she had before . . .

After a while, Belinda seemed to wake up from a dream of sobbing and disorientation. She was aware of what had just happened, but her mind was trying to stop her from believing it. No man had ever done such a thing to her before, and the strength of her own responses confused and confounded her. Shame and horror vied with delicious wonder. She didn't know what to think, but she couldn't deny what she had felt. The pinnacle of pleasure from the basest kiss of all.

As her shoulders heaved and her teardrops fell down into the garden below, she sensed André rise behind her. What he had just done should by rights have abased him, and yet it dawned on Belinda that precisely the opposite had happened. If anything, her awe of him had increased. He was remarkable. Uninhibited beyond belief. A sexual prize she was unworthy of and had not earned.

'Do not weep,' he whispered, leaning over her. 'There is no shame in enjoying the *feuille de rose*.' His arms slid around her and lifted her from the stone, and when she was standing, he gently turned her to face him, using the very tips of his fingers to erase her tears. 'And it pleased me to kiss you there. Your *cul* is enchanting. I cannot imagine a man who could resist its tender beauty and its tightness.'

Belinda buried her face in the lapel of his dinner jacket, very aware of her own vulnerability. Her pretty chemise had slid down over her back but her buttocks were still

138

naked. She could feel herself blushing again, thinking of André's cool aristocratic face pressed tight between the cheeks of her bottom.

'Hush ... hush ...' A long, graceful hand settled on the back of her head, ruffling and smoothing her short hair. Belinda felt a great calm flow over her, a feeling of being exactly in the right place in the world. What André had done had been wonderful. How could she possibly have perceived it as wrong?

'That's a pretty name for it,' she said at last, looking up into his lambent blue eyes.

'*Feuille de rose*?'

'Yes. Trust the French.' She suddenly found herself laughing.

André chuckled too. 'Yes, as a nation they have an aptitude for the *bon mot*,' he observed, smiling at her. 'But the description is valid. Have you never taken a glass and studied yourself?' His eyes twinkled. 'The entrance is soft and a dark, dark pink, and it is ruffled like the petals of a rosebud.'

'I-I've never looked,' she said nervously. Would he think her less of a woman if she wasn't fully familiar with her own sexual anatomy? She had taken her body for granted until now; perhaps not revelled in it as much as she should have.

'Never?'

'Never.'

'Then why not begin tonight?' He eyed her intently, his expression indicating an order rather than a question.

'I – ' Belinda began, then she fell silent as André slid his fingers beneath the hem of her thin chemise and whisked it up over her head.

'But how can I look at myself here?' she protested when it too fluttered down on to the flags of the terrace. She fought the urge to cover herself, especially her nipples, which were as hard and dark as plum stones.

'You cannot,' he replied, reaching gently for her breasts and cupping them, 'but I can.' He bent down, kissed each delicately pointed crest, then met her eyes again. 'And I have been promising myself this privilege all night.' He reached out and enfolded her in his arms, crushing her near-naked form to his fully-clothed body.

If Belinda had felt vulnerable before, she felt doubly so now. She was standing on an open terrace, at night, virtually nude. Her flimsy suspender belt, her stockings and her ballet shoes were no protection, especially from the mysterious, audacious man who held her. Any second now, he might bend her over the parapet and perform whatever outrage he so desired on her unprotected body. It might be more than his tongue that entered her this time – and yet, snuggling closer, she longed for the deepest of debasement.

For a while he just kissed her and held her, his mouth quite circumspect as it roved across her face, exploring briefly but always returning to her lips. Occasionally, he would mutter a scrap of a sentence against her skin, something unintelligible in his own language that nevertheless made her quiver.

Presently, his mouth settled firmly on hers again, his tongue pressing for entrance then possessing her completely the instant her lips yielded. At the same time, his hands began to range across her body, visiting her breasts, her thighs and her buttocks. In sliding circles, he rubbed and aroused her and his fingers delved repeatedly into the grove between her legs, touching her sex and the sensitive 'rosebud' of her bottom. Aflame anew, she couldn't stop herself from moaning, uttering her muffled entreaties around his tongue.

'You want me,' he said, releasing her mouth and looking down at her. It was a statement of fact, not a question.

Belinda tried to look away, but he cupped her jaw in his fingers and prevented her.

'You want me ... I know that,' he said again, with a strange expression on his face that puzzled her. She watched him bite his lip in perplexion, then heard him sigh.

Sensing the sudden return of his melancholy, Belinda moved her body against his invitingly. She found it difficult to say the words, but actions were easy enough. She shimmied sinuously, rocking her belly against the bulge of his erection.

'Would that things were different . . .' he said quietly, his eyes on her face, their brilliant blue suddenly darkened to indigo. He was aroused, she could tell. There was no denying the truth of his hard, swollen cock against her. But the very fact of it seemed to cause him sorrow instead of joy.

'What's wrong?' asked Belinda, thoroughly puzzled by the contradictions. She suddenly realised that she had perhaps never wanted a man this much ever in her life, and she couldn't bear the idea of being thwarted now. A second ago, she had been sure he desired her.

'I *will* tell you,' he said, placing a cool hand on either side of her face and making her look at him. 'But first we will share pleasure as best we can.' Releasing her, he stepped back a pace, then reached for her hand. 'Come. We will go to your bedroom. We can be more comfortable there.' He gave her a small, almost nervous smile, and began to lead her across the terrace towards the house.

'But my clothes – ' She looked back towards the pools of pale silk that were the dress and the lingerie. 'And I left my bag and my flower in the dining room.' Why was she protesting? The things were André's so what did it matter?

'You do not need clothes,' he said, urging her forward, his playfulness returned. 'Come, I want you to walk naked through my house. I want to see your breasts and your bottom sway as you move. Indulge an old man, Belinda. Please be kind.'

More confused than ever, she obeyed him, very conscious of the bounce of her breasts with each step and

141

the way her bottom rolled voluptuously from side to side. And what on earth had he meant by 'indulge an old man'? He had been flirting with her as he had said it, yet the words themselves had seemed to carry an odd significance.

He wasn't old, not by any means. Not really. Yet as she thought about it, Belinda wondered exactly how old her intriguing host was. It was hard to put a precise age on him. His features were peculiarly ageless; neither old nor young. He could have been anywhere between his early twenties to his late thirties, and his streaky hair made him even more of an enigma.

'Why are you frowning?' André asked suddenly as he stepped aside to let her pass into the main hall. 'Please do not spoil a masterpiece with such a worried look.'

Wondering what he was referring to, Belinda spun around and saw herself and André reflected in a long mirror which she hadn't noticed before.

The contrast between them was stunning: André was a dramatic and ominous figure in his sombre black clothing, while she was a pale, gleaming vision of delicate curves. The minimal scrap of lace around her hips and her gossamer fine stockings only appeared to increase her nakedness rather than cover it, and the glossy amber of her pubic curls was a brilliant splash. Once again, she felt an overpowering urge to try and cover herself, but before thought could become deed, André grasped her arms.

'Do not hide, Belinda,' he whispered, drawing her arms back and making her straighten her shoulders. Her breasts lifted proudly as if displayed. 'Your bare body is sublime. A treasure. You should exhibit it as often as you are able.' Starting to blush again, Belinda looked away, but André released her and made her turn her head. 'Look ... Look into the glass,' he murmured. 'See your own beauty.' His hand passed across her breasts, then down over her belly to rest briefly against her pubis, the dark sleeve of his coat making her skin look white and pearly. There seemed no trace left of her holiday tan. 'Would you like to watch while I caress you?' His voice was low, like velvet in her ear, and the expression on his face was almost predatory. 'Would you like to see your own face when you are in the throes of ecstasy? See it grow savage as you reach the peak of pleasure?' His mouth was against her neck; she could feel his teeth. 'Would you, Belinda, would you?'

'No! I can't! I don't want to!' She jerked away from him, aware that she was lying but also frightened. Her body was moistening at the thought – the image of her naked hips bucking, her face twisting. Her thighs spread wide while a strong hand worked ruthlessly between them. 'Please, no,' she whispered, turning in towards him then almost collapsing against the dark-clad column of his body.

He held her again, soothingly. 'Do not worry,' he said into her hair, 'there is no compulsion. You need only do what you want to do, Belinda. I would never force you to do anything against your will.'

Belinda snuggled against him, breathing in great lungfuls of his heady rose cologne. Within her, she could already feel her fears transforming into desires. It was on the tip of her tongue to tell him she had changed her mind and that she would be glad to fulfil his wishes, when he patted her back and then released her from his arms.

'Come along, to your room. We can relax there and feel comfortable.'

Belinda nodded and gave him a small shy smile, wondering how it was that she could suddenly change from a self-possessed and rather bossy young woman into a creature so pliant and submissive. It was less than a day since she had first set eyes on André von Kastel, and already she was obeying his every word.

The strangest thing, she thought, as they ascended the staircase together, arm in arm, her breast brushing the fine cloth of his dinner jacket, was how easily it had happened. André was a puzzle to her, and mysterious sexually, as well as on every other level. Yet despite this, she somehow felt strangely safe with him. She sensed he was keeping secrets from her – probably a good many of them – but she also knew, without knowing how, that he wouldn't harm her. At least not intentionally.

Turning to him, she smiled again, and as they reached the top of the stairs, he returned her smile and nodded infinitesimally.

Belinda shrugged her shoulders. How long would it take her to remember that while André could hide his secrets effortlessly, hers were an open book to him?

When they reached her door, he opened it, then stepped back, executing a slight bow to let her pass.

The room was filled with candles and their flickering casting a moving veil of light. Some were in elaborate candelabra, wrought out of iron and bronze and more precious metals; while other, thinner candles stood in a variety of small, individual holders of porcelain, crystal and brass, scattered on every flat surface to be seen. The result of all this was eerie but also welcoming, and Belinda gasped, feeling sheer delight at the magical effect.

'How lovely!' she cried.

'My servants know their duties well,' said André from behind her, a note of satisfaction in his voice.

Belinda moved forward into the room, looking around at the array of dancing lights, then down at her own body where the radiance played on it. It was something of a cliché that candlelight flattered the human body, but this was the first time she had seen the phenomenon for herself. The shimmering glow seemed to lend a soft peachy radiance to her skin, as well sleekening her curves and creating a subtle mystic shading. Without thinking, she ran her hands down her flanks and watched the shadows of her fingers leap and race. From behind her she heard a male sigh of appreciation.

When she turned around, she found André staring at

her fixedly, his eyes filled with both excitement and what appeared for all the world to be exquisite nostalgia. Seeing her body by candlelight obviously brought back a memory of some kind, a recollection that was both erotic and deeply poignant. His face shining, he held out his arms, then fiercely embraced her.

What is it? she wanted to ask as they were kissing. Who does this remind you of? The questions faded as André's kiss bewitched her senses.

Belinda had never been a great one for kissing on its own, but with André the simple act brought a ravishing pleasure. His mouth was soft, yet active and strong; as cold as ice-cream, and figuratively, just as sweet. She found herself swaying again, almost swooning; quite lost in the experience. And it was André, with a sigh of regret, who at last drew back.

'Do you need a moment to yourself?' he asked, nodding towards the bathroom.

Belinda felt confused for a second, then realised what he was asking, and was thankful.

'Yes. Just a minute,' she said, breaking from his arms. 'I won't be long.' Conscious of his scrutiny, she walked as smoothly and gracefully as she could into the adjoining room.

What am I letting myself in for? she thought, doing what she had to as quickly as possible. He scares me, and yet I let him do exactly what he wants with me.

Why is that? she asked her reflection in the mirror, studying the wild eyes and passion-flushed face she saw before her. She was in unknown territory, the realm of the imagination. After having read so many tales of the supernatural – and half-believing them at the time – she was now in the presence of a real 'phenomenon', a man who could very well not be human. And yet she trusted him.

So, what *do* you think he is? she mused as she sprayed on a little scent, then ran her fingers through her hair to smooth it. He says he isn't a vampire, but he is *something*.

No normal man can do what he does and feel how he feels.

Standing with her hand on the door handle, she had a last irrational urge to pull back, to lock the bathroom door, and shout for André to go away. But then she remembered his kisses, and his touch, and she could no longer wait a single minute to be near him. She flung open the door and strode back into the bedroom, her heart pounding madly.

André was waiting in bed for her, his clothes flung everywhere on the floor. His smile was almost shy as she approached him, and he held up the blood-red coverlet to reveal the crisp, lace-trimmed linens that lay beneath it. She caught a fleeting glimpse of his long bare flank as she slid in beside him.

'Belinda . . . The beautiful one,' he murmured, as they lay facing one another, propped up on a mound of pillows. He reached out to touch her cheek, but otherwise kept his distance, as if reluctant to press his unclothed body against hers. His face bore an expression of disbelief, an almost boyish befuddlement at the simple fact that they were together, sharing a bed.

'Why are you staring at me like that?' she asked, feeling the hairs on the back of her neck rise. André looked stunned, yet extraordinarily focused. 'You said I reminded you of someone. Is that what it is? Do I look like a woman you once made love to? Someone you've slept with already?'

'I never made love to her,' he said quietly, his mouth twisted in a quirky sorrowful little smile. 'At least, not the way I would have liked to.'

'What happened?' asked Belinda, moving closer, then clasping his arm so he couldn't retreat. As her thigh touched his, she felt the coolness of his skin, but suppressed her flinch of shock. It seemed that his entire body had the same unnaturally low temperature that his lips and his hands did.

'Did ... did she die?' She felt compelled to ask, even though she suspected his answer would cause him pain.

André looked away, and for a long time he didn't speak. His cold body felt so still against her that he might just as well have been carved out of stone. 'Not exactly,' he said eventually, 'although sometimes I wonder if it might have been better if she had died. And that I had died also.'

The wistful expression on his face was so affecting that Belinda surged forward, wrapped her arms around him, and kissed his cheek, his throat and his cool chest. Now that she was accustomed to his chilliness, she began to find it exciting. She pressed even closer, forcing him back against the pillows, gasping with relief as his body moved against her. His penis was no warmer than any of the rest of him was, but at least it was imposingly erect.

'You must have loved her very much,' she whispered, rising up over him and looking down into his face. His eyes were closed; his expression was unreadable.

'I love her still,' he said, his lashes flicking up. His eyes were clear and frank, their blueness like the light of a distant star.

'And you want me because I look like her,' stated Belinda, swirling her pelvis and stimulating his engorged sex with her belly. She couldn't understand why she wasn't feeling jealous. Under any other circum-stances she would have felt so.

'Yes – ' He paused. 'And no.' He grinned, then grasped her hips, pulling her down, hard, against him. 'It is difficult to explain ... I know in my heart that you are not Belle, and yet you seem so much like her.' He frowned, as if his own emotions were hard to compre-hend. 'To hold you like this is to experience something I thought was forever lost to me. And yet ... and yet at the same time I know you are Belinda Seward, a new friend whose intelligence and beauty enchant me, and whose naked body excites me beyond measure.' He

147

shrugged, making his penis slip and slide against her hip. 'I am at a loss to know what I feel, and what I *should* feel. You must bear with me, Belinda. I find this very strange.'

'So do I,' said Belinda, wanting to touch him and feel his hardness – to explore flesh that by any normal standards should be hot. 'Everything's strange here. The house is strange. Your servants are strange. Even time itself is strange. I know I should be scared to death – ' She paused, holding his brilliant, unnatural gaze, and fighting not to look away ' – but I'm not. Even though the strangest thing of all here is you!'

'You are right, Belinda,' he said, staring up at her, his eyes unblinking. 'So right. The source of all that is strange here *is* me.' He moved again beneath her, inveigling his thigh between hers; opening her and letting her feel the strangeness, right there, against her sex. 'And yet still you lie with me.' His mouth surged up towards hers just as his hand gripped her head, and he overwhelmed her with a long, demanding kiss. His cool tongue subdued hers, and as it did so, he slid an arm around her and rolled her effortlessly on to her back, pressing her down with great force against the mattress.

A million fragmentary thoughts and impressions rushed through her. She did feel fear, and it made a lie of her earlier statement. But she also felt a bigger, wilder excitement than she had ever felt before. The fear and the excitement were mirrored emotions, and both stirred her heart and her body profoundly. She became aware that this man – this being – who was caressing her, could probably kill her or worse at any second, and yet her body still burnt with desire. Her essence was flowing; she was open; she was ready.

Struggling to manoeuvre herself into position without their mouths breaking contact, she moaned in her throat when André wouldn't allow it. Exerting what Belinda sensed was only a fraction of his strength, he held her motionless beneath him, her womanhood spread by his

148

cool, firm thigh, her throbbing clitoris pressed hard up against it. His hands slid to her buttocks and he began to rock her – at first slowly, then faster and faster and faster – against the unyielding column of muscle and sinew.

'No! Oh no!' she protested into his mouth, feeling the wave of her orgasm break and her unfilled vagina contract and pulse. The pleasure was blinding, like a white light imploding in the core of her; yet it was spiked with a vein of dark denial. She had so wanted to have him inside her as she came.

'Why – ' she began as he lifted away from her, only to have the question suppressed by his mouth. The kiss was quick and peremptory, and she understood that it meant 'don't ask'.

'Caress me!' he commanded, sliding on to his side next to her. His penis was still stone hard, and he took her hand and folded it around himself. 'Please ... oh please,' he said, sounding less sure of himself as he moved her fingers with his own. 'Grant me pleasure, I beg of you,' he gasped, his hips lifting as their nested hands slid.

'But – '

'Please. Do it my way,' he groaned, gripping her tighter when she tried to release him so she could straddle his body.

Confused, she reseated her hold on him and began her task, creating a rhythm as best she could.

Why is he so reluctant to penetrate me? she wondered as he seemed to swell in her hand, his cold flesh juddering as if he was already about to ejaculate. Does he think he'll hurt me? Or is it me that might hurt *him*?

But how could she hurt such magnificence? His penis was thick. Long. Covered in skin that was as fine as oiled velvet. Even its very coolness was a turn-on. Warm was normal; any man could be warm. But cool was exotic and forbidden. She imagined pressing her hot mouth against his glans.

'Soon,' he gasped, as he arched and thrust himself through her fingers. 'But not yet.'

Oh God, thought Belinda. He can even read my mind when he's almost coming!

'Yes ... oh yes ... yes!' André murmured, his body jerking, his penis pushing, pushing, pushing.

Was he answering her? she wondered. Or just crying out with pleasure? It didn't matter as she swirled her hand around his shaft.

After a few moments more, André cried out loudly and froze against her, his member a rod of crystal in her fingers. The sound was inarticulate at first, then he let forth a string of tangled words in his own language, and at the same time jerked violently sideways – making her lose her hold on his sex as he came. Belinda got a momentary impression of a cold, silvery slipperiness – a thin, silk-like fluid that almost evaporated as it splashed across her wrist – then he had swivelled away, the tangled sheet around his loins.

'What are you?' whispered Belinda into the silence that settled over them afterwards. She remembered asking the question earlier – what seemed like a lifetime ago – and getting no satisfactory answer. Would he still continue to evade her, even now?

André rolled over in bed and sat up. Turning to face her, he tucked his bare legs into a yoga-like position, then let his arms rest loosely on his thighs. His gaze was gentle, resigned and utterly human, and Belinda began to wonder if she had been imagining things. Even his soft, subsiding penis looked exactly like a normal man's.

Abruptly, he looked up towards the portrait that hung over the bed. Belinda had barely noticed it when they had first entered the room, but now the candlelight seemed to be shining on it more powerfully, and showing every detail of the figure it depicted.

'That is what I am, or should I say, *who* I am.'

Belinda stared at the image, acknowledging the likeness but confused by the antiquated clothing.

'I thought he was your ancestor, like the rest of the pictures,' she said.

'All the portraits are of me,' said André softly, a little smile playing around his lips – a rather sad little smile.

'I d-don't suppose you were in fancy dress?' said Belinda, smiling herself, with trepidation, as an inkling of the truth began to come to her.

'No, I am afraid not,' answered André, shrugging. 'Just in clothes that rather appealed to me at the time ... or times.'

'Then you *are* a vampire?' Belinda said, knowing the issue had to be faced sometime, especially now, after what had just happened between them. They hadn't had sex as such, but it was close enough. Would she slip beneath a hypnotic spell any minute?

'No, as I told you before, I am not,' he said, reaching out to take her hand and squeeze it reassuringly. 'Vampires do exist, believe me, but I am not one of them. I endure a similar plight, but my needs are slightly different. Far less dangerous.' He paused for a moment, frowning, and Belinda felt a moment of doubt. Was he lying to her, trying to lull her into a false sense of security? 'To the best of my knowledge, I am still human,' he went on, rubbing his thumb across her knuckle in a way that did seem very much the action of a tender, human lover. 'Changed, but still a man. Still flesh and blood.' He smiled, more brightly this time, as if the fact that he was still mortal cheered him up.

'How old are you?'

André appeared to think carefully. 'I was born in 1760, so that would make me – ' He counted silently ' – well, over two hundred years old.' His thumb stilled and his gaze levelled to meet hers.

Belinda swallowed. Her head felt light and she experienced a sudden detachment from reality, as if she had been dreaming and had woken up too quickly. What André had just told her was more or less the secret she

151

had been expecting, but when framed in actual words, it seemed preposterous.

'Will you live for ever?'

'I do not think so,' he said matter-of-factly. 'I am extremely long-lived, yes, but as I have aged slightly since my misfortune – perhaps four or five years – I believe that I will grow old and die eventually. But it will not be for several centuries yet.'

Belinda was lost for words, yet from somewhere deep inside she found a question.

'You said you weren't a vampire, and that your needs weren't dangerous – '

André forestalled her. 'Were you not listening to me when we spoke on the terrace?' He turned her hand in his grip, then kissed her palm, licking her skin slowly and sensually.

Belinda remembered the terrace. She remembered being befuddled by shame and sensation. He had told her something, but she had desired him too much to be able to think straight. It was a miracle she remembered her own name.

'My need is very simple,' he said, drawing her towards him by kissing his way up her arm. 'And exactly as I described to you.' Rearranging his limbs, he was suddenly looming over her, his mouth swooping to brush her shoulders, then her breasts. 'I feed on your senses, Belinda. Your ecstasy, your bliss, your gratification.' His lips grazed her nipple as his tongue laved it softly. 'The erotic pleasure that you experience while making love.'

Chapter Nine

Japanese Whispers

*H*as she understood me? thought André, arranging his star-strewn cloak around him as he lay down among the books and parchments tumbled across his bed. It was close to dawn, and soon he would be compelled to go to sleep again, but until that happened he could nurture his hopes and dreams.

To his great relief, Belinda Seward had expressed no horror at his unusual longevity and shown very little fear of him, but he did sense that she harboured many questions. Questions, and an instinctive awareness of her own importance in the scheme of things; an importance that transcended simple dalliance.

Not that the love they had made had been insignificant, he realised. Far from it. Abandoning himself to memory, he lay back and hugged his silken cloak around him, thinking of the pleasure he had experienced just hours ago.

Touching and caressing Belinda Seward had been frighteningly like his recurring dreams of Arabelle. Their bodies and faces were so similar, or at least alike in the fact that Belinda was his Arabelle matured to womanhood. If Belle had not been taken from him before she had even achieved her twentieth birthday, she would have looked very much as Belinda looked now. He smiled, wondering if Belle would ever have considered cutting off her lustrous titian hair and sporting the short, elfin crop that Belinda favoured. He would have to ask her. What he was sure of though, was that she would certainly have had the same sensual nature; the same sweet blend of naïveté and daring. A rich amalgam of the pure and the profane.

As his penis began to rise again, stirred both by recent acts and by long-lost dreams, André sat up, squared his shoulders, and reached for a book. It had always seemed odd to him, but he had discovered that he did his best and clearest thinking while he was aroused. Whenever he cast an enchantment, he incited a state of desire for the process – either by stimulating thoughts or by touching himself – and he ascribed much of his magic prowess to the powers of lust.

And he would need every last scrap of that prowess if he were to achieve the difficult goal that lay ahead of him. Opening the grimoire, he turned quickly to the relevant pages, to a ritual that he already knew by heart yet which was so hazardous it had never been given a name.

Would it work? he wondered, wrinkling his nose as a familiar but hated perfume rose up from the age-darkened paper. This grimoire might be the only means by which he could achieve what he wanted for himself and Arabelle, but its origins inspired a deep revulsion. It seemed like only yesterday that he had snatched it up from among the clutter on Isidora's work table, then fled into the night, taking only it and Arabelle's crystal vial.

The book of enchantments had not come to Isidora by fair means though, he knew that. She had probably stolen it, most likely from the esoteric collection of one of her previous victims; it was a treasure that had already been antique two hundred years ago. Within its weathered pages was the lore of more than a dozen revered mages – alchemist wizards who had sought eternal life and the secret of creating gold – and even to them the knowledge had been a received wisdom. It contained lore from the Orient, from the Middle East and from Ancient Egypt; where death and rebirth and allegorical erotic ritual had been central to their complex pharaonic cult.

Where would he and Arabelle go if the rite described in the grimoire was successful? he wondered. To the stellar heavens – as the Egyptian kings had believed – or to another world entirely? To nothingness even? There was no way to tell in advance exactly what would happen, but he knew that in some form at least they would be together, freed at last from their state of separation.

There were many hazards though. The ritual might fail and condemn him to live on even longer, his mind affected, his body weakened. He might even lose the spirit of Arabelle, setting her adrift in some dark and unknown void. The greatest danger was that Belinda, as his beloved's mortal host, might be extinguished too; many ingredients of the elixir were deadly poison when taken under normal circumstances. Belladonna; mercury; azarnet, or arsenic as it was more commonly known. All these were fatal in their unenchanted forms.

Did he have the right to risk Belinda's life? And if he explained the dangers to her, could she still care for him as the ritual also demanded?

There was no way he could avoid telling her. He already felt a particular fondness for her after just one day's acquaintance, and besides which, any deception would void the magic. The host had to be aware and completely willing.

Putting aside his qualms for the moment, André considered what other elements he must assemble for his endeavour. Sacred ground was easily found – the priory's ruined chapel was the perfect site. Candles; incense; bindings? Yes, he had all those in abundance. They had been prepared for decades, in anticipation of a suitable host's arrival. The one facet he did not have to hand was an attendant sorceress to preside over the final stages of the spell.

This was a most critical requirement indeed. Michiko, his dear friend and comforter, had told him once that she was always awaiting his call, but was he yet sufficiently strong enough to summon her? Their mind-link was tenuous across great distance. And if he could contact her, how quickly would she be able to reach him?

'Michiko,' he murmured, closing the grimoire and putting it aside. 'Michiko-*chan* . . . Where are you? I need you . . . Come to me . . .'

Almost immediately, a vivid image appeared to him, not of the present but of many decades past. It was Michiko clad in the gorgeous formal kimono she had been wearing when he had first met her, back in Japan, in a period when he had been relatively strong, and travelling extensively to escape detection by Isidora.

In need of his particular kind of 'sustenance', he had arranged to be introduced to a famous courtesan, Madame Michiko, a great lady from the elite of her profession. When she had ushered him into her boudoir and they were sitting cross-legged, facing each other across the tatami mat, it had taken him only a second to discover what she really was; a Miko, or white sorceress, who was blessed – or cursed – with the same long life as he.

'I perceive your dilemma, my lord,' she had said to him from behind her fluttering fan, in his native tongue. André had been impressed by her superb command of language, although her mental gift meant she had little need to speak. 'Please accept my humble assistance in this matter. I will do everything within my power to aid your success.' And with that she had snapped shut her fan, risen to her feet and shuffled gracefully towards him, then begun, with fastidious fingers, to unfasten his clothes.

156

'Michiko,' he whispered now, remembering her imagination and her gentle, arcane skill. Her poise, above all things, was a wonder to experience, and she created art in the realm of sensual dealings.

Each garment she had removed from him she had meticulously folded and placed on a low cedarwood table. Each accessory she had arranged with reverent flair. His stiff collar had encircled his silver collar studs, and his cufflinks had been positioned one on either side. It had seemed, at first, that she was taking more care of his clothing than she was prepared to lavish on his body, but André soon realised that that was not the case at all.

'Be at your ease, my lord,' she had murmured, when at last he stood naked before her. 'I am here to serve you and to bring relief to your hungering flesh.'

Though he had a hundred years of dealing with women behind him, André felt nervous with this bright exotic creature. That she was a sorceress, possessing the same longevity that he did and most probably far greater powers, put him at a disadvantage in her presence; something he had not experienced since his seduction by Isidora. Michiko's beauty, too, condemned him as her slave.

Her oval face was painted chalk-white in the traditional geisha style, but the heavy make-up wasn't in the slightest mask-like; on the contrary, it seemed to enhance the exquisite bone structure that lay beneath it, much in the way that a glaze increased the loveliness of precious porcelain. A vivid, blood-red lip paint outlined a mouth of glorious symmetry, and her long dark eyes were boldly outlined by jet-black kohl. Her hair was hidden by an elaborate traditional wig, adorned with carved ivory combs and paper flowers, but André knew instinctively that it would be long and black and glossy. Similarly, though her body was concealed beneath her ornate many-layered kimono and its huge folded obi, he was certain she would be the very acme of slender shapeliness.

As he watched her, his penis already erect, she took a thin padded futon from a cupboard, then unrolled it on to the mat, bidding him to lie on it.

'You are very vigorous, my lord,' she said softly, sinking down in a cloud of silk beside him, her painted gaze settling intently on his penis.

'My name is André,' he told her, conscious of his own flesh swaying as she studied it, 'and you are the most beautiful woman I have ever seen.'

'I think not,' Michiko observed, her smile oblique but her eyes full of sympathy. 'There is another . . . You love her, yet she resides in a place that is neither earth nor heaven. I believe that *she* is the true beauty that you treasure.'

Unmanned for a moment, André turned away, conscious – as he often was at times like these – that he had never been fully naked for Arabelle; never given her the gift of his rampant body. She was aware of his unclothed appearance, of course, and was present in his chamber each night while he undressed, but she had never looked upon his nakedness with corporeal eyes; only 'seen' him with her strangely powerful psyche.

When Michiko's narrow hand settled on his thigh, André flinched.

'I know your pain, André-*chan*,' she said, her voice like a bell lilting in the breeze, 'and I know too, what it is that soothes it.' Her fingers drifted upward. 'Fear not for the sensibilities of your beloved. My mind has touched hers. I sense her, and she urges me to minister to your needs.'

With a great, relieved sigh, André rolled over on to his back, knowing that his clever, exotic companion spoke the truth. He too could feel Arabelle's approval, her tender urging that he empower himself through sex.

Expecting Michiko to disrobe, as he had, André was surprised when she continued to caress him, her fingers fluttering across his skin with nimble purpose. She did not touch his penis straight away, although it was standing up proudly to tempt her, but instead stroked the tender creases of his groin. Her touch was so light yet so effective, and the contact was so near to the seat of his arousal that he experienced it almost as pain instead of pleasure. He groaned, wanting her long, slender fingers to strum his aching hardness and their dainty tips to titillate his glans.

But still Michiko denied him, exploring his belly and his flanks with a studied thoroughness. André tried to reach for her, but with a strength and swiftness that astounded him, she dashed his hands away then deftly snared them in her own. In a rare feat of legerdemain, she took both his wrists in a single-handed, long-fingered grip and pressed them down against the futon at his side, leaving him helplessly pinned and at her mercy.

'Remember what I am, my lord,' she said quietly, her near-black eyes narrowing inscrutably as she surveyed him. 'I have all the power that you possess, and much more that is different and unknown to you. I am your equal, and I will have my way in this.'

Her determination suddenly reminded him of Isidora, and he shuddered.

'I am not like she, either,' said Michiko immediately, demonstrating again her undeniable mental gift. 'I wish to control you for a time, André. To play with you and give pleasure to us both.' She touched his cheek with her free hand. 'But when that is over, you are sovereign. And I serve you.'

Relieved, André relaxed against the futon, expecting Michiko to instantly release him. She did not however, and set about fondling as much of his body as she could reach with her one roving hand. André was constricted, his torso twisted awkwardly to one side, but the feeling of being bound was insidiously delicious. In the past, he had always had supremacy in such matters, and the sensation of being controlled was a piquant thrill.

As she touched him, Michiko stared deeply into his eyes, making a lie of the Japanese woman's reputation for submissiveness. She had pledged to serve him but there was nothing soft or pliant about her nature. Her fierce dark eyes were filled with an almost warrior-like zeal, and André felt a great relief that she had taken to him. With powers like hers, and her indomitable personality, she would be an enemy who made even Isidora seem weak.

'You are quite right, my lord *gaijin*,' she murmured, her crimson mouth an inch from his throat. 'I could destroy you ... or make your constant anguish a thousand times more frightful.' Her lips came within a hair's breadth of the line of his jaw, and at the same time her fingernails skimmed his twitching penis. 'But I like you ... and I offer you my help.'

André moaned, his body in thrall to his slender Nippon goddess, while his intellect, riding above it, blessed her name. She would be as awesome an ally in his cause.

Thrashing ineffectually, he tried to brush himself against her silk kimono. The pressure building in his sex was almost agonising now, and he was at the point of begging for her touch; pleading for it, crying out for any kind of friction.

'Oh no, my lord!' cried Michiko gaily, flirting her brightly-clad body away from him. The solemn herons on her kimono seemed to mock his captivity, the shimmer of silk creating the impression that they were taking flight. From out of nowhere, Michiko produced a length of woven white cord, and before André could really absorb the fact that his hands were free, they were restrained again, caught behind his back this time, the cord wound around his wrists. Jerking against his captivity, André found the simple bonds unyielding, and taking a ragged breath, he subsided sideways on to the futon. Michiko inclined over him and trussed his ankles with the same uncompromising cord.

'What are you going to do to me?' he asked, as she

knelt beside him, a speculative expression on her regal, pearl-white face.

'What if I do not do anything at all?' she said, her eyes glittering and her red mouth curving wryly. 'What if I ignore you now ... and go about my toilette?' She slid her hand into the layered folds of her kimono's bodice and quite clearly cupped the curve of one pert breast. A tiny gasp escaped her lips and her head tipped back gracefully on her slender neck, as if weighed down by her heavy, formal wig. Her narrow eyes closed and crumpled as if she were enduring some intense sensation, and André saw little movements beneath the thick brocaded silk.

The pure sensuality of her action made his own state of arousal increase alarmingly. She was blatantly pleasuring herself, manipulating the sensitive tip of her breast, and he was left immobile and unable to ease his growing torment.

'What if I bring myself to orgasm, my lord? Finger my own body, coax it slowly to the pinnacle of pleasure? Could you endure that, and expect nothing for yourself?' Michiko's low, soft voice was slurred, and the movements within her kimono grew faster, more frenzied, as if some small animal was trapped against her bosom and struggling to get free. The rest of her body was quiescent, a placid statue clad in robes of coloured silk.

'I ... I do not know.' André's teeth were gritted as he imagined what he might have to go through. The idea of seeing Michiko masturbate, again and again, while he grew increasingly engorged, was horrific, not to be dwelt upon. And yet he did dwell on it, savouring the build-up of denial, the ever-increasing stiffness of his flesh, the slow throb of blood gathering in his shaft. The condition of his groin was taxing him to his limits; he felt dizzy with need. It was pure torture, but something dark in him exulted.

'Perhaps we sh-should try to discover what your limits are?' Although her telepathy was obviously unimpaired,

Michiko was having trouble with her voice now. The words seemed to catch in her throat, as if clogged by sensation, and beneath her kimono her action was small but rhythmic. Against his will, André imagined her pinching her nipple; squashing the nub of flesh time after time, using acute pain to trigger her rise to joy.

'*Amida ... Amida...*' she murmured, her free hand fluttering in a gesture that appeared peculiarly liturgical. It stilled for a moment, then she clenched it into a fist, her whole body stiffening. A second later, she relaxed and breathed a sigh.

'That was most delightful,' she said, withdrawing her fingers from the depths of her kimono. 'I feel refreshed ... and I am ready to begin binding you in earnest.' Performing another exquisite sleight of hand, she produced a further length of the finely-plaited cord, which she twirled evocatively in tight coils around her fingers.

As she shuffled towards him, her sharp eyes were focused upon his penis –

Returning suddenly to the present, André groaned, ejaculating heavily between his fingers, his cool essence splattering the bed and the gathered books and papers. As always, his recollection had been so real that he had become totally absorbed in it, and he felt a vague disappointment that his orgasm had brought matters to a halt.

Back in Japan, in the previous century, he had not come nearly so quickly. Michiko had almost covered his body in her infernal white ropes, then used a finer cord to firmly bind his penis. After that she had ridden him. With his hips raised by a hard cylindrical cushion, and his tethered arms wedged uncomfortably beneath him, she had ridden him for what had seemed like the whole night, forcing him to suffer while she had countless orgasms.

When, finally, to the accompaniment of his tears and wails of blissful agony, she had released him and rubbed his member briskly, the resulting climax had rendered him unconscious, so concentrated was the surge of his deliverance.

'Michiko,' he whispered, sending his thoughts across the aether to try and find her.

To his astonishment, within just seconds he heard her mind-voice. It seemed incredible but she was nearby somewhere, within the watery frontier, on this same English soil –

'My lord *gaijin*,' came the soft, exotic tones of her sensuous spirit, 'I am close by. In what manner may I serve you?'

'Oh, Michiko,' he answered thankfully, then told her quickly of his dreams, and of his hope.

He's not telling me everything, thought Belinda as she opened her eyes the next morning. She felt as if she had been dreaming of her near-immortal lover since the moment she had gone to sleep, and he was still in her mind now she was awake.

He had 'fed' on her again, if that was what one called it. Exciting her with his fingers and his lips, and the weight and force of his body, he had brought her effortlessly to several more orgasms, then held her in his arms until an exhausted sleep had claimed her. He had not come again himself throughout all this, and whether he had pleasured himself afterwards was something she had no way of knowing.

She had so many questions in her brain it seemed to buzz.

Principal among them was: how had André come to be the way he was? It must have taken quite a trauma to change him so thoroughly.

Furthermore, why was it that he considered himself unfortunate? Long or never-ending life wasn't something Belinda had ever given much serious thought to. She had read about it often enough, in horror stories and fantasies, but now, with the perfumed presence of a 200-

year-old man all around her, the impact of his longevity really hit her.

All those years! Did he remember it all? Every place he had ever lived, every person he had ever met? Every woman or girl he had made love to? There must have been plenty of them over the decades, she deduced, if sexual pleasure was the prime source of his nourishment.

Stretching, Belinda became aware that she was now wearing a nightgown: an exquisite, pin-tucked Victorian affair that covered her chastely from throat to ankle, and had long sleeves that ended in ruffled cuffs.

'Did you put this on me?' she asked, turning to the portrait above the bed – the painting of André in eighteenth-century dress, at the time of his mysterious and undefined changing. 'I suppose you must have ... but I swear I don't remember you doing it.'

The idea of him handling her inert body made her quiver. It was one thing to participate consensually in love-making and permit him to touch her and fondle; but to be unconscious and have him do exactly what he wished without her knowledge? That was scary, but it was also exciting.

Running her finger over the fine smocking and embroidery at the nightgown's yoke, Belinda wondered if it had belonged to a former lover of his. Perhaps even the one he had loved and lost.

That was something else she would have liked to have asked him about. The woman she looked like, the one he was obviously still devoted to; had he known her before his 'changing' or after?

The biggest puzzle of all was his peculiar reluctance to penetrate her. Once he had brought all her senses to life and primed her desire, there had seemed to Belinda nothing more fulfilling than to finally join their bodies. It seemed unnatural not to.

But that, she supposed, was the kernel of the matter. Nothing about André von Kastel was natural. Or normal. Or commonplace. There had been a definite reason for him not entering her, something critically important. But whether to him or to her, she couldn't tell.

What a shame, she thought, remembering the erect majesty of his penis as he pressed against her. There had clearly been nothing wrong with his sexual anatomy, no physical impediment to the penetration she had so wanted. And still wanted, she admitted ruefully. If André were to come to her this moment, she was ready.

Suddenly, as if thought could summon deed, there was a knock at the door.

'Come in!' Belinda called, her heart racing, her body reacting.

Her visitor was Jonathan, however, and her rush of disappointment brought guilt in its wake. Jonathan looked handsome and well rested and she should have been glad to see him so, not irritated because he wasn't someone else.

'Hey, you! How are you feeling?' To make amends, she sprang out of bed and hurried towards him to give him a hug. 'You were out like a light last night. I came to your room to see you and you were sleeping like a baby.' She slid her arms round him, enjoying the sure, familiar feel of him and his warm body beneath his T-shirt and shorts. 'I was just going to get up and come and see whether you were awake yet.'

Jonathan reciprocated with an embrace of his own, a strangely heartfelt one, then a quick, hard kiss. 'I'm fine now,' he said, giving her a quirky smile. 'But I feel such a fool. I must have been more tired than I realised. I keep thinking of how it must have looked. I sort of flaked out, and that great big bloke just picked me up like a doll – '
He shuddered in her arms, an odd expression on his pleasant, open face.

'So the mighty Oren put you to bed, did he?' Belinda enquired lightly. The image that Jonathan had just conjured had a strange effect on her. Without thinking, she suddenly saw a picture of the two men together: Oren masterful and silent, and Jonathan in his arms, naked and pliant.

'Yes,' Jonathan continued, as together they walked over to the bed and sat down, side by side. 'And I think I've met the guy in charge here too ... The owner or whatever he is. It must be him, because he's a dead ringer for that guy over there.' He paused and nodded towards André's portrait. 'He must be his descendant or something – '

'André?'

'Is that what his name is?' Jonathan looked at her with a hint of suspicion, and Belinda immediately blushed, realising as it happened that she was giving herself away.

'Yes ... He's Count André von Kastel, to give him his full title. He owns the priory, and Oren, and Elisa and Feltris, your two girls, they're all his servants.' She took Jonathan's hand and began to stroke his palm with her thumb, the way he liked her to, hoping to distract him from asking awkward questions. 'When did you meet him?'

'It was sometime after our big blond friend put me to bed.' It was Jonathan's turn to blush, as if he too was experiencing ambiguous thoughts. 'I felt very weird, sort of spaced out. I closed my eyes, then the next time I opened them, there was this other guy there. Long hair, sort of aristocratic looking, bright blue eyes. He said, "Here, drink this. It will make you feel better", and he gave me this herbal drink in a fancy china goblet. Funny-tasting stuff, but quite pleasant really, after the first sip or two.'

'And did it make you feel better?'

'Yeah, I think it did,' replied Jonathan thoughtfully, studying their clasped hands. 'I felt a sort of instant sense of well-being ... and then I went straight to sleep. A really good deep sleep, not the sort of dozy feeling I had before.' He brought her hand up to his lips and gave it a shy little kiss. 'I slept right through ... I only woke up about quarter of an hour ago, and the first thing I wanted to do was find you.' His grey eyes brightened as he kissed her hand again.

I want him, thought Belinda, experiencing a weird sense of detachment. After all I've done and felt since I got here – I've had more sex in the last forty-eight hours than I've had for months, but I still want more.

It's you, isn't it? she accused André in her mind. You've done this. You've increased my libido to make me of more use to you. She would have looked up at the portrait, but it seemed important right now to lavish her whole attention on Jonathan. He was a good man, a sweet, sexy man; and she owed him for her recent infidelities – the ones she was certain beyond all doubt that he suspected.

'You look lovely in this,' said Jonathan suddenly, touching her shoulder through the fine cotton of her nightgown. 'It's sort of . . . innocent. You look like a Victorian maiden, all untouched and naïve.' He trailed his fingers downward, across the smocking and the lace trim, until they were resting very lightly on her breast. He turned his hand and cupped the firm curve through the delicately-woven fabric. 'As pure as a nun, but inside simply dying for it!'

How true, thought Belinda, her nipple tensing beneath his touch. Because of André and the magic he seemed to weave around her, she *was* dying for it – dying for anything. She had roused in a matter of seconds at the first hint of impending eroticism. Her particular need was for penetration – for straightforward, unelaborate sex – with the familiar body of a man she was fond of. Moaning softly, she twisted towards Jonathan, hoping he would caress her other breast too.

'You're a naughty girl, aren't you?' said Jonathan, entering into the spirit of the thing as he held both her breasts and flicked at her hardened nipples with his thumbs. 'You're thinking about rude things, I can tell. That's what makes *this* happen – ' He pinched each teat,

167

pulling them out slightly, creating a small but delicious jolt of pain.

Her eyes closing, Belinda gasped, sensing the presence of a new facet to Jonathan's sexual persona. Was André at work on him too? she thought, wriggling her bottom against the mattress. She could feel her vulva responding to the tugging sensation on her nipples; she was flowing wantonly, wetting her nightgown where it was bunched up beneath her.

'And I'll bet you're not wearing any panties either, you little slut.' Jonathan continued his pinching, giving a little jerk which made Belinda's eyes snap open. In the eyes of her partner, she saw no malice or cruelty, but just a teasing streak of humour. He was only paying her back for her own actions earlier, but his masquerade severity was a goad to her senses. She thought back to being with André last night on the terrace, and how, for a moment, she had wanted him to hit her, to spank her bare bottom and infuse her with shame. Was this a new twist to her own sexual persona? she wondered, unable to keep still as her thighs scissored and her sex pulsed. Was she a secret masochist? Would she get off on pain? Real pain; not just her breasts being nipped?

'Come on, I think we'd better have a look, hadn't we?' Abandoning her breasts, Jonathan placed his palm on her midriff and tipped her back on to the bed. With one hand, and a dexterity she had not realised he possessed, he snagged both of her wrists and held them tightly, while with the other hand he swiftly raised her skirt.

'Just as I thought,' he crowed, when the soft white cotton was bunched at her waist and her belly, and thighs and pubis were exposed. 'You're a wicked little thing, Belinda Seward, going to bed without your panties ... I bet that was so you could diddle yourself in the night, wasn't it?'

Belinda nodded, sinking happily into the fantasy of being a 'naughty little girl'. 'Yes, that is why I did it,' she whispered. 'I'm very sorry.'

'I should think so,' replied Jonathan, clearly relishing the shadowplay too, 'and you know how I feel about that, don't you? I'm going to have to inspect you now. To see how far this wickedness has gone.' He hesitated, and Belinda guessed he was either working out where to go next or trying to suppress his laughter. 'Assume the position, please.'

Belinda had no idea what the position was, but she improvised, her body shaking as she shifted on the bed. Hitching her bottom to the edge of the mattress, she slid her hands beneath her thighs, then hauled them up, at the same parting her legs. With her knees squashed against her breasts, she was in the most revealing position she could imagine for 'inspection' purposes, and Jonathan's low, delighted growl confirmed her instincts. Giddy with arousal, she lifted herself higher.

'So eager to show off, aren't we?' commented Jonathan, his voice revealingly husky as he leant over to get a better view. 'That's it, open right up. Let's see everything.'

Belinda pulled harder on her thighs, straining every muscle to expose herself completely and lifting her bottom up from the bed so he could see the dark crinkled portal of her anus. For an instant she imagined André seeing the same view, but from a different perspective, and the image made her weeping sex contract.

'This is an inspection,' said Jonathan gruffly, his breathing uneven. 'You're not supposed to be enjoying it. Come on – open wider!'

Belinda did her best, but she was beginning to climb now, to ascend towards pleasure, and her mind filled with rude, inflaming images.

Behind her closed eyes, she pictured the whole household assembled in the room, all watching the proceedings with great interest; all observing her vulgar struggles to display her sex.

She seemed to see André, sitting in one of the beautiful gilded chairs, his eyes languorous, his cool penis clasped loosely in his fingers. Before him knelt Elisa and Feltris, their golden bodies naked, their bare nipples hard and dark and rosy, while in the foreground, imposing Oren advanced towards her. He too was nude, and his huge erection pointed straight towards her vulva. She seemed to feel it touch her, and the imagined impact made her squeal.

In reality, the contact was with Jonathan's fingers, two of them, which curved slightly as they entered her vagina.

'Hmmm . . . Just as I thought,' he muttered, waggling the intruding digits inside her. 'Extremely wet.' He pressed determinedly, finding her G-spot and making her cry out again as she felt the phantom urge to urinate. Her inner muscles grabbed greedily at her assailant.

'I think this calls for the special treatment,' Jonathan observed thoughtfully, his fingers still exerting the teasing pressure. 'Don't you?'

'Yes! Oh yes!' Belinda croaked, not knowing what he meant but wanting it anyway.

Jonathan quickly slid his fingers from her body, and with a speed and assurance that she blessed high heaven for, he took her by one thigh and lowered the tilt of her body with one hand, while the other rummaged urgently in his clothing. Within seconds, the head of his penis was nudging at her entrance, and a heartbeat later he was pushing it inside her.

'Oh God, yes!' Belinda's cry was strangled but joyous. How many hours now had she been longing for penetration? It seemed like a lifetime . . . no, much longer . . . an eternity.

As Jonathan began to thrust, she matched his rhythm with her thankful sobs.

Chapter Ten

Inertia

*B*elinda felt as if she were pinned to the mattress by inertia. She couldn't get up because her limbs were too relaxed and too glowing to function. It was ten o'clock, but she simply couldn't stir.

Beside her Jonathan was equally still, although his even breathing told her he was sound asleep.

'You deserve the rest, sweetheart,' whispered Belinda, rousing herself just enough to sit up and look down on his peaceful, boyish face. It wasn't all that long ago since he had made love to her like a veritable demon, deploying a strength and authority that she had never previously seen in him – a dominant aura that seemed to suit him very nicely.

After he had given her 'a good seeing to' – while she was folded awkwardly on the edge of the bed – he had pulled out, still erect, and bade her move. Then, once she was lying in a more comfortable, less contrived position, he had pushed into her hungry body for a second time, his thrusts longer, less staccato, and more gentle. This considerate lover had been the Jonathan she was used to; the one who fucked her as an equal and made no attempt whatsoever to bend her will.

'And I like *both* of you,' she said, smiling fondly down

171

at him. 'Mr Discipline *and* my dear old Johnny.' She touched his face but he just mumbled and hugged his pillow.

The temptation to do the same; to lie down, snuggle up to Jonathan's bare warm back, and go to sleep again, was enormous. She felt as if she were floating in a delicious pool of lethargy, her limbs bathed in a glowing sexual silkiness. She knew that if she did lie down again, she would be sleeping within seconds; but at the back of her mind there were questions that needed answering. As she accepted that, she woke up once and for all.

The biggest question was, 'What the devil are we still doing here?' It was well over twenty-four hours since she and Jonathan had abandoned the Mini in the rain, and yet neither of them had made the slightest effort to go back and see if it would start, or to check on their belongings. This sort of behaviour was fairly typical of Jonathan – he was rather happy-go-lucky over things like possessions and time-keeping – but she was a compulsive organiser and it was not like her at all. Under normal circumstances, she would have had them back on their way by now, if the car was functional, or at least made some arrangements to get it fixed.

But somehow, most of her business-like qualities seemed to have been washed away by the storm, and all she wanted to do was drift around this peculiar, brooding house, and have sex in a variety of novel forms. And she had a strong suspicion as to how this had come about.

'What are you doing to me, André?'

As she spoke the words, she made a concentrated mental effort to project their meaning outward. It seemed a rather esoteric thing to do, but she was almost certain that their strange host could sense her thoughts.

Just what powers did he possess, this handsome young 200-year-old nobleman? His claims of abnormal longevity should have seemed a complete cock-and-bull story, but somehow, right at the heart of her, she believed him.

He was still withholding part of his story from her, she sensed, but she was certain what he had told her was true.

André? she probed again, then shook her head, laughing softly to herself. What was she expecting? An instant telepathic answer or a knock at the door in response to her summons? Or even that he materialise in the centre of the room from a cloud of blue mist? She smiled again, deciding she had read far too many spooky stories.

The count's extrasensory radio clearly wasn't switched on this morning, however, because nothing happened. Did he sleep during the day? she wondered. She had accused him of being a vampire, and though he had denied it, he had admitted to sharing some of their characteristics. Resting during the hours of daylight could well be one of those. He had been asleep yesterday, when she had first seen him in the tower room, and by the time she met the conscious André, it had already been the early hours of evening.

Rising cautiously from the bed, she held her hand to her head. All this deliberation over matters 'fantastic' was giving her a headache. She decided to wash her face and get a drink of water.

Proceeding languidly across the room, she bent down to pick up the Victorian nightdress which Jonathan had flung triumphantly on the floor during the course of their love-making – another symptom of his brand new sexual dynamism.

Fifteen minutes later, a slightly refreshed Belinda discovered that there was no other female clothing to be had in the room. All the things she had worn last night had disappeared, as had the shift she had been supplied with yesterday. Of her own shorts and T-shirt there was no sign at all. Neither was there any underwear of any kind.

I'm trapped, thought Belinda, recalling her presentiments that André had some secret purpose in mind for her. He's stolen all my clothes so I can't escape from him. 'Well, we'll see about that,' she muttered grimly, unfolding the nightdress again and pulling it on over her head. Giving Jonathan a kiss – to which the only response was a drowsy snuffle into the pillow – she set out to find some life in the silent vastness of the priory.

The upper corridor was completely deserted, as she had expected, and she debated making her way through the gallery towards the high tower where André 'slept'. One part of her wanted to confront him immediately and voice her suspicions, while another part told her to be wary. She had to be sure of her facts first – and find out more about him, if she could. A deeper study of his house and his possessions might help, and the library in particular had been crammed with books and documents. There was bound to be something there that could enlighten her.

Descending the stairs barefoot, Belinda felt conspicuous despite the absence of any company. The house was very still, yet there was a teasing breeze coming from somewhere. It seemed to creep beneath the hem of her nightdress and remind her that her bottom and sex were bare, and as she moved, it did too, making balmy air flow across her naked skin.

On the landing, a particularly striking portrait of André in some kind of antique military uniform seemed to smirk down at her, as if its blue eyes could see straight through the thin lawn that covered her. Pausing to frown up at him, Belinda ground her teeth in mortification. The damn thing was ogling her! And the body it perused was responding. She felt her nipples stiffen, coming to their hard, erect state so fast it was almost painful, while between her legs, her female groove began to moisten.

'Leave me alone!' she cried to the smiling portrait. 'I can't take this! It's not natural to be aroused all the time!'

Shocked by her outburst, she looked around, fearing that someone might have heard her, which was ridiculous because Jonathan was fast asleep, André was probably the same, and there was no sign whatsoever of the three blond mutes. All this weirdness is getting to me, she thought, smoothing the inadequate cotton of her nightdress against her. I'm talking to the bloody pictures now!

Fired with new determination, she hurried down the rest of the stairs, trying to ignore her sudden feeling of sharp arousal. She could even smell herself now; she caught a strong, disturbing hint of her own sexual musk as the thin nightgown billowed and flapped around her.

'Stop it!' she snapped, not sure whether it was the absent André she was castigating or herself. 'It takes two to tango,' she muttered, pausing in the lofty hall, the stone floor pleasantly cool beneath her feet. She had to be just as interested in André von Kastel as he was in her, or she wouldn't have responded to him. She had let him make love to her. Let him coax liberties out of her that her boyfriend never had. It was quite outrageous when she really stopped to think about it.

The terrace . . . As if falling through time, she imagined herself suddenly back there, lying prone across the parapet while André assaulted her with his fingers and his mouth. The way her senses recreated the incident was uncanny, and stunned to a halt in the middle of the hall, she seemed to feel again the wet intrusion of André's tongue: first into her vagina and then into her anus. As she relived it, her swollen clitoris began to ache.

'No! Oh no!' she cried, the sound almost pitiful. Her sex felt so heavy with blood that it was difficult to stand straight. Her thighs were parted of their own accord, in an attempt to ease the sudden pressure, and clenching her fists, she resisted the urge to do what her sex was silently screaming for – to reach down, where she stood, and wildly masturbate.

Around her all the portraits seemed to whisper. A dozen Andrés murmured, 'Do it! Do it! Do it!'

'No! Oh please, no!' keened Belinda, while her body betrayed her and she shifted her feet further apart, widening her stance. She tossed her head, her eyes

175

closed, refusing to see the portraits but pinned to the spot by their seditious blue gazes. Her hips tilted and her vulva twitched and rippled. Liquid began to ooze between her labia, escape her pubic hair and crawl in a single stream down her inner thigh.

'Go on,' the heard but unheard voices urged her. 'Amuse me . . . Surrender to your lust and caress your dripping jewel . . .'

The line between engorgement and real pain beginning to blur, Belinda took a step forward, biting her lips at the resulting jolt of pleasure. Her nipples were so tensed they were tugging on the sensitive tissues of her breast and creating friction against the thin stuff of her nightdress. It was woven cotton lawn of the finest, lightest texture, but she might as well have been wearing a hair shirt.

Beyond words now, she whimpered, wrapping her arm about her chest and squeezing tightly to assuage the subtle torment. She was just about to clutch her vulva when a creaking door froze her actions. Spinning around, almost coming, she expected to see André walking purposefully towards her, his brilliant eyes glinting sapphire in his triumph.

'Who's there?' called Belinda, her fingers creeping, of their own volition, towards her sex. She almost didn't care any longer if there was anyone there; they could watch her as far as she was concerned; she was too deep in her own desire to hold back now.

A door on her left swung a little way, but no one came through it. The shadows offered up no hidden voyeur. There was no one. She was alone, as she had been all along, but the interruption, she realised, had thwarted her. Suspicion had drawn her just far enough back from the brink of orgasm to return control of her actions to her brain, her thinking mind.

She still felt aroused and she still yearned for relief, but she was no longer a mindless animal led by lust. She

176

wanted to masturbate, but she couldn't stand here and
do it.

'I hate you, you bastard!' she cried out, her every
instinct pointing accusingly at André. Even when he
wasn't with her, he *was* with her, taunting her. He had
control of her while he probably wasn't even conscious.

Belinda could feel fury welling. There was nothing she
hated more than to be a man's puppet. At least, not
when she didn't want to be. The games she had enjoyed
last night had been consensual, inspired by delicious
wine and the magic, brooding darkness. Even the little
'performance' this morning with Jonathan had been
tempered by a sense of fun and their mutual familiarity.

But right now she was being used – relentlessly
manipulated – and all to serve a man's unnatural needs.

She was just about to storm back up the stairs, along
the convoluted corridors and galleries and then round
and round the circular staircase to André's eyrie, when
an irresistible aroma tickled her nostrils.

Coffee. Sublime, strong, revivifying coffee. Healer of
psychic ills and restorer of lost tempers. Belinda immediately began to salivate and to long for a steaming cupful.
A mugful. Several mugfuls. Suppressing her inner complaints against André – but not forgetting them – she
turned in the direction of the fabulous smell. It was Blue
Mountain, her favourite; she would put good money on
it.

Her nose led her to the terrace, and she hesitated in
the doorway from the house, recalling fragments of last
night's alfresco debauch.

There was no sign of the peach-coloured dress or her
abandoned underwear, and in the hazy sunlight, the
long, stone-flagged expanse didn't look in the least bit
gloomy and ominous. The terrace was like the rest of the
priory: its character seemed infinitely mutable. On a
pleasant, normal, holiday morning like this it was difficult to remember what this house had looked like in a
thunderstorm.

At the far end of the terrace, a white, circular patio table had been set up, and over it a large sunshade was inclined. Belinda could see that this table and its contents were the source of the delightful smells, because it was set for breakfast, with a tall insulated coffee pot in pride of place.

Plucking at the thin fabric of her nightdress, and weighing its flimsiness against her craving for coffee, Belinda continued to hover a little longer.

'Oh, bugger it!' she exclaimed to herself, when the aromatic lure finally became too much for her and she traversed the warm stone towards the table. Virtually everyone in the house had seen her naked already anyway, so what did it matter if she took breakfast in her nightie?

Alongside the jug, she found a basket covered with a thick blue linen napkin, and once she had helped herself to her first hit of coffee, she investigated it. Her mouth began to water all over again.

Croissants. Thick, light, sinfully and outrageously buttery, they were the exact breakfast she had hankered after yesterday. Like a starving child, she grabbed the nearest one and bit into it, sighing with pleasure as it seemed to melt on her tongue. The pastry was still warm and flakes of it fluttered down over her front and on to the table, but the flavour was so exquisite that she just didn't care.

Belinda hadn't realised she was so hungry, and could have gobbled down several of the delicious croissants without a pause, but she forced herself to be more civilised with her second, breaking it open and applying a little conserve from the lidded dish that had thoughtfully been provided. Taking smaller bites, and chewing each one properly in between sips of the glorious coffee, she surveyed her surroundings from her idyllic vantage point.

Although the gardens and the grounds beyond were overgrown, they did not appear derelict or sterile.

Whereas in the thrashing rain and sky-splitting thunderstorm everything had taken on shades of black and grey and midnight blue, they now appeared green and gold and mellow. It was difficult to believe she was staying in the same place.

Looking out along the terrace to her right, she espied an additional building she hadn't taken much notice of before. Beyond a rioting and unruly rose garden, there appeared to be a small chapel, complete with more or less intact stained-glass windows and a solemn liturgical aura. This must have been the place of worship for the religious community that had originally inhabited Sedgewick Priory, Belinda decided, feeling a sudden curiosity. Perhaps after breakfast a walk that way would be in order.

'Better get dressed first, I suppose,' she muttered. The heat of the morning was gathering itself now, and though the sunshade had created a cooler area and a slight breeze played across the terrace, Belinda still found herself sweating. Her sexual tenor had calmed a little since those almost insane moments in the main hall, but she still felt a remnant of lingering desire, like the pilot light for a greater, fiercer flame. Concentrating solely on her coffee, she tried to ignore it.

I'll try and keep a clear head from now on, she pledged. And I'll get organised. As soon as I'm dressed I'll set off to find the car, then I'll see if there's somewhere to charge the mobile, and failing that I'll find out if there's a public phone box anywhere nearby.

Belinda knew that she should have done – or at least tried to do – these things yesterday, but for the life of her she couldn't recall where the time had gone. But today would be different, a day of achievement. Hopefully, before nightfall they would have made contact with the world beyond the priory.

More determined now, she sipped more coffee and nibbled the last of her croissant. She was just about to rise and make her way back to her room, when a light tread behind her interrupted her thoughts. Turning in her seat, her heart pounding, she expected to see André, but once again, the newcomer was Oren. In one hand he was carrying a fresh pot of coffee and in the other a slim notebook and a pencil. He was almost naked, his only garment a pair of frayed denim cut-offs.

'Hello,' said Belinda quickly. 'It's a lovely morning, isn't it?'

Oren put down his burdens and favoured her with a smile that was more than a replacement for his unfortunate lack of speech. He gestured to the fresh coffee and Belinda accepted a top-up. Then, to her surprise, he sat down in another chair. The expression on his face was both open and attentive, and it dawned on her that he was waiting for instructions.

'I'm glad you're here, Oren,' said Belinda, leaning forward. 'I really need to go back to our car today, to see if it'll start and that our things are OK.'

Oren's grin widened and he shook his head.

What on earth was he on about? 'No, really, we have to get to our car and get it started again,' she insisted, feeling anxious. Was she being obstructed again? Had André given orders that she mustn't leave? 'It's important. We're supposed to meet someone.'

Oren shook his head again but this time reached for the notebook and pencil.

Please do not worry, said the note he handed to her a few seconds later. *Your car is here, and all your possessions are safe.*

'But how?' she demanded, looking up at him. 'It wouldn't start the other night.' And what was more, she realised, Jonathan had brought the keys with him, in his shorts pocket.

Oren gave her a shrug and a modest look which seemed to indicate he was a man of many talents.

'Well, thank you,' said Belinda, a little shaken. This gentle giant had just hot-wired their car. 'I'd better get dressed and then go and check it out.'

Oren's warm brown eyes seemed to assess her body beneath the inadequate protection of the nightgown, and after a second or two his blond eyebrows quirked in a way that seemed to suggest that he rather liked her in what she was wearing now. Belinda felt herself colouring as she remembered the sheer nature of the cotton lawn. The mute was observant – he could probably see everything!

After sipping the last of her coffee, Belinda stood up. 'Right, I'll go and get dressed, then,' she said firmly, ignoring the merriment in Oren's expression. 'See you later!' Flipping her fingers at him in a cursory salute, she set off towards the house –

Then stopped almost immediately, yelping and hopping.

In the time she had taken over her breakfast, the sun had climbed quite high in the sky overhead and had been beating down consistently on the terrace. Consequently, the stone flags were now baking hot, and Belinda's bare feet felt partially fried.

'Ouch! Oh God,' she squeaked, hitching up her skirt and preparing to make a run for it.

She got no further than a couple of steps before she sensed a swift, feline movement behind her, then felt herself being literally swept off her feet. Scooping her up in his arms, Oren carried her effortlessly across the remaining portion of the terrace, his own bare feet presumably too weathered to feel the burning heat.

'Thanks. Thanks very much,' Belinda said, breathless with shock as Oren made a neat sideways twist to negotiate the door.

Once inside, she expected him to let her down, but instead, Oren continued to carry her through the much cooler house. Her female form seemed to make no impact whatsoever on his giant, muscular body, and he was able to walk quite quickly with her in his arms.

The sensation of such perfection of strength and vitality against her was so exciting that Belinda forgot to protest. The wall of Oren's chest, which she was cuddled against, was like a slab of living stone, but she could feel his heart beating beneath it. His body smelt very fresh and clean, though not of any particular cologne. He was just man, pure and simple, freshly showered. And so powerful that even the long staircase didn't agitate his steady breathing.

'It's OK, I can manage from here,' Belinda announced when they reached the top of the steps, although she was aware that she was still clinging to him tightly. Her arms seemed to be ignoring her dictate, and instead of loosening her hold on him, they gripped steadfastly around his strong neck.

She felt a little worried when they reached her room and Oren switched her weight to one arm to negotiate the door. What would Jonathan think if she was carried in by Oren?

But her room was empty, with only a scribbled note on her pillow to indicate a man had shared her bed. Belinda picked it up when Oren set her on her feet, then sat down on the disordered bed to read its contents.

Gone for a quick shower. Something made me all sweaty. Love you lots. Jonathan. Short and sweet and underlined with a long row of 'X's, it made her smile and think fondly of him. It had been a bit of an adventure ending up here, what with the thunderstorm, Feltris and Elisa, and André and everything. But in a bizarre twist it had also drawn her and Jonathan closer, when by all that was logical it should have pushed them apart. Impulsively, she showed the note to Oren, and he smiled and nodded as if he too endorsed Jonathan's show of sentiment.

Strange, she thought, eyeing the tall, magnificent blond. A moment ago, she had felt herself beginning to want him, and had sensed – very definitely – that he wanted her. Yet he showed no animosity over Jonathan's note, and seemed to approve of the relationship it implied. Count André wasn't the only unusual and

182

unfathomable person here at Sedgewick Priory. In their own ways, his servants were special too.

I should have asked him to stay and wash my back for me, thought Belinda a little while later as she was dressing.

It had been an odd little 'blip' of feeling that had passed between her and Oren – a hovering on the edge of something. If he had stayed to help her with her toilette, she was certain she would have allowed him to make love to her, and though she had desired him, she was still in two minds about it. It was just too much that she should have sex with everyone in the house. It felt like a kind of 'rampage' somehow; yet each encounter so far had seemed inevitable – a natural event at the time. And she now she was regretting that she had missed her chance with Oren.

She imagined him stepping into the curiously antique yet fully-functional shower with her. There would not have been much room for the both of them in the shallow china tub together, but for her purposes that would have been an advantage. Oren's massive body would have been pressed against hers. Hugely strong, he would probably have picked her up again as they stood in the teeming water, and mounted her effortlessly on the thick shaft of his sturdy prick.

Although she had not yet seen him naked, Belinda could well imagine that Oren was phenomenal. If he were all in proportion, as the bulge in his shorts had suggested, his magnificent penis would stretch a woman in all directions.

'For crying out loud!' she exclaimed, wishing she could temper her thoughts and think of something other than sex. Concentrating on her clothing instead, she tied the drawstring at her waist in a bow. The skirt she had been left while she was in the bathroom looked sus-piciously like an Edwardian petticoat. Just as yesterday, today's clothes were really lingerie in disguise. Lingerie from past times, but perfectly cared for and preserved.

Her camisole top had tiny sleeves and an embroidered front, and both it and the full petticoat were made of ivory cambric. Her knickers were loose-legged and French style, made from the same very fine pale cloth.

Staring at her reflection in the mirror, she fancied herself as a nymphet from a continental movie, her gamine hairstyle completing the impression to perfection. She remembered seeing a picture of Brigitte Bardot, wearing a wig probably, but dressed similarly in thin white clothes. Pouting for an unseen cameraman, Belinda flicked her fringe into pixie-like points.

'This is getting me nowhere!' she chastised herself, slipping a pair of flat canvas shoes on to her feet. 'I'd better make a move and check out the car.'

Striding past the many portraits of André, Belinda hurried downstairs, across the hall and out of the front door, wondering if what Oren had written about the Mini was true. Apparently it was, she discovered almost immediately, espying Jonathan's cheerful yellow vehicle parked in the gravel drive where it curved out around the gardens. The car appeared so ordinary, so unremarkable and so much a part of the normal life she had led two days ago, that she laughed out loud in relief.

The Mini was open and the keys now in the ignition, but when she tried to start it, the engine was completely dead. 'You stupid thing!' she cried, leaping out of the car and feeling a strong urge to kick it. 'Why did you work for them, but not for me?'

Striding to the boot to check that their bags and belongings were intact, it occurred to Belinda to wonder who had driven the car this far.

Certainly not André. Instinct told her he was asleep now, resting during the day as she suspected his strange nature demanded. So that left Feltris, Elisa and Oren. The two blonde girls looked as if they wouldn't know what a car was, let alone be able to fix a wonky one and drive. Belinda imagined them being pulled by unicorns in a fairy chariot made of diamonds.

184

Too weird, she thought, rummaging among the luggage and finding – to her relief – that nothing was missing. She and Jonathan would have to get away from here soon because she could not believe some of the notions she was having.

'Bingo!' she cried, fishing out Jonathan's mobile phone. But her sense of satisfaction was short-lived. On pressing the usual buttons, she got a display of peculiar symbols she had never seen before, and no sound that in any way resembled a dialling tone. The battery needed charging, obviously, but even so the compact gadget was behaving oddly.

'Like everything and everybody else,' she muttered grimly, retrieving the charger from Jonathan's bag, then hurrying up the stairs towards the house. She would come back for their clothes and sundries later; the first priority was to make contact with real life!

In the hall, she met Jonathan, looking bleary-eyed and munching a piece of toast.

'I keep asking you this, love, but where have you been?' he said amiably. 'There's all sorts of breakfast stuff on the terrace if you're hungry.'

'I'm fine. I had something earlier,' replied Belinda, a little perturbed by Jonathan's vagueness. 'First I was having a shower and then I came down to get this.' She gestured with the mobile phone. 'Would you believe it, the Mini's parked outside! I've no idea how it got here because the engine's dead as a doornail now.'

Jonathan frowned, chewing his last bit of toast. 'Maybe we should ring the AA?' he suggested, rubbing his eyes then passing his fingers through his dishevelled hair. He looked as if he had only just crawled out of bed that very minute – his T-shirt was crumpled and his trainers weren't laced.

'Are you all right, Johnny?' Belinda asked, moving closer.

'Yes, it's nothing, I just feel a bit zonked again, that's all.' He gave her a crooked grin. 'It must be you, you're wearing me out. I can't resist you.'

Belinda smiled at him. He had been pretty impressive back in her bedroom, she thought fondly. Strong and intuitive; the best he had ever been for her. But now, on top of the growing heat and the lingering exhaustion he seemed to have sustained with the driving, his fine, lusty performance had taken its toll on him.

'You were wonderful. You deserve to be tired,' she said, sliding her free arm around his waist. 'Let's go to the library where it's cooler, and sit down while we decide what to do.'

'Good idea,' replied Jonathan, giving her a squeeze that proved there was still life in him. 'Now lead me to this library of yours. I'm totally lost around here.'

'We ought to move on,' said Belinda, when they were in the library, with Jonathan stretched out on one of the leather sofas while she looked for an electric socket for the mobile phone's charger. She had ascertained that the house did have electric power – there were bulbs in the light fittings and something must be providing the abundance of hot water and firing the stove that cooked all the delicious food. She couldn't imagine Oren or the girls tending an Aga. But she couldn't seem to locate anywhere to plug in the charger. Abandoning the idea, she sat down beside Jonathan and savoured the cool, shady atmosphere of the huge room.

'We can't stay here,' she said, then noticed Jonathan was already dozing. 'Hey! Did you hear what I said?' She gave him a gentle poke in his middle.

'Yes,' he sighed, 'I heard you.' He opened his eyes and gave her his most boyish, appealing grin. 'But why can't we stay here? It's comfortable, it's restful. His lordship or whatever seems to want us to stay.' He slithered across the leather and slipped his arm around her. 'And it's very romantic,' he whispered, leaning closer. 'Exactly what we hoped for.' He kissed her neck, and almost before she realised, he had the lower edge of her cami-sole eased out of her skirt waistband.

'But what about Paula? She'll be wondering what's

186

happened to us,' Belinda insisted, wanting to sort things out but feeling distracted by Jonathan's roving hands. One was stroking her back, the other sneaking upward across her ribs.

'Phone her,' said Jonathan reasonably, cupping her breast and beginning to flick the nipple. 'I'm sure your André won't mind another guest. We can try and get her off with Oren. She is on the look-out and she always did like big men.'

It was preposterous and also so rational. Despite her protests, Belinda knew she did want to remain at the priory. It was beautiful and strange and its very mysteriousness seemed to seduce her in to staying. And she had to find out more about André. She had to discover *exactly* what he was.

'Don't be silly,' she said to Jonathan, knowing as she said it that her resistance was empty. The touch of his fingers, moving expertly in circles around the hardening peaks of her breasts, seemed only to increase her returning sense of inertia. She wanted to stay here for this, too. For the pleasure that seemed to stalk her from all directions; from every last corner of this house and its environs. She groaned, her earlier frustration reactivated, and began to shift her bottom on the slippery leather couch. The vivid memory of being masturbated in this very same place by André excited her, and she opened her legs to invite a repeat performance – only this time from a more familiar lover.

'Oh Lindi,' gasped Jonathan, getting her message. 'You're so beautiful.' She felt him raising her skirt then sliding his hand inside the loose cotton of her knickers. 'And so wet,' he went on, his middle finger finding the core of her.

As he palpated her delicately, and she kicked her legs and climaxed, the mobile phone slid off the settee, unnoticed.

Chapter Eleven
Open House

Some time later, a familiar beeping roused Belinda from drifting, non-thinking sensual stupor.

The mobile! Good grief! Someone was ringing them! It ought to have been impossible – the batteries were flat – but a call had come through anyway. Rolling to the edge of the settee, away from Jonathan's dozing form, Belinda slithered inelegantly on to the floor and picked up the phone.

'Hello?' she said cautiously, tugging at her French knickers which were tangled around her knees.

'Belinda?' queried the caller. 'It's Paula. Where the devil are you? I've been trying to call you but getting the "not switched on" message. What's happened to you? Have you fallen off the edge of the earth?'

What *has* happened to us? thought Belinda, at the sound of her friend's pleasant, extraordinarily normal voice. How do you describe to someone that you're shacked up in a weird old priory with a 200-year-old Middle European nobleman, and you've had enough sex in two days to last six months?

'Well, it's a long story,' she began, lifting her hips so she could pull the knickers up over her bottom. 'But basically, we broke down in the middle of the night and took shelter in the grounds of this old priory ... and now the owner's asked us to stay with him for a while. As his house guests.'

Why am I telling her that? Belinda mused, instead of making arrangements to meet.

'You jammy things!' exclaimed the distant Paula, sounding so clear she could have been right there in the room. 'Does this mean the rendezvous is off? I can go to Aunt Lizzie's for a few extra days instead, if you like?'

'No! Don't do that!' Belinda said quickly, as behind her Jonathan yawned and stretched. 'Why not come here – to Sedgewick Priory. It's fantastic and there's loads of room. I'm sure Count André won't mind. It's open house here. And there's a fabulous garden. A river. A folly, even.'

'Wow! It sounds amazing,' replied Paula, audibly impressed. 'Who's this Count André? He sounds a bit exotic to me ... Is he a hunk?'

Belinda considered the question. Was André a hunk? Sort of, perhaps, though certainly not by conventional standards.

'He's very nice, actually. A perfect gentleman.'

'Obviously not too much of a gentleman, from the sound of your voice.' Paula laughed. 'What's he look like? How old is he?'

'An angel' and 'about two hundred and thirty' were the answers, but instead Belinda simply said, 'He's very good-looking. Sort of thoughtful ... with blue eyes and streaky, blondish hair.' She thought hard. 'I've no idea how old he is really, but he looks around the thirty-something mark.'

'He sounds divine!' said Paula. 'Are you sure he wouldn't mind if I just turned up?'

'Not in the slightest, I'm sure of it,' answered Belinda, realising that she was sure. She had a feeling that André would grant her whatever she desired, possibly without her even having to ask him.

'OK then,' said Paula, sounding pleased and excited.

'Gimme directions, and I'll be with you as soon as I can. This is far too good an opportunity to miss.' She paused and made a little 'mmmm' of satisfaction. 'Count André, eh? Good grief, I can hardly wait!'

Belinda was instantly aware of a dilemma. How could she give directions if she didn't know where she was? They had been entirely lost the other night, even before they had abandoned the car. And there had certainly been no Sedgewick Priory on the map.

'Give me the phone,' said a voice behind her, making her nearly drop the mobile. It had been Jonathan, yet he had sounded quite peculiar. Expressionless, almost robotic. And when she turned to him, Belinda saw a face that matched the spaced-out voice. Jonathan was reaching for the phone, but he was not looking at it, or at her, or at anything else. He looked as if he was in a trance, but at a loss for anything better to do, she handed him the mobile.

What followed was the most eerie thing Belinda had ever seen – and that was saying something, given the weirdness of the last two days.

Jonathan delivered a set of clear and very detailed instructions on how to get to the priory from the last town they had passed through. And throughout them he neither moved a muscle nor blinked his eyes once. Belinda heard Paula ask a question, and he replied, 'Just a guess . . .', continuing to stare into some inner middle distance. Without another word, he handed the phone back to Belinda.

'Is Jonathan OK?' queried Paula. 'He sounds a bit out of it.'

'He's just tired,' said Belinda, watching in perfect astonishment as Jonathan lay back again and promptly went to sleep. 'It's the driving and the heat. That's one of the reasons I want to stay here. So he can have a nice relaxing time.'

'Sounds great to me,' said Paula cheerfully.

They chatted for a few minutes more, then said

190

goodbye, the plan being that Paula would join them after visiting her aunt.

The instant the call was over, the mobile phone went completely dead in Belinda's hand. No ready signal, no dial tone, no nothing. She gave it a shake then dropped it on the settee, feeling vaguely scared of it. Turning to Jonathan, she found him still fast asleep.

This is creepy, she thought, reaching out to brush a love-lick of hair that was dangling on his forehead. Just who the hell was it that had given those directions? It certainly hadn't been Jonathan, she was quite sure of it.

Isidora Katori was shaking with excitement, although she strongly doubted that the average observer would have noticed.

Her powers serving her as well as ever, she had taken a route south from the city, letting her instincts choose the roads and the turnings. After an hour or two behind the wheel, she had felt an urge to pull off for a while, take refreshment and consider her next move, and a pleasant country pub with a beer garden had beckoned.

Not one for bucolic pursuits at the best of times, she had nevertheless experienced a growing anticipation as she sat in the shade with a cool drink and a light lunch. Her psychic awareness had sharpened to a degree that was almost painful when a young woman, carrying a lunch and a drink of her own, had asked politely if she could share the same table as there was nowhere else available in the sun.

Hiding her interest, Isidora had said, 'Of course', and after a few moments her new companion had taken a mobile phone from her bag.

The conversation that followed had been exactly the set of clues Isidora had been waiting for, and it had taken all her considerable self-control not to shout out in triumph as she had listened with her enhanced hearing to its contents.

He was here! Less than thirty miles away! And this

191

rather ordinary young woman, with her phone and her shoulder bag, was expected as a guest in his house. It was high time to make some introductions.

'Isn't it a beautiful day?' said Isidora to her dining companion, gracing the woman with her most brilliant of smiles. 'I do so love this part of the country, don't you?' She edged a little closer, along the wooden seat, towards her victim. 'By the way, my name is Isidora ... What's yours?'

Jonathan had slept for half an hour after the strange phone call, and it was only when Oren entered the library, carrying sandwiches and a jug of juice, that he woke up and looked around, his face puzzled.

Belinda – who had been nosing around the library and discovering erotic literature which made her own recent exploits seem profoundly naïve – moved to sit down beside him as Oren served their lunch.

'I had the weirdest dream,' said Jonathan, when the blond servant had discreetly made his exit. 'It was really vivid ... Gives me the shakes just to think about it, although there nothing much actually happened.'

'What do you remember?' Belinda reached for a sandwich, and, taking a bite, realised they were smoked salmon, a delicacy she had only very rarely indulged in.

'Well, I was in this stone-lined room, sort of round – ' He paused to sample his own sandwich, and his eyebrows shot up in appreciative surprise. 'Anyway, it was dark, but there were candles burning all around. And there were draperies of some sort.' He finished the sandwich. 'These are brilliant!'

'But what happened in the dream?' prompted Belinda, recognising an uncannily accurate description of André's tower room.

'Someone held this card up, with blue writing on it. And I had to read it out aloud. That's all I remember.' He took another sandwich, put it on his plate, then added a couple more.

'What did it say? The blue writing?'

'No idea!' said Jonathan blithely between bites. 'I don't remember a single word.'

I do, thought Belinda, eating her own sandwich but too preoccupied to appreciate its deliciousness. She herself could remember those directions almost perfectly, and the ghostly way they had been issued from Jonathan's lips.

After their lunch, Belinda and Jonathan ventured out into the park for a walk.

Belinda said nothing to Jonathan, but the incident in the library had spooked her. André had intervened in their lives again and prevented them from leaving his house, but there didn't seem to be any way to go back on their decision and leave. The mobile phone was dead again and there seemed to be nowhere to charge it, so they couldn't contact Paula and make a new plan. They were trapped here until she turned up to release them.

Jonathan took his sketching gear from the Mini and Belinda had a book from the library – one of the risqué ones she had been looking at earlier – and they set off in the direction of the river. No one appeared on the steps to stop them as they left, so it seemed it was all right that they explore.

'How old do you think André is?' asked Belinda, a while later. They had walked all the way across the park and found a path through the woods, and were now settled on the bank beside the stream. Belinda had a suspicion that this was the very site where Jonathan had watched Feltris and Elisa make love, but she didn't say anything. She just smiled at the way his gaze darted to one particular spot, and his expression became both dreamy and excited.

'I dunno ... Thirty. Thirty-five. Something like that,' he said after a while. 'I only saw him for a few minutes, And I was half-asleep anyway.' He gave her a puzzled look. 'Why do you ask?'

'No particular reason,' she said quickly, opening her book. 'I just wondered.'

'Well, he's definitely older than us,' observed Jonathan, as if that was the end of the matter. Holding up his pencil, he closed his left eye and measured the size of an object on the far side of the river, already deeply absorbed in his drawing.

You can say that again, thought Belinda, turning her attention to what lay on the page before her. She had discovered this treasure of perversion while Jonathan had been dozing, and been so intrigued – and shocked – by it that she had been compelled to bring the outrageous thing with her.

Not an entirely unsophisticated woman, Belinda was aware of some of the weirder practices people indulged in for pleasure. She and Jonathan had experimented a little when they had first got together, but they had never tried what was depicted in this lavishly-produced volume – the dark, cryptic delights of erotic punishment. It was all new to her, but the images were affecting.

The content consisted almost entirely of photographs of women being spanked. Some were from the very earliest days of photographic art, before the turn of the century, and some were from far more recent eras.

Paradoxically, it was the older, fuzzier prints that were most exciting. The women in them were swathed in voluminous layers of frilly underwear, much like the garments she was wearing now, and often trussed into tight corsets too. But in every case, their pale bottoms were exposed. Rounded cheeks appeared out of peepholes in the most decorous of knee-length drawers, or were visible only between rolled-up petticoats and the dark tops of snugly-gartered stockings.

Other girls and women were more lewdly presented, with legs raised or stretched apart in a variety of uncomfortable-looking poses, suggesting it was not only their bottoms that were being smacked. Seeing these willing victims – for almost all the faces visible were smiling, and others were clearly only feigning distress – Belinda found herself thinking again of last night on the terrace. Suddenly she wished André had spanked her when he could have done – when her bare bottom was pushed rudely out towards him.

She had never been punished for pleasure, but now she wanted to be, desperately. She glanced at Jonathan but he was engrossed in his drawing.

Returning to the book, she found that each successive page made her more and more excited, but one photo made her jaw drop in astonishment.

It was a picture of André – André chastising the bottom of a half-dressed, dark-haired girl. He was laying about her vigorously with what looked like a strip of leather; his face stern yet his eyes bright and lusty. The girl appeared to be sobbing, and her pretty mouth was twisted in an exaggerated moué of suffering, but between her legs there was a clearly visible glint. She was wet because her buttocks were being lashed.

Belinda came to a quick decision. 'I'm going for a bit of a wander,' she said casually to Jonathan. 'I won't be long.' She paused, watching to see how he would react. 'You don't mind, do you?'

'No, not at all,' he replied, looking up and giving her a quick grin, then looking down again. 'I'll be fine.' His pencil moved across the paper with a swift fluidic purpose, and Belinda knew he was totally absorbed.

Striking off down a path that paralleled the riverbank, Belinda walked as quickly as was practicable. She felt hyped-up, manic, and extremely naughty; and the leather-covered book seemed to burn her where it was tucked beneath her arm.

After five minutes, she found a little hollow just a few yards from the river. The mossy turf underfoot was soft and rather dry, and bushes around her provided a semblance of secluded privacy. A shaft of sunlight shining down through the canopy of trees provided just the right degree of illumination.

When she lay down, on her side, Belinda suddenly felt shy. Her actions felt calculated, sneaky, rather grubby. Why did masturbation always seem unsavoury when it was planned?

It didn't bother you the other night out here, did it? she demanded of herself, as she opened the book at the photograph of André. She thought again of the way she had wet herself in the clearing and of how the forbidden act had felt so voluptuous, then she grinned as her qualms dissolved like mist.

André looked extraordinarily handsome in the antique photograph. His long tied-back hair seemed a little anomalous for the date in the corner of the picture – 1899 – but his striped trousers, double-breasted waistcoat and high starched collar made him very much the fashionable gentleman of that age. And his rolled-up shirtsleeves showed he obviously meant business. His arm was a poem of grace; a raised arc of readiness. Belinda could almost hear the leather swishing through the air.

When she turned her attention to the girl in the picture, she suddenly felt a wash of disorientating giddiness. She rubbed her eyes, then looked again, not believing what she saw.

The clothes and the pose were the same as they had been earlier; the flounces, the lace, the exposed buttocks, the flexed, entreating body. But the long dark hair and the slightly Latin face were gone, and in their place was a short, anachronistically elfin hairstyle and features that were impossibly familiar.

How? How on earth? Rolling on to her back, Belinda felt the book slip from her fingers, the pages rustle, and the covers clop shut and conceal the picture that couldn't exist.

Suddenly, she felt herself falling, when there was physically nowhere to fall, and she realised that she needed to see more than just an image.

* * *

196

A knock on the door woke her.

Had she been dreaming? She felt very strange. Very peculiar. For a moment she didn't know where she was, but then she remembered. She was at Count André's house, the home of her handsome new benefactor. The exquisite continental nobleman for whom she would do anything: because he was kind and she simply adored him.

Belinda looked down at her booted feet, her stockinged calves and the hem of the most dainty and frilly petticoat she had ever seen. She had never been able to afford anything so pretty for herself, but Count André had lavished her with a positive mountain of expensive lingerie: chemises, bodices, corsets, petticoats, drawers – every extravagant frippery of lace, embroidery, and ribbonwork she could imagine. His only stipulation was that she wore them to be seen in – that she wore them at his special, private parties.

Thinking of the evening ahead, Belinda quivered.

'Just one or two friends who might appreciate you,' he had said, stroking her face as she sat on his lap. 'You are a jewel, my darling. You know how I love to flaunt you.' His gentle hand had begun to stray downward then. 'I feel like a king when I see the envy in their eyes.' Still descending, his hand had settled on her breast, squeezing it through the delicate lawn of her chemise, then sliding downward across the firm, unyielding panels of her corset before dipping into the open drawers she wore below. 'I love to watch them covet you. Your magnificent breasts, your pearly bottom, your beautiful quim ... I love their jealousy. The way they wish themselves in my place, so they could have use of you every day and every night.'

And yet Count André did permit his friends certain liberties. Belinda supposed he only did it to increase their envy, but he often allowed them to touch her. To play with her; intimately. To chastise her bottom and to cause her pain and shame. The idea was, she deduced, that what they could have for only a short time, they were bound to desire even more.

Tonight, Count André was holding open house for several of his most valued friends. They would have good wine, fine food, and entertainment. An erotic diversion of which she was the chief ingredient.

'Come in,' she called, responding at last to the rapping on her door. It was typical of Count André – even though he had rescued her from poverty, and to all intents and purposes owned her – that he should have the courtesy to knock before entering her room.

The door swung open and he took a step inside – a perfect picture of male sartorial splendour in his dark cutaway, his striped trousers and his dashing neckwear.

'My dearest,' he said softly, walking towards her, taking her hand and bidding her rise. 'Let me look at you.' He led her towards the mirror. 'Let *us* look at you,' he amended, as they stood before the glass.

Belinda saw herself as a fairy-tale figure, clad all in white. She wore an almost transparent white muslin chemise trimmed with embroidered lace flowers and ribbons, a fierce white silk tricot corset that made her breasts bulge and oppressed her already tiny waist, and a white cotton petticoat adorned with flounces, frills and bows of pure silk ribbon. Hidden by this, but to be seen eventually, were her drawers – also white, also frilly, and conveniently open – and her white stockings with their frivolous lacy garters.

'You are a vision,' murmured Count André, so elegant yet so predatory behind her. He was caressing her throat slowly with the fingers of one hand while with the other he was cupping her womanhood through her undies. 'A perfect plaything.' Nipping her ear, he pressed harder against her mons.

'My lord,' gasped Belinda, beginning to wriggle. The constriction of her corset was making her sex doubly sensitive at the moment. All her lower organs were bearing down on it from within. 'Oh please . . . Oh please –

'Later, my sweet,' he said, squeezing harder, just once, then releasing her. 'You must contain yourself and give up your pleasure to amuse my guests.' He stepped away from her, then took a length of soft white ribbon from her dresser. 'Let me tie your hands so you do not touch yourself until we are ready – '

'Oh, please, don't do that!' she cried, begging for a different boon this time. She felt so vulnerable when she was bound; so frightened. The sense of being quite helpless was almost too exciting, and even though she would never dash away exploring hands for fear of offending Count André, at least when she was free, the opportunity was there in theory. When she was secured, she could do nothing, and her body was available –

'But I wish it,' he said softly, his voice as kind as ever but shot through with a thrilling steeliness.

Bowing her head, Belinda held out her hands at an angle behind her and meekly let her slender wrists be tied.

It was difficult to descend the stairs in high-heeled boots when your hands were bound, but Belinda managed it, with Count André's guiding help. He supported her elbow solicitously, letting her lean on him if she needed, his attention as courtly as if she had been a royal princess.

'Do not be frightened,' he said, when she balked on the lower landing after hearing convivial voices in the parlour. 'Remember how proud I am of you ... How I prize you above all others ... Now hold your head up, and show them your perfect, graceful posture.'

'Oh, well done, André old chap,' said an English voice as they entered the room. A hearty-looking fellow gave Belinda a long appraising glance.

'She's divine,' said a woman, her tones aristocratic, her eyes filled with lust.

'You lucky thing, André,' said another, older woman. 'What I wouldn't give for a tender morsel like that – '

'Is she as good a looker underneath all those fancy

clothes?' said a second male, this one florid and rather coarse in appearance. 'What about her tits, her arse and her fanny?'

'She is perfect in every aspect,' said Count André evenly. 'And you may inspect any part of her you wish in a little while.'

There were one or two others in the small appreciative group, but for the time being they confined themselves to looking at her.

'Come along, Belinda,' said Count André, leading her forward into the centre of the room. 'Stand here and let my friends admire your charms.'

While the count attended to the needs of his guests, refilling their glasses and making idle smalltalk, Belinda stood still where he had left her, blushing furiously. She knew the fragile material of her chemise barely hid her breasts at all, and she could feel the heat of many eyes upon her nipples. Her maid had rouged her there, in preparation for just such eager scrutiny.

'André darling,' said the woman who had called Belinda 'divine', a handsome brunette with a small and petulant mouth. 'May I uncover her breasts? They look so delightful. I'd rather like to hold them.'

'Of course, Mabel,' said Count André genially. 'Please proceed.' He took a sip of champagne and winked at Belinda over the glass.

Mabel hurried forward and began unfastening the buttons of Belinda's chemise. 'Oh, she is just the prettiest thing,' she exclaimed, folding aside the thin muslin and easing Belinda's aching breasts forward. 'And rouged nipples too. How droll! André, you are so naughty! I do so love that, especially when they're firm and pink to start with.'

Belinda clenched her jaw as Mabel began to handle her. Pinching, rolling, pulling, inflicting little pains that did diabolical things down below. She felt desperate to move her hips, to work them to and fro a little; to do anything that might assuage her growing tension.

200

'Do you whip them?' enquired Mabel, cupping both Belinda's breasts and pushing the nipples inward until they touched. 'I'm sure they'd look absolutely glorious if they were wealed.'

'No, I do not,' replied Count André, coming across to where they were standing and touching each of Belinda's nipples with one forefinger. 'I prefer to see her breasts unmarked. It is more aesthetic, in my opinion.'

'A pity,' said Mabel, sounding slightly thwarted. 'What about clips? Have you tried them on her? Apparently the best ones can be quite excruciating.'

'Oh yes, clips can be very becoming,' said Count André thoughtfully. 'If you wish to experiment, you will find a selection of appropriate ornaments in the usual drawer.'

'Wonderful!' cried Mabel, releasing Belinda and nearly skipping across to the secretaire. 'Oh yes, these are just the thing,' she said, reaching in and bringing out some tiny silver objects, then returning to stand in front of Belinda. 'The very thing. These will look so pretty.'

Taking each breast in turn, Mabel screwed on the wicked silver clips, tightening each one to a terrible, crushing pitch. Belinda felt tears trickling down her face as they were adjusted, as much from shame as from the clips' fierce effect. The horrid pressure on the tips of her breasts only increased the arousal that surged within her. She bit her lip in a hopeless effort to keep still.

'Does it hurt, my dear?' enquired Mabel, brushing away Belinda's tears, then kissing her on the mouth. When Belinda nodded, she gave each clip an additional turn. 'Don't worry. We'll take them off in a minute or two.' She grinned devilishly. 'And that will hurt more than having them on.'

'Courage, my darling,' whispered Count André, when Mabel had retreated in search of more wine. 'See how beautiful you look,' he said, directing Belinda's attention to the large mirror that had been set up at one side of the room for the express purpose of letting her see her own humiliation.

Belinda observed her flushed face, her glowing skin and her maltreated nipples, and knew that she was indeed beautiful; the very picture of submissive, erotic suffering. She wanted to lift her petticoat and open her knickers too, so she could show all the party how aroused the pain made her.

Like a white-clad living ornament, she stood waiting while Count André and his friends drank their wine and discussed her appearance. Some of the observations they made and some of the things they proposed to do to her made her blood run cold. If she were to belong to any one of the others, she knew she would suffer unimaginably, but at least she felt safe in Count André's possession. He respected her and his limits were hers too.

'Let's see her arse then!' said the crude man after a while, breaking away from the others. 'It's high time she felt a taste of the lash.'

'Yes, perhaps you are right, Henri,' Count André said pleasantly, obviously humouring the man. 'Come along, my sweet,' he said to Belinda. 'Let me undo your hands so you can pose more comfortably to receive your punishment.'

'You're too soft with her,' said Henri, licking his lips. 'If she were mine, I would have thrashed her by now, bonds or no bonds.' He moved closer, then grabbed her cruelly, his fingers digging into the softness of one buttock. 'And I'd have sodomised her too. It's plain as day that she needs it. She's got a loose, wanton look about her, André old man. She needs a proper taming.'

'You're probably correct, Henri,' murmured Count André as he unfastened the ribbon around Belinda's wrists.

Belinda trembled as she looked into her beloved's eyes. If he wanted his friend to possess her backside, she would endure it, but only because it was his – her master's – wish. And if Count André would hold her

202

hands and kiss her lips while his friend took his pleasure, she could almost believe she would enjoy it too.

'Now, my dear, perhaps you would kneel on the chaise-longue?' said André encouragingly, as if she were a nervous fawn to be coaxed out of hiding. Taking her elbow, he helped her up on to the padded, velvet-covered chaise, and then pressed down on her back so she assumed the right position – resting on her elbows with her rump up in the air.

The pose was difficult to hold, especially with her clipped breasts dangling down like pears and throbbing cruelly. Belinda swayed a little, then felt her spirits lift as André touched her cheek.

'Would you assist me, Pierre?' she heard him ask another of his friends, one who had not yet spoken. 'Perhaps you would be so good as to uncover Belinda's bottom?'

'Of course, *mon ami*,' replied Pierre, his voice refined and pleasant. Belinda felt happy that it was he who was uncovering her. Monsieur Pierre was dark and hand-some, his features exotic and Eastern, and he had always been a little kinder than the others. He would enjoy her punishment, certainly, and the spectacle of her red and fiery bottom; but she sensed finer feelings beneath the surface of his lechery.

Even so, she flinched as she felt him deftly adjust her clothing; lifting her flounced petticoat, then dividing her loose, open knickers.

A gasp of approval went up around the room, and all those assembled moved in a little closer to improve their view.

'That's a sumptuous arse, André,' observed Mabel, her voice slightly breathy. 'What I wouldn't give to have one like that to beat whenever I wanted.' Belinda heard the swish of silk as Mabel sidled close, then felt feminine fingers touch the furrow of her bottom. 'She's so sensitive too. Ooh, how lovely! Like velvet to the touch.'

Despite the awkwardness of her position, Belinda bit

her knuckle and tried not to respond. Mabel's drifting fingertips were as light as a feather, and they seemed intent on lingering. Belinda felt the whole of her bottom groove being explored, her anus being palpated, her sex-lips being patted and pushed very gently. Where she had been rough with Belinda's breasts, Mabel was tenderness itself with her nether regions; but in the pit of shame, the woman's cruelty was easier to bear. Suddenly, Belinda yearned with all her heart for the lash – the blessed instrument that would both elevate and focus her.

Surprisingly, or perhaps unsurprisingly, it was Henri who came to her aid.

'I've had enough of this shilly-shallying about,' he said, pacing the room grumpily. 'When is she to be beaten? It *is* what you invited us here to see.'

'Of course,' said Count André courteously. 'We will begin in a moment. But first perhaps another drink for you all?'

Belinda remained motionless on the chaise while Count André dispensed hospitality. For a few moments, she perceived herself as they might – not really a person but just a human entertainment. She pictured herself as such – a study in still life. A mass of white linen, a creamy rounded bottom, a set of stockinged legs, and feet in buttoned boots. And at the centre of it all, her wet, blushing pudenda and her shadowed anal crevice. The image in her own mind made her sex pulse and quiver, and she felt a great urge to gyrate her naked buttocks.

If only one of them would touch her again. Rub her. Insert something into her. Her unfulfilled need for stimulation was intolerable; she was almost beside herself. And yet she knew that if she touched herself, she would be dismissed and found wanting.

After what seemed like an interminable wait, Count André spoke up. 'And now it is time,' he said solemnly. 'Henri, will you take the strap from the drawer?'

204

Belinda heard the slight squeak of the drawer being opened, but there was no other sound. Breaths were bated and she sensed lips being licked all around her.

'I will beat her myself first.' The leather strap hissed experimentally through the air. 'And then, perhaps, someone else would care to take over?'

There was a chorus of heartfelt 'yeses', 'absolutelies' and 'with pleasures'; there seemed no shortage of candidates to torment her.

The next thing Belinda heard was a series of tiny rustling sounds – her beloved count removing and folding his jacket, then rolling up his sleeves.

'Mabel. Pierre. Perhaps you would be kind enough to hold her in position?' Belinda sensed her master moving into place somewhere close behind her. 'Henri, I think you will find that the seat by the secretaire will give you the best view.' The strap swished again. 'Julian and Madame Clermont, perhaps if you stood a little to your right you too would be better able to see.'

Unable to stop herself, Belinda whimpered when Mabel sat down beside her on the chaise and took hold of her hands. At the same time, Pierre took her by the hips, raising them higher and making her part her thighs further. 'That's it, Mademoiselle,' he whispered to her. 'Spread yourself a little more.' Belinda felt him sit down beside her, then felt one arm slide over her and secure her around her waist, while his free hand settled snugly on her vulva, middle finger crooked so it compressed her swollen clitoris.

'Oh no! Oh dear God!' keened Belinda, feeling the familiar spasms tremble beneath that fingertip.

But just as her vagina began to convulse, the leather strap lashed down heavily across her bottom. There was a moment of complete blank shock, then it was followed by a raging slice of pain.

'Oh André!' shrieked Belinda in her agony and ecstasy. At last her exaltation had begun.

Chapter Twelve
Help at Hand

'*I*s something wrong?' Jonathan asked Belinda, as they walked towards the priory.

'No, not really,' she replied, telling a little lie. The leather book-cover felt strangely warm beneath her fingertips, but she was quite at a loss to explain how she had suddenly found herself in one of its pictures, then lived in it like an encapsulated world with no memory whatsoever of her 'real' existence.

'We need to talk,' said Jonathan, obviously not fooled. He eyed her shrewdly. 'Let's sit down for a while.' He nodded to a stone garden seat at the edge of the overgrown formal garden, then guided Belinda towards it.

'OK, Lindi. What is it?' he said, taking her hand once they were settled on the sun-warmed stone.

Belinda decided to pitch straight in at the deep end. 'Do you believe in the supernatural?'

'I don't know,' said Jonathan thoughtfully. 'I'd like to ... I think ... But nothing's happened to me yet that would make me believe.'

Belinda felt relieved then slightly annoyed with herself. Why had she doubted him? Jonathan had always been an open-minded type, and of all the boyfriends she had ever had, the one most prepared to explore new ideas.

'What would you say if I told you that we've stumbled into a supernatural situation right now?' She paused and looked towards the house, which was beginning to look mysterious and secretive again, now that afternoon was slowly blending into evening. 'That nothing here's really what it seems.'

Jonathan followed her look. 'You mean André?' He turned and smiled. 'Yes, I have noticed that he's not exactly Mr Average. I mean, the hours he keeps, for one thing – ' He faltered, his smile looking a bit nervous at the edges. 'You're not trying to tell me he's really Count Dracula, are you?'

Belinda laughed, trying to diffuse her own nerves. Framed in words, it all sounded so preposterous. 'I did ask him if he was a vampire, but he said he isn't – ' Oh Lord, how could she phrase this? 'But he *is* two hundred years old!'

'You're kidding!' Jonathan's hand was shaking slightly where it curled around hers.

'I'm not. You know all the portraits of men with the blue eyes? They're not of his ancestors; they're all him!'

'Jesus wept!'

'It's true. He – '

Belinda was just about to explain as much as she knew about their peculiar host when she heard an insistent, roaring, thrumming noise. It sounded quite distant at first, but quickly grew louder as the source of it drew closer. Looking in the direction that it seemed to be coming from – the winding drive they stumbled along in the rain two nights ago – she saw the dark shape of a motorcycle burst violently from the tree line then charge towards the house, spewing stones and gravel from beneath the blur of its wheels. As it passed behind the building, the powerful engine note was throttled back-then abruptly killed to silence.

'Well, that certainly wasn't Paula,' observed Jonathan

mildly. 'Unless there's something she's forgotten to tell us.'

'It must be a friend of André's,' said Belinda.

'What, another two-hundred-year-old raver?'

'He's not a raver!' cried Belinda, not sure why she was springing to the defence of a man she hardly knew, especially as he was sexually exploiting her.

'Really?' Jonathan lifted an eyebrow in a way that said he either knew or suspected what had passed between Belinda and their enigmatic host.

Belinda was about to go on the defensive when she recalled Jonathan's own confessions. She quirked her own eyebrow back at him, and he had the grace to grin.

'OK, so neither of us is blameless, but – ' He hesitated, as if he couldn't find words to describe his feelings, or didn't, perhaps, quite know what those feelings were. 'I don't feel jealous and I don't really feel guilty.' He squeezed her hand. 'How do you feel? About everything, I mean?'

Well, how did she feel?

'About the same,' said Belinda, after a long pause. 'When I'm with André, it's as if I'm enchanted and he's the most important thing that ever happened to me. But when I'm away from him, I'm more sorry for him than anything – although I have to admit I still find him attractive.'

'Why do you feel sorry for him?'

Slowly, and very carefully, trying to piece together the big picture as she spoke, Belinda outlined what she knew of André's history.

'He's lonely,' she said finally. 'He adored this girl, his fiancée, and he lost her. And he's lived all these years missing her, and wanting to be with her. I mean ... it'd be bad enough in a normal lifetime, but with him living so long, it must be a total nightmare.'

'It doesn't bear thinking about,' said Jonathan, his voice full of feeling. Belinda looked at him sharply, but he was studying their entwined hands, deep in thought.

Silence hung over them for a few minutes, until finally she said, 'I think he wants something from me.'

'Of course he does,' countered Jonathan with a wry little grin. 'He wants you to keep on having sex so he can feed on the energy.' He gave her hand another little squeeze.

'Yes. But I'm convinced there's more to it.'

'How do you mean?'

'I think the fact that I resemble his fiancée is significant.' She stared at the house, as if its darkening grey facade held an answer. But there was none. 'But I get the impression that he's frightened to tell me why.'

'Do you think it's something that might be dangerous?'

'I don't know ... but I've a sneaking feeling it could be.'

Jonathan shook his head, frowning. 'Then we better had get out of here. As fast as we can.'

'We can't ... Paula's on her way here now. We've got to wait for her,' Belinda pointed out, knowing that it was only a superficial argument.

'We could try and intercept her,' countered Jonathan. He looked up and gave her a long, appraising, sideways look. 'You want to stay, don't you?'

'Yes,' she admitted. 'I want to find out what it is André wants from me. And if it's not too awful, I'd like to help him. I'm sorry for him,' she finished, knowing that that too was a superficiality.

'Look,' said Jonathan, seriously. 'We've covered this ... I don't mind if you want to help him because you like him ... because you're attracted to him.' He hesitated, then blushed furiously in a wild red way Belinda had never seen before. 'I ... um ... I can understand that, you know. I ...' He faltered again, as if what he were about to say was so strange to him that he physically could not get the words out of his mouth. 'Look, don't think I'm going queer on you, but, well ... I think he's attractive in a way too.' This last sentence came

209

tumbling out so fast it made Jonathan sound breathless. 'I only saw him for a few minutes but it was really strange ... Something I've never felt before. I wanted him to stay. To ... Oh God, I don't know what!'

Belinda put her arms around her confused boyfriend. 'Don't worry, I get the general idea ... I was with Feltris and Elisa, remember. That's just the same ... And you don't think any worse of me for that, do you?'

Jonathan shook his head, his smile returning.

'OK then, there you are!' Tugging on his hand, she urged him to get up. 'Now come on, let's get back to the house and see who was on that bike!'

'My lord! How good it is to see you!'

Michiko strode into the darkened tower room, an imposing figure in her skin-tight black leathers. André knew it was Michiko, even though her head was encased in a gleaming helmet adorned with the design of a ferocious fire-breathing dragon. Her electrifying aura was so strong he could almost taste it.

Yet he got a shock when she removed her shiny headgear and set it aside.

'Michiko! Your hair!' he cried – in English, the language in which she had addressed him – as he rose from his disordered bed, still naked. He knew he was awake but for a moment he seemed to be dreaming.

The last time he had seen his friend the sorceress, thirty years ago, her lustrous black hair had fallen in a water-straight curtain to her waist, but now there was no sign of that coiffure. Instead her hair was short – cut with a thick, wedge-like fringe and short back and sides – and all tinted a brilliant orange-toned yellow.

'My countryfolk are in an experimental phase,' she said blithely, flipping her lurid locks with her fingers. 'This is the latest thing, especially for girls who dress up as boys.' She rubbed her fingers across the cropped back of her head.

'Ah, the Takarazuka,' said André, beginning to under-

210

stand the metamorphosis. For her own amusement and to bring an element of variety to her long, long life, Michiko had abandoned the life of a geisha, and instead joined the Japanese all-girl theatre, the Takarazuka. She had already become something of an idol, even when André had last encountered her, and with her commanding, imperious manner, she made a perfect male impersonator. But back in the 1960s, she had always worn a wig.

'Do you like it?' she enquired pertly, sidling closer, the ultimate predator in her shiny black carapace.

'Yes. I do,' said André, after a moment, quite beguiled by the eye-catching new style. 'It is most becoming . . . even if something of a shock.' He smiled as she sat down beside him on the rumpled sheets, her gloved hands as ever straying towards his groin. 'It was a shock to find you so near to me, too,' he continued, his voice catching as she delicately touched his penis.

'We are on tour,' she told him, her slanted eyes downcast, studying the reaction of his body, 'and currently in London. Most opportune, my lord *gaijin*, is it not?' she murmured, playing her leather-clad fingers along the growing length of flesh.

'Indeed,' said André, leaning forward and inclining his mouth towards hers. At the last minute, he saw her upswept eyes dart sideways, seeking Arabelle's blue-glowing casket. 'She sleeps, my dear friend,' he said softly, placing his hand against Michiko's exquisitely-sculpted jaw, 'and even if she were awake, she would not deny us. You know full well that she is fond of you.'

'Yes, I do know it, my lord,' whispered Michiko, her brilliant mouth moving against his, 'and in a little while, when she is awakened and I have greeted you sufficiently on my own behalf, I will bring her to you.' She paused a moment, her lips perhaps a hundredth of an inch from his. 'Only briefly, I regret to say. My powers cannot sustain her all that long.'

André shuddered, relishing the hope and the expectation of that peculiar fusion, even while his spirit soared in anticipation of a greater one.

Almost against his, Michiko's eyes flew open. 'I can sense your "discovery", my lord,' she said, her normally calm voice full of excitement. 'And you are right, she *is* the one.' She cocked her head, as if listening. 'Tell me more about her, with your mind, while I pleasure you.'

And do you really think I will be able to concentrate sufficiently, while you are caressing me? observed André, obeying her even as her gloved hand moved faster on his penis. In contact like this, they could easily exchange thoughts, but it would not be long before his became disordered. *Let me pleasure you first, my dear Michiko. That way, I will still have enough of my wits to make sense of it.*

Gently removing her hand from his member, he reached for the long zip of her voluptuous leather suit, and began to describe – by means of thought transference – the arrival of the woman he hoped would help free his soul.

Michiko wore no underwear beneath the form-fitting hide that enclosed her, and the combination of the jet black suit and her honey-coloured skin made it seem as if he were unpeeling a ripe and luscious fruit. She moaned softly as he reached into the slit he had created and massaged her small, firm breasts, amazing him with the way she simultaneously assimilated what he 'told' her, even down to asking questions as she writhed with easy pleasure.

Stretching out her arms above her head, across the tangled sheets, Michiko offered both breasts to André's feverish hands. *How much does she know?* her mind asked coolly. *Is she aware that she resembles Arabelle?*

Yes, she knows that she looks like Belle, replied André, leaning down across his friend to kiss her nipples. *And she knows that I lost Belle many years ago.* He nipped first one crest, then the other, then settled down to a long, concerted suck that made Michiko lift her hips and beat the air.

212

But does she know the significance of that likeness? questioned Michiko, her inner voice as placid as the surface of a lake, while outwardly she was gasping and groaning and pulling André's fingers to her unattended breast. *Does she know exactly what you are?*

I have told her of my longevity, replied André, complying with Michiko's wishes and squeezing her nipple between his fingers. *And I think she does believe me.* He closed his teeth on the nipple in his mouth, carefully gauging the exact degree of pressure. *But she knows nothing of how both I, and Belle, can be released.* He glanced towards the casket, thinking of the pure spirit that slept within the vial. *She does not even know of Belle's continued existence.*

Despite the fact that he was the one doing the pleasuring, André suddenly found himself distracted. Lying over Michiko, he felt her body's leather covering against his own skin, the touch slick and clingingly sensuous. He rocked his hips slightly, making his penis slid back and forth over the smooth, almost living hide, his rough breathing matching Michiko's wild gasps.

Then you must tell her, instructed Michiko, her head tossing as he held her nipple between his teeth. *And tell her soon, in case there isn't much time.*

André well understood the need for urgency, but it made him angry. He twisted Michiko's teat cruelly between his fingers, re-directing his rage in a useful direction. He would not think of Isidora now; he would not accept the fact that she too could possibly be close by, and may already have detected his 'awakening'. It was something to discuss with Michiko later. Later, when she wasn't bouncing her hips around on the bed beneath him and trying to push her mons pubis against his midriff for stimulation.

Lifting himself and sliding himself along Michiko's body, André pressed his penis against her leather-clad thigh and at the same time crushed her parted mouth with his. Kissing her profoundly, he eased down the zip of her suit a little further, then discovered that – most

213

conveniently – went all the way down between her legs, up her bottom crease, and to her waist. When she obligingly lifted her rump from the bed, he whipped the zip open to bare her whole genital area, revealing her sex-lips and her silky pubic bush; a tuft of hair that was far blacker than the leather.

Will you help me? he asked Michiko while he tugged apart the unzipped aperture so he could get to the sleek rounds of her buttocks. *I have everything we need. It only remains to distil the elixir.*

Of course, she concurred, wriggling furiously, almost searching for him with her hindquarters. *I am at your service, my lord,* she said, her mental voice serene as she located his fingers then jammed herself down on them, forcing him to fondle the puckered portal of her anus.

And I am always in your debt, my faithful friend, André replied, beginning to give Michiko the caress she clearly wanted. Rubbing hard at the little hole, he got a satisfyingly violent reaction. Michiko's legs flailed and her torso shook; she threw her thighs wide apart, physically knocking André off her as she bucked and heaved on the bed. Reaching down behind her back, she took hold of her own bottom cheeks and opened herself, blatantly coaxing him to breach her darkest orifice.

'Ah!' she cried, her physical and mental voices merging when finally he pushed a digit right inside her. '*Amida,*' she murmured, her arms stiffening above her head as he used his rigid middle finger to fuck her bottom. André sensed in her an almost overwhelming longing to touch herself. She wanted to squeeze her breasts or finger her clitoris, but she was tormenting her own body by denying it. He would have done either of those things for her, or he would have curled himself up and licked her between her legs, but he knew that too would defeat her prime objective – her desire to orgasm by only anal stimulation.

'My lord, my lord,' she grunted as he moved himself around, his finger still firmly lodged inside her. Kneel-

214

ing, he positioned her in front of him, and brought her knees up to squash against her breasts. Then he grabbed a pillow and jammed it against the small of her back, making her lift her skewered bottom even higher.

What a sight she was, his contorted lotus flower. Her body was almost doubled, and her bottom was protruding like a split and honeyed peach from between the edges of her night-black leather suit. He twisted his finger inside her and she made an uncouth gobbling noise, the superb muscles of her buttocks bunching madly. The snug ring around his finger gripped and tensed.

'Do you remember the jade phallus, Michiko?' he whispered, leaning over her, studying the invasion of her forbidden amber rose. 'The one we played with in Paris. The one you made me suckle on before you put it in me?'

'Yes, my lord,' she said, her voice small as she trembled around him.

'Well, I wish I had it now. So I could insert it into you ... right here, where my finger is.' He wiggled the digit he spoke of and Michiko almost choked. 'It was very big, Michiko ... even for me.' He paused, easing out his finger a little way, playing it delicately around the inside of her sphincter. 'It was uncomfortable. Very uncomfortable. It hurt me, and yet still you pushed it into me. Right into me.' He began to push in again. 'My belly and my bowels were in turmoil. Surging. Protesting. But you were stern. You would not be denied.' His finger slid in, one joint, two, as far as it would go. 'You forced almost all of that horrid thing inside me.'

He began to pump her. Slowly, metronomically, using his finger as a miniature penis to sodomise her. Michiko's booted heels flailed dangerously near to his face, but the hazard only added to his enjoyment. She was chuntering now, yelping in Japanese as she squirmed, her Oriental reserve entirely dissipated. To squeal and struggle was an enormous loss of 'face'.

215

'You fucked me with it,' he told her, savouring the Anglo-Saxon word that somehow had more impact than its equivalent in the other tongues he spoke. 'Like this!' he exclaimed, driving his finger in and out of her like a piston and enjoying both the view and the way her bottom gripped and grabbed him. For a moment, he considered whipping out the finger and inserting his penis instead, but he knew something quite different – and almost sacred – lay ahead of him, so he concentrated his energies on pleasing Michiko.

It didn't take long for them both to reach that goal. With a cry that was softer and strangely peaceful, Michiko went rigid in every sinew of her magnificent body, while between her legs her entire vulva moved and rippled. André was torn between watching those exotic pulsations – the ones he could feel transmitted through her vitals – and observing the suddenly placid expression on her face. Within the violence of orgasm, Michiko seemed transfigured, as if she had passed over into some realm beyond his imagining, a place of rest and quiet and tranquillity which he longed to reside in himself. A haven he could share with Arabelle.

Presently, he and Michiko untangled themselves, and studying him with her clear, dark eyes, she rolled away and peeled off her disordered clothing. Nude and beautiful, she brought a scented cloth and cleansed them both, then she knelt on the bed in a pose of meditation. Observing her as she murmured some unknown sutra under her breath, André was struck again by her unexpected new hair colour. He supposed that he too should have been meditating and preparing himself, but he couldn't ignore the vivid difference in Michiko. He liked it. The brilliance of her short, sharply-cut hair matched the vivacity of her spirit and personality and negated the only thing about her that had ever troubled him – the fact that long black hair had unhappy connotations, reminding him of Isidora and the evil she had done.

'Don't think of her, my lord,' said Michiko, looking

up, her aura more powerful for her impromptu devotions. 'The lady you love is awakening.' She touched one slim hand to her bosom. 'I feel her here. She speaks to me, André.' She smiled her small inscrutable smile. 'And in a few moments, she will speak to you through me.' They both looked across to the rosewood casket and the slight increase in its weird blue nimbus.

André trembled. It had been a long time since this phenomenon had occurred, and though he yearned for it, its pleasures were bitter-sweet. The precious moments were always over almost before he had begun to relish them, leaving him lonelier and missing Belle more than ever.

And yet there was no way on earth he could refuse the chance.

Quitting the bed again, Michiko advanced on Arabelle's casket and lifted it with reverence from its resting place. Her face still, but her near-black eyes alight, she held the carved box to her naked breasts, cradling it gently and rocking it against her. André got the impression that she was already communing with his beloved somehow; that they were engaged in some intimate girlish interchange that he could never be privy to, even if Arabelle were corporeal. He smiled as he recognised a pang of jealousy.

Michiko turned after a moment, and brought the box towards the bed. Smoothing the coverlet, she placed it carefully, then fetched a length of pure silk ribbon from a drawer in the secretaire. With a swift glance towards André, she lifted the lid of the casket and waited for his sign that she could take out the vial within.

André nodded, his heart pounding far faster than it had ever done in his natural life. He swallowed, full of nerves as Michiko lifted the crystal flask and the weird blue radiance that was all that remained of the woman he loved more than life cast slowly dancing shadows across their bodies.

André? queried Arabelle, her clear discarnate voice full

of happiness. *Do not be afraid ... Michiko has told me of the hopes you share. Perhaps next time you and I will be together always ... And if not, let us take heart from what we are about to share now ...*

She was always so calm, so accepting. It made him feel weak sometimes; inadequate because he could not endure his lesser torments with the same grace. But by the same token her equanimity was a solace. He remembered the early days, and her fits of manic uncomprehending terror and raging confusion, and gave thanks that she had matured and found wisdom. In truth, the way she had accepted her fate was a miracle, because never having physically aged, she was effectively still little more than a girl. The same exquisite, innocent, sensual girl he had fallen in love with over two centuries before.

Michiko put the flickering flask on the bed, then wound the silk ribbon around her wrist and arm in a complicated pattern, leaving one long end of it trailing free. She nodded to the vial, and with fumbling, shivering fingers, André unscrewed the glass lid then very carefully slid the tail of the ribbon into the opening.

'Great *Amida*,' intoned Michiko softly, 'guide the *kami* of the lady Arabelle into the shell of thy humble servant.' Crossing her free arm across her torso, she arranged her fingers into a magic symbol and pressed them against her skin, murmuring a low incantation in Japanese. Tilting her head back, she closed her eyes tightly, then her lips parted in a tiny yielding gasp.

André watched for a moment, tense with anticipation, as Michiko's breathing quickened and a droplet of sweat appeared on her suddenly furrowed brow, then he switched his attention to the vial and the ribbon.

Slowly, oh so slowly, the blue radiance that was Arabelle began to flow along the pristine white ribbon. Through sheer power of her will, Michiko had banished her own spirit, her *kami*, to some unknown nirvana, and Arabelle was passing into the vacated body by osmosis.

218

When the blue glow was right out of the jar and just about to slide across Michiko via the ribbon, André could observe its progress no longer. This temporary fusion was unpredictable and sometimes didn't work at all. Lying back and struggling to hope, he closed his eyes. If the process was successful, he wouldn't open them till it was over.

'André ... my love,' murmured a dear familiar voice in his ear, while a slender, female form lay down beside him.

'Belle! Oh, Belle!' he gasped, drawing her into his arms and rolling over to kiss her with more power. His eyelids still firmly shut, he seemed to see the woman he was embracing with his inner vision, and every detail of her lovely face was sweetly sacred.

Arabelle returned his kiss with a quiet, nascent passion that delighted him, pressing her body against his without shame. Even though Michiko, the vessel, was completely naked, as he held Arabelle he seemed to feel the brush of clothing. She had come to him, as she had before on these infrequent occasions, dressed in the gown she had been wearing when he had last seen her – a soft, elegant dress of the palest blue sprigged muslin, bound at the neckline and at the waist with fine blue ribbons. The bodice was low cut, as the fashion had been at that time, and he had a keen, almost painful memory of her allowing him to dip his hand inside her linen and touch her breast. He groaned, recalling the puckered texture of her nipple.

Just as he received a tactile recollection of Arabelle's pretty clothing, he also seemed to feel her silky hair; the heavy fall of her cascading auburn ringlets. As a fresh young girl, not yet tainted by the excessive pursuit of fashion, she had mostly worn her hair loose and flowing and only very lightly curled, its glossy thickness a delight to eye and hand. One day, he had made her blush profusely by describing how, when they were man and wife, he would ask her to caress him with her hair –

219

to rub her lustrous satin tresses against his penis. She had laughed and told him he was a wicked man to corrupt her with such an outré suggestion, but later, when he was touching her, and she was sobbing with pleasure, she had promised him he would eventually have his wish.

Too late now, he thought, feeling a little wistful as her firm, sweet lips parted under his. There were limits to how far illusion would stretch.

'Do not be sad, André,' she whispered, as if she, or Michiko, had sensed the thought. 'Let me make love to you.' Her quiet, vibrant voice was filled with humour. 'You will be surprised how much dear Michiko has taught me.'

Gentle fingers slid down over his chest, spreading deftly to create a flat caress, then closing to catch his nipple and carefully tweak it.

The sensation was so intense that André murmured, his head tossing against the pillow, his body arching. Because he loved her, even so slight a thing could thrill him.

Arabelle laughed, the husky impish chuckle that had always meant 'beware' because she had some further naughty trick laid in store for him. Pressing her slim thigh between his legs, she massaged his erect penis with the textured muslin of her skirt, pinching his teat in the same relentless rhythm.

'My lady, have a care,' he gasped, clasping her closer and locking his legs around the one that rubbed against him, 'or I will soil your handsome gown.'

'Who cares about gowns,' she answered, continuing to roll and jerk, her lips opening like rose petals against his throat.

'Minx,' he whispered, making her stop her gyrations by gripping the lobes of her bottom. How firm and trim and rounded they felt in his hands – sheer perfection! Tightening his hold on her, he quickly turned the tables and rocked her thinly-covered sex against his hip.

After a moment or two of this, Belle went deliciously limp against him, her slender shape as pliant as a reed. Her arms slid around him and he felt her panting, her breath cool and sweet, her mouth just an inch from his ear. 'Oh André,' she breathed, her pleasure evident not only in the beautiful malleability of her body but in the unguarded message he received directly from her soul. Her whole ethereal being was ablaze with love and wonder, an emotional wavefront that stunned him to silent awe. He would do anything to make her happy, he realised, and in any way. He would risk any risk and take any chance, regardless of any perils that path incurred.

An instant later, he forgot danger, he forgot the odds against success and he forgot all the moral considerations that plagued him. Uncoiling her right arm from around him, Arabelle walked her fingers down his belly, the steps as light and tiny as those of some mythic fairy, until her fingerpads were resting on his penis, just touching the root of it through his flossy pubic hair.

Moaning, he surged against her, pressing his hard length into the billows of her skirt. Her lips were at his throat again, kissing softly, whispering and encouraging, while below, her fingers curved around his shaft, gripping firmly with the exact pressure that he craved.

'My darling, my darling,' he chanted, as that snug grip began to move smoothly on him. Up and down, up and down, sliding the mobile skin over the iron-hard inner core. Stretching; pumping; tantalisingly gloving, twisting and teasing, his virgin beloved used a whore's skill upon his flesh.

'Oh God help me!' he cried out hoarsely, as his penis leapt and juddered and his spinal column seemed to melt and turn to fire. Collapsing backwards among the sheets and covers, he held his lover close, knowing that even as he climaxed, she was receding from him.

'Oh, Belle,' he whispered, as her essence fluttered and shook like a guttering candle flame, and he felt the

221

woman he was embracing twist and struggle. She was Michiko again now, reaching out for the crystal vial that lay beside her, guiding her discarnate friend towards the safety of containment.

'I am so sorry, my lord,' she said after a moment, and André realised he was sobbing like an infant.

They had been so close, he and Arabelle, but under these conditions their joy could never be more than fleeting. Michiko was an accomplished sorceress, full of sympathy and power, and using her mental skills she could temporarily be a vessel. Fundamentally however, she was incompatible with Arabelle, and even her greatest efforts couldn't furnish what they needed.

As he snuggled into Michiko's jasmine-scented embrace, he thought again of another woman who was within his orbit.

Belinda Seward – who *was* compatible, and who could, if she were willing and brave enough, sustain Belle's essence through the erotic ritual of release.

But would she help them? he pondered, his hand moving automatically over Michiko's satiny back. Would Belinda risk her very life for two people she hardly knew?

You can only ask her, said his Japanese lover, her voice clear and assertive inside his mind. 'And you must ask her,' she reiterated – as if for emphasis – by forming the words with her perfect rose-hued lips. 'You must ask her soon before it suddenly becomes too late. We both know there is only a limited period in which to act.'

He knew it only too well. It was only a matter of time before his revived state was detected – and the pursuit that never ended resumed again. 'You are right, my friend. As always,' whispered André, touching Michiko's brilliant coiffure and remembering certain long, black tresses that he had once had the misfortune to handle – a fall of hair that was *not* that of his faithful Japanese ally.

Neither one of them named the danger they feared was coming.

222

Chapter Thirteen
Perils and Pleasures

'*T*ell me about Arabelle,' demanded Belinda of her exotic and eye-catching new acquaintance. 'How can she live like that? Without a body?'

She and Michiko were strolling in the garden after dinner, and though the night was warm, their conversation had made her shudder. Michiko had told her all the things that André couldn't. 'And you said there were dangers. What dangers? To whom? To André? To Arabelle? To me?'

Now she knew his secret, Belinda could understand her host's strange reticence. André needed her to escape. Only she could help him leave a life she had already sensed was purgatory for him; and only through her could he take his best beloved with him.

'One thing at a time,' said the beautiful Japanese softly, slipping her arm through Belinda's as they wandered along the path. The touch of her bare skin was cool, as André's was, the sure hallmark of a being more than human. 'Arabelle is a discarnate spirit. When she was drugged and killed by the black witch Isidora, the life force was teased out of her, along a silken filament, and trapped inside a crystal vial.' The orange-haired woman spoke calmly and reasonably, as if such things were commonplace. 'And once she was sequestered inside the vial, Isidora destroyed her body so she could never return to it.' Michiko paused and turned, her near-black eyes glittering with anger. 'Her beautiful body burned to ashes ... to bones and dust. And all so that foul creature could indulge her evil passions and have André to herself for ever.'

'But André told me that he wasn't actually immortal ... just very long-lived.'

Michiko released Belinda's arm, then took her firmly by the shoulders. The Japanese woman's eyes were as glossy as chips of onyx. 'The spell was never completed, which is one of the reasons why Isidora pursues him.' Strong thumbs dug into Belinda's naked upper arms. 'She created a bond with André. Linked their fates. If he achieves his goal – if he dies – then Isidora can no longer live either.'

'I see,' said Belinda, knowing she didn't – properly – see at all.

'You see a little of it,' countered Michiko, a smile softening her fierce samurai face.

Belinda couldn't speak. Michiko's momentary gentleness was far more affecting than her dominant persona, and it spoke to something in Belinda that was new-born and unsure of itself. She found Michiko intriguing, a little frightening, and quite stunningly beautiful. It was strange to feel desire again, after all that had been revealed to her within the last hour, but she felt a strong urge to touch the Japanese woman – to repeat what she had learnt from Feltris and Elisa.

She became aware that Michiko was studying her closely – a new look in her dark, upslanted eyes.

'You have questions?' she enquired of Belinda, cocking her luridly-coiffed head to one side. *Questions about me, little one*, she seemed to add, confusing Belinda completely because the words were audible but Michiko's lips had remained still.

Can you read my mind? thought Belinda, concentrating

224

earnestly on the phrase, so much so that she felt the muscles of her face tense painfully.

'Yes, I can,' answered Michiko, her smile broadening, 'but if you don't like it, I can stop.' The fingers that gripped Belinda's bare arms released a little of their pressure, and the hold seemed to take on a more subtle quality.

Something about the Japanese woman seemed to dare Belinda to accept the challenge of mental communication, but she still felt slightly afraid to rise to it. Michiko was powerful, frightening. She induced in Belinda a peculiar sensation that was vaguely reminiscent of being a child cowering before a stern, omnipotent teacher – and yet not like it at all. It was fear, it was awe, and it was excitement. A physical thrill that was completely sexual in its content. She had experienced something of the feeling with André – a need to obey and to be controlled – but his haunted aura had somewhat softened its effect.

'I – ' Belinda began, then faltered. Michiko's look, and her touch, seemed to be making weakness steal up through her. She felt her knees almost buckle and she swayed in the Japanese woman's hold. She was also aware that her body was betraying her in other ways. Her nipples were hard points beneath the thin bias-cut satin dress she had been left to wear – she suspected it was a thirties nightdress rather than a real evening gown – and she could feel a tell-tale flush seeping up across her chest and throat.

'Ask your questions, Belinda,' commanded Michiko, her tone like a sheathed blade. 'I have nothing to hide from you.' For the moment, she seemed to have forgotten about telepathy.

'Are ... are you like André?' Belinda asked, still conscious of her vulnerability. Her dress was revealing, the off-white satin poured over her shape like fluid, without underwear beneath to give even a semblance of protection. In contrast, Michiko was clothed in leather,

225

which only reinforced her personal supremacy; narrow trousers and a waistcoat in a fine hide the colour of gun-metal, worn with soft, unstructured boots in the same grey shade. Around her neck was a brushed-steel pendant, suspended from a white cord, in the shape of an indecipherable ideogram.

'In some ways,' she said, answering Belinda's question, 'only my longevity derives from a different source.' She looked thoughtful, almost amused. 'A bargain with certain gods. A twist in the laws of reincarnation, you might say. I am allowed to retain the same body, and my belief is what sustains my state of youth.'

'Not sex then,' Belinda blurted out without thinking.

Michiko laughed loudly, her slanted eyes crinkling, then she kissed Belinda full on the mouth.

'No, not sex!' she said after a moment. 'I enjoy it, but I do not need it to survive.'

'Oh,' said Belinda, feeling vaguely crestfallen. She ran her tongue across the print of Michiko's lips.

'Are you disappointed?' the Japanese enquired, loosening her grip, then sliding an arm around Belinda's waist and encouraging her to continue along the path. It felt just as if they were a pair of lovers out strolling, the male suitor guiding his mate towards seclusion. 'Were you hoping that I was desperately in need of sexual stimulation, and that you were my next intended victim?'

Uncannily, that was exactly what Belinda had been hoping, and the words crystallised her muddled yearnings. She saw now that since she had first encountered André's Japanese friend in the library, where they had gathered for a pre-dinner drink, she had been wondering about the body beneath the leather. Wondering about it, wanting to explore it and caress it; and wanting to give herself to Michiko in return.

Are you still reading my thoughts? she asked silently.

You never actually said I shouldn't, came the reply, projected into her mind by Michiko's.

'Then you know what I feel,' Belinda said, swallowing. She was aware that her whole face and throat were pink now.

Michiko nodded. 'Come! I know a place which will serve our needs perfectly.'

It's too late, thought Belinda, as her new friend hurried her along the path, through the overgrown rose garden with its almost narcotic odour of night-scented blooms, and in the direction of the building she had noted earlier. The dilapidated shell of the almost ruined chapel.

As they stood in the porch and Michiko tackled the massive door with its rusted hinges, Belinda was unable to control a jumble of mental pictures. Herself, being fondled and made love to by Elisa and Feltris; herself, being exposed and studied by André, her buttocks naked to the night air of the terrace as she experienced disappointment when he didn't smack her bottom; herself, in a new scene, one that at first seemed unknown, then suddenly became familiar. She was kneeling awkwardly, with her bottom raised and completely bare, while an unknown figure stood threateningly behind her. Belinda realised that she was seeing a representation of her fantasy, the one in which, like some kind of latter-day Alice, she had fallen into the pages of a book and been a submissive who was about to take a beating. As the image grew in detail, the figure behind her raised its hand, ready to bring it down again with raw and stinging force. The figure turned and showed familiar almond eyes –

As Belinda gasped in recognition, Michiko swung open the chapel door, then whirled to face her. The Japanese woman's smile was oblique and knowing – and Belinda acknowledged the source of the final image.

'A preference of mine,' Michiko said, her voice smooth, 'and a fantasy I perceived in you when I first saw you.' Her eyes narrowed for a moment, became quintessentially inscrutable and Oriental, then she turned and led the way into the chapel. Belinda followed, watching her companion's boyish bottom sway.

Once inside, Belinda was able to forget her nerves for a moment, swept away by the high drama of their surroundings.

At one time, the roof of the chapel had been removed altogether, although there was no sign of the rubble and debris that should have resulted. Consequently, the small building was completely open to the sky and the moon that rode across it, surrounded by the tiny brilliant pin-pricks of a host of stars. Belinda knew little about church architecture, but she could see pews and what she supposed was a knave, but of an altar or an elaborate crucifix there was no sign. They had been whisked away as comprehensively as the roof. And a long time ago, too. The forces of nature clearly had no respect for hallowed ground because there were weeds and wild flowers growing here and there inside the building; springing up from pockets of silt-like earth that suggested a flood at some time in the past. In the bright moonlight the effect was strangely beautiful.

'Is this wh – '

Michiko silenced Belinda's question with a hand across her lips. *No!* came her psychic voice, commandingly. *Do not think of that now. This is our night. Let us concentrate on us!* She drew her hand laterally over Belinda's mouth, then inserted two fingers into it, touching the quiescence of her tongue. In a reflex as old as life, Belinda suckled.

'Ah yes, my little one,' the Japanese woman murmured, letting a third finger join the other two and stretch the corners of Belinda's mouth. 'My little girl, my naughty little girl. What have you been doing while you have been here, my wicked child?'

The words should have sounded twee and rather silly, like the words of a mock Victorian nanny in an indifferent and poorly-written play, yet on Michiko's lips they had the ring of true authority. Somewhere at the back of

228

Belinda's mind was the memory of what Michiko had described as her profession in the real world. She was an actress, a principal player in a world-famous Japanese theatre troupe, and she was a very fine one, judging by this, an impromptu performance.

'I'm s-sorry,' stammered Belinda as Michiko removed her fingers. The response was automatic; she suddenly even seemed to *feel* remorse. The submissive role had completely engulfed her just as smoothly as the mantle of dominance had been taken on by Michiko.

Belinda hung her head, unable to look her Japanese mistress in the eyes.

'Sorry for what?' A strong hand cupped her jaw, lifting her face again. 'Look at me, little one. Are you not at fault?' Belinda obeyed, meeting ebony eyes that glittered. 'Should you not be punished?'

Again, a portion of Belinda's mind remained rooted in reality and recognised the absurdity of the dynamic that was emerging. She hadn't done anything wrong. In fact, quite the reverse. She had been wanton because it was the spark that André needed –

But another part of her mind acknowledged ritual, theatrics and role-play – all key elements in Michiko's way of thinking. It was clear too that the Japanese woman enjoyed pain and power exchange as a satisfying form of eroticism, perhaps even the one that most fulfilled her, but her civilised mind demanded they be presented in a framework. Hence the sudden appearance of a 'mistress' and her 'penitent'.

Their eyes remained locked for perhaps thirty seconds, during which neither of them smiled or acknowledged any kind of covenant, yet even so Belinda sensed an agreement made. Looking down again, she slowly nodded her head.

'Good girl,' said Michiko softly, her thumb brushing across Belinda's lower lip. 'You will feel so much better.' Her free hand brushed Belinda's hair, ruffling it affectionately as a mother or a sister would. Or perhaps a teacher who was old-fashioned and lovingly stern.

The gesture was sexless, but Belinda's response to it could not have been more different. She felt a wave of delicious languor sweep through her. A melting. A soft, hot weakness that seemed to pool in the pit of her belly. It was as if she had wandered into a dream within a dream, where a new set of rules and responses held sway. Just the lightest touch of her hair could set her body and her sex a-quivering, and the thought of being punished made her heart leap with a strange dark longing.

But I don't like pain, she thought, as Michiko took her by the hand and led her across the uneven stone floor of the chapel. I hate it. I'm a baby; I cry at the slightest thing. What will I do when she actually starts to hit me?

Michiko paused when they reached the area where Belinda supposed the altar had once been, and seemed torn between two possible sites where her desires might be indulged. One was a deep, high-backed oaken pew, standing parallel to the nave; and the other was a heavy, solid-legged table – also of oak – which stood against the outer wall, behind the pew. Nodding her head, Michiko studied first the pew, then the table, then the pew again. She glanced sideways at Belinda, then squeezed her hand.

'Both, I think,' the Japanese whispered, as if she were offering not one gift, but two. Drawing Belinda's quivering hand to her crimson-stained lips, she kissed it once, then gave it another encouraging squeeze. 'Come along, my dear, it's time we got started.'

Releasing Belinda's fingers, Michiko stepped smartly towards the pew, then sat down on it, her long legs manishly spread. Lifting one elegant finger, she made a curling 'come here' gesture, then pointed to a spot a foot or so from where she sat.

Belinda hurried forward but stumbled slightly on the irregular flooring. The slip was barely noticeable and she

230

recovered in an instant, but when she stood before Michiko she couldn't help blushing.

Michiko gave her a look which indicated she had taken note of her clumsiness but was prepared to tolerate it. Slowly, measuredly, the Japanese woman reached out and laid her left hand on Belinda's right hip, then with her right hand she touched Belinda's left nipple. The little crest was hard to start with, and embarrassingly distinct beneath the moulded satin of the dress, but when Michiko's finger settled on it, it puckered even more.

Belinda bit her lip. It was as if an encoded message was passing through the tiny contact – all the information she needed about this and other activities that loomed ahead of her. For a second, she had a wild urge to break away and take to her heels and run, but Michiko's narrow smile seemed to act as a shackle. Belinda could no sooner move than stop breathing in and out.

'This is a very revealing dress, little one,' observed Michiko, taking the nipple in her finger and thumb and twisting it. Her other hand squeezed quite hard on Belinda's hip. 'It's a whore's dress. What could you be thinking of wearing something like this?'

'I-I don't know,' gasped Belinda. Her nipple was hurting now, really hurting, from a combination of being tweaked and the crushing grip itself. Michiko's hands were so slender and graceful that it was hard to believe they could wield such painful force. What on earth else could they do to me? thought Belinda, feeling panicky. Without her being able to control it, her pelvis began to weave.

Why? Why is this happening? She was in pain now, and she still didn't like it; but down below she could feel her sex engorging. She was dripping with desire, but it was *because* she was suffering, not in spite of it. As Michiko pulled her breast outward, like a plump fleshly cone, she whimpered loudly.

231

Immediately, the nipple was released, though the low ache still remained. Still holding her by the hip, Michiko's warrior hand travelled downward until it hovered lightly at Belinda's pubis, then pressed on the thin satin slip and made it cling to her crisp knot of curls.

'The grove of heavenly delights,' intoned Michiko, pushing the shiny fabric inward. Belinda felt her sex-lips part and the pale satin begin to moisten with her juices. There was just a single layer of delicate cloth keeping Michiko's finger from touching her vulva, and she could feel the pad of that finger a bare inch from her clitoris.

'Take the gown off your shoulders,' said Michiko coolly. 'Come on, girl, lower the straps.'

Belinda flinched and obeyed. It felt like a miracle that she could actually move her hands and perform the simple action required of her. The situation, and Michiko's presence, seemed to inflict a paralysis upon her limbs. Flicking the thin the straps of the slip-like dress off her shoulders, she allowed the garment to slide down her body and expose her swollen breasts. With a struggle, she slid her arms out from the straps, leaving her torso naked and the satin rumpled around her hips.

Michiko just looked at her, long and hard, her pressing finger remaining quite motionless in its hazardous position. Belinda seemed to feel the Japanese woman's scrutiny like a strange, liquid ray cruising her body at a slow-motion pace. Her nipples stiffened even more and almost seemed to jump. Despite being exposed to the night air, her body began to sweat. She imagined perspiration forming in visible pools in her armpits, beneath her breasts, and in her groin. Phantom streams of it trickled over her skin and oozed down her flanks like jewelled, betraying rivers.

Suddenly, Michiko withdrew her left hand for a moment and let the bunched satin slip off Belinda's right buttock. The Japanese then grasped the naked lobe and squeezed it firmly, the tips of her fingers digging crudely and suggestively into Belinda's bottom-cleft. The whole weight of the dress now seemed to be hanging from her one probing finger.

Belinda moaned softly, desperately wanting something to happen, but afraid that it would. She no longer moved her hips; she dare not. Michiko's fingertips were so close to her most sensitive zones that the slightest of movements would bring them into contact with bunches of nerve receptors that screamed silently to be triggered.

'Oh please,' she whispered, remembering the same begging situation with André, the same state of being driven almost to madness in need of something.

'Remember what you are begging for,' warned Michiko, palpating the muscles of Belinda bottom-cheek. 'Remember what I want of you – '

'I don't care!' cried Belinda, rocking, and getting the most minuscule of half-nudges against her clitoris. She felt a brief but brilliant shard of sensation, then the hand was withdrawn and her dress slithered to the ground, leaving her bare but for the white stockings she wore gartered at her knees, the only other garments, except her shoes, that she had been provided with.

'Do anything with me! I don't care,' she repeated, waggling her bottom in the Japanese woman's hold. 'I don't care,' she sobbed, her eyes filling with childish tears of thwarted lust.

'As you wish,' said Michiko, her face a mask, her eyes as fierce as supernovae. She released Belinda's buttock. 'Step out of your dress, then let's have you across my knee.'

Belinda stepped clear of the pooled satin around her ankles, then dithered, feeling a wanton in just her stockings. Michiko gave her an intent look and she stepped to one side of the Japanese woman's braced thighs, then with as much grace as she could summon, she went across them.

The pose wasn't as easy to hold as she had expected. Though Michiko's thighs were muscular and firmly braced, Belinda still felt an alarming sense of vertigo.

She felt as if she were falling both literally and figuratively – tipping head-first off Michiko's lap and cartwheeling wildly into a new and frightening world. She was more relieved than she could have imagined when Michiko's left hand settled securingly in the small of her naked back, while the other lightly toyed with her buttocks.

'Hmm ... Nice and firm,' the Japanese murmured. 'Resilient – '

Almost while she was still speaking, the first smart slap landed unannounced.

'Oh God!' shouted Belinda, in total shock.

It felt like a slab of wood had crashed down on her bottom, a seasoned timber that had been pickled to make it harder. After a second of blank whiteness, her right buttock flamed, then almost immediately its twin caught fire too.

Michiko's rhythm was immaculate, each blow timed so that the previous one's impact was given time to fully develop. Crying within thirty seconds, Belinda could not believe how hard the smacks felt, how hard Michiko's hand felt. How stunning and painful a simple spanking could be.

Wriggling and squirming, she felt heat building and building in the muscles of her bottom, and at the same time sinking through into her quim. It was difficult to credit the way the sensations began to blend.

Michiko was really hurting her now, making her suffer far more than she had expected to, yet between her legs, Belinda was slippery and excited. Her brain seemed to be in a state of short circuit somehow, sending all the wrong responses to her breasts and her genitals. She was being hit, punished, belaboured; being made to experience excruciating pain and profound humiliation. But instead of despair, she felt jubilant, elated; her heart soaring with a wild, sweet desire.

'Oh Michiko,' she groaned, lifting her bottom high to meet a slap, then riding down on it to grind her crotch

234

against her mistress's thigh. Each hard blow made her clitoris jump and pulse. 'Oh Michiko, I can't bear it,' she squealed, opening her flailing legs wider so her tormentor could seek out more tender targets.

When her climax finally came, she felt stunned and fought for breath, enduring pleasure waves so powerful she nearly fainted. Her throbbing, blazing bottom and the deep spasms of her vagina seemed to fuse into one huge, amorphous feeling, a fabulous sensation that transcended all description. It was ecstasy; it was pain; it was both of them and better . . . and it seemed to last for hours and hours, yet fade far too quickly.

As her senses wavered, she heard, *Well done, my little one.*

'Is Michiko a lesbian?' asked Jonathan, apropos of nothing.

Of all the questions he could have asked, having heard the bizarre story his companion had just told him, it surprised him that this was the one he had posed. What did it matter which way the Japanese woman's preferences swung? And what difference did it make to their involvement in André's future?

'Sometimes,' said André, staring back at him over the rim of a rounded crystal glass. They were in the library, drinking brandy, while the women walked in the garden. 'And sometimes not. It depends,' he continued, then took a sip of the amber-toned spirit.

Jonathan drank some brandy too, although rather more than the count had done. This was the first occasion that he had spent any length of time with their mysterious host, and the conversation alone would have been enough to drive the most abstemious puritan to the bottle, dealing as it had done with gothic magic and abnormal longevity.

It's more than that though, thought Jonathan, studying the other man. André was sitting at the other end of the

235

leather-upholstered settee, and seemed to be lost in deep, dreamy fugue.

It's *him*, as well, Jonathan told himself. Him, and the weird effect he has on me.

Reaching for the bottle which stood before them on a low table, he sloshed a little more into his glass, then gestured towards André's glass with it.

'Why yes, I will,' said the count, his smile still a little distracted.

Jonathan poured more of the glowing fluid into his companion's glass, wondering as he did so whether it would have the same effect.

Is he still human? Can he even get drunk? he pondered, watching André's throat undulate as he sipped the warming spirit. The count was wearing a loose royal blue silk shirt with a tiny tab collar, and the vibrant colour made his smooth skin appear very pale.

'About Michiko,' he prompted, returning to the subject of the Japanese woman because his thoughts about André von Kastel were too alarming. 'You said "it depends". Depends on what?'

'On how beautiful the other woman is,' said André mildly. 'How spirited. Michiko is a great admirer of physical beauty, but if there's no spark there, no fire of individuality, she's not interested.'

Jonathan sighed. 'I suppose that means she's seducing Belinda right now, even as we speak.'

'Probably,' replied André, his blue eyes so bright that Jonathan couldn't look away. 'Does that bother you?'

Did it? He really didn't know what to say. Or to think. The idea of two women making love was a classic male fantasy, he knew, and it had worked for him well enough in the past – in general terms. But he had never visualised Belinda with another woman. Not even here, when the way she had spoken of her dealings with the two mute girls seemed to suggest that Feltris and Elisa had been as affectionate to her as they had to him.

'I detect that your feelings are ambiguous,' said André,

into the quietness of the big high-ceilinged room. The only sound, apart from the occasional creak of the leather sofa, was their breathing.

Jonathan opened his mouth, but still couldn't seem to form a word.

'The idea of Belinda with another woman is new to you, is it not?' the count continued. 'And puzzling. You wonder why you do not feel more jealous.'

'I-I'm not sure what I – ' Jonathan faltered, swirling his glass then lifting it to his lips, trying desperately to analyse his feelings. About Belinda. About Michiko. About all the strange revelations. About the man with whom he was sitting and drinking; the man who suddenly seemed far closer than he had a moment ago. So close that their thighs were almost touching. So close that he could see the toned shape of the musculature beneath André's tight, faded denims – and the size of the firm bulge at his crotch.

With brandy in his mouth, Jonathan spluttered furiously and felt himself choke and start to cough, his face turning a bright, blushing red. Eyes watering, chest heaving, he felt his brandy glass being removed deftly from his hand, and the impact of a solid, well-placed thump against his back. He coughed again, gratefully this time, and suddenly found he could breath deeply and evenly.

'I'm sorry,' he muttered, wiping his bleary eyes with the sleeve of his shirt. 'Maybe I've had too much to drink.'

'Perhaps you have not yet had enough?' countered André, and Jonathan felt the hand that had struck him stroke his back.

The caress was so light and innocuous it was almost illusory, but coming after the realisation of a moment ago, it made Jonathan start to shake and blush again.

'Here, but drink slowly this time.' André held out the refilled brandy glass. 'Sip by sip.'

When Jonathan took hold of the fat, rounded glass, he

was alarmed to feel André's hand curve around his, lifting the drink to his mouth. The count's skin was extraordinarily cool, yet its very coldness was exotic and exciting, and sent a thrill through Jonathan's shocked body.

I can't feel this! thought Jonathan helplessly, feeling it anyway. He's two hundred years old. I don't know him. Dear God in heaven, he's a man! He's a man! He's a man!

'Sip,' André urged again, his free hand returning to Jonathan's burning back.

Jonathan sipped. Far faster than was wise, but he was desperate for some kind of anaesthesia. He was experiencing something he had never felt before, and something he had never in his wildest dreams or darkest nightmares expected to feel – and the worst part was that it was ravishingly delicious. The brandy seemed to be having no effect on him whatsoever, but as he was allowed to take a breath, André's cologne made his head whirl. It was the smell of roses, and a sharp visceral musk.

'Think of Belinda and Michiko,' whispered the count in his ear. 'Imagine them together.' That long cool hand was still on his back, moving a little, rubbing him through the cotton of his shirt. 'How does that make you feel?'

'I don't know!' cried Jonathan, horrified by the strange sound of his own voice; its shrillness, its girlishness.

'Does the idea of same-sex love repel you?' André's voice was deep now, very masculine and cajoling. 'Surely not.' The final two words were not a question but an observation – and not one about Belinda and Michiko.

I'm being seduced, thought Jonathan. Just as Belinda was, here on this couch. And for all her single-mindedness, all her steadfast resistance of any kind of exploitation, she succumbed to this man within moments of meeting him.

238

'Jonathan?' prompted André gently, his hand still now, and so chilling through Jonathan's lightweight shirt.

'I don't know,' repeated Jonathan, feeling broken apart but somehow strangely resigned. He looked up, staring into the middle distance, intensely aware of the alluring figure beside him yet knowing it was he, himself, who had the choice.

'Look! Get it over with, if you're going to,' he said suddenly, unable to cope with the growing tension any more. If André made a move and it was thoroughly repellent, well, at least he would know. He would know, and he could leap up and flee from the room as fast as his feet would carry him. And if it wasn't? He couldn't know until the moment came.

'It is your choice,' said André quietly, as if he had viewed the brief debate in Jonathan's mind. Maybe he had?

Jonathan turned his face, and found his lips just inches from his companion's. He could smell the brandied sweetness of André's breath, and almost drowned in the aquamarine pools of his eyes.

He's so beautiful, thought Jonathan. He attracts me. I want him. But my body doesn't quite know how I want him. He shuddered, filled with thoughts and fears of buggery. 'I don't know what to do,' he said, his voice extraordinarily small.

'Do not worry,' said André, reaching up and undoing the thong that tied his striated locks back. 'I know what it is we need to know.'

Jonathan bit his lip to restrain a gasp. André's hair was soft, thick and shiny, despite its peculiar coloration. Jonathan felt a strong urge to bury his hands in it.

'Go ahead, do it,' urged André.

His breathing shallow, his heart racing, Jonathan put up his hands and slid them through André's silky tresses until he was cradling the other man's head. He watched André's lips part, almost in ecstasy, revealing the soft rosy interior of his mouth. Without thinking, Jonathan lunged forward and kissed him.

It's just like kissing a woman, he thought, feeling André's strong, slender arms come around him. The sensations were the same: velvety lips under his, parting provocatively and admitting his tongue. He was so used to kissing like a man – probing strongly and taking the initiative – that he continued to do so, while André seemed perfectly happy to let him, relaxing back on to the settee and drawing him down.

'Mmmm ...' murmured the count as they broke apart for a moment, and he reached up to touch Jonathan's chin. 'Not so bad, is it?' He smiled, then took Jonathan's hand, from where it still held his head, and turned his face so he could moistly kiss its palm.

'No ... no, it isn't,' stammered Jonathan, disconcerted as André surged up against him, kissed him again, actively this time, and at the same time began unfastening his shirt buttons. Before he knew it, the garment was open to the waist and the loose tails pulled out, then André was shimmying along beneath him and sucking at his nipple. He felt the count's teeth close wickedly and he groaned.

Jonathan had always had sensitive nipples and loved to have them played with and nibbled. For a moment, he thought of Belinda and how beautifully she did this for him, but the next instant he was dragged back to reality, his body excited by the extra layer of piquancy that having a man's mouth on him created.

The pair of them rocked and wrestled. Jonathan on top, his hands rubbing and stroking at every bit of his partner he could reach; André beneath, holding tight, his teeth still nipping. As he wriggled and struggled and cried out in excitement, Jonathan was embarrassingly aware of his erection. It was as big and hard as it had ever been before, and it was poking André somewhere in his mid-section. The count too was erect, his organ pressed against the side of Jonathan's leg. His bulge felt enormous, even through two layers of denim, and wriggling faster, Jonathan wondered what it looked like. Would it be smooth or veined? Circumcised or uncut? Would it be long and thin, or shorter, but very thick?

Exhibiting, once again, the telepathic ability that Jonathan suspected him of, the count suddenly slithered out of the peculiar clinch and got to his feet.

'Let us make ourselves comfortable,' he said, with a playful little grin that almost reminded Jonathan of Belinda. What a conundrum the man was; one minute he was the archetypal alpha male, all effortless command, and the next, he was more feminine, more languorous. The weird contrast was confusing but still attractive. Jonathan watched, rapt, as André first unbuttoned his shirt, flicking the tails out of his waistband, and then, standing elegantly on one leg, then the other, removed his boots. He wore no socks, and when he had unbuckled his belt and unfastened his jeans, then removed them, Jonathan discovered he wore no underpants either, and his penis was both sizeable and rigidly hard.

'Now you,' said the count quietly, still wearing his lustrous blue shirt.

Nervous, embarrassed, yet excited too, Jonathan began the same procedure. He was convinced he could not get his clothes off with the same graceful ease that André had, but nevertheless he tried, and was rewarded with an encouraging smile. Off came his trainers and his socks, then his belt and his jeans, and finally he slid down his boxer shorts and kicked them away from him.

André said nothing, but regarded him steadily for a few moments, his frank gaze ultimately settling below the waist.

Jonathan felt himself blushing again, all over, and his penis growing so rigid that it hurt him. He knew his body was reasonable, and he had never had any complaints from the women he had made love to, but beside this male lover he began to feel inferior.

After what seemed like a lifetime, André spoke. 'You have a handsome body, Jonathan. Strong. Straight. And very manly. It is no wonder that a woman like Belinda chooses to be with you.'

Still speechless, Jonathan stood like a statue, too timid now to move forward. With a gentle smile, the count moved towards him.

'No need to be scared,' he whispered, wrapping Jonathan in his arms and pressing his cool, smooth body to Jonathan's warm and sweaty one. 'No need at all,' he said, guiding him back towards the couch.

Then, as they settled down on to the leather, their limbs entwining, their sexes duelling, it dawned on Jonathan that his strange new friend was right.

He sighed contentedly. He wasn't scared at all.

Chapter 14
Preparations for Departure

'*H*e didn't fuck me,' said Jonathan, his voice solemn in the shadows. 'And I didn't fuck him. I didn't seem to need to.'

Belinda touched his arm reassuringly. It must have cost Jonathan a lot to reveal what had happened between him and André. Men were touchy about their masculinity, and Jonathan was as much a man as any other. To admit to a homosexual tryst was a major catharsis.

'What did you do?' she asked quietly, glad for him that it was night and that the darkness was dense.

It had been after midnight when she had left the chapel with Michiko, and a strange cloudiness had passed across the sky. She had felt tender as they walked through the garden towards the priory; her bottom had been glowing from the spanking she had received, but she had been filled with another radiance too. A glow of satisfaction. The nurturing of a special secret. The knowledge that she had followed a hitherto untrodden path – with yet another charismatic new lover – and that despite the pain, she had loved every second of it!

She had also been hoping that Jonathan would come to her, so she could tell him about it; and here he was, with his own tale to tell, which was equally wild.

'He took me in his arms,' her boyfriend said, sliding his own arm around her shoulder and drawing her close. Belinda rested a hand on his chest and felt his heart beating furiously within. 'He kissed me and touched me and I kissed and touched him. It wasn't a lot different to the things we do together–' He paused and seemed to ponder a second '–up to a point.'

'And then?'

Belinda could feel the heat of Jonathan's blush; his chest was hot beneath her face. 'He rubbed me until I came. Then he put my hand on his ... his cock and sort of rocked against me until he came too.' He halted again, and Belinda sensed awe in him now and not a little fear. 'It was cold, Lindi ... Like his skin. Cold and sort of thin; not like ordinary semen at all.' Belinda reached for his hand, and squeezed it tightly. 'That was when I really believed him. About what he is. It never really sank in until I felt that weird, cold stuff trickling over me.'

She had been going to tell him about Michiko and the spanking, but now it seemed they could no longer avoid the bigger, more dangerous issue. The strange service that she alone could perform for André and Arabelle.

'Are you going to do it?' Jonathan asked, as if the tenor of his thoughts had altered too.

Although she paused for a while, as if considering her answer, Belinda had already made her decision. She had made it quite some time ago, she realised. When she had first seen André asleep in the tower room, she had felt a strange bond with him. Perhaps even before that, when she had been caught in the thunderstorm with Jonathan and had sensed another presence observing them. She wasn't sure if she believed in fate and destiny and events being mysteriously preordained, but somehow she had known right from the beginning that her life and André von Kastel's were entangled.

'Yes, I am,' she said at last.

'It's dangerous,' said Jonathan, his arm enclosing her

244

tighter. 'If what André told me is correct, there's a chance that you might die too.'

His voice was even, resigned, lacking argument; and Belinda was aware that Jonathan had not only accepted her decision, but was glad of it. She smiled. How clever André was. By making love with Jonathan, he had bound him to the cause too – quashed his objections with the power of affection.

'I know,' she said calmly, 'but I have no choice. I can't bear to think of them going on for centuries and centuries like that. So near, but apart. Loving each other, wanting each other, but unable to do anything about it.'

'I certainly couldn't cope with it,' said Jonathan. 'If it were you and me, I would've gone mad.'

For a moment, Belinda forgot the plight of André and Arabelle. Jonathan had spoken spontaneously, without thinking, and revealed feelings for her that were deep and all-encompassing – feelings she suddenly realised she shared. They had had their troubles – only weeks before this holiday they had even discussed splitting up – but the thought of losing him now was suddenly appalling, as much if not more than the thought of losing her life altogether.

Lost for words, she struggled in his hold, then scooted upward, pressing her lips against his jaw, then his mouth. Despite everything that had happened in the last two days, despite her still smarting bottom that reminded her of pleasure at the hands of Michiko, despite even her fear of what was to come and the very real possibility of death, she wanted desperately to express her love for Jonathan now. Right now. She wanted, no, needed to let him know, while she was still able, that she shared his deep but unarticulated emotion. That she loved him as much as he loved her.

As his tongue entered her mouth, she felt his body harden against her. Embracing him tightly, she knew that it wasn't yet too late.

* * *

'It must be tomorrow night,' said Michiko, pacing the tower room, something André had observed she always did while thinking and planning.

'So soon?' he said, feeling a frisson of jumbled anticipation.

'Yes, it is imperative,' said Michiko, smoothing the voluminous sleeve of the thin green kimono she now wore in readiness. 'I sense her. I feel her approach.'

André watched her shudder, feeling the same revulsion himself, and more than that, a blank, all-consuming rage. Time after time, he had eluded Isidora, knowing she had the power to enslave him for ever if she came close enough, but now the tables were finally beginning to turn. With the help of Belinda, Michiko, and even Jonathan, he had the power to destroy her, and to be free; but if she perceived that fact she could well unmake his plans.

'Would that my powers were as sensitive as yours,' he said, rising and wrapping his own robe around him. 'Then perhaps I would not have had so many perilous moments in the past. Do you believe she already knows what we intend to do?'

'No, I think not,' replied Michiko, pausing in her circuit and moving towards André. 'Remember, her psychic powers are incomplete.' She took his hands and smiled at him. She was reassuring him, for which he almost loved her. 'She can sense your consciousness over great distances but she cannot read your mind. Or any other.' Her dark eyes narrowed conspiratorially. 'And even if she has employed some new spell and gained the ability to read thoughts, I know a stronger spell to counteract that. I can protect all the minds beneath this roof.'

'What would we do without you, my dear friend?' said André, smiling at Michiko, then glancing towards Belle's glowing box.

'You would find ways to prevail, my lord,' replied Michiko pertly, giving his fingers a fierce squeeze that

246

made him yelp. 'Now come, we have much work before us! And when dawn comes, you will be no help at all!'

There was a great deal of apparatus set up on his workbench – burners, flasks of various shapes, pipettes, a pestle and mortar, earthenware vessels and several thuribles. And the great black grimoire lay open at the fateful page.

'First things first,' André said, smiling at Michiko and feeling focused now the work was in hand. Picking up a white linen handkerchief, he unfolded it, then plucked from its smooth white surface a single red hair about four inches long – which Feltris had deftly retrieved from among Belinda's clothing. This André placed on a thurible, then tugged a single hair from his own scalp to join the red one.

Next he strode to the night-table beside his bed and picked up a small rosewood casket, decorated in the same style as Arabelle's refuge, but smaller, and from this he took another single hair – one strand from the long coiled lock that lay within. It was as red as Belinda's, almost exactly the same shade, but in this case approximately three feet in length. Twirling it around his finger, he pressed his lips against it with reverence. 'All that I have of you,' he murmured, letting Arabelle's strand of hair uncoil, then carrying it across and adding it to the others in the thurible. As he lit a taper, he felt Michiko touch his arm.

'Soon you will be with her, my lord,' the Japanese woman whispered, as they watched the three strands burn to minuscule ashes.

'There have been times when I believed I would never make these preparations,' he said thoughtfully, stirring the charred mixture with a small glass rod and then tipping it into a fresh vessel. Although he knew this ultimate enchantment by heart, having spent many hours – during his last wakeful period – learning it in readiness, he consulted the grimoire to affirm the next step.

247

Hallowed water from the underground stream that ran beneath the chapel, this time lovingly distilled for him by the ever-faithful Oren, was placed in an open-necked glass flask and set to heat over a burner, ready to receive the rest of the ingredients of the potion.

In other containers, Michiko was mixing components of the complex, many-faceted elixir. Herbs: bettony, agrimony, cedar. Spices; nutmeg, cloves. The magic poisons: belladonna, azarnet and mercury – the monarch among metals. Each mixture was stirred with its own particular pattern – here a square, here a triangle, here a hexagram – and as both the magicians worked, each of them chanted in accord with their beliefs. André called on the Christian trinity of his upbringing, and then on other patrons he had come to understand later. Hecate, the queen of the spirits. Hermes Trismegistus, the mediaeval god of alchemy. Beneficent Isis, the matriarchal goddess of the Ancient Egyptians. The good offices of all these would aid his cause.

As he chanted, he was aware, too, of Michiko's liturgical murmurings. André understood very little of her native language, but he knew that for her part she would be calling on the air spirits, the *kami* of the sky and the heavens beyond, who would also wield their forces to assist him.

Finally, when all the separate conglomerations were prepared, it was time for the final combining. 'Be as one,' whispered André as each vessel yielded up its contents into the flask. 'Be as one that she and I may be as one.'

The resulting melange was dark and murky, an indeterminate mud-like dark brown. André agitated it carefully with the point of his black-handled dagger, stirring in all the magic symbols that he had used with each ingredient, while repeating the appropriate chant with each separate shape. Beside him Michiko whispered in Japanese. The last step was to apply a flame to heat the flask.

Slowly, very slowly, as the contents became tepid,

then warm, then hot, a startling transformation took place within the vessel. What had been a dirty, odiferous blend of disparate constituents very gradually took on a hue of beauty, and by the time it was bubbling steadily it had changed nature completely. Within the glass now there was a clear, jewel-like liquid of the most intense lapis blue – the same brilliant colour as André's own eyes in the mirror.

'It is ready,' he said quietly to Michiko, as they both gazed at the contents of the flask. He was glad that they had achieved the transmutation so successfully, but he still felt a slight pang of uneasiness. Although it had not been precisely this mixture that Isidora had added to his wine that fateful night two hundred years ago, what he had before him now was only a variant of the potion that had damned him.

'It will not work unless you believe that it will, my lord,' said Michiko softly from beside him. 'Your faith is the most potent of all ingredients.' She slid her slender arm around his waist, beneath his robe, and gave him a squeeze.

'I hope you are right,' he replied, still gazing at the enigmatic fluid.

'Of course I'm right.' Michiko's voice was confident but tender, and her slender fingertips slid down across his hip. 'And now, my lord, I am going to make love to you.' Her hand cupped the muscled curve of his buttock. ' – because this could well be the last chance we'll ever have.'

Realising she was right, André turned to her, his throat choked at the finality of her words. He would miss his old friend – miss her spirit and her loveliness – and he would miss the closeness that their strange condition had forged in them. Opening the folds of her kimono, he pressed her naked body to him, then brought his lips down on her mouth in a long kiss.

Her face was wet, but were they her tears or his?

* * *

249

The sun was high in the sky when Belinda woke.

Shifting Jonathan's arm from across her body, she slid as quietly as she could from the bed and padded to the window, naked. The grounds and the garden looked as ordinary as they had looked at any time during their short stay at the priory, but what caught her eye was an express delivery van trundling along the drive towards the house. It was the first real sign she had seen of an interaction taking place between the inhabitants of this strange place and the outside world – but instead of reassuring her, it made her feel nervous.

The problem was, while she was completely cut off from her everyday life, with its patterns and its artefacts, she could believe in things like magic, extreme longevity and discarnate spirits trapped in bottles. But when evidence of the commonplace and the mundane presented itself, the veracity of the supernatural world wavered. And when she thought of what she had done – and what she might do – she felt ridiculous. And frightened.

As the delivery van pulled up outside the house, she saw Michiko and Oren walk down the steps to meet it. The driver opened the back and pulled out several large white cardboard cartons – which Oren took and carried back inside – then proffered a clipboard, which Michiko signed. The whole transaction was so utterly unremarkable that when the van sped away, Belinda wondered whether she had dreamed it. That was until Michiko looked upward and gave a wave.

As Belinda waved back, the Japanese smiled broadly and blew a kiss.

'Who were you waving at?' enquired the waking Jonathan, when Belinda stepped away from the window after Michiko had gone inside.

'Michiko. She was outside. Taking delivery of some packages.'

Jonathan said nothing, but climbed out of bed and wandered towards the sideboard, on which – Belinda noticed for the first time – was a tray containing their breakfast.

'This looks nice,' he said, lifting an immaculate white napkin. 'Brioches, butter, preserves.' He flipped up the lid of an insulated jug. 'Mmmm. Fresh coffee! Just what I need!'

A few moments later they were both sitting cross-legged on the bed, tucking into the food, with big white French coffee cups balanced precariously on the bed beside them.

'What do you suppose everyone is doing now?' said Jonathan, chewing. He had brioche crumbs in his sparse, dark chest hair, Belinda noticed, and she smiled. He had never looked younger or more appealing.

'Well, as I understand it, André will be sleeping,' she said thoughtfully, breaking off a piece of her own brioche and popping it in her mouth. 'But Michiko and the others could well be getting things ready for tonight. Those boxes might be something to do with it.'

'Tonight?' Jonathan looked quite shocked, and his cup trembled in his hand as he conveyed it to his lips, letting a little of his milky coffee drip on to the sheet. 'How do you know it'll be tonight?'

How *did* she know?

Belinda was surprised at the certainty of her own intuition. She had not been told when the freeing ritual would take place, but she couldn't shake the powerful feeling that it was scheduled for tonight. Had Michiko imparted the knowledge to her subconscious somehow? Anything was possible given the Japanese woman's esoteric talents.

'I just know,' she said quietly.

Jonathan studied the coffee stain, jabbing at it with his fingers. 'Oh God, I just thought of something,' he said, looking up again. 'We've told Paula to come. She'll probably arrive today. What are we going to do with her? Tonight? She'll probably expect us to stop up until

251

the small hours, drinking and talking. I mean, that's what we've always done before, isn't it?'

Belinda saw the problem, and just as quickly the answer. The coolness of her own logic astounded her. 'You'll just have to keep her occupied on your own then, Johnny, won't you?' She looked at him levelly, willing him to comprehend her.

Jonathan frowned, and she knew he had got the message.

'She's always fancied you. It'll be easy.'

'But . . . won't you mind?'

Belinda considered the idea. 'If you'd asked me a few days ago, yes, I would have minded,' she said, musing on the way she and Jonathan had progressed. 'But things have changed.' Ignoring the cups and the tray, she reached out and laid her hand on his thigh. '*We've* changed.' She squeezed his wiry but muscular flesh. 'We've both had sex with other partners, but it hasn't split us up, has it?' She saw him nod then smile sheepishly. 'And there's a higher purpose behind it this time. Something important.' She grinned back at him. 'You'll just have to close your eyes and do it for the cause!'

'I suppose I can force myself,' said Jonathan, laughing now. He leant forward to retrieve the cups and plates and all the other remnants of their breakfast, then put the lot in a semblance of tidiness on the tray. 'But I'll have to be prepared.' His eyes gleaming, he slid off the bed, scooped up the tray, then put it out of harm's way before climbing back on to the bed again. 'I might need some practice,' he said in mock-thoughtfulness, as he reached for her. 'Do you think we could have a quick run-through now?'

Opening her legs and tumbling backwards, she said, 'Of course.'

Smiling with satisfaction, Isidora Katori rose from the rumpled hotel bed and stretched the kinks from her slender, shapely limbs. It was already late in the day, and she had to move.

Walking naked to the dressing table, she spared only the briefest glance towards the figure who still lay deeply sleeping. Her victim, who would now stay in a coma for three or four days.

It had been quite easy to pick up this 'Paula' in the pub garden where she had found her, then the simplest of child's play to flatter her and seduce her. With a few drinks and a little assistance from an aphrodisiac, the poor thing had almost believed that she was a closet lesbian and that she had been waiting for Isidora all her life.

Smoothing her hands over her voluptuous curves, Isidora had to admit she had enjoyed such an innocent passion. Bewitched and rendered insatiable by a few drops of the special tincture, love-struck Paula had been touchingly grateful for her orgasms, and most anxious to repay for them in kind. They had stayed in bed together for far longer than Isidora had planned on, and now it was afternoon and high time she was leaving.

Even so, she took a moment to study her face.

Paula Beckett was pretty enough, Isidora supposed, lifting her fingers to touch the features that were now hers. The girl wasn't stunning nor really beautiful, but her face would be quite passable for a limited period. The best thing about Paula's appearance was that it was sufficiently similar-looking – in general terms – to Isidora's own, and could be copied quite well enough to fool observers.

What she was seeing now, Isidora knew, turning her head this way and that, was a clever psychic projection, a mental mask that would fool any person without special powers. And it would fool André von Kastel until it was too late for him to flee.

Isidora smiled again, watching the curve of her unfamiliar lips and finding them pleasing.

'I will have you, André von Kastel,' she whispered,

trying her borrowed voice for the first time out loud. 'And this time I'll finish what I started. This time there will be no chance for escape . . . and I'll destroy that red-haired milksop bitch of yours completely.' She laughed Paula Beckett's laugh, and found it light but acceptable. 'Before this day is out, André, you will be mine for good and all.'

It was afternoon before Belinda and Jonathan rose, and even then a strange lethargy hung over them.

At first, Belinda felt nervous, thinking she should be doing something, making preparations of some kind, or even just finding Michiko and discovering more of what might happen to her, but it wasn't long before she felt too dreamy to care. After Jonathan had gone to his room to dress, she took a long and leisurely shower, then dressed slowly in the clothing that had been left for her – another shift-like petticoat in the flounced Edwardian style.

When she left her room, she was torn between going to the library and trying to seek out background reading on the ritual that lay ahead of her, or going out on to the terrace to enjoy the sun. She knew that anyone in their right mind would choose the library and 'preparedness', yet somehow she couldn't seem to make that choice. Her head felt light but in a rather amenable way, and all she wanted to do was just relax and float along.

On the terrace, it seemed that someone had anticipated her decision, or perhaps even initiated it. In addition to the table where she had breakfasted the day before under the sunshade, there were also now two surprisingly modern loungers. And on one of these, she found Jonathan half-reclining, his attention already embroiled in a charcoal sketch. His fingers were smudgy and he was naked apart from his shorts.

'So?' she said, sinking down on to the adjoining lounger and arranging her skirt so she could get the sun on her legs. 'Is anything happening? Have you seen Michiko? Or the mutes?'

'Oren was here a minute or two ago,' Jonathan replied, setting aside his drawing pad and wiping his sooty fingers down the side of his shorts, 'and I think he asked me if I wanted a cool drink, but I'm not quite sure.' He shrugged and put up a hand to shield his eyes from the sun. 'Anyway, whatever it was I told him yes ... and make it two.'

'Lovely,' said Belinda, seeing the image of a tall cold cocktail, and feeling thirsty. 'But what about the others?'

'They seem to be busy, apart from André, that is.' He blushed a little at the name of the man he had made love with. 'I keep seeing them taking things over to that ruined building over there.' He nodded in the direction of the chapel.

'What sort of things?'

'Armfuls of flowers ... What looked like rugs or something ... Books, wooden boxes ... All sorts of stuff.' He frowned slightly, as if the list of paraphernalia troubled him. 'I suppose that's where it's all going to happen, isn't it?'

'I believe so,' she replied quietly, feeling fear stir in her mind then quickly subside again. 'It's funny, I still can't seem to get my head around it.' She paused, wondering how to explain herself. 'I know I should be worried. Scared stiff. But I'm not.'

'Perhaps there isn't anything to be scared of,' said Jonathan, touching her arm and leaving a smear of black on her skin. 'Michiko seems very capable. Very organised.' He grinned. 'I don't know. I know she looks a bit exotic, but she acts like a businesswoman. A high-powered motivator or something. She seems too real somehow to be a witch!'

'Oh, she's real all right,' murmured Belinda ruefully, her fingers settling suddenly on her flank. The soreness in her bottom had disappeared quite miraculously, but she could still remember the impact of being spanked.

Jonathan eyed her with sudden interest. 'You never did tell me what happened with her last night,' he said, his voice full of curiosity. 'I'm not the only one who learned something new, am I?'

'No, you're not,' admitted Belinda. 'I had a lesson of sorts too.'

It was on the tip of her tongue to describe the whole incident, but just then Oren appeared in the doorway to the house, and he walked towards them, carrying a loaded tray. When he reached them, he nodded politely and set it down.

'Oh Oren, this looks wonderful!' cried Belinda, with feeling. The tray contained a tall jug full of some reddish Pimms-like concoction, complete with tiny fruit pieces bobbing on the surface. There was an insulated ice container – not the bucket that she had seen in the library, she noticed – and beside it a couple of heavy crystal glasses. Also on the tray were several bowls of savoury nibbles: tiny cheese biscuits, potato chiplets, salted nuts. One final item was not immediately identifiable: an alabaster jar with a fat cork in its neck.

As Belinda sat up in anticipation, Oren poured the fruity cocktail into the two glasses, then added several rocks of ice to each one. Belinda took a sip of her drink as soon as he handed it to her, and gasped at both its deliciousness and potency.

'Phew!' she said, then sampled it again, trying to analyse what made the taste so special. It was similar to many of the kinds of fruit cup or punch she had tried before, but with a pungent aftertang that was totally unfamiliar.

It's drugged somehow, she thought, setting the glass down. It's either full of aphrodisiac or it's to prepare me for tonight. After a moment's thought she settled on the former; if the same drink was being served to both her and Jonathan, its effects weren't specifically for her.

A model of efficient service as ever, Oren set the jug and the tray of food down between the two loungers so

256

it was in easy reach for later. He also set down the alabaster jar, and when Belinda frowned doubtfully at it, he gestured upward towards the hot afternoon sun, then made a rubbing motion along his bare arm.

'Sunscreen?' she queried, and the tall man nodded, then gestured again towards her own bare legs, and crouched down to retrieve the chunky jar. He tilted his head questioningly, then tapped his chest.

'No, it's OK, Oren, I can manage,' she said, putting her hand up for the jar.

Oren smiled amiably and gave it to her, clearly not offended that his services weren't required, then nodded briefly and turned, leaving Belinda alone once more with Jonathan.

'Tactful, isn't he?' observed Jonathan, reaching for his drink and taking a long swig. Belinda watched his eyes light up as he savoured its effects. 'Wow!' was his only comment as he set the glass down again, before picking up his sketch-pad and stick of charcoal. After drawing a line or two, and then smudging them, he looked up at Belinda and prompted, 'You were going to tell me what it was you learnt last night.'

Unable to look him in the eye, Belinda picked up the jar, twisted off the lid and stuck a finger into the soft, cream-coloured substance within. It had a slick texture and a sharp but very pleasant, vaguely citrus smell. When she daubed it on to her calf, it felt cool.

'Lindi!' shouted Jonathan playfully.

Slowly, and in as much detail as she could bring herself to go into, she described her painful tryst in the chapel with Michiko. As she spoke, she smoothed the sun balm on to her lower legs and thighs, the sensuous movement complementing the eroticism of her account. Pausing for a moment to admire the glistening sheen on her skin, Belinda seemed to remember her spanking even more vividly than she had earlier. Her bottom, although it showed no sign of what had happened, and had ceased to hurt quite some time ago, started to tingle again, as if her flesh had a separate memory of its own. She could almost feel hands gliding over it then crashing down with a remorseless, fiery force.

'It was painful,' she conceded, dipping her fingers into the jar again, and beginning to work the cream over her shoulders, 'but it was erotic too. I wouldn't have believed how much.' She paused, switched hands, began creaming her other shoulder, then spread the cream in a thin film down her arm. 'I – I had several orgasms.'

Jonathan set his glass down with a clatter and poured in more fruit cup, sploshing quite a bit of it over the side.

'Jesus,' he murmured, then took a long, long drink, his eyes unfocused as if he were seeing the picture she had just painted.

Belinda smiled, seeing the bulge in his soft jersey shorts. Men were so easily excited, and clearly he was responding to both of the two classic fantasies she had outlined for him: lesbian love-making and a girl's bottom being spanked.

Not that her account and her memories hadn't stirred her too. She felt lightly aroused, but not uncomfortably so. Her whole body felt warm and sensitised and it was a condition she did not dislike being in for its own sake, rather than a prelude to something more powerful and more passionate. As she watched Jonathan shift uncomfortably on the lounger, trying to find ease for his engorged penis, she had a sudden revelation of quite extraordinarily startling clarity.

Although it sounded rather silly when framed into words, she knew she had to 'save herself'; to conserve the sexual energy and the desire within her so that tonight she would be ready for, and want, André. The ritual demanded a willing partner, and more than that, it needed her to genuinely need and care for him. If she satisfied a simple and fairly low-key bodily itch with Jonathan now, she could destroy the last hopes of two desperate people later. It was not too much to ask of herself, she decided, letting her fingers drift dismissively across her crotch.

But that didn't mean Jonathan had to suffer.

Rising gracefully from her lounger, Belinda took the couple of steps it required to stand before him, then sank on to her knees, her floaty skirt drifting out around her. Jonathan watched her over the rim of his glass, his eyes filled half with lust, half with awe, as he sipped nervously at the ruddy fruit-filled cocktail.

With a confidence that felt new to her, Belinda took the glass from him and set it aside. He started to protest but she laid a finger across his lips and he subsided, then obediently lifted his bottom when she reached for the waistband of his shorts.

His penis sprang up bouncily as she slid down the garment; a column of hungry flesh, prime and vigorous.

'Belinda!' he moaned almost querulously as she cupped his balls in one hand and with the other delicately enclosed his straining shaft.

'Shush!' she said, then settled her lips around his glans.

259

Chapter 15

The Freeing

*B*elinda stared at her reflection in the mirror, already feeling her identity start to blur. The soft, periwinkle-blue dress she wore couldn't actually be Arabelle's, she knew that, but instinct told her it was a good facsimile.

'It's no wonder he misses her,' said Jonathan, moving up behind her and slipping his hands around her waist. 'If she looked like you she must have been very beautiful indeed.'

She met his eyes in the mirror. 'Thank you, Johnny.'

'My pleasure,' he murmured, smiling shyly. 'It's true.'

She put her hands over his. 'I'm scared.'

'I know.' His smile turned to a small frown.

'But I can't back out. He may never find anyone else who can do it. You understand that, don't you?'

'Yes. Yes, I do,' he replied, his fingers flexing against her waist. 'And I want you to help him ... them. If there was anything I could do myself I'd do it. I just wish it wasn't so dangerous for you!'

Belinda was about to reassure him, to lie to him, but just then there was a sharp rap at the door, and before they had time to react, Michiko swept into the room, an expression of concern on her face. She was wearing what looked like a sumptuously elaborate kimono, which she hadn't had time yet to fasten, and on her feet were bifurcated white socks. Her elegant Oriental face was heavily painted in purest white, her lips were crimson, and her eyes were lined with black.

'She's coming!' she cried, hurrying towards them, her steps silent in her socks. 'We must be ready. And Jonathan, you must help us!'

'What do you mean?' demanded Belinda, feeling Jonathan's embracing hands drop away. 'Who's coming? What's the matter?'

The Japanese woman reached out, took each of them by the hand, and squeezed hard. Her eyes were burning coals in her whitened face. 'Isidora is on her way here. I sensed her. I think she may well arrive within the hour.'

'Can't we just lock the gates or something? Or lock the house itself?' suggested Jonathan. 'What about Oren, can't he stop her? He's big enough.'

'Poor Oren is helpless against her powers,' said the Japanese woman. 'He would surrender his life to protect André, but it would do no good. Isidora would find some way around him.' She squeezed Belinda's hand again, then released it, taking hold of both of Jonathan's hands. 'You, on the other hand, I can protect. And you must act as a diversion while we complete the rite.'

'Why would she take any notice of me?' demanded Jonathan. Belinda saw doubt in his face, and real fear. It was clear he now believed completely in the supernatural.

'Because she is approaching in disguise. I was able to catch a glimpse of her mind without her detecting me,' said Michiko intently. 'She is using subterfuge. Hoping to get close enough to André to act, before anyone even realises she's here, and she knows her new face is welcome at the priory, because she has an invitation!'

Belinda had a horrible thought. She remembered a phone conversation, just yesterday. 'Paula!'

'Is that your friend?'

'Yes,' said Jonathan, speaking up while Belinda considered exactly what they had done. They had created a loophole for André's worst enemy to sneak up on him. 'But what has she done with our Paula, the real one?' Jonathan demanded.

'Put her to sleep for a while,' answered Michiko, her smooth brow puckering. 'I think. I didn't seem to sense anything that indicated permanent harm.'

'Dear God,' whispered Belinda, letting out the breath she hadn't realised she was holding.

'But what can I do?' demanded Jonathan. 'I don't have any special powers.'

'You have your manly charms,' observed Michiko, her fine eyebrows quirking with wry humour. 'If there's one thing that we know Isidora delights in, it's to steal another woman's lover. She simply can't resist it.'

'But how will she know?' persisted Jonathan, looking down at his hands which Michiko still held.

'She's not a mind reader,' said the Japanese, releasing him with an encouraging little shake, 'but she's an expert at making people say more than they want to. She uses her persuasive powers. Drugs. Flattery. Her body.' She smiled narrowly. 'She will know a great deal about you two and your relationship.' Suddenly, although it was well nigh impossible, Michiko seemed to blanch beneath her make-up. 'Your friend ... Would she have carried any photographs of you with her? Any image of any kind?'

Belinda considered. 'Not to my knowledge,' she said, desperately trying to remember the last time she and Jonathan had been photographed. 'Why?'

'If Isidora realises how like Arabelle you are, she will stop at nothing to destroy you, as well as Arabelle's vial.' Michiko clenched her hands together, clearly thinking and scheming. 'She knows about the ritual of the freeing. Even though André has her grimoire. It's not something she's likely to overlook.'

'Look, I'm almost certain she won't have any snaps of us,' offered Jonathan hopefully.

'And if she does,' Belinda continued for him, trying to rationalise even though it wasn't easy, 'it'll be pictures of you, Johnny boy, not me.' She flashed him a reassuring grin. '*You're* the one she fancies!'

'Really?' said Jonathan, momentarily distracted.

'Good! Excellent!' said Michiko, her voice suddenly strong and resonant. 'If Isidora knows there's a relationship to be split up, then she will be interested in you, Jonathan. Would you be prepared to have sex with her? As a distraction?'

Jonathan went very pink and Belinda didn't know whether to laugh or protest. The whole situation suddenly seemed to her like a kind of black, or deeply gothic blue, comedy, and she looked from her boyfriend to Michiko and back again.

'It seems only fair,' she observed, her lips shaping themselves without her permission into a grin. 'I get to make love with a sorcerer, and you get a sorceress.'

'I – I don't know if I'll be able to get it up,' said Jonathan, his face so serious that Belinda did laugh. Michiko too.

'Your friend, Paula, are you attracted to her?' enquired the Japanese woman frankly.

Belinda listened carefully for the answer, but Jonathan said, 'She's quite attractive, but I've never really thought of her as fanciable . . . Not really.'

'I think you will find her a good deal more "fanciable" tonight, my young friend,' said Michiko, eyeing him. 'Isidora's powers of seduction are prodigious . . . I don't even think a change of face will cramp her style.'

He's here! He's here somewhere, thought Isidora, slamming the door of the car she had purloined along with Paula Beckett's face.

Glancing towards the house before her, which seemed to brood in the soft amber twilight, she could sense the presence of André all around her. She could already feel the delicious thrill of conquest, a sensation so erotic it

263

almost made her knees go weak. Or it would have done so if she had been other than what she was. Her quarry – so long pursued – was almost hers for the taking, and if she had felt like it she could have sought him out immediately. But it was so much more satisfying to savour the dénouement, to stretch it out, and make the most of the build-up.

As she walked determinedly across the gravel, a young man appeared at the top of the steps. She had never seen him before, but all the laws of probability pointed to him being Jonathan – the one a slightly drugged and very drunk Paula had admitted she was half in love with. Totally confident, Isidora called out to him. 'Jonathan! Hello!'

The young man's smile seemed a little guarded as he came down the steps, and in the few seconds before he reached her, Isidora studied him.

Was something wrong? Did he know something?

'Hi! So you found us all right,' he said. 'I was a bit worried with it being so late.' After a moment's hesitation, he slid his arm around her. 'Boy, am I glad you're here!'

'I'm glad to be here,' replied Isidora, rather liking the feel of his arm. She had not expected much of the gullible Paula's most likely just as gullible friends, and had been prepared to simply brush them aside now she was here. But this dark, wiry youth was quite tempting. A toothsome morsel she could toy with while anticipating her triumph.

'Where's Belinda?' she asked, as Jonathan led her up the stairs, his arm still around her. 'I thought she'd be here to meet me too.'

'God knows!' he replied, sounding cross. 'She said she had a headache and she wanted to lie down. But ... well ...' He faltered, his face tight.

'What is it?' demanded Isidora, stopping in what was a most impressive hall, with – she noted gleefully – several portraits of her prey upon its walls. 'Something wrong between you?' She reviewed her memory for things Paula had said. 'The holiday spirit not bringing you together after all?'

The young man appeared to hesitate, then his words tumbled out in a jerky rush. 'I – I've been really exhausted since we got here ... I think I was ill or something, and I slept a lot. And I thought Lindi was taking it easy too, but it turned out she wasn't.' His expression looked set, and his rather seductive mouth was tense. 'She was ... She was ... Bloody hell, I think she's been playing around with this fucking André ... this Count Whotsit ... Our oh so gracious, oh so generous host!'

'Oh, that's awful!' exclaimed Isidora, putting her arm around him, her loins almost melting with pure delight. 'How could she? You poor thing!'

It was too delicious. Dissent in the camp. Perhaps she could set about seducing both of these delightful young things? Deprive André of his comforts, and flaunt a fresh pair of conquests in front of him, before she finally took away his freedom? The slut Belinda obviously deserved punishing rather than pleasuring, but perhaps there would be time to do both?

'Come quickly! We must hurry now,' urged Michiko, leading Belinda down a narrow back staircase. The Japanese woman was negotiating the narrow stone treads with the greatest of ease, despite the fantastically elaborate beauty of her clothing. In her traditional geisha garb she was almost unrecognisable.

Hurrying as best she could behind Michiko, Belinda knew now what had been in the boxes delivered this morning. A many-layered kimono in sumptuous brocade; a sash or obi, which fastened in an immense, folded bow of enormous complexity; a formal wig, shaped into high, stiff coils and adorned with flowers and delicately beaded combs. All these elements – combined with her white, painted face and her peculiar clog-like footwear – seemed to transform Michiko into a creature of even greater mystery, and of complete refinement and total femininity, yet they detracted not one whit from her power.

The foot of these particular stairs led out into a small courtyard at the back of the house, which was only a few strides away from the chapel. With any luck, Jonathan had already steered Isidora towards the library – luring her with his sob story and his willingness to be seduced – but it was still not wise to linger long outside.

The heavy door of the chapel was pushed to, and when Belinda opened it and entered with Michiko, she felt a frisson of cool excitement ripple through her. In the gathering twilight, the old nave looked very different to the way it had looked when she had last visited the chapel.

There were hothouse flowers everywhere; their scents heavy in the air, their brilliant colours muted in the strange light. Candles were burning in various candelabra and torches stood in wall sconces, but the radiance they all exuded was fuzzy. It seemed to hug itself unto itself; and Belinda realised she hadn't seen the slightest hint of it outside. There was nothing visible to alert the predator to their presence.

The heavy oak table had been moved – by Oren's massive strength, no doubt – and now stood more or less in the centre of the chapel. Its surface was covered with a beautifully embroidered quilt and a selection of cushions, and the very sight of it made Belinda's loins clench. It was there that she would lie entwined with André.

She did not at first see her prospective paramour; it took her a moment to notice his presence in the shadows. He was sitting on the gleaming old pew where Michiko had sat, only last night, to inflict punishment. He was wearing what appeared to be a long cloak of lustrous silk, decorated with stars picked out in silver thread, and his head was bowed as if in private contemplation. On his lap he had a small rosewood box, the one Belinda had seen in his tower chamber, and as his fingers moved across it, it seemed to glow. When Michiko called his name, he looked up slowly, his hand still possessive on the box and its intricate carvings.

'It's time,' said Michiko gently, gliding towards him. 'We must do it now, before Isidora detects our purpose.'

André rose, still cradling the box, and stepped forward in readiness, but when his eyes met Belinda's own, they mirrored her fears.

Jonathan trembled as Isidora's cool arm slipped around him. This was the most terrifying thing that had ever happened to him in his life, but what was so astounding was that the danger seemed to rouse him.

Charged with one of Michiko's spells, he seemed to be seeing things. It was Paula's familiar face before him, and for some of the time he could see nothing untoward in it; her features were the same as they had always been; pretty but to him not particularly exciting. She was just his friend. But every now and again, reality seemed to slide sideways somehow, and he would see something he could only define as a doubling. Paula was still there but behind her was a presence that was infinitely threatening. A face more beautiful – by far – yet hard and deadly as a shaman's painted mask. The face of a woman with seductive powers that made all others seem like pale impressions. Jonathan instinctively loathed her, but his penis ached like fire.

'She's been hanging around him, throwing herself at him at every opportunity,' he said, trying to make his voice poignant with complaint, 'but when *I* tried to make love to her she didn't want to know.'

Of course, some of it was true, he thought wryly, as a look of carefully crafted sympathy appeared on his companion's face. Belinda had been with André, but by the same token, so had he, as well as with Feltris and Elisa. The difference was that their various combinings

267

had been consensual and free. He didn't resent Belinda's involvement with André, but here on the front line, he had to pretend it hurt a lot.

'The bitch!' he cried, looking down at his clenched hands, then feeling Isidora tighten her hold. 'How could she do that to me?'

'I don't know,' she answered, reaching over to stroke his hands, then his arm, and then his thigh. 'I really don't – ' She paused, and Jonathan felt her fingers edge a little way towards his groin, their pressure insidious. 'Although, sometimes . . . just sometimes, I've wondered about Belinda. She's a little bit fickle. She doesn't always think. And – ' She paused again, her face drifting closer to his, her perfume somehow thickening and becoming mesmeric, ' – I've never mentioned it before, but I've seen her with other men too.'

'The bitch!' repeated Jonathan, feeling full of a peculiar unfocused resentment, as if he genuinely had been cuckolded.

'Don't let it upset you, Jonathan,' came the silkiest voice in his ear. 'You're a handsome man. Intelligent. You don't have to take such treatment. You could have any woman you wanted.'

As she kissed his neck, so delicately he almost didn't feel it, Jonathan fought to retain a hold on reality. This was the enemy, the creature who would damn his new friend, his first and possibly only male lover, for ever. He was supposed to seduce Isidora, or to allow her to seduce him, but it seemed quite wrong to feel so attracted.

'Jonathan,' she whispered, planting kisses along his jaw and across his cheeks. 'Forget her.' Her hand slid the last few inches up his thigh, out of the neutral zone, and became a positive caress against his groin. 'I've always been attracted to you. I've always wanted you. I'll make you happier than Belinda ever could.'

Her touch was so light yet so commanding that Jonathan groaned. His cock leapt in her cradling hand, as if trying to burrow out of his jeans and get at her. He felt her lips settle at the corner of his mouth.

Realising now that he would have no trouble feigning or generating desire for this woman he knew and yet didn't know, he lifted his hand, cupped her cool chin, and angled her face to his for a kiss.

Immediately, her tongue shot into his mouth, brooking no resistance as it explored and moistly probed. Even as he yielded, he could feel her deft fingers tackling his zip, whizzing it down effortlessly, then parting his fly. Within seconds his cock was in her hand.

'You don't know how long I've wanted this to happen,' murmured Isidora huskily, nibbling at his lower lip as she manipulated his penis.

'Same here!' gasped Jonathan, for a moment half-believing it was true, then almost immediately hating himself for what he was feeling. There was a sort of loathsome voluptuousness to the way she was touching and rubbing him, and he suddenly understood the sweet, sickly lure of forbidden fruit – and how bad women down the ages had been adored.

'Shall we go to my room?' he said, almost choking on the words, he felt so aroused. His sex had swollen and hardened so much that it seemed to be an iron bar dragging on his belly; a rod of engorged flesh that would explode if he didn't soon find release.

'No, why wait?' growled Isidora, sliding herself sin-uously off the sofa and on to the rug, and dragging Jonathan down with her by his cock. 'Let's get comfort-able right here,' she urged, and with one last provocative squeeze, set free his cock. 'You're not scared of being found out, are you?' she teased, beginning to undress for him with no apparent qualms.

Jonathan had seen Paula in a bathing suit on several occasions, but as Isidora slipped off her last garments – a thin white bra and panties – he experienced a lack of phase between image and illusion. The revealed body was undeniably Paula's, but it had never seemed so irresistible until now.

'Touch me!' the sorceress ordered, lying back on the antique rug and parting her legs. Jonathan could instantly see every detail – her copious juices trickling down over her inner thighs and bottom, the swollen puffiness of her vulva and her clitoris enlarged and standing out, as if to invite the ministrations of a man.

'Jonathan, I command you to touch me!' Isidora cried hoarsely, reaching down to part her outer labia with her fingers.

Jonathan obeyed. He felt both entranced by what was so blatantly offered, and afraid of what would happen if he refused it. As he slipped the tips of his fingers into her furrow, he found that the unusual coolness of her skin did not extend to her genital organs. The wet terrain between her thighs was burning hot, and he felt it ripple as if further to entice him. When he began to rub her, her thighs trapped his hand like a vice.

'Yes!' she crooned, reaching up and wrapping her whole self around him. Her body rocked and she ground her nakedness against his still clothed torso, then she growled like a lioness in evident pleasure, her vulva tensing and relaxing beneath his touch.

Isidora's orgasm seemed to last for an eternity, exciting Jonathan beyond measure in return. He felt as if he were hovering on the edge of a brink of some kind, engaged in a dangerous sport that could kill him at any second; holding his breath, ready to soar up or descend. Adrenalin pumped and his heart was thudding wildly.

As he hesitated, Isidora ceased her writhing then sat up straight and pushed him backwards, looming over him.

When she murmured, 'Your turn,' he felt his perilous plunge begin.

Belinda suddenly felt embarrassed as well as frightened. How could she just make love like this; in cold blood, in plain sight, with no preamble? How could she even begin when she knew how it might end?

And if she had doubts, might not André have them too?

As if reading her thoughts precisely, he looked up from his contemplation of the glowing rosewood box. 'Come here,' he said softly to Belinda, his face a little eerie in the rising blue radiance.

She went to him and sat down on the pew beside him, as Michiko set about some complex, arcane task which involved muted chanting and the burning of incense.

'I know,' said André as Belinda sat down. 'This must seem so contrived to you, so strange.' He smiled, and his blue eyes twinkled in a way that was so normal and boyishly appealing that she felt the first twist of sweet desire in her belly. 'And you are right. It is the most unnatural reason to make love, under the most unnatural of circumstances. But if things were different . . .' He shrugged and let his breath out in a sigh.

Noticing a fluctuation in the quality of the light, Belinda looked down at the box on André's lap, resting among the folds of his luxurious silken cloak.

How could someone live in there? And that someone; how might she feel about what André had implied? That in other circumstances, he would happily have betrayed her with Belinda.

She looked up again, and saw that he had been staring at the box as well. 'You could have been friends,' he said, his voice barely audible. 'Sisters even, soul sisters. You are so alike, so akin in many ways . . . Here!' he said suddenly, lifting the box and offering it to Belinda.

She hesitated, her fingers pleating the thin muslin of her dress.

'She will not bite,' assured André, smiling.

Belinda took the box and immediately felt a diffuse impact. A force. A presence. The wood was cool to the touch, but her brain twisted the message in its interpretation somehow, and Belinda perceived it as warmth.

271

She felt a great rush of emotion, a recognition, a kindred feeling that was so powerful it was almost erotic. Without thinking she found herself stroking the box, almost petting it. She felt a great urge to open it and look inside.

'Go ahead,' said André.

Or was it André? There had been a strange almost ringing quality to the words, as if it had not only been him who had spoken.

Within the box was a stoppered crystal flask which was filled with a swirling hazy substance that could be defined as neither liquid nor gas. The colour was incredible – the simple word 'blue' was not sufficient to encompass it. It was sky; it was ocean; it was the most exquisite jewel-blue, sapphire or lapis lazuli. The substance – the 'personality' – was formless, yet Belinda's senses told her she was looking at a smile. The essence of a greeting, of a touch; the feeling of love.

'Hello,' she whispered, letting her fingertips rest on the vial, and experiencing another surge of the disembodied impression of welcome. It was the psychic equivalent of a hug. An embrace of sisterhood and all that it entailed, an emotion that dispersed her fears and doubts. She felt a sudden eagerness to know this, her strange sibling, better; to share her life and her mind, if only briefly.

'Come, it is time,' said a voice that sounded as if it came from miles away. Belinda looked up and saw Michiko standing over them, an imposing figure in her ornate wig and her layered silk finery. She was holding out her hands, ready to receive the precious container. Belinda kissed the vial, feeling its cool surface tingle on her lips like sherbet, then closed the box and passed it reverently to Michiko.

'So we begin,' said André, rising at Belinda's side and offering his hand to assist her to her feet.

As Michiko bowed, holding the box in her slender white hands, Belinda let André lead her courteously towards the table.

* * *

272

'Oh God!' moaned Jonathan as hot sensation surged through him in waves. Isidora was above him, astride his loins, her naked body bouncing up and down on him, her cool vagina a tight sleeve around his cock.

'It's nothing to do with him,' she growled, swivelling her hips in a way that seemed more animal than human – if that was what she was, or ever had been.

Jonathan hardly dared look up at her as she rode him. The more he saw of her in the throes of copulation, the less he could see of familiar Paula. The features above him were those of his friend and colleague, but the expression and the frenzy were dark and alien. He had never really fancied Paula, much less been to bed with her, but instinct told him she could never be like this.

Isidora was using him, engulfing him, overwhelming him. He felt as if he were being drained dry by a bottomless black void; his vital energy being siphoned from him through his cock. Yet again, she circled her pelvis, then jerked down hard.

'Caress me, Jonathan,' she urged, her voice harsh and raw with sex as she clasped his limp hands then clutched them to her breasts.

He groaned, feeling the resilient orbs of flesh against his fingers, and hating himself for the way his body reacted. His penis stiffened and lurched within the confines of her body, and his balls felt like boiling fiery stones. Without conscious thought, he began to knead her breasts.

'Yes!' she squealed, squeezing him in return, her inner muscles flexing on his shaft.

Jonathan whimpered, bucking his hips up against her and getting a low, feral grunt of appreciation. This was the wildest, darkest most breathtaking sex he had ever experienced, the whole process rendered profoundly thrilling because of the danger. He had a strong but illogical feeling that Isidora was fully aware that he knew she wasn't Paula, and was putting him through the grinder in order to drive that awareness home. She was fucking him into submission, and making him too much hers to protest. And though he didn't know how, she was keeping him hard beyond his endurance. Under treatment like this, he should have ejaculated many minutes ago.

'Oh, this is so good,' she growled, grabbing his hair and wrenching him up from the rug beneath them to kiss his gasping lips. His hands, still holding her breasts, were squashed between their bodies. 'Isn't this good?' she demanded of him, the words distorted by the mashing of their mouths and the duelling of their tongues.

Jonathan's scalp hurt furiously where she pulled at him, and his back felt ready to snap in two, but his entire groin was one pulsating well of ecstasy. It was as if his cock was about to explode in the very next second, and that when it did it would kill him, but he couldn't summon the energy to care. His pelvis juddered, and he knew his climax was imminent –

But when he hit the leading edge of it, Isidora cried out in fear.

'No!' she shrieked. 'The devil take you, no!' And even as Jonathan spurted, she was leaping up and off him, a startling transformation beginning before his pleasure-blurred eyes.

Staggering to her feet was a woman he had never seen before.

Belinda sighed. She licked her lips. André's kiss had expunged the bitterness somehow. She could no longer taste the potion's astringent flavour.

She felt weak now, too, but pleasantly so. She didn't complain when André eased her on to her back on their makeshift but comfortable couch. She simply smiled at him, then smiled again, over his shoulder, at Michiko, who was studying the huge book on the lectern before her, and murmuring softly in what sounded like Latin.

The chant was soothing, and Belinda let her eyes flutter closed. In a dreamy, pleasant cocoon, she felt André's lips roving over her throat and her chest in an arcane pattern that must have been decreed a thousand years ago by the gods. His mouth was cool but exciting, his tongue flicking out to lick her skin. After a few moments, she felt his hands slide beneath her, lift her a little way off the quilted mattress, and deftly unhitch the fastenings of her blue dress. She giggled a little as he drew it off her then just as cleverly removed her thin cotton shift. All these actions seemed to be occurring a long long way away from her, yet she still received delicious messages from her body when André's chilly fingers touched her skin.

'I want you,' she purred to him, the words slipping from her without conscious volition. Reaching for him, she tugged at the corded silk fastening of his floating blue cloak, then pushed the garment off his shoulders. She heard a swish as it fell to the chapel floor.

They were both naked now, in the balmy night air, their bodies quickly pressing and fitting together. Belinda was aware of a thick rush of moisture between her thighs, her channel flowing as if to invite André's penis. He was hard and enticing against her leg, and she put a hand on him as he pressed a finger to her sex.

Michiko turned a page, and whispered on.

After a moment, André began to rub in earnest, and Belinda heard herself laugh with delight as her vulva quivered.

'This is for you, Belinda,' he said, pressing his lips against the skin of her arching throat. 'Just for you, and you alone.' His fingers curved cleverly, pressing on either side of her clitoris and making it roll like a bearing in thick oil.

After a moment, she came – a very clear, light orgasm that was so effortless she cried out happily. Her legs scissored and she scrabbled at his back to pull him closer, feeling her quim pulsate and joyful tears run down her cheeks.

Drifting in a perfect aftermath, she felt André lift her upper body away from the mattress; but she was so loose with residual pleasure that she could do nothing to help him. As he held her, draped forward across him, Michiko was suddenly beside them, and Belinda sensed something narrow and silky being threaded around her. When she looked down she saw it was a long length of white satin ribbon, which the Japanese sorceress was winding loosely about her bare waist. When she was finished, one tail was left dangling over the side of the table and the other was run down over Belinda's belly and then drawn meticulously between the swimming folds of her still-aroused sex. She could feel its ghostly presence against her clitoris and just touching her entrance.

She did not seem to need to question the arrangement, and she was unsurprised when André positioned himself gracefully between her thighs, then pushed deeply and surely inside her, his cock brushing the trapped silk ribbon.

'Oh my dearest,' he groaned, sliding his arms around her waist.

Belinda felt her head begin to lighten strangely. She could feel him in her and feel the satisfaction of it, but the sensations were still coming from a great, great distance. Even further than before, and through time now as well as through space.

She kissed his throat, and had the sudden impression that she was watching another woman kiss him, even though she could feel his smooth skin beneath her lips. His penis was stretching her, yet seemed to be lodged in some other vagina. The condition was peculiar, but she felt no trace of fear.

As André began to move gently inside her, Belinda felt an urge to turn her head. Looking to one side, and peering through what seemed like an oscillating nimbus of light, she saw Michiko standing beside them, her lips still moving. She was not reading from the book now, but reciting something she must have known by heart. In one hand she held the silky end of the pure white ribbon, in the other the crystal vial that contained Arabelle.

Slowly, still murmuring, the Michiko tipped the vial, and the blue radiance poured out and seemed to gather in the ribbon. When the transparent vessel was empty, the shifting blueness began to flow swiftly along the inch-wide strand of white.

Belinda would have watched, but she felt André shift his position a little so he could reach up and touch her cheek. Angling her face towards his, he looked down at her, his eyes like twin blazing sapphires, his whole face transfigured.

'It is happening ... Oh dear God, it is happening!' His mouth pressed down on hers, still moving in a final kiss that stole her senses. 'Oh thank you ... Oh thank you, Belinda,' was the last thing she heard.

Epilogue

'What happened? Did it work?' cried Jonathan, bounding into the chapel, his face blanched and wild.

Belinda felt a reassuring squeeze, Michiko's strong arm supporting her and revivifying her, and with a quick glance at the Japanese woman she said, 'I think so.'

'Yes, it worked,' said Michiko quietly, her face radiant beneath its white cosmetic mask. 'Completely. My friends are free now.' Belinda saw her shoot an enquiring glance at Jonathan. 'There is nothing more to fear.'

'Are you all right?' he enquired, moving towards the table where Belinda was sitting supported by Michiko. She had André's starry cloak around her, and she felt cold and more than a little shaky, but she could not say that there was anything really wrong with her. She was suffering from mild shock, she guessed, but otherwise all felt well.

'I'm OK,' she replied, giving him a smile, but not sure it would convince him. Then, looking more closely at her boyfriend, she frowned instead. 'But what about you? You look terrible!'

Jonathan's face was still unnaturally pale, and his hair

was standing up in tufts, as if he had run his fingers through it again and again. His clothes were rumpled and half unfastened, and he was barefoot. His eyes were almost starting out of his head.

'I've never been so scared in my life,' he said, a slight quiver in his voice as he sat down beside her. 'One minute, I'm getting it on with Paula – ' He flashed Belinda a shamefaced look, but she touched his arm to reassure him ' – and the next minute, she's leaping up off me and she isn't Paula at all. And she's screeching and whirling about, almost as if she was on fire or something. Then suddenly, "poof", she disappears! I was so terrified I damn nearly wet myself!'

Belinda could feel his arm shaking beneath her fingers. She squeezed it gently. Jonathan's experience obviously hadn't been quite the lyrical one she had participated in. Not that she knew properly what had happened. She had woken up a few minutes before, cradled in Michiko's arms, but of André and his spirit lover there had been no sign at all.

'She is gone for ever now, Jonathan,' said Michiko calmly, beginning to gather up the paraphernalia of the freeing: the grimoire, the crystal flask, the limp silk ribbon. 'Her original spell bound her existence to André's. So when he went, so did she.' She shrugged her kimono-clad shoulders. 'But not, I'm afraid, to quite the same place.' Wearing a wry smile, Michiko continued her task.

Belinda looked at Jonathan and they exchanged a glance of tacit agreement, then both got to their feet to help. Belinda felt slightly rubbery at the knees at first, but after a moment, she regained enough strength to move around carefully.

'What will happen to Oren, and Feltris and Elisa?' asked Jonathan, a little while afterwards, as they were walking back towards the moonlit house. Michiko had left the accoutrements of the ritual gathered together on the table for Oren to collect later, but in her arms she was carrying the great grimoire.

'I will take them into my service, if they wish it,' the Japanese sorceress said. 'I am thinking of making a home in England. Perhaps I will even settle here at the priory. That way they can continue to live here undisturbed.'

'Good,' said Belinda, 'I'm glad about that. I didn't like the idea of them suddenly being left on their own.'

When they reached the house, Michiko bade them both retire to their beds and get some sorely-needed sleep, while she went down to the servants' quarters to break the news.

Functioning with the same sense of mutual understanding that they had experienced earlier, Belinda and Jonathan both made their way to Belinda's red room. Deep in a thoughtful but companionable silence, they got ready for bed, then snuggled up together underneath the covers. They were both naked but Belinda felt no urge to make love, and neither, it soon became obvious, did Jonathan. The peculiar events of a peculiar night had taken their toll.

Although she hadn't expected to be able to sleep, Belinda soon found her thoughts losing focus. She felt loose and drowsy, and Jonathan's presence at her side was warm and calming.

The descent into refreshing sleep was more welcome than it had ever been, and she embraced rest with a relief that was almost blissful – seeing André's smiling face as she succumbed.

The next day, in the afternoon, Belinda and Jonathan left Sedgewick Priory. Not for ever, because they had promised to visit its new châtelaine in the future, but it was good to be heading back to a normal life.

A normal life where life's appliances worked as normal.

The Mini started first time, and Belinda, who had

chosen to drive, felt convinced it had never run so smoothly.

The mobile phone also functioned perfectly, even though they had never actually got round to charging it. Jonathan rang Paula's mobile number and got through on the first try. He spoke to a nurse and discovered that their friend was in hospital in the nearest big town.

Paula had been found unconscious in a hotel room, it seemed, but she had come round now, and apart from remembering nothing whatsoever about the last couple of days, she was completely unharmed and resting comfortably. It also turned out that she had been most concerned at missing her meeting with her friends, and that her car had been stolen. Belinda smiled as she listened to Jonathan instructing the nurse to tell Paula not to worry, and that it was probably just a joy-rider and the car would soon be found, most likely in a lay-by on some quiet country road.

Jonathan's sense of direction and his ability to read maps had been reinstated too. Without the slightest problem, they located the hospital where Paula was sequestered, but as it would be too late to visit by the time they got there, they made their way to the hotel instead. As luck would have it there was a room vacant for the night.

'You know, these last few days,' Jonathan said, as Belinda walked naked into the room after her shower. 'It was all so weird, so different, like a dream somehow.' He was lying on his back on the bed, wearing only his jockey shorts, staring up at the ceiling as if its tiled surface held an explanation of some kind. 'I keep wondering if any of it really happened.'

Belinda looked at him sharply and closely, and found her body reawakened by the view.

Jonathan's limbs were strong, his torso lean, and his groin full of bulging erotic promise. She experienced a jolt of yearning at the sight of his cock so snugly contained in his close-fitting briefs; and his face too, cast in lines of thought, had a sweet allure. Her familiar boyfriend wasn't a patrician, mysterious André, or a massive, golden Oren, or even a Michiko, so female and exotic; but he was truly hers, he was always willing, and he loved her. In repose, he was an innocent male temptation.

'Oh, it happened all right,' she said in answer to his musings. Turning away, she stood before the mirror and studied her own shape.

Her breasts, her waist and her hips she found pleasing. It had never before occurred to her that she was beautiful, but now, with a clear new perspective, she saw she was. Or at least, she had certain possibilities. She ran a slow, searching hand over the curve of her belly until it reached the fragrant grove at her rousing crotch.

'Lindi?' Jonathan's voice held a new note, and as she turned, still touching her vulva, she discovered him watching her.

Smiling, she withdrew her fingers and looked down to see them glistening. Without conscious thought, she raised them to her lips and tasted desire.

'Oh, Lindi,' said Jonathan again, his lust undeniable as he moved up from the pillow and held out his arms.

Belinda went to him, lying down at his side then rolling towards him. His skin felt warm yet somehow invigorating where their bodies touched.

'You're cold, sweetheart,' he muttered, pressing himself lovingly against her breasts and against her belly. 'Don't worry, I'll soon warm you up.' He slid his hands around her and stroked the swell of her bottom, while between her legs he rubbed her genitals with his thigh.

Belinda moaned, grinding herself against him, humping the taut muscle and feeling a familiar pleasure bloom. Reaching around behind herself, she took Jonathan's hand and drew his fingers to her anus.

'Oh yes! Oh yes yes yes!' she shouted out joyfully, while she rode him – and he industriously stroked. Within seconds she was coming against his skin.

'Oh Lindi, you are really something special,' he crooned to her as she fell back against the pillows, slack and sated for the moment. 'I didn't think you'd be interested just yet, what with . . . I dunno . . . André and all –'

'But of course I am,' she said, smiling and opening her eyes, reaching up to touch his face and make him look at her.

Jonathan complied, his own eyes filled with affection, then suddenly, with abject puzzlement.

'Oh dear God,' he whispered, his voice almost nothing, his body trembling furiously against hers. His cock was still hard, but the strange shaking wasn't sex.

'What is it?'

'I – ' he began, 'It – ' He faltered again, then sat up, climbed across her, and slipped off the bed. Taking her hand, he drew her with him towards the mirror. Then, making her face it, he stood behind her and said 'Look!'

'What at?' she demanded, although deep inside her the answer was rapidly dawning.

Reaching around her, Jonathan brushed her fringe from her brow, then slid his hand under her chin to move her a little closer to the glass.

Belinda blinked. And blinked again.

'Oh, I see . . .' she murmured, studying the change she had half-expected with fear and wonder.

Her eyes, which had once been hazel, were now bright blue.

Visit the Black Lace website at
www.blacklace-books.co.uk

LOOK OUT FOR THE ALL-NEW BLACK LACE BOOKS – AVAILABLE NOW!

All books priced £7.99 in the UK. Please note publication dates apply to the UK only. For other territories, please contact your retailer.

THE BOSS
Monica Belle
ISBN 978 0 352 34088 7

Felicity is a girl with two different sides to her character, each leading two very separate lives. There's Fizz – wild child, drummer in a retro punk band and car thief. And then there's Felicity – a quiet, polite, and ultra-efficient office worker. But, as her attractive, controlling boss takes an interest in her, she finds it hard to keep the two parts of her life separate.

Will being with Stephen mean choosing between personae and sacrificing so much of her life? But then, it also appears that Stephen has some very peculiar and addictive ideas about sex.

Coming in March 2007

FLOOD
Anna Clare
ISBN 978 0 352 34094 8

London, 1877. Phoebe Flood, a watch mender's daughter from Blackfriars, is hired as lady's maid to the glamorous Louisa LeClerk, a high class tart with connections to the underworld of gentlemen pornographers. Fascinated by her new mistress and troubled by strange dreams, Phoebe receives an extraordinary education in all matters sensual. And her destiny and secret self gradually reveals itself when she meets Garou, a freak show attraction, The Boy Who Was Raised by Wolves.

MÉNAGE
Emma Holly
ISBN 978 0 352 34118 1

Bookstore owner Kate comes home from work one day to find her two flatmates in bed ... together. Joe – a sensitive composer – is mortified. Sean – an irrepressible bad boy – asks her to join in. Kate's been fantasising about her hunky new houseshares since they moved in, but she was convinced they were both gay. Realising that pleasure is a multi-faceted thing, she sets her cares aside and embarks on a ménage à trois with the wild duo. Kate wants nothing more than to keep both her admirers happy, but inevitably things become complicated, especially at work. Kate has told her colleagues that Joe and Sean are gay but the gossip begins when she's caught snogging one of them in her lunch hour! To add to this, one of Kate's more conservative suitors is showing interest again, but she's hooked on the different kind of loving that she enjoys with her boys – even though she knows it cannot last. Or can it?

COOKING UP A STORM
Emma Holly
ISBN 978 0 352 34114 3

The Coates Inn restaurant in Cape Cod is about to go out of business
when its striking owner, Abby, jumps at a stranger's offer of help – both
in her kitchen and her bedroom. Storm, a handsome chef, claims to have
a secret weapon: an aphrodisiac menu that her patrons won't be able to
resist. It certainly works on Abby – who gives in to the passions she has
denied herself for years.

Bat can this playboy chef really be Abby's hero if her body means
more to him than her heart, and his initial plan was to steal the
restaurant from under her nose? Storm soon turns the restaurant
around, but Abby's insatiable desires have taken over her life. She's never
known a guy into crazy sex like him before, and she wants to spend
every spare moment getting as much intense erotic pleasure as she can.
Meanwhile, her best friend Marissa becomes suspicious of the new
wonder-boy in the kitchen. Before things get really out of control,
someone has to assume responsibility. But can Abby tear herself away
from the object of her lustful attention long enough to see what's really
going on?

Coming in April 2007

WING OF MADNESS
Mae Nixon
ISBN 978 0 352 34099 3

As a university academic, Claire has always sought safety in facts and information. But then she meets Jim and he becomes her guide on a sensual journey with no limits except their own imagination – and Claire's has always been overactive. She learns to submit to a man totally, to be his to use for pleasure or sensual punishment. Together they begin to explore the dark, forbidden places inside her and she quickly learns how little she really knows about her own erotic nature. The only thing she knows with absolute certainty is that she never wants it to stop . . .

THE TOP OF HER GAME
Emma Holly
ISBN 978 0 352 34116 7

It's not only Julia's professional acumen that has men quaking in their shoes – she also has a taste for keeping men in line after office hours. With an impressive collection of whips and high heels to her name, she sure has some kinky ways of showing affection. But Julia's been searching all her life for a man who won't be tamed too quickly – and when she meets rugged dude rancher Zach on a business get-together in Montana, she thinks she might have found him.

He may be a simple countryman, but he's not about to take any nonsense from uppity city women like Julia. Zach's full of surprises: where she thinks he's tough, he turns out to be gentle; she's confident she's got this particular cowboy broken in, he turns the tables on her. Has she locked horns with an animal too wild even for her? When it comes to sex, Zach doesn't go for half measures. Underneath the big sky of Montana, has the steely Ms Mueller finally met her match?

Black Lace Booklist

Information is correct at time of printing. To avoid disappointment, check availability before ordering. Go to www.blacklace-books.co.uk. All books are priced £7.99 unless another price is given.

BLACK LACE BOOKS WITH A CONTEMPORARY SETTING

☐ ALWAYS THE BRIDEGROOM Tesni Morgan	ISBN 978 0 352 33855 6	£6.99
☐ THE ANGELS' SHARE Maya Hess	ISBN 978 0 352 34043 6	
☐ ARIA APPASSIONATA Julie Hastings	ISBN 978 0 352 33056 7	£6.99
☐ ASKING FOR TROUBLE Kristina Lloyd	ISBN 978 0 352 33362 9	
☐ BLACK LIPSTICK KISSES Monica Belle	ISBN 978 0 352 33885 3	£6.99
☐ BONDED Fleur Reynolds	ISBN 978 0 352 33192 2	£6.99
☐ BOUND IN BLUE Monica Belle	ISBN 978 0 352 34012 2	
☐ THE BOSS Monica Belle	ISBN 978 0 352 34088 7	
☐ CAMPAIGN HEAT Gabrielle Marcola	ISBN 978 0 352 33941 6	
☐ CAT SCRATCH FEVER Sophie Mouette	ISBN 978 0 352 34021 4	
☐ CIRCUS EXCITE Nikki Magennis	ISBN 978 0 352 34033 7	
☐ CLUB CRÈME Primula Bond	ISBN 978 0 352 33907 2	£6.99
☐ COMING ROUND THE MOUNTAIN Tabitha Flyte	ISBN 978 0 352 33873 0	£6.99
☐ CONFESSIONAL Judith Roycroft	ISBN 978 0 352 33421 3	
☐ CONTINUUM Portia Da Costa	ISBN 978 0 352 33120 5	
☐ DANGEROUS CONSEQUENCES Pamela Rochford	ISBN 978 0 352 33185 4	
☐ DARK DESIGNS Madelynne Ellis	ISBN 978 0 352 34075 7	
☐ THE DEVIL INSIDE Portia Da Costa	ISBN 978 0 352 32993 6	
☐ EDEN'S FLESH Robyn Russell	ISBN 978 0 352 33923 2	£6.99
☐ ENTERTAINING MR STONE Portia Da Costa	ISBN 978 0 352 34029 0	
☐ EQUAL OPPORTUNITIES Mathilde Madden	ISBN 978 0 352 34070 2	
☐ FEMININE WILES Karina Moore	ISBN 978 0 352 33874 7	£6.99
☐ FIRE AND ICE Laura Hamilton	ISBN 978 0 352 33486 2	
☐ GOING DEEP Kimberly Dean	ISBN 978 0 352 33876 1	£6.99
☐ GOING TOO FAR Laura Hamilton	ISBN 978 0 352 33657 6	£6.99
☐ GONE WILD Maria Eppie	ISBN 978 0 352 33670 5	

BLACK LACE BOOKS WITH AN HISTORICAL SETTING

- [ ] THE AMULET Lisette Allen   ISBN 978 0 352 33019 2   £6.99
- [ ] THE BARBARIAN GEISHA Charlotte Royal   ISBN 978 0 352 33267 7
- [ ] BARBARIAN PRIZE Deanna Ashford   ISBN 978 0 352 34017 7
- [ ] DANCE OF OBSESSION Olivia Christie   ISBN 978 0 352 33101 4
- [ ] DARKER THAN LOVE Kristina Lloyd   ISBN 978 0 352 33279 0
- [ ] ELENA'S DESTINY Lisette Allen   ISBN 978 0 352 33218 9
- [ ] FRENCH MANNERS Olivia Christie   ISBN 978 0 352 33214 1
- [ ] THE HAND OF AMUN Juliet Hastings   ISBN 978 0 352 33144 1   £6.99
- [ ] LORD WRAXALL'S FANCY Anna Lieff Saxby   ISBN 978 0 352 33080 2
- [ ] THE MASTER OF SHILDEN Lucinda Carrington   ISBN 978 0 352 33140 3
- [ ] NICOLE'S REVENGE Lisette Allen   ISBN 978 0 352 32984 4
- [ ] THE SENSES BEJEWELLED Cleo Cordell   ISBN 978 0 352 32904 2   £6.99
- [ ] THE SOCIETY OF SIN Sian Lacey Taylder   ISBN 978 0 352 34080 1
- [ ] UNDRESSING THE DEVIL Angel Strand   ISBN 978 0 352 33938 6
- [ ] WHITE ROSE ENSNARED Juliet Hastings   ISBN 978 0 352 33052 9   £6.99

BLACK LACE BOOKS WITH A PARANORMAL THEME

- [ ] BURNING BRIGHT Janine Ashbless   ISBN 978 0 352 34085 6
- [ ] CRUEL ENCHANTMENT Janine Ashbless   ISBN 978 0 352 33483 1
- [ ] GOTHIC BLUE Portia Da Costa   ISBN 978 0 352 33075 8
- [ ] THE PRIDE Edie Bingham   ISBN 978 0 352 33997 3

BLACK LACE ANTHOLOGIES

- [ ] MORE WICKED WORDS Various   ISBN 978 0 352 33487 9   £6.99
- [ ] WICKED WORDS 3 Various   ISBN 978 0 352 33522 7   £6.99
- [ ] WICKED WORDS 4 Various   ISBN 978 0 352 33603 3   £6.99
- [ ] WICKED WORDS 5 Various   ISBN 978 0 352 33642 2   £6.99
- [ ] WICKED WORDS 6 Various   ISBN 978 0 352 33690 3   £6.99
- [ ] WICKED WORDS 7 Various   ISBN 978 0 352 33743 6   £6.99
- [ ] WICKED WORDS 8 Various   ISBN 978 0 352 33787 0   £6.99
- [ ] WICKED WORDS 9 Various   ISBN 978 0 352 33860 0
- [ ] WICKED WORDS 10 Various   ISBN 978 0 352 33893 8
- [ ] THE BEST OF BLACK LACE 2 Various   ISBN 978 0 352 33718 4
- [ ] WICKED WORDS: SEX IN THE OFFICE Various   ISBN 978 0 352 33944 7

To find out the latest information about Black Lace titles, check out the
website: www.blacklace-books.co.uk or send for a booklist with
complete synopses by writing to:

     Black Lace Booklist, Virgin Books Ltd
     Thames Wharf Studios
     Rainville Road
     London W6 9HA

Please include an SAE of decent size. Please note only British stamps
are valid.

Please send me the books I have ticked above.

Name ....

Address ....

....

....

....

Post Code ....

Send to: Virgin Books Cash Sales, Thames Wharf Studios, Rainville Road, London W6 9HA.

US customers: for prices and details of how to order books for delivery by mail, call 888-330-8477.

Please enclose a cheque or postal order, made payable to Virgin Books Ltd, to the value of the books you have ordered plus postage and packing costs as follows:

UK and BFPO – £1.00 for the first book, 50p for each subsequent book.

Overseas (including Republic of Ireland) – £2.00 for the first book, £1.00 for each subsequent book.

If you would prefer to pay by VISA, ACCESS/MASTERCARD, DINERS CLUB, AMEX or SWITCH, please write your card number and expiry date here:

....

Signature ....

Please allow up to 28 days for delivery.